Maid for Majesty
Forbidden Fruit

Book One of the Maid for Majesty Series

AJ PHOENIX

1

BOOKS BY A J PHOENIX

Maid for Majesty Series:

Forbidden Fruit (Book One)

Absence (Book Two)

Black Swan (Book Three)

Forbidden Fruit Erotica Version (Book One)

Absence Erotica Version (Book Two)

Black Swan Erotica Version (Book Three)

ACKNOWLEDGEMENTS:

I'm grateful to the following people for their encouragement and support:

To my husband, James, for giving me time to write the world of Maid for Majesty, looking after the little ones, and for the first edits.

To my family and friends who tolerated me as I lived in my own little world.

To CB, thank you for all the words of wisdom and telling me like it is.

TL for all the edits.

To J.M. Frey for all the advice.

To all my Majesties for believing in me.

To James, the ruler of my heart.

1

ENSLAVEMENT AT WATSON MANOR

"Blast! Michel, you'll have to finish this pudding. I have to get going," Madeline said as she undid her apron.

"Are you mad?" he said, dropping his whisk in a bowl. "I need your help, the party—"

"Getting Lady Watson ready is going to take hours," she interrupted, putting her hands on her hips. "If you'd like we can switch places. You can cinch up her corset, get her dressed and ready. I can finish preparing tonight's meal."

The rest of the servants in the room stopped to stare at them.

He said nothing. No one wanted the duties that Madeline Black had. If Lady Watson was in a bad mood, doing her makeup and hair would be a nightmare.

"Well, I am the chef," he said as he slowly picked up his whisk again, "I know best how to prepare the puddings and cakes."

"Don't forget she'll want them on the Wedgwood platters," she said, pointing to a large china cabinet full of dinnerware and silver platters.

"Right."

"Tonight is important to her and her reputation. We'll all pay if something isn't perfect."

"Tonight is only about impressing the King," one of the servant girls whispered. Madeline rolled her eyes as she walked out through the kitchen corridor. It was true. The Watsons had invited everyone at court over for a dinner party to celebrate their twentieth wedding anniversary, even though they had only been married for eighteen years.

Aside from trying to impress the nobles, Lord and Lady Watson felt it would be an opportunity to climb the social ladder at court. Their titles wouldn't change from Baron and Baroness, but Lady Watson felt that, if everything went as planned, the party would be one of the biggest social events of the season. This would lead to a plethora of invitations to other occasions. If it didn't, she would delight in all the anniversary gifts received.

She entered the main hall, where other servants were busily decorating every corner of the room. Upon seeing her, Will eagerly walked over to her. "What do you think? Will this be up to Lady Watson's standards?"

She looked about, tapping her finger to her cheek. The crystals hanging in the chandeliers sparkled like new; the pillars were wrapped with garlands of silk flowers. Oversized gold silk festoons hung from the large windows and gold, silk furniture, imported from France for the event, was randomly placed around the room. The tables were all cloaked in cream taffeta, and silk petals were strewn amongst the gold china place settings.

"Looks good," she said, walking through the room, with Will following her about, "But these statues need to gleam as I walk by them. Did you dust all the wall panels and ceiling moulds?"

"Yes, we did. Got every nook and cranny."

"Waxed the floor?"

"Yes."

"Why are the silver vases empty? Where are the flowers?" she asked, looking about the tables.

He raised his brow. "We had sent for someone to drop them off this morning. They arrived, but, uh ... I'm not sure where they have gone."

"They've disappeared? Who was sent to get them?"

"Sissy."

She pressed her lips together, "I guess Lady Watson didn't like them?"

"She never likes anything Sissy does. You know that."

"Funny how Lady Watson didn't tell me or anyone else she didn't like them. She just threw them away."

They exchanged dark expressions. "Lately, things always seem to be difficult for Sissy," he commented. His voice dropped to a whisper, "I think Lady Watson has it in for her."

She nodded in agreement. "I'll be sure to go to town to get some flowers."

"Will you have enough time?"

"I may have to rush to get myself ready, but if I don't, well, God only knows what will happen to Sissy."

"Just get the flowers. I'll make time to put them into the vases so you can get yourself ready for tonight."

"Thanks, Will."

The organization of the event seemed never-ending and making time to thwart Lady Watson's plans to punish Sissy made it worse.

She pressed on into the entrance with its marble floor, statues and oversized paintings. Unfortunately, much of the decor was borrowed from noble friends or businesses in downtown London. It was going to be a lot of work returning to the businesses what the Watsons couldn't afford to keep. It was also going to be annoying to hear all the knocks on the door in the following weeks. She had a suspicion that the Watsons had no intention of returning their friends' possessions. Strangely, many of the gentry whom they borrowed from were not invited to the party.

The Watsons never returned anything. Over the years there had been numerous times that nobles would stop by and politely remind Lord and Lady Watson that they wanted their things back. This was met with a couple of well-practiced lies by the Watsons; they either claimed that they had already left it with their friend's servant (who must have stolen it) or pretended they thought it was a gift and acted insulted by the request to return it. Embarrassed, most of their noble friends wouldn't question the matter. In time, when Lady Watson became bored with what she had stolen, she would gift it to higher nobility to win favour or try to make new friends.

Because of the constant borrowing and gifting, the Watsons hardly knew what was in their home. It didn't take long for Madeline to figure out that she could pocket small trinkets or figurines from

9

time to time, which she sold at shops in London. However, learning that Lady Watson didn't know what was under her roof was not an easy lesson.

On her first day as a servant, she was brought to the main hall to wash the floors and dust the mantles and tapestries. The Watsons were holding a party that evening to celebrate the homecoming of Lord Watson, who had been away in the Caribbean. While dusting the mantles, a beautiful figurine of a woman with dark hair, glowing olive skin and a white dress was knocked to the floor where it shattered into tiny pieces. She swept up the figurine, and headed to the kitchen to throw it into the trash. But a brash older maid barked, "Girl, are ya mad?"

"Uh, well um, I'm not … sure what you mean … mad?"

"If ya don't cover that up with somethin' that Lady Watson will find it, and she will 'ave yer head."

"Well, I have to tell her, don't I?"

"If she sees it missin'. Otherwise, I wouldn't."

Madeline was an innocent, honest girl; she didn't cover it up. At the time, it seemed unthinkable that Lady Watson wouldn't notice such a beautiful figurine missing. Until that day, she hadn't seen any home as magnificent as the Watsons. It seemed that the logical thing to do was to tell the truth. It was better that Lady Watson knew now, rather than discover its disappearance later.

As she re-entered the main hall to get back to work, Lady Watson was there, surveying her cleaning job. "Did you wash the floors?" she asked, her eyes narrowing on her.

"Yes, ma'am."

"Beat the dust from the tapestries?"

"Yes."

"And the drapes and windows?"

"Yes."

"Mantles?"

"Well—"

"—'Well'? WELL WHAT?"

"I ... I" she stuttered.

"WHAT IS IT, GIRL? SPEAK UP! THE MANTLES? WHAT OF THEM?"

"There was a figurine. A figurine of a dancer with dark hair and— "

"—Where was she? Which mantle?"

It was at this moment that she realized what the older servant woman meant. The Watsons had so much around the house the figurine could easily be overlooked, or forgotten. But she had already mentioned the statue. There was no backing out.

"It was the on the mantle on the east wall," she said softly.

Lady Watson raised her hand.

SMACK

Despite the ringing in her ear, Madeline managed to hear her next words. "A whipping will serve you best, it will teach you to be careful, not a daft, clumsy girl."

After smacking her, Lady Watson pulled her by the ear outside. Being dragged to their mews was one of the scariest experiences in her life. Imagining the impending pain sent tears of terror down her cheeks.

SMACK

"You pathetic girl. Crying won't help." She let go of her ear and pulled her by the hair into the stable. There were several horses in different stalls. The wooden walls between the horses seemed dilapidated and in need of repair; the horses were scrawny and malnourished.

"Alfred? Alfred?" Lady Watson called.

An old man with grey hair appeared from around one of the stalls, a brush in one of his hands.

"Alfred, I need you to whip this incompetent girl."

His eyes widened as he saw Madeline. "My lady, she seems quite young. I'm guessing that this is the new girl? It is her first day. She is just learning."

"Who is the master? Who is the servant? I ordered you to do something. Are you incompetent too?"

He knew that defying Lady Watson would end with more punishments and whippings for Madeline and himself. With a heavy heart, he dropped his brush and removed a whip hanging on the wall.

"Outside!" Lady Watson shrieked, "I want the servants to see from the windows of the manor. If they see it, it'll encourage them to focus and work harder." She grabbed a length of rope, and they followed her through the stable doors. She tied Madeline to a lone wooden pole sticking up from the ground.

Seeing it, Madeline shivered. She could see some blood stains along its sides. It was obvious that whippings were a regular occurrence at Watson Manor. After tying her to the pole, Lady Watson began unbuttoning the back of Madeline's dress.

"I'm sure you thought you could put a sweet smile on your pretty face and get away with this," she whispered. She pulled apart the dress, popping the buttons off, exposing her back. "But that's not how things work around here, missy." She stepped alongside Alfred. "Get to it then!"

Madeline held her breath and squeezed her eyes shut. She could sense the whip fly up through the air. It landed on her back, a soft sting with a little numbness. The experience of being whipped was indescribable. It was painful but not as terrible as she would have imagined. The first few lashes she was given were light and brought a tingling in her body that made her feel alive. However, this didn't last long.

"Alfred, you must be joking! What a shoddy job! Argh! Why is it I have to do everything myself?"

She tore the whip from his hands and threw it up. It made a whistling sound as it cut through the air. Madeline clenched all her muscles in fear and it relentlessly cut into her back.

"AAAHHHH!"

Several more shrill cries were followed by the whip's thunderous cracks. Warm blood trickled down her back, and tears streamed down her cheeks. When it was over, a group of servants ran from the house to untie her.

"She doesn't get out of work tonight," said Lady Watson evenly, "I expect you all to see that she does her fair share."

The entire night of the party, Madeline had the sympathetic eyes of all the other servants. They tried to assist her while she slowly worked in excruciating pain. The lashes had cut deeply.

Although the other servants did a decent job of tending her wounds and applying her bandages, every step she took she could feel her flesh on fire and her eyes welled up. But, she refused to cry and she refused the help of the other servants. She knew that, if she did, Lady Watson might see her as weak and beat and whip her regularly. Before selling her, her father, Isaac Black had played similar mind games with her. He had a dangerous temper and if she showed any disrespect or weakness of character, he'd hit her with whatever object was within reach.

It was six years ago, but the scars from the whipping were still visible. It was a reminder of what failure to meet expectations meant in Watson Manor. Nonetheless, it didn't deter her from taking valuables from the Manor and selling them. If anything, she got pleasure out of doing it. Seeing the scars on her back angered her and getting her own little private revenge felt good.

Since the incident with the figurine, she would not allow herself to make mistakes. From time to time, the Watsons made up excuses to punish her, but that wasn't unusual, it happened to everyone at Watson Manor.

She meticulously checked over her work, paying particular attention to little details. Eventually, Lady Watson noted that she barely made mistakes in her daily chores and she was punished less and less. Soon all the servants asked her to check over their work.

She was given more responsibilities; dressing Lady Watson, powdering her wig and applying her make-up. In time, she unofficially became the head maid. No one questioned her when she delegated work to other servants. The servants treated her as if she was the authority on Lady Watson's particular ways. Lady Watson had a belief on how every chore should be done, and Madeline innately understood these quirks. So much so, she was left in charge of the occasion that evening.

But what Lady Watson said would be an evening soiree snowballed into a seven-course meal, including some theatre, music and of course dancing.

Though planning the party was a burden for her, it was also an opportunity. With the mountains of gifts the Watson's would receive, it would be easy for her to nick a few for herself to sell.

She reached the end of the hall and stood at Lady Watson's door. Inside, Lady Watson was taking her afternoon nap. She dreaded waking her up. While Lady Watson was somewhat attractive in her waking hours, she was a drooling, snoring animal in her sleep. Once awake, she was somewhat incoherent for some time and grouchy. Lord Watson never slept next to his wife. Though he said it was because of her sleeping behaviours, everyone knew it was just an excuse. He didn't like to be in his wife's presence, which was why he worked abroad.

She tiptoed up to the large four poster bed with is canopy. The silk drapes were drawn to a close. She pulled them back carefully and began to rub circles into her mistress' back as she coughed and snored.

"Miss?" she began, speaking in a normal voice. She always called Lady Watson, 'Miss'. Once she overheard her tell a friend that she preferred being called 'Miss' because it made her feel younger. It was silly. Lady Watson was married and in her forties, and being called 'Miss' was not going to change that. But Madeline did it anyway. Swallowing her pride and doing so had given her favour over many of the other servants.

"Miss?" she spoke a little louder.

"Miss?" she said as loud as possible without yelling.

She stared slack-jawed at her, picturing herself smacking the cruel woman hard across the face. It was exasperating trying to get her up. Slowly she began to rock her back and forth on the bed.

"Miss!" she nearly yelled. Lady Watson's eyes finally fluttered open. "Wha- Oh- right," she said softly and began to drift off again.

"No, Miss!" she began shaking her hard, "You'll be receiving guests in a few hours!"

"Oh! Guests! The King!" She sprung up from the covers.

She should have mentioned him earlier. Though getting gifts and gaining popularity amongst nobles was important, the biggest highlight of the evening for Lady Watson was the fact that King Alexander had accepted her invitation. He was quite a bit younger than Lady Watson. He was only twenty-four. He was quite popular with his female subjects. According to Lady Watson, he had a certain 'je ne sais quoi'.

Aside from being handsome, he was also was a military genius and a good match' politically speaking. Often, there were princesses from other European countries visiting his castle, falling all over themselves hoping he'd ask for their hand. Because of this and all the other noble women he surrounded himself with, he gained quite the reputation.

He was often the talk of the London. Whenever Madeline went to town, she would see articles written about him on the front of The Society Pages, noble girls and ladies gossiping about what he did, how stylish he dressed, or their latest conversation with him at court. Of course, any little excursions or gifts he gave were always bragged about and sometimes this would lead to catty fights amongst them. Then the girls would get physical.

But to her, he sounded like a scoundrel with a crown; conquest after conquest. None of the women at court seemed to know that he was seeing several of them at a time. Naturally, servants of different households compared notes in the marketplace. On the other hand, the women probably did know, they just didn't care.

Despite knowing so much about him, she had never laid eyes on him. She had no idea what he looked like. For some reason, King Alexander had banned all publications from publishing any likenesses of him. In all the images, he was portrayed as a tall man with a wig and crown. No details were drawn on his face. Though she knew she wouldn't be impressed by him, she was curious.

Lady Watson had rushed over to her vanity stool and sat looking up at her eagerly. This was unusual. She wished King Alexander came every day. Lady Watson's vanity was white with and had drawers with silver handles. There was a matching white and silver pitcher and basin. Madeline poured some water into the basin and began, "We will start with your hair. Would you prefer to wear a wig?"

"A wig is suitable for the occasion."

To Madeline, a wig was not suiting to any occasion; she thought it looked like Lady Watson wore fluffy clouds with curls on her head. She was not a fan of her own jet-black hair, but a powdered wig full of pomades and ornaments was literally a pain in the neck. To Lady Watson, pain was nothing in her quest for beauty. She liked to think she was keeping up with the trends, but many of her styles were outdated. They were all styles she wore as a young debutante, which was more than twenty years ago.

"Get the one with the big poof in the front and the dangling curls in the back. It's my favourite."

She wished her mistress was like most other English women who powdered their own hair. Wigs were dirty. Not many ladies wore them anymore either. She turned on her foot and stiffly walked over to Lady Watson's armoire full of wigs and searched for the white ball of hair. She took it along with its stand and placed it on the vanity table and with a put-on grin, began powdering it.

"How's that Miss? More or less powder?"

"I think more."

She slowly sprayed on more powder.

"Whoa! That's it. Stop!"

Madeline always felt that it was senseless to spray the wig before adjusting it to Lady Watson. But again, this was one of her 'particular ways' the servants referred to. She liked it sprayed before, and after it was adjusted.

"Now give the powder time to set," she instructed.

"Right. Let's move on to your make-up then?"

"Indeed."

It always took some time to get Lady Watson primped. Like her wig, her make-up application also had an odd routine. It started with washing her face with a cloth and primrose water. Twice. Then patting her face dry, and applying lotion. Twice. After the lotion, Madeline lightly patted a whitish base onto Lady Watson's skin. Twice. White foundation was also an outdated trend, like the wigs. But making suggestions was out of the question.

She pressed the first layer on her skin lightly with the powder. Lady Watson would throw a tantrum if she wiped it on. After applying her face twice, she continued applying the white base to her neck, back, shoulders and bosom.

"All right, the foundation is on. What kind of colours would you like to use?"

"I think the Parisian rouge and that Egyptian kohl, oh and why don't you get that beautiful red lipstick Lord Watson just got from the Caribbean? Tonight is a special occasion after all."

Many of Lady Watson's beauty products had come from other parts of Europe and the Caribbean. Lord Watson spent much of his time abroad and never came home without heaps of beauty products. Some of her make-up did come from shops and boutiques in London, but she preferred her imported make-up for her parties. For tonight's occasion it seemed that she was only requesting the most expensive and rare products she had.

She brushed on the rouge, outlined Lady Watson's eyes with a light hand and dabbed on the lipstick. Its colour was vivid and brought life to Lady Watson's normally thin, pale lips. She adjusted and attached the wig to her head and sprayed it again.

Sissy, entered the room.

"Good timing Sissy," said Lady Watson curtly, "We were just about to get my garments, you can help get me into them."

It was not good timing. Only Madeline was allowed to see Lady Watson without her make-up and hair. She would throw a fit if anyone else entered the room. Madeline had instructed Sissy to be there at one thirty in the afternoon. Though Sissy was a bit of a scatterbrain, she had remembered to peek through the chamber door to see if Lady Watson was prepped.

It took them almost an hour to help Lady Watson put on her dress. Throughout, Sissy was harassed for everything she did; from the way she tightened the laces to how she presented Lady Watson her shoes. After several mistakes, she slapped Sissy and sent her away, which left Madeline to continue to work alone.

19

When Lady Watson was finally ready, she swayed in front of her full-length mirror admiring her reflection.

"Miss?" Madeline began timidly.

"What is it?"

"Would you like me to head to the market to get any last minute things for the party?"

"Yes. That would be a good idea. Anything you think we may need for this evening, I want to be prepared for any mishaps. You know where the change purse is."

She did a quick curtsy and left the chamber smiling. She was finished much sooner than she thought. It was only two thirty. Not only did she have time to get some fresh flowers, but she could also sell some goods too. She collected the change purse then hurried through the servants' common room between the men's and women's bunks.

The common room was full of rickety old wood chairs, a beaten couch, and damaged tables. It had a pantry, full of bland or nearly rotting food. Sadly, Lady Watson starved servants if she felt they were being incompetent, which was most of the time. She always had a complaint about something or someone.

The women's bunk room was a simple room with walls of brick and several piles of folded blankets laying on the floors at the walls. There were no beds. They used the blankets and slept on the cold stone floor. There were two mirrors and two dressers on the opposite wall from the blankets. The men's bunk room was the same. Unless ordered, there were rules that Lord and Lady Watson had about men entering the women's room and vice-versa.

She quickly ran over to the wall where she hid her valuables. When she first came to the Watsons, she discovered a loose brick by her pile of blankets. She removed it to uncover a hole. The breach was quite deep, and she often wondered if other servants that had worked there before she did hid things in there. She reached into the wall, grasped her bag and put it in her dress pocket.

2

MEETING THE KING

Madeline took the servants' wagon down to the market. She loved the ride, she usually took Oxford Street, which was filled with shops full of interesting items from all over Europe, the Americas and India. Not all the buildings were businesses; large brick homes filled with stained glass windows also lined the busy street. She wished she could own one of the homes, and this was why she stole and sold things from the Watsons. She knew that someday she would grow old and they would want to be rid of her. After years of being a slave, she'd finally have her freedom. But she would be left with nothing. The money she made from the stolen items was a retirement fund. She would never own one of the houses on Oxford Street, but a small home in the country would be better than living on the streets.

After she sold the valuables, she would go to England's First Bank and deposit the money into an account under her mother's name.

Fortunately for her, she was able to use her mother's name. She never tried, but she knew it was unlikely that they would allow a slave girl to open an account. Luckily, none of the bank managers suspected anything of her depositing money there. Many of them figured she must have been depositing money for her mistress.

She typically sold things to the shopkeepers on Oxford Street. Many of them knew her, what kind of goods she sold and not to ask too many questions. Most times, the shopkeepers gave her a fair price. Very few shopkeepers tried swindling her. She knew what kind of money her items could bring in from their customers. If the haggling wasn't going in her favour, she would bring it to another shop down the street. She would keep moving to the next shop until she got the price she wanted.

She usually dealt with Sheffield's first. Mr. Sheffield was always kind to her. He had known Madeline's mother and had a soft spot for her. Her mother had been a frequent customer of his when he bought and sold things from his home. With her mother's help, (who was a noble), Mr. Sheffield became so successful that he was able to open a shop on Oxford Street.

Mr. Sheffield was also her saviour. Madeline was fourteen when her father sold her off to a brothel. It was Mr. Sheffield who convinced Madam Ravine, the owner of the brothel, to sell her to Lady Watson. Madam Ravine was bitter about this decision later. She often made comments on how she should not have listened to the sob story of a sympathetic shopkeeper whenever she saw Madeline in the marketplace. On several occasions, she tried to coax her into working at the brothel. She had even made several offers to the Watsons to buy her back. Once, they came close to making a deal, but Lord Watson refused, saying it was immoral.

Sleeping with strange men for money disgusted her. It was another kind of enslavement, and she feared it more than her abusive servitude at the Watsons'.

"Hello, Mr. Sheffield," she said as she entered the shop.

"Madeline, my dear! I swear you look more like your mother every day," replied Mr. Sheffield as he raised his head from his accounting books, pulling his glasses down the bridge of his nose.

He often told her she looked like her mother, and she figured he was only being pleasant. Her mother, Elizabeth Swan, had quite a reputation. She was thought to be the most beautiful girl in London when she was alive. She had a string of beaus that were vying for her hand. Though there were many offers for her hand, Madeline's grandfather held out for a rich Duke or Earl. Finally, a noble made an offer Lord Swan could not refuse, but Elizabeth had her sights on one man, Isaac Black. He was an actor and the two had met at court while he was entertaining the King and Queen. Shortly after meeting Isaac, Elizabeth ran away with him and had Madeline out of wedlock. Soon after Madeline's birth, Elizabeth mysteriously died.

She did not like to think or talk about her mother. She despised her for being foolish and falling in love with the wrong man. Isaac was a selfish, sleazy, alcoholic, abusive father.

"I've got a few things you might be interested in Mr. Sheffield," she opened her bag and placed a set of faux pearl earrings, a small silver platter and a detailed hand carved wooden box on the counter.

"Let's see here," he said as he began inspecting the pearls. "Are these real?"

"I think they are real," she lied with a doe-eyed expression.

"Madeline-"

"Oh all right! They're fake, but if I told Mr. Burnham down the street that, you know he'd believe me. He isn't very bright."

He laughed. "I'll give you two shillings for the lot."

24

"Are you kidding? Four shillings at least."

"Three?"

She smiled, "That's fair."

Mr. Sheffield handed her the money from the register as the Honorable Susanna walked through the door. Madeline quickly curtsied, as tension filled the air.

The Honorable Susanna was the daughter of Lord Bathory and she embodied everything that Madeline hated about the upper class. As horrible as the Watsons were, she knew working for the Lord Bathory would be as terrible, if not worse.

Everywhere the Honorable Susanna went she was always dressed in her finest gowns, and only bought what she knew others could not afford. The rich prat was so full of herself she tried to avoid speaking to anyone below her class. Unless it was her servant and she was making a demand, she acted as though commoners did not exist.

The Honorable Susanna summoned her chaperone to speak to Mr. Sheffield. Her chaperone curtsied to the Honorable Susanna then walked over to the counter. Madeline stepped back allowing her to pass.

"Excuse me, Mr. Sheffield, Lady Susanna Upton of Bathory was wondering if you might have some earrings from India. She heard you recently received a shipment."

Another thing that annoyed Madeline was that Susanna insisted on people using the title 'Lady' and not 'the Honorable'. Technically, her mother was the 'Lady' of the household. For someone as well-bred as Susanna was, it was odd that she would ignore her proper title.

"Well, we still have some lovely gold earring sets," said Mr. Sheffield and began placing them on the counter. As he did so, Susanna pushed past Madeline and she toppled to the floor. This behaviour did not shock Madeline, it was not the first time the 'Honorable' Susanna had done it. Ignoring the urge to grab her dress and pulled her down with her, Madeline got on to her feet and dusted herself off.

"I've seen nicer earrings from India than these," Susanna said, pushing them aside. She put her hands on her hips. "With shipments like Mr. Sheffield's, London is getting less fashionable by the minute. I should really travel to France sometime."

Madeline shook her head and made her way to the door, opening it, she paused. A grin grew from ear to ear, as she turned back and curtsied, "Good day Mr. Sheffield … Miss Susanna," she said.

As she shut the door behind her, she saw from the corner of her eye, Susanna's face go red and her hands clench into fists. Madeline bolted down the steps as she heard the chaperone rushing after her. Madeline ran down the street towards the wagon, pretending not to notice Susanna's chaperone on the sidewalk yelling at her, "You cannot speak to Lady Susanna Upton of Bathory that way. Come back and APOLOGIZE."

The chaperone chased after her, but tripped on the sidewalk. Madeline hopped onto her wagon into the drivers' seat and took the reins, as she released the break. She felt somewhat guilty. There was a good chance that the chaperone would be punished for this. But she wasn't going to go out of her way to apologize to someone who shoved her about like a barnyard animal.

After depositing her money at the bank, she made her way to the food market, where mostly everyone was talking about the Watsons' party and King Alexander. She kept to herself, ignoring the conversations around her. She no longer had much time to get ready for the party and stopping to chat about it wouldn't help.

She bought the freshest flowers she could find in the market. When it came to flowers, she knew that Lady Watson did not care about the price. If they looked fresh and were fragrant, she would want them. There were plenty of colourful roses in season. She decided to get the lighter coloured ones, it was spring and red roses were cliché.

As she helped the vendor pack the flowers into the open carriage, she noticed a copy of The Society Pages on the cobblestone street. Seeing the ridiculous cartoon of the King, she picked it up and read the headline.

HIS MAJESTY WINS ANNUAL TENNIS TOURNAMENT

She read the article with little interest. Apparently, his Majesty was athletic. Or at least that is what she heard. He was also quite the huntsman and swordsman. She raised a brow and turned to the vendor, "Do you think his Majesty actually wins tournaments? Or do you think being royalty no one would dare try to beat him?"

The vendor laughed, "You're talking about the King's latest victory I suppose? With his military victories, I doubt his Majesty needs to win a tennis match to impress."

"Perhaps," she admitted, "but is winning a tennis tournament really that interesting to report about? Doesn't he have royal duties to attend to?"

"I doubt the nobility care much about his royal duties." He pointed to the article, "Just look at that drawing. It has the

Hampton, Davis, Cavendish and Upton families in there. If The Society Pages were to report on the King's royal duties, I doubt the nobility would enjoy reading it."

"Right," she said and climbed onto the wagon. "I suppose The Society Pages wouldn't exist if the nobility couldn't find themselves in the pages either."

She got back to the manor and gave Will the flowers so he could arrange them, then went to the Main Hall. She surveyed it carefully, before getting changed into the new uniform Lady Watson had provided for the staff. When she reached the quarters, she could hear the commotion of the other maids getting ready. Sissy, dressed and ready, sat in the common room on an old, rickety rocking chair, grinning at the floor. She was admiring her new shoes that went with the new uniform, bought for the nights' occasion. Madeline walked up to her, "You look lovely, Sissy. Stand and turn slowly."

Sissy did as she was asked and modelled the dress, proud as a peacock. It was black with a built-in corset and a white apron sewn around the waist. The apron had small lace appliqués on it. It exposed Sissy's bosom, which was startling because she did not have much for breasts. 'Amazing,' Madeline thought her eyes widening. It was unbelievable what a corset could do. Sissy blushed, "I stuffed it."

"Your bosom?" she confirmed, stunned.

"Yes. There were these little pads that came in the shoes. So, I took them out and popped them in."

"They look fairly natural. Lady Watson could use a tip like that."

"I wouldn't do any favour for that witch if I didn't have to."

"Nor would I."

28

"Do you want me to help you get ready?" Sissy asked, excitedly clasping her hands together.

"I would love your help. I don't think we have much time now."

"Okay, I'll get started on your hair, and you can do your make-up, Lady Watson got us some for the party."

"My, my. She really is trying to impress, isn't she?"

"King Alexander, I suppose," Sissy said, leading the way to the ladies' bunk. "But it's kind of enjoyable for us, isn't it?"

"I suppose."

Inside, the other maids were getting ready. Madeline sat on her bed applying her make-up with a mirror in hand, while Sissy began braiding her black hair. She was thankful, Sissy made the most exquisite braids.

"Honestly, do you think this is all just to bed the King?" Sissy whispered in her ear.

Madeline howled, "I didn't want to say anything, but yes, I think Lady Watson has an eye for him. Have you noticed she seems to talk about him more and more? When I served her and her friends afternoon tea the other day, they were giggling about him like a bunch of young debutantes."

"She's foolish. Hoping that a king, more than fifteen years younger, would want to be with her."

"Lord Watson does not have much interest in her. She has to find comfort somewhere."

"Maybe. But she could be realistic."

After they finished doing her hair and make-up, she stood in front of a large mirror that was hung on the bricked wall. Sissy had made a beautiful French braid that went half way around her crown, the rest of her hair was pinned up in curls in the back. It was seldom she adored her black hair; usually, she could do nothing more with it than a simple ponytail.

"You're naturally beautiful Madeline," she said, adoring the reflection. "If you were some noble's daughter, I'm sure there'd be a fight for you."

"You're sweet, but I doubt that. There's no man interested in me now."

"I think Will might have a bit of a crush on you. He'd just never say so. The Watsons wouldn't be pleased with that."

It was true. None of the servants at Watson Manor had romantic relationships with each other. It was too dangerous. Lady Watson used relationships to make their lives as miserable as she was.

"Make-up does work wonders, doesn't it?" she said trying to change the subject.

"I don't think there's much to improve with you."

Sissy grabbed a uniform and began to help Madeline get into it. Sissy tightened the laces to the corset, Madeline's waist shrank, and her bosom grew.

"Goodness!" giggled Sissy, "This corset certainly shows off some of your best assets."

Madeline stood staring open-mouthed into the mirror.

"Surely we can take them down a bit? You know, loosen the laces?" She began pulling down at the corset and pushing down her breasts. Sissy stopped her, "Why would you want to do that? Besides, I can't wait to see the look of envy on Lady Watson's face."

Neither could Madeline, "Good point."

Sissy brought over her shoes and helped her slip them on.

"Thanks for all the help."

"No problem, Mad. Thanks for getting the flowers. Will told me what happened."

They were the last to leave the servants' quarters. When they reached the foyer, all the rest of the servants were in position, ready to receive the guests. Madeline went over to Lady Watson, curtsied and stood on her left. Lord Watson stood on the other side of Lady Watson and she could feel his roving eye creeping over her body. Lord Watson disgusted her. He shamelessly looked at other women. He had somehow come to the deranged idea that all women were attracted to him, despite his grotesque looks and tobacco breath She tried to ignore being around him. He made her skin crawl, and she was thankful that he spent most of his time abroad. Lady Watson looked over at Madeline, "These uniforms certainly compliment you, don't they?" she said folding her arms.

"Yes. Thank you, Miss, for being so considerate and getting us such nice uniforms for the occasion. Good luck for tonight."

"I won't need luck. I'm sure you organized every detail, and there will be no hiccups?"

"None at all," Madeline said swallowing hard.

"I don't mind the fresh flowers you got."

Then she grabbed Madeline's jaw tightly, "But next time, if there are red roses, get them," she said hoarsely.

31

SMACK

She stumbled back, next to Sissy.

"That's got nothing to do with flowers," Sissy whispered beneath her breath.

Within fifteen minutes guests were being ushered into the manor. Piles of gifts were brought in. Sissy along with some other maids arranged them on a large table in the entrance. Statues, silver platters and goblets, paintings, ottomans, and Persian rugs, were among the presents. Soon the gift table was overflowing and the servants could no long find any room on or around it. They began carrying them into the Main Hall and displayed them next to one of the pillars.

Once the guests arrived and had been greeted by Lord and Lady Watson, they were then escorted into the dining hall, where their names and titles were announced to the other guests.

Mostly everyone invited had arrived. Madeline was surprised that some of the upper nobility came. Most Dukes, Earls and Viscounts, didn't have much to do with the Watsons. The manor hall was nearly full when she noticed a commotion by the front door. Hurriedly, servants rolled out a red carpet and got into position. The King. Looking out the front doors, she could see a gold and black coloured carriage, drawn by several Clydesdale horses. She rose slightly on her toes to see if she could see him, but there were so many bodies in the way, it was difficult to see anything. Surrounding the carriage were servants, the driver and his entourage of advisors and valets. They all crowded around him as he climbed up the steps of the manor to the front door. As he went through the threshold, his entourage finally stepped back. The atmosphere changed. Some of the maids looked down shyly, and everyone became silent as he walked towards the Watsons.

"Oh my goodness! He is gorgeous!" Sissy whispered.

Madeline gawked at the sight of him. Gorgeous was an understatement. 'Godly' might suffice. He was tall, well built with chiselled features and smooth tan skin. He had shiny jet black hair. His eyes were sparkling blue and he had the sexiest smile with perfectly straight white teeth. She was expecting to see some skinny prat in an ugly powdered wig. Instead, she was faced with a man she could not help but undress with her eyes.

He stood in front of Lord and Lady Watson, then his eyes met hers and he gave her a warm smile. Every muscle in her weakened. She couldn't help herself from ogling him. She felt like a hypocrite. She was no different from the noble girls she thought were ridiculous for wanting him. But unlike her, they had a chance of being with him.

"Congratulations on your twentieth anniversary, Lord and Lady Watson," he said.

She melted into a puddle on the floor. His accent was refined and gentlemanly. He looked over to her again smiling.

Lord and Lady Watson both curtsied and bowed greeting him with 'Your Majesty.' In a daze, Madeline forgot to curtsy.

"Madeline this is royalty!" Lady Watson said through gritted teeth, pulling at her skirts, "Curtsy!"

She looked about embarrassed; it seemed all the other maids had remembered to do this. But he only looked on smiling his dashing, flawless smile. "Exceptions can be made," he said.

Maybe she was imagining it, but as she curtsied she could feel his eyes wander over every inch of her body. She nervously pulled herself to her feet, then moved to his back to take his overcoat, feeling the soft, smooth, silky material as she pulled it down his arms.

His muscles felt solid and she blushed. Then she noticed the intricate details of the red and gold coat he wore underneath. She had never seen a man with such style. Once she removed his coat, Lady Watson quickly took his arm, ready to parade him into the large Main Hall. But, he turned and gently grabbed Madeline's arm, "Thank you, Miss …?"

"Black, your Majesty," she said timidly.

"Promise you won't let me forget my coat Miss Black?" he said gazing into her eyes.

"I won't."

"Good. Then I'll be sure to see you again before the night is through?"

"Yes, Sire."

"I'm going to hold you to that," he said, smirking.

He felt a tug on his arm and turned as Lady Watson pulled him into the Main Hall. She watched as Lady Watson showed off the decorations and the hall itself. Madeline had been responsible for the entire event. Yet, knowing Lady Watson, she would take credit. She would have loved to have heard what he thought of everything. She continued to stare as Lady Watson continued pointing out the festoons hanging from the windows and ceiling and the garland. She could not stop watching him. He had a manner about him, a kind of confidence as he moved swiftly about the room. She noticed that she wasn't the only person that could feel his presence, other guests watched him too. Some of the ladies were already making a beeline toward him.

"Oi! It would be excellent if someone could do their job," said a strange man in a humorous tone.

She turned to see a tall, thin man with unkempt brown hair standing before her. Having waited for some time for her to remove his coat, he decided to do it himself. He dangled it in front of her, trying to contain his laughter. She turned bright pink and quickly gathered his coat in her arms. "Pardon. I'm so sorry, Sir? Lord?"

"Umbridge, Sir Gregory Umbridge, Miss."

"Sorry, Sir Gregory. I'll um ... put this away for you. Are you with anyone this evening?"

"Yes, I'm with the King."

She looked down feeling like an idiot, "Oh. Right."

He gave her a sympathetic look, "Don't worry about it, love." He patted her shoulder and casually walked into the hall.

"Next time Miss Black," Lord Watson began in an exasperated tone, "don't insult the King's best friend by treating him as if he doesn't exist."

"I'm so sorry, Lord Watson."

He grazed her body with his eyes again. "It's all right. You can make up for it later."

Confused, she wondered how she could make things up to Sir Gregory, but the thought was quickly dashed out of her mind as more guests entered the home. She continued assisting them with their coats and gifts.

After the last of the guests had arrived, she and the other servants went to the kitchen. Appetizers were served to each table in turn, starting at the head table where King Alexander sat. His chair was positioned higher than everyone else's since no one's head could be higher than his. She thought it must be awkward to be the guest of honour at every social occasion. This was the Watsons' celebration, yet all eyes seemed to be on him. He took it in stride, and before dinner was served, made a well-spoken toast to the Watsons congratulating them.

As the music played and the guests ate, Madeline moved through the tables, making sure each course was served promptly to everyone. Now and again, she'd steal glances at the King. He sat in his chair, the most elaborate one Lady Watson could find, and ate his dinner, talking to Lady Watson and Sir Gregory Umbridge. Every so often, Lady Watson running her fingers through his black hair or flirtatiously touch his shoulder or arm. At one point, she was sure she saw her run her hand up his chest. She was disgusted not only with her behaviour, but her lack of proper etiquette. No one, not even a noble, had the right to touch the King. Through all of this, he was genteel towards Lady Watson, smiling and laughing. At the end of the dinner service, Lord and Lady Watson led their guests in a dance.

Madeline watched the party from behind the punch and refreshments table. As much as she detested aristocrats and their pompous ways, she loved watching the dancing. She thought it was sophisticated how the gentlemen and the ladies bowed and curtsied and that everyone knew the choreography of each traditional dance. She paid particular attention to King Alexander, who was dancing with Miss Hampton, Lady Wiltshire and Miss Cavendish. He was swift on his feet and kept to the rhythm and beat of the music. Between each dance, a crowd of ladies would circle around him, hoping he'd pick them for the next dance. She was envious of all of them, even the girls he did not dance with. At least they had a hope of dancing with him.

After several more dances, he bowed out, and the noble ladies whined in disappointment. Madeline grunted, pathetic, she thought. He couldn't dance all night, and there were probably other people he would want to speak with. Strangely, after he finished dancing, he walked directly to her at the refreshments table.

"Could I have a glass of punch, Miss Black?"

She quickly curtsied, "Yes, your Majesty."

She shakily dipped the ladle into the crystal bowl and poured it into the glass and presented it to him.

"Are there cherries at the bottom of the bowl? Could you get some in the glass for me, please?" he asked as he took the glass from her, grazing her hands with his fingertips as he did. Warm to the touch, she could feel herself growing weak again. By the look on his face, he knew what kind of effect he had on her. It wasn't often she felt shy and unsure of what to say. She bent down and began trying to fish out the cherries with the ladle, her breath uneven. He waited patiently, watching her bosom heaving as she tried to capture the cherries.

It was difficult, but when she got five cherries, he finally grinned, "That'll be fine Miss Black, thank you."

Lady Watson pulled away from the crowd and stood next to him, "Are you having a lovely time your Majesty?"

"Yes, the punch is quite good." Madeline cocked her head.

It was an odd comment since he hadn't tried any yet.

Lady Watson continued, "It's an old family recipe."

"And Miss Black did a wonderful job making it," he said gazing at her again. "You did prepare it, didn't you Miss Black?"

"Yes, your Majesty."

Lady Watson jabbered on to him about the food, decor and how she had had a difficult time deciding what to wear. She eyed him from time to time as other guests came up for food and punch. But he wasn't really paying attention to Lady Watson. She noticed his gaze wander back to her as he took sips of his punch.

"... just look at these flowers, your Majesty, are they not lovely?" Lady Watson said pointing to a vase next to Madeline.

"Oh, yes, Lady Watson," he said amusedly while smiling at Madeline, "There's nothing like rubbing your face in a fresh flower, and drinking it all in." He quickly winked at her.

"Oh! Oh!" she continued, "then you must smell the flowers I picked out for tonight, they are absolutely delicious."

Madeline took her cue, and picked up the vase of roses and offered them to him. He leaned toward her to smell them. She swallowed hard. His sensuality, the way he breathed them in and slowly opened his eyes. Her mind began to wander to perverse places it hadn't before. She immediately shook her head trying to erase the thoughts.

"Mmm, what a divine flower," he said looking up at her through hooded eyes.

She looked down, her face hot. It was probably just wishful thinking, but it felt like he was flirting with her. If he were, then Lady Watson was oblivious to it. Her back to Madeline, she stood facing the King fanning her bosom, prattling on.

Sir Gregory Umbridge, now inebriated, stumbled across the floor, bumping into guests as he went. He eventually reached them and put his arm around King Alexander.

"This has been a lovely celebration," he extended his wine glass into the air and red wine splashed to the floor. King Alexander's eyes bulged. Lady Watson's jaw dropped as she looked down at the spilt wine.

"What is going on over here? Huh?" Sir Gregory said, hanging off King Alexander he began to point to Lady Watson and the other guests. "What'z going on?"

The King grinned, raising his brow, "Lady Watson, and I were just discussing how delicious fresh flowers are."

Sir Gregory laughed loudly, slapping his thigh. Lady Watson looked aghast. He abruptly stopped and regained his composure.

"I totally agree, Lady Watson, fresh flowers are lovely!" Sir Gregory said pretending to sound genteel, "On an unrelated note, I also like peaches and pussy ... cats!" He fell back onto the King, his laughter carrying through the room. He did his best to raise his friend back from his chest. Lady Watson crossed her arms, her face scarlet.

"You must forgive my friend Lady Watson, it only takes him a glass of wine to forget where he is, and the company he keeps."

"Oh, of course, your Majesty," Lady Watson said in her prettiest tone. "Any friend of yours is always forgiven."

"Excellent. Then perhaps you could help my friend find a place to sit? He's no longer able to stand on his own two feet." He flashed his perfect teeth.

"Of course," she said grabbing his and the King's arm.

"Oh Lady Watson," he said releasing his arm from hers, "Could you take Sir Gregory? I need someone to escort me to the lavatory."

"Oh," she said, disappointed that she no longer had his company. She snapped her fingers in Madeline's direction and added, "Escort his Majesty to the lavatory."

Madeline curtsied, made her way around the table, curtsied again in front of him and began to lead the way to the foyer and up the stairs. He followed, "Pardon Miss Black, are there no facilities downstairs?" he asked as they climbed the stairs. She tried to keep from giggling. In his genteel accent, 'pardon Miss Black' was somehow seductive and endearing at the same time.

"Oh, there are, but someone may be using them."

As they made their way, Miss Hampton and Miss Cavendish walked to the foot of the stairs and goggled up at him. She could not help to think how annoying it would be to be followed by women that looked like anxious little puppy dogs. Upon reaching the top of the stairs, she led him down the hall, out of their sight to the bathroom door. She turned to him and curtsied again and rose to her feet.

He paused a moment watching her. Her breath hitched and she cast her eyes downward. She felt a fluttering inside of her. Her skin was hot her palms were clammy, feeling his eyes soaking in the curves of her body. He lifted her chin with his hand and penetrating his gaze at her emerald eyes. She averted her gaze to the floor. A predatory smile lined his lips, "Look at me," he said softly.

Awkwardly, she looked up at him and curtsied. She could feel her skin grow goosebumps at his touch. He chuckled and released his hand from her face.

"All these curtsies. Are you trying to make up for earlier?" he asked.

"No," she said, embarrassed. "I'm just trying to give you the hint that behind this door is the lavatory."

She grinned and jokingly curtsied again. He laughed. Her heart beat fast. His laugh was as warm as his touch. Again, her mind went to naughty places. It would be great to take him into one of the guest rooms. Then, she felt stupid for thinking it. She was just a servant, and she was reading into everything he did and said.

"You don't have to wait here," he said, "I'll be able to find my way back to the party."

She watched as he went in. As she stood gawking at the door, she had to admit that she now understood why he was the talk of afternoon teas, the marketplace, and parties. He was handsome, sweet and kind to everyone. His joking with her was a moment she could never share with any other. As she stood there in her dream world, she realized it would be strange if he came out and she was standing there staring at nothing.

Now would be a perfect opportunity to go through Lady Watson's closet and pick out a few pieces to sell. Lady Watson would only be concerned with the whereabouts of the King for the rest of the evening. She walked past the stairs, and Miss Hampton, who now waited alone at the bottom of the staircase, and continued down the hall to Lady Watson's room. She lit several kerosene sconces in the room and went into the closet.

She rummaged through the back of the drawers, looking for items that she had not used or seen in ages. She pulled out a pair of lace stockings that had never been worn. She rolled up the socks and put them in her dress pocket. She continued to sift through a drawer until she heard voices in the hallway. She gasped, put out the kerosene sconce in the closet and peeked out the door into the bedchamber.

"This is the perfect place. We'll do it here."

3

THE NAUGHTY KING

It was Miss Hampton. She giggled as she pulled King Alexander by the front of his waistcoat into the room. He had a firm grip on her hip and bottom and began to kiss her, passionately.

Madeline's blood began to boil. Even though it wasn't her place, she was jealous. But then, he pulled away from her, having second thoughts.

"Maybe we shouldn't do this? I mean this isn't one of my or your residences," he said as he glanced around the room. "Actually, I think this is Lady Watson's chamber."

"Well, if she comes walking in, she'll get a good show, won't she?" she said, pulling him further into the room. "Everybody knows she wants one from you."

She propped herself onto the canopy bed and began lifting her petticoat. He gazed at her hesitantly, his eyes shifting about the room. "Do you feel there may be someone in here?"

He looked at the vanity, then his head darted to the closet.

Madeline moved back further in the darkness, hoping he didn't see her.

He shook his head. "Never mind," he said.

Miss Hampton lay back on the bed, with her skirts over her belly, her legs wide open, awaiting him.

"You need it that badly?"

"I take every chance I can get to be your whore."

Wow, thought Madeline staring at the pair. She thought Miss Hampton was the naive, innocent type. She had a reputation for being a sweet, proper woman. It was odd to see her begging for sex and calling herself a whore.

"Darling, I think we should talk first."

"I don't want to talk about it. You owe me," she said, her eyes fierce. "I don't want to hear excuses. Besides, if you want to know-"

He put his finger to her lips. There was a silence. They looked at one another as if to stare each other down. Then, he got onto his knees and began kissing her thighs. Madeline sat in shock, that kind of act was never spoken of. It was taboo. Was the King really that wicked? Miss Hampton jolted up.

"Your Majesty," she said coquettishly tangling her fingers in his hair and looked down at him. "I want it. Your cock. Now."

He got up and began unbuttoning his trousers as she pawed and rubbed him through the material. He pulled his trousers down.

Madeline moved forward from the darkness to sneak a peek. It was a shame his back was turned to her. Though, she had to admit he had a cute backside.

"Mmmm," Miss Hampton crooned the moment he entered her.

He began slowly thrusting into her, and she moaned and murmured. Madeline began to get excited. She knew what sex was, but she had never done it or seen it. Judging by Miss Hampton's moaning, he was all he was rumoured to be. Oddly, the entire time, he barely made a sound. Madeline wondered if this was normal for a man. From what she gathered, she thought men were supposed to like sex more than women. As he began pumping faster, she became louder. Soon she began squealing and crying 'yes' again and again. But as her first orgasm passed, he continued thrusting and she became louder than before, screaming obscenities and 'your Majesty' as if she were possessed. Orgasm after orgasm was happening, and he didn't seem to be letting up.

After some time, he slowed down his thrusting, and her body became listless. He withdrew from her as she lay on the bed exhausted, panting heavily. For the next several minutes, she was disoriented. He tried to rouse her, softly kissing her. Eventually, he helped her to her feet. She stood shakily her glazed eyes staring into the closet.

Madeline quickly ducked down to the floor. As she did, she noticed Miss Hampton going down on her knees and she glanced up at him seductively. "I suppose you want this, your Majesty?" She began tonguing his inner thighs.

It was then, he turned slightly, and Madeline could see his cock. She gasped, clasping her hand over her mouth. Though she was some feet away, she could see he was well-to-do in more ways than a crown.

Miss Hampton just barely wrapped her hand around it as she stroked him. He began to touch her lips with his fingers and gently opened her mouth and guided her toward him. She began to kiss his length.

Madeline was stunned. To see the King doing it was unthinkable. People never spoke of it. It wasn't proper. It was dirty. Tsk! Tsk! Naughty boy, she thought trying to keep herself from giggling. Then Miss Hampton turned away.

"You don't want to?" he asked as if her change of mind didn't surprise him.

"Not anymore," she said simply.

"Fine," he said helping her up from her knees.

Madeline sat in the darkness, taken aback, she furrowed her brow. He could have easily commanded Miss Hampton to do what he wanted. But he didn't. She couldn't help to feel put out. If she couldn't be Miss Hampton, it still would have been great to see the look of pleasure on his face the moment he came. It looked as though Miss Hampton only cared about her own needs.

"Prude," she said beneath her breath, crossing her arms.

He stopped buttoning his trousers and tilted his head toward the closet. Miss Hampton adjusted her skirts and made her way to the door. But he didn't follow. She turned back toward him, her dress sweeping across the floor, "Your Majesty, I would like the pleasure of your company," she demanded.

"Go on without me. I need a moment alone."

She rolled her eyes before turning on her heel and walking out.

He looked over at the closet entry. Madeline's chest constricted, her muscles tightened. He knew she was there. She quietly walked further into the dark closet and hid in amongst Lady Watson's largest, most elaborate dresses. A moment later, he came in carrying a lamp with him. He stood at the closets entrance staring into the darkness beyond the light of the lamp. She breathed unevenly. She slowly pulled back a small piece of material and saw him as he began to walk through the closet, lifting the lamp.

Then, he stopped next to her. She held her breath, her face hot and palms sweaty. If she stretched her arm, she could touch him. He paused there for some time. She could no longer hold her breath, so she exhaled as soundlessly as she could.

He closed his eyes and inhaled deeply. *Vanilla pudding,* he thought. A small devilish smile grew on his face. It was that cute servant, Miss Black. He was tempted to pull her out from the dresses and press her lips to his. He was certain that a kiss from her would be warm, welcoming and more satisfying than the sex he'd just had with Miss Hampton. He wished he could take back what he just done. *Not the impression a gentleman leaves,* he thought. He sighed and left the closet.

She exhaled deeply, her heart racing, she wiped the sweat from her forehead with a handkerchief. She couldn't shake the feeling that he had seen her. Panicked, she decided to wait awhile in the closet. It wasn't a good idea to be absent from the party for long, but she feared that he could be waiting for her outside the closet door. She sank down amongst the dresses.

After some time, she crept out of the closet. If she didn't go back to the party, someone would notice her missing and search for her. Before making a quick exit out of the bedroom, she checked the hallway from the door to be sure no one would see her leaving. When she saw no one was in sight, she casually made her way back to the stairs, and back to the Main Hall. She slipped behind the buffet table and began to hand out glasses of punch. For several minutes, she surveyed the room.

It seemed no one had noticed her long absence. As she watched the festivities, she thought it was silly that she even worried. Lady and Lord Watson along with their guests were busy enjoying themselves.

Relieved, she looked about for Sissy. Sissy had the responsibility of cleaning the tables, and she wanted to be sure she was done before the party was over. She spotted her petite figure by the musicians, clearing some glasses. As her eyes moved back across the room, she saw King Alexander. He stood amongst some gentlemen who were speaking animatedly to him, competing for his conversation. She gazed at him, admiring his body. She daydreamed about running her hands up and down his sculpted chest and abs, and soon, her hands stroked him a little lower. She grinned.

But, then he smiled back at her. Embarrassed, her eyes darted in another direction. She pretended to look busy, rearranging the snacks. She could feel his eyes on her as he began walking over to the table. Quickly, she collected all the empty plates in her hand as well as some cheeses that were no longer looked appetizing and turned to go to the kitchen, "Excuse me, could I have some of those?" he asked innocently.

"Some of what, your Majesty?" She turned around, giving a small curtsy.

"Whatever it is you have on your tray."

"These cheeses are not so appetizing your-"

"Oh yes they are, bring them back here, Miss Black."

She walked back to him and put the cheeses back on the table and crossed her arms.

"Most times my servants hold the tray up for me," he said flashing his gorgeous smile.

She looked up at him suspiciously. He knew she was in the closet. At least she was quite sure. If he did, then what was he playing at? She held up the tray with one hand, and he picked a cheese and ate it, cringing as he swallowed.

"Miss Black, maybe you should come work at Buckingham. You need to learn how to serve royalty properly. You should use two hands to hold the tray." Obediently, she put her other hand on the tray.

"I don't think I could work at Buckingham."

"The living quarters and pay are better."

"No matter," she said as she organized some of the trays on the table. "Lady and Lord Watson own me, so I don't have a choice."

He looked at her sympathetically, having a loss for words. She felt sorry for making him feel awkward. It was a rude thing to do to a king, she looked down, shamefully. He bent down and caught her eyes with his, "Well," he said with a little smirk, "I think Lady Watson would own me too ... if she could."

She guffawed, "She had me send out the invitations early, just to be sure you would reserve the date."

He laughed, "You're quite plain about Lady Watson. Anything else you'd like to share?"

"Yes, check your carriage. I think she may have persuaded one of the servants to break the wheel, that way you'll stay the night in one of the guest rooms here," she joked.

He leaned towards her, "If that does happen, and I do stay here, should I expect an 'unexpected guest' in the middle of the night?"

"Oh yes."

"You'd protect me though, right?" he whispered, leaning closer so close she could smell the scent of sandalwood on his neck.

She giggled, "If you'd like, I could leave a dagger under the pillows in the guest bed."

"Daggers? Pillows?"

Greg Umbridge had come from out of the crowd, still drunk, fumbling about, "Alex, what on earth are you two talking about?" Madeline was surprised that Sir Gregory casually referred to King Alexander as 'Alex'.

"Why aren't you dancing or singing, Greg? You love to sing."

"I could ask you the same question. Miss Hampton has been looking for you, she would love to dance," he said as he nudged him with his elbow.

He rubbed his temples, "Why don't you go dance with her then?"

Greg scratched his head. Then, he noticed Madeline and raised his brow, "I would dance with Miss Hampton, but I already promised a dance to this lady."

He bolted behind the table and grabbed Madeline's arm. The silver plates fell from her hands and came to the floor with a loud clatter. He dragged her out onto the dance floor as he wrapped his arm around her waist, swaying her to and fro to the music. She looked over her shoulder at the King, who stood tightening his lips. The guests stopped to stare as she struggled to push Sir Gregory off.

He overpowered her wrapping both his arms around her. Over his shoulder, she could see Lady Watson storming through the crowd, a scathing look on her face as she watched her and Sir Gregory.

King Alexander cut into her path.

"Lady Watson, may I have this dance?" he asked.

An elated expression appeared on her face, "Of course, your Majesty."

He bowed, Lady Watson curtsied and the two started dancing. As he circled around, Madeline could hear him whisper crossly to Greg,

"Let Miss Black go."

"Why?" he teased. "She's such a good dancer."

"Now."

Greg stopped, and escorted her back to the buffet table. As she left the floor, she could overhear King Alexander making excuses to Lady Watson for her, "Poor thing. Sir Gregory's too drunk. She had no idea he'd try dancing with her."

"Still no way for a servant to behave, your Majesty."

"I'd prefer that you don't punish her, Lady Watson. I command that you don't."

She stood from behind the buffet table staring at him as he continued dancing. She had never had someone come to her defence like that. Ever. Not even her father. Nobles did not do that for servants, and servants knew better than to try to defend other servants. She began to want to work at Buckingham. Even if all she could do was clean, serve and watch him from afar.

The evening wore on unto midnight. As guests began to leave, Lord and Lady Watson began seeing them out the door. King Alexander left but, not before mentioning a promise that had been broken.

"I'm sorry Lady Watson," he said, "but one of your servants promised to see me out the door tonight. I believe her name is Miss Black?"

"Sissy, go fetch Madeline."

Sissy found her in the pantry, "The King wishes you see him out the door, Madeline," she said excitedly.

"I didn't think he was serious."

She shrugged, "Well, he's wondering where you are."

She quickly went to the entrance as he waited to be given his coat. She fetched it out of the closet and checked it over to see that it was still clean. She re-entered the entrance where he stood, his face beaming.

"Miss Black, you promised me that you would see that I would get my coat back."

"I know, and here I am, keeping my promise," she said as she opened his coat, holding it out for him.

"Oh no. You forgot again, Miss Black."

"Sorry, your Majesty, what did I forget?"

"To curtsy."

She glanced over at Lady Watson, who stood glaring at her.

"She's not the sharpest knife in the drawer your Majesty. I apologize."

"It's all right Lady Watson. I was only teasing her."

Nonetheless, Lady Watson was not pleased, "Sissy, can you help his Majesty with his coat. Madeline hasn't a clue."

Humiliated, she stepped next to Greg Umbridge and the King's other valets and advisors, who had witnessed the scene. Sissy grabbed the coat from her and held it out to him.

"Never mind," he said gruffly, adjusting his coat. "Miss Black while I put on my coat you can give me another curtsy. You can show Lady Watson that you can do it."

She stepped in front of him and curtsied. He grabbed her hand and kissed it. His lips were soft and warm. He gazed at her through hooded eyes.

"Thank you for all your assistance this evening."

He kissed her hand again, and out of the corner of her eye, she could see Sissy's dewy eyes widen. Lady Watson pushed Madeline aside, and positioned herself in front of the King.

"Thank you so much, your Majesty, this evening would not have been the same without you. Lord Watson and I are so pleased you came." She curtsied and looked up at him expectantly.

"Yes," he said, in a dismissive tone, looking about. "Well, we really must be going. Something tells me that Sir Gregory will be nursing a hangover, tomorrow."

"And how," laughed Greg.

"Good night, Lady Watson, Lord Watson."

"Good night my Liege," Lady Watson curtsied again, this time with her hand raised slightly in front of him. Her gesture seemed to go unnoticed. He nodded to Lord Watson and walked out the door to his carriage, his entourage following. Sissy walked over to Madeline and whispered beneath her breath,

"Did he just snub Lady Watson?"

As they rode off into the night, the carriage bounced them about the purple velvet seats, the wheels rolling over rough dirt. Drunk, Greg Umbridge looked at his friend suspiciously. Alex looked at the shaded trees out the window, trying to avoid him.

"You've been acting strange all night," he started, "First you ignore Miss Hampton's advances, then you walk out of Lady Watson's without thanking her or kissing her hand. I don't think much of Lady Watson, but you're not one to be thaaat rude publicly," he said in a drunk tone, wagging his finger at him.

"I did not ignore Miss Hampton's advances. She would not leave me alone, she begged me to dance and after we did, she followed me to the lavatory. To get her off my back I took her to Lady Watson's room. Later, she followed me about the ballroom. It was annoying."

"Annoying? I thought you enjoyed Miss Hampton's company. Are you telling me you're no longer interested?"

"I'd be interested if she could be interesting. She doesn't trust me. It seems she wants me to keep playing her games."

"Why did we come tonight then? Do you have a thing for Lady Watson?"

"I accepted the invitation because just about everyone at court decided to go."

"Right, Alex."

He gazed back out the window, hoping the conversation had come to an end. The last thing he wanted was Greg questioning him about his odd behaviour with Miss Black.

"So you've got a new interest then?"

"What? No. What makes you think that?"

"You don't have to limit yourself to just one, do you? Are there a few others?"

"No. But what does it matter? Even when I'm seeing more than one, and they find out, they play stupid and act like I'm committed only to them."

"Aren't we a little egotistical?"

"It's true. They all just want to be a queen. To be honest, I'm getting tired of spending time with these 'noble' women, competing for a crown."

Greg lunged to the other side of the carriage next to him. "If you'd like, I could take off the pressure ... I'll be the next Queen of England." He raised his hand to his brow and pretended to faint onto his lap.

He chuckled, "Get off me, you arse."

"So is there someone else then?"

"No one," he said slowly, his expression vacant.

Madeline Black was 'no one' and because of that, she would never be his. She was naturally beautiful, witty and did not seem to try so hard to impress him like so many other women he knew. Hell, she was a little cheeky with her jokes and curtsies. He felt a huge hole grow, deep inside him. Unless he made an odd request that she come work at Buckingham and raised suspicion from the entire nobility, he'd never see her again.

4

FIGHT TO FLIGHT

"All right, now listen up! All of you!" Lady Watson yelled as soon as the last guest had left, "I want this place cleaned top to bottom. I don't want to see any sign that we had a party tomorrow when I wake up. I know Lord Watson feels the same."

With that, she stomped up the stairs in a huff. Obviously, the King deliberately ignoring her hand bothered her. She didn't ask for Madeline's assistance undressing and prepping for bed. That was unusual.

Lord Watson quickly went over to Madeline, "I would like some chamomile tea before I rest. Bring some to my room," he said putting his hand on her shoulder. It felt slimy and made her uncomfortable, but she nodded and made her way back to the kitchen to prepare the tea. As she put the kettle on, Sissy came in and handed her a tray with one hand.

"Oh, thanks Sissy. It's been a long night."

"So, what did you think of the party?" asked Sissy in a low voice.

"Interesting. Very interesting."

"I'll say! You won't believe some of the things I saw. That Sir Gregory Umbridge is quite wild when he gets a few in him. He tried to take off his trousers at one point!"

"What?" she sniggered, placing the teacup and saucer onto the tray. "So, this will probably be the one and only time we meet the King. What did you think of him?"

Sissy smiled, "He's absolutely divine, isn't he?"

"That's putting it mildly."

"Could you imagine being one of the debutantes? To have the chance?"

A huge grin grew on her face; thanks to Miss Hampton she had an idea.

"And he kissed your hand. He treated you like a lady with a title," said Sissy timidly. "He paid no attention to Lady Watson when she said goodbye. Do you know what that was about?"

"No idea."

"Hmm."

The kettle whistled. Madeline grabbed it and poured the hot water over the leaves and placed the ceramic top on the pot as Sissy talked about the party. She left the kitchen with Sissy at her heels, talking about the ladies at court. "That Miss Hampton is a striking, isn't she? Everything she does; dancing, eating, speaking she does with such grace."

When they reached the top of the stairs, Madeline looked down at the tray and realized that she had forgotten the tea cosy.

"Damn," she whispered under her breath. "I've forgotten the tea cosy. Could you grab one from the kitchen and bring it up to Lord Watson's room, Sissy?"

Sissy nodded and went back down as Madeline continued down the hall to Lord Watson's room which was on the opposite side of the manor from Lady Watson's in another wing. She knocked on the door.

"Lord Watson?" she called timidly.

"Come in, dear," he called casually.

She turned the knob and found Lord Watson, standing beside the foot of his bed in his bed clothes. This made her uncomfortable, male servants usually tended to Lord Watson when he was in his bed clothes or getting ready in the morning. It was far too personal and she questioned her presence in the room. She hesitated at the door.

"Well, come in dear, the tea won't serve itself," he said.

Not wanting to offend him, she stepped into the room. As she walked, she felt him ogle her body, and it made her feel sick to her stomach. She avoided making eye contact by glancing about the room. His room was similar to Lady Watson's. It had sconces adorning the walls, a fireplace and several armoires and tables. There was a small vanity and a large four poster bed. It had a more masculine look with dark maroons and reds, and the detailing on the furniture was rugged not dainty. She placed the tray on the table and began pouring the tea into the cup. He stepped next to her, and brushed a strand of her black hair behind her ear.

"When you first came here, I never really thought of you as the daughter of Elizabeth Swan. You certainly did not look like her," he said as he stroked her arm. "But every time I come home, you grow older, and you look more and more like her. Your mother and I had a thing you know."

It was a lie. She wasn't fond of her mother, but she could not imagine her in love with someone as repellent as Lord Watson. He moved his greasy hand across her cheek, and she felt chills go up her spine. He leaned in to kiss her.

"Well, I'm not my mother," she said as she brushed his hand away from her face.

"You should be proud to be compared to your mother," he continued, "looking like your mother could be to your advantage." He slowly ran his finger down her cleavage.

She tried to dash to the door, but he grabbed her by the arm and hurled her to the floor, she rolled and crashed into a table. Two wood candlestick holders and a small silver box fell to the floor as he seized her shoulders and tried to drag her over to the bed. She struggled trying to dig the heels of her shoes into the floor.

"No! NO! SISSY!" she screamed desperately for help.

Just then, Sissy ran to the door, a tea cosy in hand staring. Lord Watson released her to the floor and walked over to the door.

"Be gone, you stupid girl!" he yelled as he shut the door in her face.

"SISSY!" Madeline shrieked as she scrambled up from the floor.

He turned to her as she bent down and grabbed a candlestick holder that had fallen to the floor, he clasped her wrists so tightly she released the candlestick with a cry. He smacked her hard across the face and she fell to the floor again. Beneath her she could feel the small silver box. She clutched it in her hand as he dragged her over to the foot of his bed. He lifted her and threw her onto it. She held the silver box behind her back. As he moved closer to her, she smashed it hard across his face. He howled in pain. She kicked him in the stomach, leaving him on the ground gasping for air.

"YOU WHORE! YOU BITCH!"

Madeline wheeled around to see Lady Watson at the door, Sissy standing in her wake.

"GET AWAY FROM HIM!" Lady Watson screeched again.

Madeline dropped the bloodied silver box and ran to the door as Lady Watson ran over to her husband and got down on her knees.

"Oh, darling, are you all right?" she asked, touching his cheek. The girls stood looking at each other astounded. It was obvious what he had been trying to do. But Lady Watson pretended to not know.

There was a long silence, and a tension filled the room. Finally, Lady Watson got up from the floor. Her lip a gash of anger, "We can't have a servant that beats her master. Madeline will simply have to be sold off at the market first thing tomorrow morning. With any luck Madam Ravine will put her where she belongs."

"Dearest is that really necessary? It's all right. If I can forgive her, surely you can," he said leering at Madeline.

"No," she said with a firmness that no one at Watson Manor would question. "I'll have someone take you in the morning, Madeline. For now, the both of you can finish cleaning the mess downstairs."

Madeline and Sissy turned to leave, when Lady Watson grabbed them both by their hair, pulling them back to her, "Neither of you will ever speak of this to anyone. Do I make myself clear?"

"Yes, Miss."

Sissy nodded meekly.

She released them and the two went down the stairs and helped clean the areas of the manor that the guests had used. Neither of them said anything about what happened upstairs to anyone or each other. Once the work was finished, they went to bed, leaving them one hour to sleep before they woke for their daily chores.

But, Madeline didn't have to do her daily chores. Sleep deprived, she stood looking at her reflection in the mirror. She was dressed in a plain white cotton dress, the only thing she owned. She wore it the day she arrived at Watson Manor. She was fourteen when she first came, so the dress fit rather snug around her waist and hips and came up short around her ankles. Sissy stole a white table runner from the kitchen linen closet to tie around her waist. She was able to bring the waist down a little with the sash, but the dress barely covered her ankles.

"I look like a gypsy girl with this sash."

"The Watsons would have your head if you took one of their uniforms," Sissy replied.

Madeline shrunk away from the mirror, "I suppose it's better than having no modesty and showing my ankles."

Sissy smirked faintly, then quickly teared up, "I don't know what I'm going to do without you here. Lady Watson, she'll ... she'll ..."

She wrapped her arm around her, "Next time Lady Watson makes things difficult for you, just tell her if she does not stop, you'll tell everyone why I suddenly left."

"Do you think that will work?"

"Has to," she said confident. "There's nothing Lady Watson cares about more than her reputation."

"True."

Madeline hugged her tightly, "Don't be afraid to try it. You'll be punished either way."

"I suppose," Sissy said, clasping her hands behind her back.

"I should get going. I know Lady Watson said she would have someone to take me. Hopefully I don't run into either of the Watsons before I go."

They hugged.

"Bye Madeline. I hope you end up in a place nicer than this."

"Me too," she whispered, her voice cracking. She gave her a kiss on the cheek and turned to leave.

Walking into the common area of the servants' quarters, she saw Will was sitting at a table, a leather scroll case sitting next to him. She immediately recognized it. Inside were her ownership papers. It seemed the Watsons did not wish to say goodbye to her either.

Will usually dealt with business dealings for the Watsons, as well as buying and selling in the market. He was usually able to get a good price for them and was one of the few servants that knew arithmetic. She sat next to him.

"I suppose they've asked you to take me to the market to sell me?" she asked eyes downcast.

"I'm still shocked that Lord Watson asked me. Did you know they planned to sell you?"

"Yes."

"Really? Why?"

"I'm not really sure," she lied. "Perhaps last night's party didn't quite reach the Watsons' expectations?"

He gave her a look, "If that's true, that's bollocks."

"What more can you expect from the Watsons?"

"I'll be sorry to see you leave," he stopped, hesitating as he looked about the room. "Maybe leaving is what's best for you."

He took her in the servant carriage down to Covent Garden market. In the square, there was a stage set up to auction off servants, furniture and other odd ends. She sat in the line of items and people waiting to be called up onto the stage.

"I'll try to make sure that the organizers and the auctioneer know all your good qualities, so maybe you'll end up going to a nicer home, maybe even the castle."

Strangely, she had never thought of the castle or King Alexander until Will mentioned it. Her body trembled. What would the King think of her getting fired by the Watsons? She shook her head. It was unlikely she would go to the castle. To get a job there you needed a connection. She knew no one.

As she waited in line, next to all sorts of items, she watched as the auctioneer sold some pedestals, a beautiful red fainting couch, a painting, a collection of rare plants and a sixteen-year-old girl. Will came back over, "I let the auctioneer know that you're literate and oversaw the event last night at the Watsons. That should help a bit I'd think?"

She looked up at him. Though he spoke calmly, an angry expression was across his face.

"If I'm not sold, it'll be your head when we get back to the Watsons," she reminded him.

"Our next item for bid is a twenty-year-old servant girl, Madeline Black," the auctioneer called out.

Her palms went clammy, "I promise to do my best to sell myself," she said to Will before she climbed up the steps and looked down into the crowd. There were people from all over the city, from all different social classes. This seemed a bit strange. Never did she see people of different classes together. Then she reminded herself that all of them were there to find a cherished object that might make them feel more classy and refined. For some it could be a clock, for another a human being.

She stood in the middle of the stage as the auctioneer introduced her, giving details of her physical appearance, weight and mentioned that she had helped plan the Watsons party. As he spoke, she noticed a familiar face in the crowd.

"Thirty pounds!" the woman screamed out. It was Madam Ravine. Madeline's stomach churned, her skin crawling with fear. She wanted to run off the stage. Taking her chances on the streets was better than Madam Ravine's brothel.

"Fifty pounds!" called another voice. Relieved, her eyes went to the crowd to see whom it was. A much older man stood next to a young girl, his eyes greedy as he gawked at her. He reminded her of the creepy old men she would see at the bar when she went looking for her father. She knew his home would be no different from Lord Watson's or Madam Ravine's.

"Excellent!" said the auctioneer, "We have a few serious bidders."

She kept her head down not wanting to learn what her fate was going to be. Then another voice boomed from the crowd, "One hundred pounds!"

Her head popped back up. To the back of the crowd, there was a familiar face. He had attended the Watsons' party. She was quite sure he was a part of the King's entourage. As he pushed through to the front of the crowd, she could see that he was wearing a double-breasted overcoat with the King's coat of arms on it.

"We have one hundred pounds!" yelled out the auctioneer, "Do I hear one-fifty?"

The creepy older man looked annoyed, but raised his hand "One fifty!"

The gentleman from the King's entourage quickly yelled out, "Two hundred."

The auctioneer began to close, "Two hundred going once, twice – sold for two hundred!"

Her jaw dropped. Two-hundred pounds? That was more than a years' salary for a footman. She didn't know the name of the man that bought her to serve the King. She remembered him at the party, he was quiet, meshing into the background, observing what was going on about him. He climbed up the stairs and escorted her off the stage.

"Hello, I'm Miss Black," she said, wanting to hug and thank him a thousand times over.

"Sir Ashton Giles, at your service. The palace has plenty of servants, but we can always use another," he said casually. He led her through the large crowd, to a carriage that looked similar to some of the carriages the King brought to the Watsons the night before, but less detailed. She climbed into it.

"Wait here while I go take care of some business," Sir Ashton said.

She watched him as he walked back to the organizer's desk and spoke to them. In a little less than a half hour, he came back holding some papers and the leather scroll case, and climbed into the carriage.

The ride to the palace was quiet. Sir Ashton did not seem to want to make any conversation with her. She watched him as he looked out the window observing the people on the streets. She tried to think of something to say, but went blank. She knew that any conversation they might have would be artificial. She really wanted to thank him for saving her from a very unhappy life, but that would only be awkward. She gazed out the window, her thoughts on what her new life at Buckingham would be like. Nicer living conditions, better food and serving a gorgeous master.

She became a little shaky. As thankful as she was to be going to Buckingham, the idea of seeing King Alexander again made her feel faint for some reason. She could feel her hands grow clammy again. What would he think of her being fired by the Watsons? She looked down at her dingy white dress and closed her eyes. She couldn't imagine how run down she must look. She'd manage an hour sleep. What would he think of how she looked? Would he be as kind as he was the night before, or did he treat his own servants differently?

"Are you all right dear?" Sir Ashton asked, concerned.

"Um, yes," she said coming out of her reverie.

It was then she realized that Sir Ashton Giles had some influence. He had been given the privilege of being able to go to the market to buy things for the King. He most likely knew King Alexander quite well. She tapped her finger to her lip in thought.

For the sake of pleasing her new master, she had to start asking questions. "What's the King like?" she asked abruptly.

Sir Ashton looked away from the busy London streets to her. "Very wise. Not much gets past him."

"Is he very particular?"

"About certain things, yes."

"Is he very dedicated to his country, or does he spend most his time with other activities?"

"His Majesty is a well-rounded individual Miss Black. He's intelligent and handles most of his affairs independently. He doesn't like to be surrounded too much by valets and the like. He's a different kind of king. But, I have more confidence in him as a king then his father, and that's saying something."

"You served King Charles as well?"

"Yes, but that was some time ago now."

She looked out the carriage window and could see that they were riding by a large marble archway in front of the royal residence.

"What is that archway?" she blurted out before she thought of a polite way of asking.

"That is the Marble Arch, it is used for ceremonial purposes."

The carriage pulled up to a large stone path and stopped at Buckingham's front door. The driver opened the door and she stepped out of the carriage, taking Sir Ashton Giles's hand.

"First, I will briefly introduce you to the King. Afterwards, I will have one of the other maids give you a tour. That will take the entire day. Buckingham has hundreds of rooms along with the grounds you'll need to be familiar with."

"Hundreds of rooms?" she repeated slowly.

"Yes, but no worries dear, they won't take you through all of them. Just the State Apartments and some private apartments."

She stood marvelling at Buckingham Palace, feeling small. It was majestic in every sense. It seemed ridiculous that anyone would call it a house. It looked more like a palace. Its yellow bath stone was constructed in a classical style with columns surrounding the windows and pediments filled with Greek mythological figures of war. There were also other scenes of war carved into the walls and statues surrounding them.

"I imagine the King would be either hunting or practicing his swordplay," he said looking at his pocket watch. "On the other hand, today is Wednesday. There's a good chance he will be in the library."

The entryway to Buckingham was surrounded by several guards. She followed Sir Ashton inside.

The entrance was the most elaborate room she had ever seen. It made the Watsons' manor lacklustre in comparison. The ceilings were very high and had eight king-sized mahogany lanterns. There were large windows and three stone staircases on each side of the room.

She admired the large statues in the alcoves in the walls, the huge marble pillars that surrounded the room, and a massive Indian carpet with elaborate detail. She bit her lip wondering how long it would take to clean the carpet. Let alone the room. She could hear the echoes of their footsteps as they walked through.

She stared around in wonder as Sir Ashton had plodded on ahead, unfazed by the luxury. When he reached the staircase, he turned to noticed that she was still standing in the centre of the room.

"Are you coming Miss Black?" he asked politely.

"Oh yes," she said awakened out of awe. She trotted over to him, and climbed up the stairs into a long, wide corridor full of oversized paintings that covered the walls. The hallway was so large it could be used for parties. She slowly walked down the hall, surveying the paintings around her, then stopped to look at one of them. A beautiful woman held a man's plate on a silver platter; it was grotesque and she wondered how anyone could have such a chilling imagination. Again, staring at the painting, she fell behind.

"Are you coming Miss Black?" he asked again when he reached the end of the corridor.

"Um, oh I'm so sorry," she said in embarrassment. She hurried over to him.

"Down this wing is where most of the private apartments are. We are just near his personal library now."

They continued down another hall. It did not have as many paintings, but the walls were filled with panels and silk tapestries. There were plenty of large columns as they walked down the halls, along with large vases, some that were taller than her. She tried not to gaze at the splendour surrounding her. But it was difficult. Buckingham and everything within it was a piece of art and something to behold. Anyone, even a simple servant, could respect and appreciate it.

The King's private library was a large room with more books than a person could read in a lifetime. The books filled all four of the walls of the room from floor to the wide arch windows above the shelves that emitted a natural light into the room. There were a couple of marble top writing desks. King Alexander sat at one of them, immersed in a book.

"Excuse me, your Majesty," Sir Aston said bowing.

Peeking from behind Sir Ashton, she got a closer look at him. Her heart beat out of its chest. It had only been several hours since she seen him, but she felt as though she forgotten how handsome he was. He was dressed in a brocade tailcoat with a dark red vest and black trousers. He wore a pair of glasses as he read. Until that moment, she believed that glasses didn't look good on anyone. She pulled down at her old dress trying to cover her ankles.

"What is it, Ashton?"

"Given that Ms. Brody will be retiring, I thought that perhaps we would need an extra hand." He stood aside, and she stepped forward and curtsied unsteadily. He pulled his glasses down the bridge of his nose and peered at her with his crystal blue eyes, smiling.

Though he was flabbergasted that she was there before him, he maintained his composure as Sir Ashton continued, "I bought this girl in the market today. She's literate and she organized last night's party at the Watsons'. I think we could use her here."

"Thank you, Ashton. Ms. Brody does need a replacement," he said. "Miss Black I remember you from last night. You did a fantastic job. I'll make you in charge of the Tuesday and Thursday tea."

"Yes, your Majesty," she said giving a small curtsy.

Sir Ashton stepped forward objecting, "Your Majesty, perhaps maybe that's quite an undertaking for someone who is new to Buckingham?"

"Ashton, I have faith that Miss Black is capable of tea time," he said dismissively. "Besides, someone must shoulder Ms. Brody's responsibilities."

"If you insist," Sir Ashton said, "I have her ownership papers here." He pulled out the leather scroll case and handed it over. He opened it and briefly checked the papers. She looked at him hopeful. Maybe he would grant her, her freedom.

"Everything looks in order," he said in a stiff tone. He took out a quill, signed them, and handed the scroll back to Sir Ashton.

"I'll have the papers filed then. Come along Miss Black."

She followed Sir Ashton, arms crossed. The King she talked to last night seemed sympathetic towards her plight of being owned by the Watsons. Not a day later, he had no problem owning her himself.

"Wait."

She stopped and turned alongside with Sir Ashton, maybe he would at least offer to pay for her services.

"Give me the ownership papers Ashton," he commanded, "I have some other documents to file, so I might as well take those too."

Sir Ashton gave him a strange look, but handed him the leather scroll case. Sir Ashton left with a cross woman in tow.

Left alone, King Alexander pulled the ownership papers out from its leather casing again and gaped at them in disbelief, his heart racing with excitement. Last night she was the last thought he'd had before he drifted off to sleep. But now, he owned Madeline Black.

5

BUCKINGHAM PALACE

Sir Ashton brought Madeline to the servants' quarters. They were lavish compared to the Watsons'. There was not one common room for all the servants to share, but several. There was an oversized kitchen with cupboards and shelves filling the walls, a parlour with a large cobblestone fireplace and an absurd number of cushioned chairs, dark oak oval tables, couches and several ottomans. She smiled to herself as she thought of the old, rickety chair in the common room at the Watsons'. Being put up for auction this morning was a blessing in disguise.

They entered a dining hall with six long dark oak tables. Sir Ashton led her to a group of young maids sitting at one of the tables enjoying their break. He pulled aside a long blonde haired girl with a small black feather hair piece placed in a bun.

Madeline watched as the girl and Sir Ashton talked several feet away from her. The servants attire was a little like what Lady Watson had bought them for the anniversary celebration. It was black and white apron with appliqués with a built-in corset, but also had lace trim around the neck, apron and sleeves.

"Miss Madeline Black, this is Miss Marie Greenwood," he said introducing her to the blonde haired girl. "You'll be sharing a room together, and she will also be giving you a tour of Buckingham today."

Marie beamed at her, "Hello."

"Hi," Madeline said embarrassed, as she pulled down at her drab dress.

"Excellent, I'm sure the two of you will get on quite well. Miss Greenwood, be sure that Miss Black sees most of Buckingham. Perhaps another day she can be taken to St. James Castle and Westminster."

"Yes sir," said Marie.

"All right. Goodbye, ladies. Enjoy your tour, Miss Black," he said and left the servants dining hall.

"I'm kind of glad you came today," Marie said excitedly. "After the party at the Watsons' last night, Sir Gregory Umbridge went to the Billiards Room and had a little after party. Guess who is assigned to clean it today?"

Madeline laughed, "You and no one else."

"That's right. The room is a disgusting mess now. I don't have to worry about it now though," she said giddy, "I get to take you on tour instead."

It was good to get Marie out of cleaning the Billiards Room. Getting off on the right foot with other servants was important. Marie invited her to sit down and eat with her before the tour.

73

"You'll need all the energy you can get," said Marie. "There's a lot of walking."

"Oh," Madeline said wishing that she had a better night's sleep. "How long is it?"

"Several hours."

Madeline grabbed a sandwich from a plate that the servant girls had been sharing, "So what kind of party did Sir Gregory hold last night?"

Marie and the other servants chuckled. "He usually tries to get a bunch of ladies, valets, footmen...and the King down for drinks and cigars." The servant girls giggled at the mention of Alex, but Marie continued, "Once Sir Gregory has a few drinks in him, he always ends up doing something crazy."

"Yes," another piped up, "Unfortunately for King Alexander, it was just him and Sir Gregory Umbridge last night. Sir Gregory got so rowdy he started a fist fight. The King, of course, had to put him in his place."

All the girls howled with laughter.

Madeline listened, shocked, "Who starts a fist fight with a king? Won't his Majesty punish him?"

"Greg Umbridge does. He never gets in trouble for anything. The King treats him like a brother," said Marie. "You should see the room though! Paintings on the floor, cigar ashes all over the billiards, broken cue sticks and chairs. And that's not the half of it."

She raised her brows in disbelief. Had something like that happened at the Watsons', the servants would have been slaughtered.

"We should get going," said Marie, "you've got a lot to see and know before you start tomorrow."

They went to their dormitory room. It was simple; two dressers, two mirrors, two small beds and two armoires, but to Madeline it was posh. All the furniture was made from the beautiful dark oak wood she saw in the common rooms, there was even art on the walls.

"I figure you might want to see where you'll be staying first. It's not much, but we just sleep here."

"It's wonderful," Madeline said looking around the room gratefully. "I used to work at the Watsons', I had to share a single room with all the other female servants."

Marie looked as though she were about the ask something, then hesitated. She waved her hand around to the walls of the room. "I hope you don't mind that I have decorated the room myself, with my own drawings." She looked down blushing.

Madeline moved closer to one of the drawings and examined it. It was a gorgeous charcoal drawing of a woman's face that looked somewhat familiar to her. Marie's shading and contrast almost gave the woman's face aglow.

"You have quite a talent," she said earnestly.

"Thank you. Do you recognize the face?"

"Sorry, no. Should I know her?"

"Well, some people do," she said moving to the drawing. "It's Miss Elizabeth Swan. Have you heard of her?"

"Yes," she answered crestfallen. "I've heard of her."

"Gosh, you look like her," said Marie looking from the drawing to her.

Madeline stared into the woman's eyes for a moment, stunned that a servant girl her age not only knew her mother, but had managed to find an image of her, and draw her. She wondered if there was a painting of her somewhere in Buckingham. But it was unlikely. She wanted to ask Marie where she got her inspiration, but could not bring herself to ask.

"You know, we should get your maids uniform, Madeline. You'll also be needing some shoes I think."

She was grateful Marie did not poke fun of her dingy dress that didn't fit her properly. She had been pulling down on it every so often since putting it on, hoping it would not ride up too high and expose her ankles.

"What size are you, Madeline?"

"About yours," she said, sizing Marie.

"You look a little smaller I think. What about your shoes?"

"I'm not sure about the size. I have bigger feet."

Her shoes were in a sadder state than her dress. Marie looked down at Madeline's toes crunched at the end, pushing the leather into a bumpy form.

"Those are large feet. You poor thing, must be awful finding a good pair. I'll get you what you need."

Marie left the room. While she was gone, Madeline wandered about the room. She pushed down on the bed mattress as she sat down. It was comfortable. Better than the small pile of blankets on the floor at the Watsons'.

She pulled open both the armoires. Marie had several dresses, uniforms, shoes and shoe polish. It was a relief to see. At the Watsons' she only had two uniforms, and it was hard to keep them clean.   The dressers were full of crisp white stockings, handkerchiefs, aprons and other accessories for special occasions.

As she walked about the room, she found herself staring at the drawing of her mother.   Elizabeth Swan was as stunning as everyone had said.   It was depressing looking at her and realizing that this was the only image she had ever seen of her.   Looking at the details and lines of the charcoal, she wondered how Marie knew of her mother.   Elizabeth Swan lived twenty years ago.   Why was Marie interested in her?

Marie came back in with several uniforms hanging over her arm and a few pairs of shoes in the other.   "Here you are," she said placing the uniforms on her bed.   "I put my uniforms in the armoire, along with my day dresses.   We could go shopping to get you a few."

Madeline looked down at her dress, humiliated again.   She had no day dresses.   Nor did she want to buy one.   The money she had saved in her mother's bank account could not be used for frivolous things like a dress.   She sighed as she placed her things in the armoire, she didn't want to tell Marie that she was owned by the King and could not afford a dress.

"Well, hopefully in time I can save up a few pounds and pop out to London to get a new dress," she said smiling faintly.

"You deserve one!" said Marie, helping her hang her uniforms.   "If we get days off on the same day, we should go together."

She could not believe her ears.   She never dreamed she would have days off.

"We get time off?" she asked, holding her breath.

"Yes. You didn't get time off at the Watsons'?"

"Never."

With Marie's assistance, she got dressed in her uniform and put on her black shiny new shoes. It was strange, but she felt rejuvenated putting on her uniform. Shedding the old, threadbare white dress and putting on her new maid outfit was a turning point. This would not be like her stay at the Watsons'. No one would slap her across the face or refuse to feed her. Life was not going to be excellent, but it was going to be better.

After she got dressed, they left the dormitory room. Marie led Madeline down several small corridors, up some stairs and back to the gallery full of paintings Madeline had seen earlier.

"We are out of the servants' quarters now; this is the King's Gallery. It has all sorts of paintings from famous artists and paintings of monarchs of the past. This one is of the King's father, King Charles."

Madeline looked up at the larger than life painting that was framed by large mouldings on the walls. The painting went from the detailed French credenza beneath it to the ceiling. As she stared, Marie quickly moved along.

"Sorry, you can't admire the work. We really do need to see the rest of the residence."

"Is St. James' as luxurious?"

"Yes and no. They are building some additions to Buckingham. Once they are finished, they'll call this place a palace. They still use St. James Palace for different things, political meetings."

They came to a large set of opened doors, "This is the White Drawing room. It's one of fourteen State Rooms when they finish the additions to the castle."

Madeline surveyed the room, admiring the lengths the designers had gone to. The room was white with gold mouldings. There was sculpture work around the mantels of two fireplaces in the room. Above the entry ways of the room, plasterwork formed large frame ovals around paintings of previous monarchs. Cherubs were mounted around the ceiling, and crown moulding surrounded four large chandeliers. French gold silk furniture was placed about the room. Gold dust silk drapes adorned the large windows. A large red rug with blue and dusty gold designs filled the room.

"Now I know why my former mistress Lady Watson wanted fine French gold couches at her reception," she said shaking her head.

"Bet it was nothing like this."

"Not even close."

"If you head through those doors over there," she said pointing to the south wall, "you'll find several more State Rooms."

"Are they all as magnificent as this room?"

Marie laughed, "Only the best for royalty."

They exited the White Drawing Room and headed down the King's Gallery again. They walked past several drawing rooms before they came across a staircase to a set of doors.

"These are the Mistresses' Chambers."

"The Mistresses' Chambers? The King has a lady?"

Marie cackled, "No. The King seems to enjoy his current relationship status I reckon. But if he did have a lady, this is where she'd stay. "

Marie did not take her into the room and continued walking down the hall.

"Why are we not going in?" asked Madeline, following Marie.

"The tour really is that long. There's no time to look through every room."

After touring some of the private apartments, they passed a small set of stairs, Marie casually pointed them out.

"Up these stairs are the King's Apartments. The King is particular about who cleans his room. Usually, the head maids do this job."

They went to the Dining Hall, where again Madeline was impressed by the grandeur of the room.

"They really do not hold back," she said looking around at the intricate gold designs about the red walls and ceiling. There was a large oblong table in the centre of the room that sat sixty to seventy people.

"How often would you say the King uses this room?"

"He does not eat here every night, just when he has many guests. There's another room where the King receives smaller parties."

By the end of the tour, Marie had shown her the courtyards, the gardens, several gallery halls, the tennis courts, the Armoury, the Throne Room, the Grand Staircase and several State Rooms. The last attraction was the Royal Mews. It was exhausting walking up and down so many flights of stairs, but each room was worth seeing.

"I think we should check the Billiards Room," Marie said as they finished the tour. "I just want to be sure that someone has looked after it."

"I suppose if it's not finished it's your head."

They headed down to the Billiards Room by way of another gallery, unlike any Madeline had seen yet. To her right there were floor-to-ceiling paintings, with thick gold frames of royalty and on her left gargantuan pillars with gold encrusted rails between them.

"This is quite the gallery."

"Oh yes, this gallery is also a balcony overlooking the Throne Room," Marie said pulling her to the gold gilt railing. "You're not afraid of heights, are you?"

"Oh no, I'm fine," she said looking down at the Throne Room from the rails admiring the magnificence of the room.

"We ought to get going."

Marie opened the door to the Billiards Room, forgetting to knock and Madeline followed her in. To their embarrassment, the King and Sir Gregory Umbridge were playing a game of billiards. Madeline noticed a military tactics book with some papers between its pages sitting on the billiards table ledge. It was the same book he had been reading earlier in the library. She and Marie curtsied, "We are so sorry your Majesty, Sir Gregory."

"It's quite all right ladies," King Alexander said. "Sir Gregory and I are only finishing a game we started last night." He looked over at Sir Gregory and patted him on the back.

"If I was not three sheets to the wind last night, then I would have beaten his Royal Majesty."

"Sure, Greg."

Madeline snickered to herself. They seemed like a pair of brothers teasing one another.

"I take you are giving Miss Black a tour of Buckingham Miss Greenwood?" asked King Alexander as he watched Greg taking a shot with his cue. She was impressed, there were tons of servants, but he knew Marie's name. She wondered if he knew them all.

"Oh, we've just finished, your Majesty," said Marie.

"And how does Miss Black find Buckingham?" he said looking towards Madeline with interest.

"It's magnificent, your Majesty."

He smiled as he nonchalantly chalked his cue, "What was your favourite room?"

"Oh the Royal Mews, I think."

"Why's that?" he asked as he took a shot.

"The horses are absolutely stunning, the carriages are quite lovely, and the stalls are ... well, I've never seen any like that."

He laughed looking at her intrigued, "The stalls? Why's that Miss Black?"

"They're immaculate."

"Only the best for such fine specimens," he said, swivelling his cue on the floor casually.

Madeline took this as an insult. Her living quarters were probably nothing in comparison to his.

"Are you a fine specimen then your Majesty?" she blurted out.

She put her hands to her lips, Marie stared at her stunned. Greg Umbridge fell on a couch in a fit laughter.

"She got you good Alex, losing this game today was worth hearing that!"

Alex moved towards Madeline, his eyes probing hers, a calm expression on his face. She felt vulnerable, almost bare. Then a sexy smile grew on his face, "The finest specimen you could ever have, Miss Black."

She looked down her face burning up. Greg Umbridge rolled off the couch still howling.

"You wish you were the finest specimen, Alex. I could disprove that by just dropping my trousers."

"Greg, not in the presence of ladies," said Alex as he walked back over to the billiard.

"Well, we ought to be going your Majesty," said Marie chortling as she curtsied, "there are other things I need to show Miss Black."

Madeline curtsied, and the two left the Billiards Room and headed back to the servants' quarters.

"There's nothing else you need to show me, is there?" asked Madeline.

Marie smirked, "No, but Sir Gregory Umbridge has a bit of a reputation."

"That doesn't surprise me, but what do you mean by 'reputation'."

"Well, let's put it this way, if he pulled down his trousers today, it would not have been the first time he did that in front of a servant."

"He sleeps with servants?" she asked, disgusted that Sir Gregory would take advantage of his position.

"Oh no. He's not like that. He's just, shall we say, 'free spirited'."

She giggled, "Who was the victim?"

"Ms. Johnson. She's an old, timid type. Never got married. Actually, I don't think she had ever been with a man. So, you can imagine how traumatizing it was for her!"

The two fell into one another in a fit of giggles.

"An older lady seeing a young man? Maybe she enjoyed it," Madeline said. They howled louder, and Madeline realized that it was not the first time they shared a laugh that day. Marie was easy going. She did not keep anything from her about Buckingham and the people that lived within it while they toured it. She was relieved to have been set up with a great dormitory mate.

6

THE VASE

In the evening, Madeline and Marie went down to the servants dining hall to join everyone for dinner.

"So with there being so many servants, how does everyone get the chance to make their food?" asked Madeline as they walked through the kitchen.

Marie cocked her head, "Pardon?"

"Well, the kitchen is big, but I doubt that everyone can be in there at the same time to make their dinner."

"Is that how things were done at the Watsons'?" she asked in disbelief.

"Yes."

"Well, we do things a little more traditionally here. Look at all the tables Madeline."

She looked up at all the tables noticing that many people were already seated, and piling food onto their plates. Young servant girls brought out simple porcelain tureens and platters of food.

"You take turns making dinner?"

"No. See the table at the far left?"

She nodded.

"That table is for the head housekeepers and butlers. We don't have a head butler here. Sir Ashton Giles is probably the closest thing we have to a head of household. King Alexander trusts him with all sorts of things. He's a very busy man. He comes down here from time to time to dine with us."

"So he's pretty much in charge of Buckingham?"

"Yes. He has a few head butlers that do assist him though. Then there is the valets and cooks table over there." She said pointing to the table next to the head butlers table. "We don't have any ladies-in-waiting in Buckingham since we don't have a queen or princess."

"What do the valets do?"

"Oh, they look after the King's personal care. They'll accompany him on outings, clean and lay out his wardrobe. The King doesn't have many valets, just three," she said pointing to them. Madeline looked over at the three strapping young men. They sat several feet down from the cooks, laughing as they ate.

"It's a 'little boys' club," she said shaking her head. "They think they're something special because they are in the King's presence sometimes. He dismisses them most of the time. Greg Umbridge is probably the only company the King really likes to keep."

"What do those valets do then?"

"Tsk, not much! They're good for nothing but small favours. Of course, you have to pay them to do it."

She furrowed her brow, "What kind of favours could you get?"

"Some of the maids like to know the King's personal schedule, which they are privy to. Just information and gossip really."

"What are their names?"

"Why are you curious about the King?"

"No," she blushed, "But there are only three of them."

"Ben Caston, Jack Caston and Richard Baker. Anyway, the table next to that is for the grooms and coachmen of the horses."

"What about the royal guard?"

"Oh, the guards don't eat here. They are on shift work, so their schedules are different from ours. The table next to the horsemen is the footmen and pages table. If you look there are some decent looking gentlemen there," she said with a smile. "There not as pretentious as the valets."

Madeline smirked knowingly. Obviously, Marie had a crush on one of them.

"Next to them is the housemaids table. That's where we will sit. Then finally there is the scullery maids and kitchen maids table, and they take care of meals- not us."

"So dinner is served? We just sit and eat?"

"Sure do," Marie said and grabbed her hand leading her to the dining room table. They sat down next to each other and Marie introduced her to the maids sitting around them. However, Madeline did not have much to say. She mostly kept to herself and ate the delicious meal served. She could not remember the last time she had a square meal like this one, if ever.

She looked about thinking of all the things that Marie had showed and explained to her that day. It was a lot to take in. She knew how to clean the rooms, but remembering where everything was and where the rooms were would be difficult. After finishing dinner, the servants sat in the parlour and talked for the rest of the night. Madeline went back to her room and napped on her bed in her uniform. It had been a long day for her, she felt as though she was going to crash to the floor. Some time later, Marie came into the room woke her up and, handed her a nightgown.

"Here you can have this, I have a few extras in my drawers."

"Um, thanks," she said, rubbing her sleepy eyes.

The two discreetly got changed. "What do you think of the King?" Madeline asked as she pulled off her uniform.

"Hmm, well that depends," she said with a girlish simper on her face, brushing her hair, "How do you mean?"

"Any impressions really," she said, trying to sound casual as she climbed into bed.

"He's gorgeous, there's no overlooking that face and body." Marie laughed as she brushed her hair, then paused to add, "But these ladies of the nobility and these princesses, they'll never get him."

"Why do you say that? Does he enjoy being single?"

Marie put down her brush, a thoughtful expression grew on her face. "No, it's not that."

"What do you think it is?"

"He has intellect. They just don't understand him. They all come around here and have these dull conversations with him. I can see it bores him. I served him once while he was entertaining a princess from Germany. All she could talk about was her petticoats."

She howled then sputtered, "What?"

"I think she was trying to seduce him or something. She was trying to get him to touch the one she was wearing, in front of a crowd of people. I could tell he found her too aggressive."

"Hm. Any other interesting ladies?" she asked fluffing her pillow.

"Oh plenty, Lady Alice Pye used to pretend to faint in his company, just so he'd catch her in his arms."

"That's so pathetic."

"It was. Until one day King Alex accidentally dropped her," she said with a wink.

Madeline held her fingers to her mouth giggling.

"It's amazing though," she continued, "He's a war hero, you would think these ladies realize he knows a trap when he sees one."

"He's a war hero?"

"You didn't know that?! I thought everyone in Europe and the colonies knew that!" Marie said in disbelief. "In a battle with the Irish, he killed eight men single-handedly to stop an uprising."

"Really?! How old was he then?"

"Just turned thirteen," she said as she adjusted her hair tie.

Her jaw dropped, "How did he do that?"

"No one really knows the exact details. King Alex won't discuss it. Not even with Sir Gregory."

"Must have been awful then."

"Must have. All that is known is the next day the English army broke into the enemies' stronghold." She climbed into the bed next to her. "They found King Alex locked in a room with them, sword in hand, all of them dead."

"But, he was only thirteen. Surely he couldn't ..."

"His Majesty has been taking lessons since he could pick up a sword. There's no doubt. Some Lords of the court thought it was Sir Ashton. But Sir Ashton was with several other men the night it happened."

Madeline felt foolish that she didn't know. She burrowed down into her sheets and pulled her covers over her chest. Marie blew out the candles and left her alone with her thoughts in the darkness. Madeline did not know exactly how she felt about King Alexander. She found him attractive, she doubted there would be any woman that wouldn't. He was a war hero, and from what others in Buckingham said, intelligent. He came off as pleasant, but she could not help to think there was a cocky side to him. She was annoyed with his 'fine specimen' comment he made earlier and loathed that he owned her and didn't have any misgivings about it. One thing she did know was since the day started, she could not seem to get him out of her mind.

She awoke the next morning and the two girls got ready together then headed to the dining hall for breakfast. She ate a boiled egg, a slice of bread, sausage and a small side of oatmeal. There were baskets of fruit the servants could pick from, so she grabbed an apple and put it in her apron pocket. It would be good for a quick morning snack while she worked. She was grateful. At the Watsons', breakfast was either gruel or stale bread.

"Is breakfast the same every day?" she asked Marie as they ate.

"Oh, not everything is the same every day. Sometimes they make crêpes or omelettes."

"Really? Crêpes?"

After breakfast, Marie took Madeline to the schedule, which was written with chalk on several large blackboards in the servants' parlour.

"Usually, two or three maids are assigned to clean the State Rooms, just yourself if you have a smaller room. Just find your name on the board, and the room next to your name is what you are supposed to clean."

She looked up and down the boards and found her name. "I'm in the Blue Drawing Room."

"You'll probably get some help. Good luck. See you later tonight Madeline."

She went to the Blue Drawing Room, which took some time as she got lost several times before she made it. When she arrived, she found two other maids on ladders dusting the chandeliers. One was stout, with thick red hair held back with a white handkerchief. The other was tall and wiry with a pale face.

"What took you so long?" the short one asked in an Irish accent.

"I'm sorry," Madeline apologized, "I just started yesterday and I had a bit of a time finding my way here."

A peeved expression grew on the stout woman's face as she dropped her feather duster to the floor.

"Did someone not give ya the tour yesterday?"

"Relax Johanna. It's not hard to get lost in this place," said the thin, pale girl.

"Mind what you' cha say, Emma. Make excuses for 'er, and she'll always be sayin' she got lost."

Madeline ignored Johanna and got straight to work. She grabbed a duster and a ladder and began cleaning another chandelier.

The ladies worked through the day until the late afternoon cleaning the windows, ceiling mouldings and mirrors, sweeping and brushing the rug, dusting the large pillars encased in the walls, and cleaning the silk furniture. They did so with little conversation as they neared the end of the work, Johanna finally spoke, "Well, girlie, since Emma and I were here firs', you can finish off the room by cleaning the mantles."

"Oh, it's okay Johanna, you go on," said Emma, "I'll help her."

"No, ya won't Emma," she said raising her hands to her hips again. "This girl needs a lesson in punctuality."

Emma gave Madeline a helpless look, clearly Johanna was not to be crossed.

"It's quite all right Emma," said Madeline, "I guess this is how things are run around here. If Johanna is ever late for reasons beyond her control, I suppose I'll have to remind her that she will be staying longer. On the other hand, if it is Emma that is late, I'll be sure to offer to help since she offered me help just now."

Emma grinned while Johanna scowled at Madeline, "Ya mind yourself missy -"

"Oh, I will, and I'll mind you too, "she said briskly and she went about the mantles. Johanna turned on her heel and left the Blue Drawing Room. Emma waited for her to leave.

"Don't pay too much attention to what Johanna says," said Emma. "I swear, she's the worst person to work with."

"Thanks. By the way, I'm Madeline," she said.

"Are you sure you don't need any help, Madeline?"

"It won't take too long."

The doors opened, and King Alexander along with Sir Gregory, Sir Ashton and two other men walked into the room. Emma curtsied to them and made a quick exit.

"Let's sit and talk in here, Lord Bathory," Alex said as he moved towards the silk chesterfields. Her eyes followed him as he walked. He looked particularly divine today. His black hair was styled and had a subtle shine to it. This made her think of when she first got a whiff of his hair and felt goosebumps. He was wearing a navy blue coat with gold buttons and a thin white shirt beneath which made her wish she could throw her pail of water on him. Or tear off his clothes. Once again, he was carrying his military tactics book. Madeline discreetly went over to the mantles and began quietly dusting.

"Your Majesty, perhaps you should give this girl leave?" said the fellow whom's name she didn't know.

"She's a woman. What does she care of war Lord Kinney?" said King Alex, dismissively. All the men laughed, except for Sir Gregory, who looked over at her, confused.

"Anyway, Bathory, what is it you want to propose to do in this Dunkirk situation and why not tell everyone in the meeting?"

She continued cleaning as they spoke paying little attention to what they were saying. She was disgusted by what King Alex had said. Just because she was a woman, she did not care for war, or what was happening to her country? Or maybe he thought she was not smart enough to understand? Why did everyone, especially women, think so highly of him? He thought of himself as a 'fine specimen' that had the right to own people! She shook her head, concluding to herself that he was just a gorgeous looking dolt.

A beautiful white and blue vase caught her eye as she dusted the mantle. She surveyed it for a moment. *Could it fit into my pocket?* she wondered, sizing up the vase and slowly putting her hand into her dress pocket. It would fit. She casually turned to see what the King and his guests were doing. She shook her head. In a heated male discussion about war, she thought as she saw Lord Bathory and Sir Gregory raising their voices at one another, she turned back. She began to pretend to dust beneath the vase, then swiftly pocketed it.

She finished dusting the mantles and left the room giddy with excitement. He nor any of his advisors had seen what she had done. It was not the first time she had stolen something right under her master's nose. Not as wise as everyone thinks. She curtsied and left the room.

Alex quickly finished the discussion, "Lord Kinney, Bathory, I will have Sir Ashton send word to Sir Dunkirk to advance. We're cornered. I'd like to take action before they do their worst."

Kinney and Bathory rose from their seats bowed to him, and left the room, leaving Alex with Greg and Sir Ashton.

"Bathory really would love to run this country, if he could," said Greg disgusted.

"Never mind Bathory. His petty little ploys to overthrow me aren't working anyway."

"I know, but he is a wanker."

Alex swiftly changed the subject, "Sir Ashton, Miss Black just stole one of my Ming dynasty vases."

"When did this occur?" asked Sir Ashton.

"Just a moment ago before she left."

"Did she really?" Greg said in amazement.

"Yes. I'm betting she thinks she got away with it too," he smiled.

"I will apprehend her immediately," Sir Ashton began, "We can arrange to have a full trial tomorrow."

"That won't be necessary, Ashton," Alex said with an even tone, "I want you to follow her, and report back to me what she does with it. Under no circumstance do you intervene. Do you understand? If she sells the vase, buy it and bring it back."

"Yes, your Majesty." Sir Ashton bowed and made a speedy exit.

Greg Umbridge looked at Alex and raised his brow, "This is interesting."

"What?"

"If I'd stolen your Ming dynasty vase, you would have chopped my balls off."

"That's impossible Greg."

"How so?"

"Well, to steal the vase, you need to have balls."

"Oh and you do?" he scoffed. "Couldn't even call her out on it … now why might that be your Majesty?"

7

PARDON ME?

After getting her mother's banking papers in her dormitory room, Madeline sneaked away on one of the small servants' buggies. She lied to one of the footmen, telling him that some cleaning supplies were needed to clean a painting. The poor dote bought it, and even assisted her in prepping the buggy.

She decided to go to Mr. Sheffield's to see what kind of price he would give her for the vase. She was sure she could be back in time for dinner.

It was daring to bring it to Mr. Sheffield. There was the chance that he would know that Madeline had just started working for the King. If he did, he definitely would not buy it from her. However, she had to take a chance on Mr. Sheffield. If he did know that she was working for the King, she could trust him not turn her in to the authorities. Any of her other regular buyers would turn her in to get a reward.

She rode the coach in front of the shop and went inside.

"Madeline," said Mr. Sheffield in his cheery voice, "how are you, my dear?"

She did not answer him. There were other customers in the shop, and she didn't want to try to get a price for the vase in front of them. She pretended to look at some items Mr. Sheffield was selling in the shop. He immediately observed her suspicious behaviour, and began assisting the other customers until they bought what they needed. He escorted them out of the shop door and locked the door behind them as they left.

"What is it Madeline?" he asked, his voice full of concern. "Has Lady Watson done something?"

"No," she said, relieved. He had not yet heard that she had been fired and was now working for the King.

"It's just, I've come across an item here," she began, as she pulled the Ming vase from her dress pocket.

Mr. Sheffield inspected carefully and was taken aback, "Madeline, was this Lady Watson's?" he asked sceptically. "How did you come across a Ming dynasty vase? If this is hers, she will notice it missing."

"How much can you give me for it?" she asked, ignoring his warning.

"Honestly Madeline, I would have to sell all the goods in my shop to buy it from you. How did you get a hold of such a priceless antique?"

"No matter. Who do you think I could sell this to?"

"Madeline, perhaps you should take this back?"

"Trust me when I say this, I don't believe anyone would notice this missing."

He was about to protest, but seeing the stubborn expression on her face, he hesitated.

"Trust me," she insisted. "The owner of this vase has forgotten they have it."

He looked at her, astonished. "All right. If I were you, I would take it to Hemingways. Don't accept less than two thousand pounds."

She looked up in shock. Two thousand pounds could buy her a small home with extra to live on. If she found another small priceless item in the castle, she could run away and live a quiet life in the countryside.

She felt uneasy. Was Mr. Sheffield right? What if someone noticed the vase missing? She thought of all the grandeur the castle held within it. There were plenty of pieces worth more than the five-inch vase. It would not surprise her if the King himself did not know the worth of the vase. She left Sheffield's and rode the carriage to Hemingways. She had never been to Hemingways before. She had seen the store front often as she rode by and knew it was a popular place for those of the upper nobility. Lady Watson often visited there with friends, but would never buy anything. She couldn't afford it.

Madeline stepped out of the carriage and looked at the shop. It had a chocolate brown awning with 'Hemingways' written in gold on it. The stone steps had gilt iron banisters and led to the shops French doors on either side of the doors were beautiful arched stained glass windows.

She walked up the steps wondering how the shop keeper would treat a servant. She imagined other servants would come to the shop to pick up items for their masters. She opened the door and saw an older gentleman, dressed in fine clothes, standing behind a white marble counter that had small pillars etched into it.

"Excuse me, Sir?" she said as she timidly walked up to the counter.

"Yes?" he asked.

"Does Hemingway's buy items as well as sell them?"

The gentleman pulled his glasses down the bridge of his nose. "Miss, we only buy items of value. Do you have something of value?"

"Yes. I believe I do," she said as she pulled out the vase, and displayed it on the counter. The man adjusted his glasses and began examining the piece.

"Miss, I imagine the value of this piece may be around five shillings. Not worth my time."

"Strange, the fellow down the street told me I should not take anything less than three thousand pounds."

"Then he does not know what he is talking about, Miss."

"Perhaps I should head to Warwick's? See what price they offer me," she said, as she casually picked up the vase. She knew that Warwick's was Hemingway's biggest competition. He frowned.

"I will give you two thousand pounds. No more, no less, and if this vase is reported stolen, I'll report you, even if you decide to go to Warwick's to sell it."

She had never been threatened by one of the shopkeepers. It was an unspoken rule that shopkeepers were never to give the identity of their so-called suppliers if an item was reported stolen. She got the feeling that he didn't want her to sell it. He probably didn't want to see her get in trouble with the law. But she was confident nothing would come of it, "Two thousand pounds will be just fine," she stammered. "The vase is yours."

He gave her a worried look, "Understand something, Miss. I'm not sure where you got this vase, but a Ming dynasty vase doesn't go unnoticed. I suggest you take this back to where you found it."

"Well, this vase has gone unnoticed. If you wouldn't mind, I would like to collect my money and be on my way."

The shopkeeper wrote her a cheque, and she left the shop. As she walked out the French doors, Susanna Bathory and her friends walked in. She held her nose in the air as she passed by Madeline.

Too excited to care, Madeline headed to the bank and deposited the money. The amount she made on the vase was the most she had made on anything. It was about twenty years' worth of a maid's salary. This would help her live comfortably for years after she retired.

When she arrived at the bank, the teller suspected nothing and deposited the money in her mother's account.

She arrived back at the castle with time to spare before dinner. As she sat alone in her dormitory room, she wondered if she should have heeded the warning given to her by the shopkeeper at Hemingway's.

Sir Ashton Giles arrived back to the castle earlier than he had planned. After following Madeline from Sheffield's to Hemingway's, he lost track of her. As she left, Susanna went into the shop and tried to buy the vase. Unfortunately, for Sir Ashton, he had to burst into Hemingway's and compete with her for it. He bought the vase for four thousand pounds – something he knew Susanna Bathory could not afford. He left Hemingway's with her cursing him as he went.

Upon his arrival at Buckingham, he went straight to King Alex who was with Greg Umbridge in the Throne Room. While Greg took the small vase and placed it on a table next to the throne, Sir Ashton explained what happened and apologized for spending four thousand pounds to get the vase back.

"No matter about the money, Ashton," he said, pacing about. "What of Miss Black? Where did she go after Hemingway's?"

Sir Ashton looked at his King astonished, "Your Majesty, surely you'd rather I secured the vase than know the whereabouts of Miss Black? We all know she'd eventually come back here."

"Of course. Yes, the vase is more important," he said, realizing that it must have seemed odd that he cared more about Madeline's whereabouts than his possessions. He continued, "Bring Miss Black here to the Throne Room, I wish to have a word with her."

As soon as Sir Ashton left, Greg broke the silence. "You wouldn't care how much money she took you for, would you?"

"Greg, I plan to get the money back. She will have to repay me," he said as he walked over to his throne.

"And just how will she do that, your Majesty?" he said, in a jest-full tone, "You own her, so what will she repay you with?"

"Never mind, Greg."

He plopped on his throne wondering what was the best way to approach the subject as he waited for her arrival. He set his military tactics book down, next to the throne. He was angry. He was not angry that she had stolen something from him. He didn't take it personally, figuring that stealing was something she did in the Watson manor. He was angry she risked her life to do it, when it was certain she would be caught.

Sir Ashton escorted her to the Throne Room. As she walked up the red carpet leading to the throne, her eyes caught the vase sitting on a small table next to him. Her heart beat out of her chest. She wanted to cry and run the other way, but that was out of the question. She curtsied to him trembling. "Yes, your Majesty?" she said her voice cracking.

"Miss Black, do you see this vase here on the table?" he began calmly.

"Yes."

"I had one of my advisors buy it for me today, at Hemingways."

"Oh?" she said innocently.

"Do you know why?"

"Ahem, why?"

"Because one of my servants stole it and sold it to Hemingways. Do you know whom that servant might be, Miss Black?"

"Well," she stopped, trying to find the right words, "I don't-"

"You, Miss Black," he said cutting her off. "You stole my vase. I saw you do it."

"But I – I-" she stammered, as tears began trickling down her face.

"What?" he bellowed. "Did you think, no one would notice Miss Black? Hundreds of servants work here. You thought that not one of them would notice or say anything?"

"I suppose I – I- wasn't thinking ..." she trailed off.

"Do you know what the punishment is for this kind of treason?"

She looked down, "I'm not exactly sure, your Majesty."

"Prison or death, Miss Black!"

She began sobbing, and got down to her knees, "I'm so sorry, your Majesty! Please! I –"

He rose from the throne and presented his hand to her. She exhaled, relieved. It seemed he was going to forgive her. She kissed a ring on his large, smooth hands. "It's all right Miss Black I'm not going to behead you. But I would like you to explain why you would do something so senseless."

She looked up flushed, knowing how idiotic she must have looked to him. She wondered if her explanation would make any sense to him.

"I, um, you own me as a servant."

"Yes," he said matter-of-factly.

"But someday you'll have no need for me, and I'll be banished from here. I'll have no place to go or live, and no money. I'll need something to get by," she said between choked breaths.

His expression softened, he wished he could kneel down and comfort her.

"Tell me the truth, were you stealing from Lady and Lord Watson?"

"Yes," she said looking down at the red carpet.

"Miss Black, you are never to steal anything from anyone again, do you understand me?" he said as put his hand on her cheek.

"Yes, your Majesty," she said holding his hand at her cheek. "Thank you."

He released his hand from her cheek and turned to Sir Ashton Giles, "See that Miss Black is paid for her work."

She looked up from her knees stunned. "Thank you so much your-"

"It's all right. You may go, Miss Black," he said waving his arm.

She rose from her knees and walked out of the Throne Room, Sir Ashton Giles followed a few steps behind her. She felt like dancing. No longer would she have to worry about her future. Since Sir Ashton was only a few steps behind her, dancing would be embarrassing. So, she continued down the hall in a reserved manner.

"Miss Black, you'd think with all the extreme generosity the King just showed you, you would be skipping down the hallway."

She stopped and turned to Sir Ashton. He grinned, "I know I did when King Charles turned me from a servant, to an advisor, and knighted me."

"Well, I suppose I should. But I'm not the greatest dancer."

"You didn't do too badly with Sir Gregory Umbridge the other night."

She stopped in her tracks, shocked that he had remembered her. He smiled and winked and continued down the hall.

Meanwhile, in the Throne Room Greg was teasing Alex, "So, let me see if I understand this. If Miss Black steals something, she will be immediately pardoned and rewarded with a salary?"

"Her situation made her desperate, Greg. It was survival. She was doing it out of necessity," he said waving his hand.

"You forgot to ask for the money she got for the vase," Greg said pointedly.

"Never mind that. It's not important."

"Right mate. I suppose giving her a salary will stop her from stealing too?"

"Hopefully, yes."

"You don't think she will spite you for continuing to keep her ownership papers and being her master?"

"Well, no," he said pausing.

"I wonder your Majesty?" Greg continued. Hearing the words 'your Majesty' or 'your Highness' from him annoyed Alex. Greg always said it with a hint of sarcasm.

"What?" said Alex irritably.

"Well, why do you keep Miss Black's papers? Why don't you just grant her freedom?"

"I suppose I didn't think of it," he said. He shifted in his throne, turning away from him.

"Oh yes, yes, possibly," Greg said, knowing Alex was trying to ignore the conversation. "But I think you like owning Miss Black, don't you? You like the idea."

"That's ridiculous."

"I imagine that these past few days you've been spending more time pondering Miss Black than the destiny of our beloved England."

"I love my country, don't question that." Alex said through gritted teeth.

"You're right. I'm sorry to question your love for cuntry."

Greg walked up next to the throne and quickly grabbed the military tactics book from the floor. Alex held his breath, watching the book.

"You've been carrying this military tactics book everywhere you go. To the Billiards Room, to your meals and your meetings. You even brought it to your chambers last night. Your commitment to your country cannot be questioned." With that, he flipped through the book, and loose papers fell to the ground. Alex stared down at them. "What this?" Greg asked as he picked them up off the ground. He chortled, "Miss Black's ownership papers. How curious."

"Can't I have my own interests?" Alex smirked, trying to make light of the situation.

"Interests? More like obsession. You're carrying her ownership papers everywhere you go for Christ's sake."

Alex sprung up from his throne and snatched the book and papers back, "Can you do me a favour and drop it?"

"Oh, I'll let this go. But I get the feeling that Miss Black is soon going to be the topic of conversation on a regular basis. Isn't she?"

"I said drop it."

"Alex, you can't show her much favouritism. If you do, the other servants will make things difficult for her. As for your reputation as a king, well, having a fascination with a servant will never be accepted. The nobility would be disgusted with you. Your dear cousin Bathory will find more supporters to help overthrow you."

"You don't think I know that?"

"Just don't be careless."

Greg walked out of the Throne Room leaving Alex alone with his thoughts. He understood what his best friend was trying to tell him; having a relationship with Madeline Black was out of the question. Bathory had been trying to overthrow him since his father's death. If he did anything that would displease the nobility, his reign could end. He tapped his finger on the armrest. *Never mind the nobility*, he thought, *if I'm smart about it, the nobility will never know.*

8

RULER OF THE THRONE

Madeline woke up the next morning with some pep. Knowing she was working for pay gave her some dignity. She got her schedule, serving afternoon tea during the House of Lords meeting, and washing the Throne Room floor. She folded her arms in a huff, "Err! That's going to take me all day."

"What'd you get stuck with?" said Marie coming up from behind her, tying her apron about her waist.

"Oh, I've got to wash the Throne Room floor."

"Rotten luck. It hurts the knees. I've got to clean the Music Room," Marie said happily.

"There's a Music Room?"

"Oh yes. It's a different kind of room. It's circular with a bunch of windows. His Majesty's quite the accomplished musician. He's actually written music himself."

"Really?"

Marie laughed. "Madeline, honestly! He's a king, he's been educated to play different instruments, learn several languages, defend his country and proper etiquette. I imagine his whole childhood was nothing but tutor after tutor."

"Wouldn't it be wonderful to be so educated? Probably was difficult though."

"Not for him. Apparently all his tutors called him a 'natural'."

Though she did not say it, she disagreed. The King was intelligent, but acquiring those kinds of skills took time, determination and patience. King Alexander was given an education, but he did not have to be an excellent pupil. It was common knowledge that many tutors of noble children did the work of their students when the student refused to do it themselves. Otherwise, the tutors ran the risk of getting fired. Lady Watson once said that she had never learned much arithmetic. She said she did not enjoy it, and just ignored doing it, until her tutor would do it for her. Even as a child, Lady Watson knew no tutor would tell her parents that she was being a prat and not doing her lessons.

She decided to get an early start on the Throne Room. She went in and began with the floor furthest from the throne, at the entrance, and began to make her way across to the other side. She saw another servant washing the floors of the balconies that looked over the Throne Room and wished she had that floor to clean. She worked non-stop until lunch, then went back to the servants' quarters to take a break and eat. Marie was already there. Having just finished the Music Room, she had plans to visit the Royal Mews.

"Are we allowed to visit the stables when we are not working?" she asked sceptically.

"Oh … well no," said Marie, "But as long as no supervisors or any one of importance finds out, it's okay. The horsemen never really say anything. I imagine the punishment would be a slap on the wrist, like an extra room to clean or something."

She looked down smiling, luckily for her, she got paid for stealing the King's vase. She stifled a giggle. Marie looked over at her.

"I looked over at your schedule on the board. You have to take care of tea time today?" Marie asked in a concerned tone.

"Yes, I think perhaps I should get started on it now, I don't want to make any mistakes."

"I'm surprised that you were given the responsibility. It's a very serious job … and burdensome."

She chuckled, "What could be so difficult about serving tea?"

"Madeline, this is no ordinary tea!" Marie said anxiously, "There are twenty or so men in there, all have different tea and snack preferences. You're supposed to serve the tea with the milk, honey or sugar in it you know!"

"What?" she said and took a deep breath, "I didn't know that! No one told me!"

"I know what you can do. A girl named Cecilia does the tea Monday, Wednesday and Friday. She can give you the list."

Marie ran out of the servants' quarters to find Cecilia. Meanwhile, Madeline thanked God she made friends with Marie. When she came back, Marie was out of breath, "She said the list is in the pantry at Westminster," she said huffing.

"Westminster? Why on earth would it be there?"

"I suppose you know nothing about government? Westminster Palace is where most meetings are held. If I were you, I wouldn't have started on the Throne Room." She frowned. "You'd think Sir Ashton or someone would have given you some training. I'll get us a carriage. Meet me at the front entrance of the palace."

Marie drove Madeline down to Westminster, and escorted her through the rooms of parliament trying to get her down to the kitchen. Once there, Marie retrieved the list out of one of the many drawers.

"Okay, so how shall we go about this?" Marie said staring down at the list of paper. Madeline watched her a moment and realized that Marie was illiterate. She was looking at the paper upside down, and seemed uncomfortable as she ran her fingers across the words.

Madeline slowly took the paper from her and turned it right side up. "Thanks so much Marie for helping me."

"It's not a problem," she said. "You'd do the same for me."

Madeline began reading aloud what each Lord requested for tea, and the two began setting up individual trays of tea and scones.

"How will you remember whose is which?" Marie asked looking at the trays helplessly.

"Do you have any little pieces of paper? I can put their names on them and their preferences on the back."

"Brilliant."

They worked together until two o'clock preparing the teas and letting them steep. Marie helped Madeline load her cart and led her down to the House of Lords Chamber. She stood outside the doors, next to some guards. A grandfather clock nearby struck two, and the guards opened the large oversized doors. Madeline entered, pushing the tea cart in front of her. She knew she would have to serve the King first and then those of most importance. She had the list, but who was who? Blast! She wished she had asked Marie.

King Alex was at the other end of the meeting hall, in front of some large arched windows. He towered over the Lords in a tall pulpit. The long aisle she stood on led to the pulpit, with the Lords and advisors sitting on either side of it on red velvet chairs. The floor had a black and white harlequin design. She took a deep breath then nervously started walking toward him, the eyes of all the Lords on her as she pushed the cart. When she reached the pulpit, she looked up at Alex who was speaking.

"Earlier in the House of Commons meeting this morning, Sir Peregrine Grey read some interesting letters that had been intercepted. They were written by Napoleon to his wife. Napoleon had made some interesting comments about his wife. Sir Peregrine I'll allow you the Lords' attention."

Sir Peregrine Grey stood up from one of the red velvet chairs, "I won't bore the crowd with everything your Majesty, just the interesting parts."

Alex nodded.

"Ahem," Sir Peregrine began, "this letter was to his wife, 'I hope before long to crush you in my arms and cover you with a million kisses. A kiss on your heart, and one much lower down, much lower!"

Madeline heard derisive laughter, sounds of disgust and words like 'obscene', 'filthy', and 'only a Frenchman' as she took Alex's tea tray. Sir Peregrine continued reading the letter.

"I write you, my beloved one, very often, and you write very little. You are wicked and naughty, very naughty, as much as you are fickle. It is unfaithful to deceive a poor husband, a tender lover! You don't write to me at all; you don't love your husband; you know how happy your letters make him, and you don't write him six lines of nonsense.'"

All the men were red, laughing hoarsely. Sir Peregrine sat back down, a huge grin on his face. She tried not to snicker, but she couldn't help it. A dictator like Napoleon lovesick was hilarious. She giggled as she climbed the steep steps of the pulpit with Alex's tray of tea. He turned to Sir Peregrine Grey upon hearing her laughter. "Sir Peregrine, that truly is amusing. I think all of England would have a good laugh. Send it to the papers to be published."

She set his tray down and tried to manage an awkward curtsy.

"Tea time?" he whispered beneath his breath.

"Yes, your Majesty."

She shyly watched him as he surveyed the men in the room. Even in his royal robes with the ridiculous crown on his head, he still looked incredible. She glanced and saw his military tactics book lying open in front of him, loose papers between its pages. Noticing her eyeing it, he flipped it shut. She was amazed by how much he cared for the well-being of his country. It really was honourable of him; every time she had seen him he always had the book.

The men of his assembly seemed to prattle on about the war that was taking place throughout Europe. She picked up his card and looked on the back. Just honey. No milk, no sugar, just honey. She swirled the dipper into the honey and raised it about the tea cup, letting it drizzle into the tea.

"Smart girl," he whispered again beneath his breath as he watched the conversation.

She looked up at him.

"The cards" he continued, "no mistakes."

114

She wished that were true. She knew she had to serve a gentleman named Lord Bathory next, but she had no idea whom he was.

"Who to go to next?" he whispered knowingly. He discreetly pointed his finger to the gentleman sitting on his left. He was in his early to mid-forties and she recognized him as one of the men in the Blue Drawing Room. She stepped down the pulpit stairs and went to the cart taking the tray with the place card 'Lord Bathory' on it. As she walked over to the Lord, she finally made the connection. This man was the father of Susanna Bathory. As she came closer to him, she could feel him looking down on her. She timidly poured the tea, and then looked on the back of the place card. 'No milk, no sugar, no honey.' She was about to make her way when she realized she did not know which the Duke of Axford was. She looked about the room and at King Alexander for a hint, but he was busy commenting on the war.

"We cannot bring more men to Dunkirk's troupe. There is not enough time," he said. "We've already discussed this. Let's move on to the possibility of taking two of-"

He was then cut off by an agitated Lord Bathory, "Your Majesty, I believe this girl hasn't a clue what she's doing," he said pointing at Madeline.

He turned to Lord Bathory, "Is that news worthy enough to interrupt me?" he asked, indignant. There were a few chuckles from some of the other Lords.

"Well, my daughter Lady Susanna could do better than her. She is familiar with everyone in the room."

"Miss Susanna could do better than this? Can she even boil a pot of water?"

The Lords roared with laughter. Lord Bathory turned red with anger, "Boil a pot of water? My daughter is an educated, talented woman as you well know your Majesty."

"Yes, I hear she very talented with horseme-" he stopped, smiling devilishly. "Oh, I mean horses."

The laughter continued. Then Greg Umbridge stood up and yelled out, "HORSEMEN!" The men howled louder than ever.

The laughter finally died out, but Madeline still stood in front of the pulpit, confused about who the Duke of Axford was.

King Alex spoke to Bathory again, "Next time you interrupt me or the House of Lords, have something relevant to say. For now, just use your common sense and tell Miss Black where she should go next!"

"Over there," he said to her in an irritated tone, motioning his head to the Duke of Axford, a man that looked to be about sixty or so. She found his tray on the cart and set it down in front of the Duke. She began preparing his tea to his specifications. He watched her every move, a strange expression on his face. He whispered, "Thank you Miss, sorry what was your name again?"

"Black," she whispered back.

He put his fingers to his lips, his face went pale. She wondered if she done something to offend him. But, he said nothing and pointed shakily to Greg Umbridge.

She dismissed the Duke's odd behaviour and went over to Greg, setting his tray down in front of him. She looked at his card, 'no milk, no sugar, no honey.' She poured the tea into its cup. Greg leaned toward her and whispered, "Is that tea?"

She wanted to giggle, but she stopped herself, "What else would it be? It's tea time, Sir Gregory."

"Oh. Um, you should know that usually the ladies don't serve me tea. They serve me something to help me get through these awful meetings. You know so it's more of a blur."

She bit her bottom lip, trying not to crack up. In the middle of all these talks of war, there was Greg Umbridge trying to hustle her for a drink.

"Sorry Sir Gregory. Next time."

"I'll let you get away with it this time," he said, giving her a wink.

She smiled.

"Geez, you get away with a lot, don't you love?"

She blushed. He pointed to Sir Ashton Giles, and she continued with her work about the room until all the men were served. When she left, they were still discussing war, and she understood why Greg wanted a drink. The arguing was nauseating. Back in the kitchen, she washed and dried the dishes. When she finally finished, she left Westminster and took the carriage back to Buckingham. It was exhausting, so she had a light snack before continuing the Throne Room floor.

Hours later, as she washed the Throne Room floor, the King stormed in, angrier than she had ever seen him. Lord Bathory, Greg Umbridge and several other Lords were at his heels.

"Enough already!" he yelled. "We've spent hours, days, no — weeks debating this. We haven't much time now. I refuse to hear any more arguments of what should be done."

Though he was angry, she couldn't help but to gaze up at him dreamily from the floor. He always looked handsome and well put

117

together. He was no longer wearing his royal robes and crown from before. He now wore green coat with gold embroidery detail around the buttons adorned his broad shoulders. It was matched with a fitted green vest and a cream shirt. She noticed his eyes sparkling as he looked down at her. He flashed his perfect smile and she nervously looked away, and went back to cleaning the floor.

His demeanour changed and he calmly addressed the men around him, "I'd like some time alone to figure it all out," he said abruptly. "I'll draw up a plan before tomorrow's meeting. Leave me."

He walked over to his throne and sat down. The Lords turned and walked out of the entrance. She was ecstatic to be finished earlier than expected. She picked up the pail and wash cloth and was about to leave.

"Miss Black," he began. "You're of no consequence, you may stay."

She sighed and put her pail and cloth back on the floor. She knelt back down on her hands and knees and continued washing, as the men shut the doors behind them.

He opened his military tactics book and pretended to read. Slowly, he lowered his book and peered at her. It was impossible to focus on the war with Madeline in his thoughts all the time. She was a natural beauty. He learned earlier that it was a bad idea to have her look after tea. After she had entered the room, he hadn't been able to focus much on what the other Lords had suggested. Her uniform accentuated her curves and he knew he wasn't the only man that noticed. As she went about the room, he watched her through his peripherals and fantasized that they were the only two in the room.

Now she was in front of him, on the floor; enticing him again, her milky white breasts nearly spilling out of her dress. He snapped his book shut.

She looked across the large floor, as she dropped her rag back into the pail. She had just passed the throne in the centre of the hall and was now three quarters finished. Tired, she rubbed her eyes; this was going to take several more hours. She wrung out her cloth and continued scrubbing.

"I believe no naughty deed should go unpunished Miss Black."

Madeline cocked her head up and saw him towering over her with his military tactics book in hand, its loose papers between its pages. On her hands and knees, she looked up timidly, feeling small under his muscular stature.

"You stole my vase. You should be punished for that," he said smoothly, his crystal blue eyes piercing hers. She felt more scared then she would if he were yelling. Most masters yelled before disciplining, this was unnerving. He sank down to his knees next to her and put his book with her ownership papers between its pages, on the floor.

"Miss Black," he continued as he moved his hand down her back, "what are the rules when a person is near or around a king?"

She felt her mouth go dry, his indecent proposal becoming clear to her. Her skin began to prickle at his touch.

"They should not sit or stand higher than him?" she said, swallowing hard.

"That's right, Miss Black," he said casting a furtive glance. "Just so there's no confusion, I suggest not moving."

He continued to stroke her back, running his fingers through her hair as he did. She felt like a horse he was considering riding. Her body froze at the expression on his face; his eyes were slight and glazed over as he devoured the sight of her.

Just touching the laces of her corset and her silken hair was intoxicating. He felt a rush inside him, unlike any other. This wasn't lifting the skirts of some noble debutante he'd lose interest in after a few weeks. He was taking advantage of a beautiful woman, who didn't have her sights on a crown. He was her master, and she was a slave. A slave that wanted it. He could see hunger in her eyes, her back arching, beckoning for him as his hand descended down the laces of her corset again.

Their eyes met. No sweet nothings needed to be said. He pulled at the laces in a frenzy. She couldn't believe what was happening. She fancied him the moment she laid eyes on him, but him wanting her was too surreal. She gasped, her arms and legs began to tremble. *Oh my God this is happening!* she thought as he pulled at her corset's chest and reached out for her soft mounds. He caressed them softly with a skilful hand and she closed her eyes and murmured. His touch was delicate. He closed his eyes, nuzzled into her neck, and began nibbling her softly, sending tingles through her. She turned to him, offering her lips and he began kissing her deeply, holding her face in his large soft hands.

"I've been wanting this since the moment you forgot to curtsy to me," he said his eyes smouldering. His lips moved about hers again in a whirlwind of passion. Madeline smiled inwardly as she felt a fluttering inside her, his heated breath and kisses nibbled up and down her mouth and neck. He pulled back whispering with a firm tone, "Since you didn't properly greet me with your skirts then, I want you to lift your skirts for me now."

She stopped breathing, stunned. She didn't know he could be so crude. She felt hot, and dizzy as if someone drugged her.

"Miss Black," he spoke softly, between kisses, "that's a king's command. Lift. Your. Skirts."

He pulled back as Madeline obediently lifted her dress and brought the hem to her hips, so her bottom just peeked out.

"Miss Black," he said in a sexy tone, "I want a good look at your arse."

Her breath fell short again. Moving quickly, he pulled up the skirt higher so it was round her waist. By his force, she rocked forward. She stabilized herself again and her bare bottom plainly stuck out in the air, his eyes staring at it as he began to rub it softly. She had never felt so vulnerable and aroused.

"That's good," he said slowly and deeply, immersed with the urge to take her then and there. Ignoring his desire, he took the military book on the floor. A naughty idea came over him, he became hard at the thought of spanking her with the book that held her ownership papers.

There was a good chance she'd refuse this, but he couldn't help himself. He tenderly pushed her shoulder down and she took this as a cue that he wanted her head on the floor. She went down, laying her face on her hands looking up at him.

"Very good, Miss Black." He picked his military tactics book off the floor and rubbed it softly against her bottom. She knew what was to come. "I'm going to have to punish you now," he said the book on her bottom, she knew she could crawl away. But she was too horny to consider it. She'd wanted this. She wanted him, his taste, his smell, his fuck.

He held the hard cover book up, she squeezed her eyes shut and he smacked her hard. To her surprise she grew more excited, she moaned, her pussy glistening.

"Again," she whispered, barely audible.

A cocky smile lined his mouth, "What's that Miss Black?" he asked, pretending not to hear.

"Again," she sighed. "Again … please."

He came down on her with the book again.

"Oooooohhhhhh!" she screamed, her body quaking.

"Sorry, Miss Black, but I'm a little envious of the book," he tossed the book back to the floor, and she looked up at him pleadingly, hoping he would not stop. He gazed at her, taken aback. Spanking her with the book to 'punish' her was just a little dirty fun. He didn't really expect she'd enjoy it as much as he did. He raised his hand and slapped her bottom with his palm. She moaned again.

"More?"

"Yes, yes."

He smacked her again, and she cried out in ecstasy, the throne room resonating her sound. After each spank, her knees would falter a little, but she brought them back up again, presenting herself to him, begging for more. After several spanks, he stopped and left his hand on her bottom rubbing it softly, her body still shaking from the pleasure. Pulling her closely to him, he slowly worked his fingers down to her inner thighs and began caressing them.

Knowing what he wanted, she spread herself, inviting him in. Surprised at her own response, she couldn't believe the effect he had on her. She rarely touched herself, and if she did she felt guilty. Now, she happily spread her legs for him without a second thought.

He massaged her sex, gently entering his digits into her.

She gasped, his clever fingers made her pussy hot and her folds and bud swelled. Her juices flowed, as he gently pushed against the wet velvet. She murmured, amazed at him. For the few times she had touched herself, she was never been able to get so titillated.

He wrapped his other arm around her waist. "My, my, you get quite wet," he said huskily.

She cocked her head back at him, as he withdrew and licked his fingers. She had never heard of anyone doing this kind of act. Watching him, she knew that every citizen of England would find it repulsive. But strangely, it pleased her to see him doing it. Her body quivered in delight as she watched him, taking his time, tasting her.

"Mmm."

At hearing him groan, an urge took over her. She felt a certain kind of yearning she had never felt before. Deep inside her, in the innermost depths of her pussy, she was calling for him. Instinctively, he answered her and put his fingers deep inside of her, and began pushing against her.

"Mmm."

"Miss Black, you please me. A lot. I want to make you cum," he said as he began thrusting and swirling his fingers deeper, and more vigorously. "Nothing would please me more."

She could not believe everything that was happening and the words he was saying. He had countless women after him. He was a king. What about her pleased him? Why would he desire to satisfy her? Without warning, he pounded his fingers into her and she wailed in pleasure. Writhing against him, her knees slid across the marble floor, her hands scratched it looking for something to dig into.

"Uh,mmm uh..."

His strong arms held her tightly. He continued probing, sweating and tiring his fingers and arms in his longing to see her crumpled up, weary on the floor.

"You're so hot. You're going to cum," he said harshly as he pushed through her teeming sex. "Cum, for me. Cum."

His words consuming her, he could feel the walls of her twat squeeze his fingers. As he pushed harder and faster her orgasm stormed through her body. She shrieked, her body shaking, she came drenching his hand and her skirts. Her legs feeling like jelly, she collapsed onto him. He withdrew his fingers and began sucking them off again. Madeline's shaking slowly died out and she lied across him, breathing heavily, her eyes heavy with the temptation to sleep.

"You're delicious," he said laughing and smacked her bottom lightly. He moved her onto her back and began kissing her lips and cupping her face with his hands. Lying underneath him, Madeline felt small, but it felt right. She began moving her hands up his arms feeling his chiselled muscles and around the nape of his neck running her fingers through his hair as they kissed passionately. He sighed. He pulled back and considered her for a moment, softly caressing her cheek. He gave her one last kiss, rose from the floor, walked back to his throne and sat on it.

She lay on the floor completely perplexed. *Is he really going to sit on his throne and act like nothing happened?* She felt like grabbing her wash pail and throwing the dirty bucket of water in his face and storming out of there. How pretentious and rude to walk away without a word and sit on a throne like a king! *Oh yeah,* she realized slowly, *he is a king, he can do whatever he pleases.*

She felt foolish. She had been used. She began tightening the laces to her uniform.

He turned to her, "Madeline, get over here, I'm not done with you yet."

She dropped her laces stunned. She had never heard him call her by her first name before. She did not know that he knew it. She walked over to him and faced him standing on the red carpet she curtsied. He smiled.

"Madeline, come closer," he said firmly.

She stepped forward at the edge of the small steps that led to the throne.

"Closer, Madeline."

She put her feet on the first step bowing her head to be sure she did not stand higher than the King.

"Closer."

She bowed further down as she rose to the next step. She was getting a little annoyed with his humiliating little game. It seemed like he wanted to make sure she knew her place in this world. All the while he kept smiling.

"Closer," he whispered.

She got on the third and final step and realized she would have to drop to her knees. As she went down, it occurred to her that he was not playing a game to humiliate her – on her knees, she was directly at his crotch.

"How loyal are you to your King?"

She looked down blushing, "Loyal," she said softly.

He waited, and she pretended to not know what he wanted next. She wanted him to ask for it. He raised his brow, "Don't you play innocent with me Madeline, you know what I want. You were in the closet at the Watsons'."

Her cheeks went scarlet. He looked straight down at her with his devilish smile.

"I am a king. I am trained in combat. I know when someone else is in the room with me."

At this point, there was no point in denying that she wanted to satisfy him. He knew she wanted to. She began to undo the buttons to his trousers and his huge cock sprung free, eagerly waiting to meet her. Madeline's mouth went dry again, as she realized she had never been this intimate with a man before. He loosened her braid and her hair cascaded down her back. Hand trembling, she reached out and touched him, her fingertips caressed his length and she began to explore him. He allowed her as he moved his fingers through her soft hair, watching her as she discovered him.

She thought it was curious how soft his skin was on the outside, yet how hard he was. She flirtatiously traced her fingers up and down along his length and touched his wet tip. She drew closer and laid it against her cheek and breathed him in, the smell of his arousal, inflaming her desire. She looked up at him.

He grunted, "Ugh, you're driving me mental."

"It's big, Alex," she said wondering how she could fit it in her mouth.

She bit her lip realizing she had called him 'Alex'. He said nothing but looked down at her, his lips curving. She looked back down at his cock and noticed the tip glistening. She moved closer breathing hot, nervous breaths on his member, until she found her nerve, giving small licks and kisses at his tip.

"Mmm ... Madeline," he exhaled.

She then took in his member into her mouth, surprised at how slippery it was. He was salty and tasty. She sucked hungrily at his head, enjoying him.

"Uhhh, you like it don't you?" he grunted, tilting his head back into the throne. Madeline murmured happily her lips suctioned to his shaft she leaned in taking his entire cock into her mouth.

"Ohh yesss," he whispered, as she began working his entire length with her mouth. He grabbed her head to guide her up and down it. She sucked slowly at first, feeling the heat rising in his loins as he moaned. Soon Madeline quickened her pace. Smacking and clenching the arms of the throne, he reached the edge of his climax. Madeline worked harder and faster, his eyes rolling back into his head.

"MMMMM GOD UGGGHHHHH!!!!"

Alex groaned so loudly it echoed across the room. Holding her face he released into her mouth and she eagerly swallowed all his nectar making sure to lick every last drop off his sex. He watched, shocked as she did this.

Madeline pulled back and looked at him. She felt somewhat empowered as she watched him slump back in his throne gasping for air, sweating.

After a few moments, he shakily propped himself up, bent down and pulled her onto his lap, still breathing heavily. He kissed her and began nibbling her earlobe. "Wow," he whispered, "that was incredible." Madeline giggled. He slowly moved down to her mounds and began squeezing them through her corset. They kissed each other's lips softly as he continued massaging her breasts.

"I've been wanting these since I first saw you at the Watsons'," he said grasping them hard.

Madeline sat up and pulled down at her corset, fully exposing her white smooth peaks to him, her shiny black hair swinging softly about them. Alex started feeling a tingling in his cock. He tweaked her pink nipples and they grew hard at his touch. Leaning down he began tonguing circles about her nipples slowly sucking and biting at them.

She could feel his penis become solid again beneath her and rubbed her bottom against it. "Mmm, Alex," she said in a kittenish tone. He smiled, he liked her calling him Alex.

She could feel herself grow moist again and began rubbing her pussy through the layers of her skirts. Alex moved back from her chest and noticed the hot, beautiful mess before him, as she kneaded her bottom against his cock and touched herself. Wanting to satisfy her again, Alex began to pull up on her skirts again.

Just then, they heard steps and talking from distant in the upper balcony. Alex and Madeline gave each other their eyes bulging.

"Damn!" he whispered hoarsely.

It was surprising to see a gentleman swear. No one would guess he could swear with such ease.

The steps seemed to be coming closer to the throne room and soon whomever it was would be able to look over and see the two of them in plain view. She darted off his lap and pulled up her corset started tightening the laces of her dress. He buttoned up his pants, then quickly turned to her and pulled the laces tight as possible. Ignoring the need to tie them, she ran over to her pail and took out the cloth. Looking somewhat dishevelled with her hair strewn about she got down on her knees and began washing, trying her best to not look suspicious. Not a moment later, Sir Ashton Giles and Sir Gregory Umbridge looked over the balcony at them. Greg Umbridge smiled.

"Your Majesty!" he said playfully, "Are you in good spirits?"

Sir Ashton Giles gave Greg an odd look. Greg knew his King quite well.

"Very well – good, thank you," Alex said stiffly, not looking directly at them.

"Have you figured out what you are going to do about the situation with Dunkirk?" he asked.

"What? Ahem," Alex cleared his throat. "Yes, still figuring it out," he said as his eyes darted about looking for his book.

"Little hard to do when your tactics book is lying next to your servant," Greg said, his brow raised.

Sir Ashton Giles looked befuddled. He seemed not to understand what he had stumbled upon. Madeline, on her hands and knees, looked across the floor and saw the book. She picked it up and began to walk over to Alex to hand it to him.

"Well, you see, Sir Gregory," she began, "his Majesty was so frustrated with the whole thing, he threw the book across the room and accidentally hit me."

He scoffed, "Hmpf! Interesting, Miss Black." He cast a sideways glance at Alex, who looked away to Madeline. She bowed her head as she handed the book to him.

"Good night Sir Gregory, Sir Ashton," Alex said quickly.

Both men bowed, Sir Gregory doing so half laughing and left.

"Miss Black," Alex began as he perused his book, "it will take you till morning to wash this floor. Retire for the night and do the job tomorrow."

She turned to him, a pout on her face, "Do I really have to do it tomorrow?"

"Come closer to me Madeline." She was about to get on her knees to avoid standing taller than him, but he stopped her. He pulled her closely to him, he rubbed his nose against hers.

"No," he chuckled, "I don't really expect you to clean it."

She giggled and he kissed her.

"Good night, Madeline."

She kissed him softly and whispered good night. She picked up her things made a small curtsy and left.

Alex sat in his throne for the next few hours staring off into nothingness. Strangely, the France situation and Dunkirk's folly was easy enough to solve. As soon as Madeline left the room, the answer came to him. However, he realized that she was another problem. A problem he enjoyed having. He ached to go down to the servants' quarters and finish what he started, he considered using the castle's secret passageways reserved for his use only to do it. But there was still the matter of finding her and not being seen by anyone once he got there.

It was more complicated than military tactics. How could a king get time alone with a servant girl without being noticed? Not only did he often have company, but she was constantly surrounded by other servants doing work. That she had been alone tonight in the hall washing the floors was a happy coincidence. How could he have time alone with her without looking suspicious? How was he going to be sure that his own company and advisors were unaware of what he was doing? Greg already seemed to know what was going on. Alex knew that he was lucky Greg was his closest most loyal friend, and wouldn't say anything. Then, at that moment, Alex realized how easy it was to have Madeline.

Madeline went back to the servants' quarters and to bed. As she lay under her blankets, she could not stop thinking of him. Dirty. Scandalous. Sexy. Those were the words she would use to describe Alex. Far from Marie's 'intellectual' and Sir Ashton's 'good' and 'wise'. It would shock the King's loyal subjects to know what she and Alex did that night. Acts like those happened in brothels. People did not speak of oral sex, much less spankings. Even though their behaviour was frowned upon, she had to admit she always thought that thinking was prudish. She found it pleasurable, what was so disgusting about a playful spanking?

9

THE MISTRESSES' CHAMBERS

It was early morning when the King and Sir Gregory Umbridge were enjoying their usual Wednesday tennis match in the courtyard. Greg bounced the ball several times on the ground looking for the right words to advise Alex. He caught the ball in his hand and looked directly at him, "You're my oldest friend" he began, "so what I'm saying to you now, I say because I care about your well-being."

Alex rolled his eyes, he knew what he was about to hear. "Out with it!"

"I know it's not my business, but you shouldn't fuck your servant."

"Why not? She is my servant," he raised his eyebrows mischievously smiling.

"That's not funny," Greg said and served the ball.

Alex hit it hard and Greg missed the return. Picking up the ball, Greg walked up to the net. "I don't care much about what's proper, but your subjects do have expectations. You're playing with fire; you'll be ridiculed by an entire country if they find out you can't keep your hands off a peasant girl. People already have a problem with your best friend being a commoner."

"Never mind that. Besides, can you blame me? I mean she's breathtaking, she makes a servant's uniform look-"

"You know that no one else cares how beautiful she may be. Parliament and the nobility won't like it if she's what's standing in the way of their country getting a suitable queen. I'd hate to see what they'd do. If your cousin Bathory can get more supporters, you know he'd overthrow you."

"I'm not worried about Bathory. Besides, I never said anything about marrying her. I'm just playing around. It's no different than having a noble girl around."

"So you say."

"I promise you," he began in his most convincing tone, "I'm not falling for her. How could I fall for someone I have nothing in common with? What kind of stimulating conversations would we have? I don't know anything about washing a floor, nor do I care to hear about it."

Greg shook his head, "Well, I suppose she could teach you to steal things," he joked.

Though he was not amused, Alex laughed. He had a favour he needed to ask, "I need you to do something for me."

"What?"

"Like I said, I'm just playing around … But I need to be put in situations where I'm alone with her."

"You know mate, for someone you're just playing around with, you're going to a lot of trouble. First you ignore the fact that she stole something from you and had her followed. Hardly caring about what she stole from you, then you dismissed your advisors during an important time to enjoy all the benefits the throne has to offer. Now, you're getting me to arrange a secret rendezvous?"

"If she were a noble, I wouldn't have to ask you to do this."

"Why don't you just play with a noble instead? Why would you want-"

"Do you enjoy tea when all you really want is a scotch?"

"So Miss Black is a stiff scotch?"

"No," he smiled. "But I am when she's around."

Greg chuckled.

"I'm tired of the noble women and princesses," Alex went on, "as I get older I swear they all think I'm looking for a wife. Maybe it would be good to get to know someone who has no hope of getting a crown."

"You don't think she's going to want something serious?"

"I think she knows that nothing much could come of it."

"Okay, so let's imagine that Miss Black is fine with the arrangement you're suggesting. Your subjects will judge this. She is also your slave."

"What they don't know, they can't judge."

Greg bounced the ball to the court in thought, "She's still just a servant girl, mate. No one will forget that."

"Don't forget your humble beginnings, Greg."

"Oi! Aren't we the master of deflection?" he said catching the ball in his hand. "Don't try bringing up the fact that I was a commoner. It has nothing to do with you liking a slave."

"You're hypocritical," Alex said knowing the power of his words. "You think it's disgusting I'm interested in Madeline because she's a servant."

"I don't think it's disgusting," Greg countered. "I have no problem with her or the fact that she's a servant. If the world were a fair place, I'd tell you to be with her and be happy. But what Kingdom would accept a servant as a queen? What nobility would accept that kind of king?"

"You afraid I might get the guillotine?"

"The French did it, and not too long ago either."

"Look, I'm going to see her whether you help me or not. But it's more likely that I'll get caught if you don't help."

"All right. All right. What am I doing exactly?"

"You'll be making changes to the servants' schedule. Change several of the servants' schedules, so it doesn't look suspicious. Make sure that every day of the week she is put into a room that only requires one servant to clean it. Also, try putting her in rooms that have been cleaned."

"So she's getting out of work and still getting paid for it?" he scoffed.

"Honestly, Greg. What man woos a woman by telling her to have sex with him after she's cleaned his home?"

"A man that's good in bed."

He rolled his eyes, "That's why you don't get with the ladies too often."

"No, I don't get the ladies often 'cause I stand next to an Adonis that wears a crown, you arse."

"Put her in the Mistresses' Chambers tomorrow. It's already been cleaned."

"And conveniently has a bed," said Greg as he walked back to his edge of the court.

Madeline had not seen Alex all of Wednesday. It drove her insane. She wondered what their next meeting would be like. Most likely awkward. The more she thought about it, she figured that Alex probably felt embarrassed about what they'd done. It was improper on so many levels, the fact that he was a king, and she was a servant, his spanking her and her obediently getting on her knees. What happened the other night with him was a one-time thing she needed to forget. If she could.

She checked her schedule in the parlour. As she expected, she was serving afternoon tea, but she was also cleaning the Mistress' Chambers.

"Oooh! Lucky you!" said Marie, "You should see all the gowns in the closet in that room! Make sure you get a peek."

She made her way down to the Mistress' Apartments, almost giddy. It would be exciting to see what kinds of things were on offer to a woman the King fancied. She walked down the hall of the private apartments and opened the large doors and stood in amazement. It was a huge room. It was surprising she was not cleaning it with another servant. But as she looked around she did not see a bed. This was the Mistress' Drawing Room, she reckoned. It had large elaborate fresco's across the ceiling, each framed with elaborate crown mouldings. There were red velvet ottomans around

136

the room, and renaissance style tapestries. She moved across the room to another set of large floor to ceiling doors and pushed them open.

It was an extraordinary room of soft pinks, sages and blues mixed with ivory and gold. All the walls had tapestries bordered with crown mouldings and hand embroidered with small flowers crawling up vines that danced across the ivory canvas. The bed was massive, with a heavy silk canopy that had embroidery that matched the tapestries and a mountain of silk pillows.

The walls were covered with small sconces made up of vines. The hardwood floor had an exquisite pattern that must have taken months to lay down. There was a small fireplace of ivory marble. On the same wall was another set of doors next to floor-to-ceiling windows that brought light into the room. *That must be the closet*, she thought trotting over to the doors beaming.

She opened the enormous ivory and gold closet doors and her mouth fell open. She was not sure which room was bigger, the bedroom or the closet. There must have been close to a thousand dresses, maybe more, hanging from racks that created a maze.

She walked through astonished at all the different colours, fabrics and textures of the gowns. She turned down another pathway of dresses, noticing the dresses were organized according to season and day or night wear. The further she walked into the labyrinth, the more vintage the dresses became. There were probably two hundred dresses that were fifty years old. The passageways of dresses also led to other areas for accessories, undergarments, hats, masquerade masks and stomachers. One area was like a powder room, it had upholstered silk ottomans, several armoires, and a large vanity bigger than Lady Watson's and a huge basin almost as big as a bathtub.

Curiosity overtook her and she began to search through the vanity drawers. She had never seen a larger selection of beauty products. They came from all corners of the world.

She pulled out a deep red lipstick from the drawer and noticed that some of the lipsticks next to it were beginning to crack and fade in colour. It was wrong. Every woman in England would have killed to have this closet. Instead, it was unused and unappreciated. She always wanted to get dressed up and go to a ball. She frowned and put the lipstick back. She had a room to clean.

She walked back into the Bedchamber disappointed. As she entered, she noticed something odd. The windows were clean. She inspected the floor, not a speck of dirt lay upon it. She went to the fireplace mantle and brushed her finger across the marble. No dust.

She shrieked and bolted back to the closet, giggling. She had to do tea time in the afternoon, but she had enough time to pamper herself. She opened all the drawers envisioning the possibilities. She pulled out some Turkish rosewater, Eastern European cold creams and Egyptian beeswax.

She stripped down and began to pump water into the basin. After filling it, she sat next to the basin and started with the wax and the straight razor. Lady Watson shaved off most her hair, but then again she was known to be an odd woman. She wondered what other noble women did. Unsure, she waxed and shaved what she felt was appropriate. She hated the wax but loved the after effect of her skin. It was silky smooth, and she hadn't started with the crèmes yet.

Once she finished carefully plucking her eyebrows, she poured some rosewater into the water in the basin. It smelled heavenly, and she tipped a little extra in. She knelt next to the basin and dipped her hair into the water, massaging her scalp and breathing in the scent. She exhaled and sniffed again and again. With her hair still in the water, she felt around the tub for the bottle and poured some directly onto her hair. She cleaned her hair thoroughly and wrung it until it was damp. She stood up, grabbed a towel from one of the armoires and wrapped it around her head. She glanced back at the basin. It was big enough to fit her. She poured some more rosewater in and sat in it. The smell was so intoxicating and relaxing, she could have fallen asleep.

It was four more hours until tea time. There was plenty of time to set her hair, slather on some cold cream and put make-up on her face. But she knew she couldn't serve tea with her hair and make-up done. She decided that once she finished tea, she would come back and dress herself up. Maybe go to her own imaginary ball.

When she finished primping, she literally smelled like a rose. Around noon, she put her uniform back on and left Buckingham with plenty of time left to prepare tea at Westminster.

Minutes before two o'clock, Madeline stood outside the doors with her tea cart as the House of Lords meeting was in session. Along with the guards, she stared at a grandfather clock, waiting for it to strike. As it chimed, the guards opened the doors allowing her in. She looked up to the King at his pulpit, immersed in some documents. It seemed as though they were still on about the war, and by the sounds of things, whatever Alex had decided, it was brilliant.

"Your Majesty, it truly is a fantastic idea. But, I think cornering the Spanish and forcing them to arms may gain us some enemies," said Lord Bathory.

"Forcing the French into their territory may be unfair Bathory, but this is war," he said matter-of-factly. "Spain and France are already having issues. There's talk of war for control over the Iberian Peninsula."

"But what of the royals? France's feeling towards-"

"Never mind that, Bathory. Since when have you been sympathetic? It's their problem to deal with. As I said, France will take them to arms either way. We are just speeding up the inevitable."

Alex paused as he noticed Madeline climbing the steep pulpit steps. She stood near him and prepared his tea with honey. His nose twitched, and he inhaled. She stared at him, her breath caught in her chest, thinking about how much rosewater she had used. A sexy smile grew on his lips and he began howling in laughter. It echoed across the room, interrupting the Duke of Axford, who was reasoning with Lord Bathory.

"Are you quite all right your Majesty?" the Duke of Axford asked, turning his head.

"Yes, yes," he sniffed, regaining his composure. "Sorry Axford, continue."

Madeline continued serving the tea as the meeting wore on. When she poured Greg Umbridge's tea, he looked at her suspiciously, "That'd better be brandy, not rosewater, love."

She did a double take. She did her best to remain poised and answered him in a hushed voice. "You've got quite the imagination. This isn't the first brandy of the day, is it Sir Gregory?"

"No," he whispered calmly, "but I'm not that drunk, yet."

Madeline finished the rest of the service, which was uneventful as the Lords droned on. She sped through the dishes, then went back to the Mistresses' Chambers and into the closet where she started primping her hair. She put in a bunch of curls, backcombed it and pinned it up. It looked elegant. She was impressed she could do such a good job without the help of Sissy, but being able to use the right tools made it easy. She continued with doing her make-up. She began to pat on some foundation. Not the pale base that Lady Watson insisted on, but a beige that gave her more colour. She added some blush to her cheekbones and used some plums and mauves on her eyelids, which made her green eyes pop. She applied the deep red lipstick she had found earlier and surveyed herself in a full-length mirror.

Gazing at her reflection, she touched it with her fingertip. It was amazing what some make-up and a little primping could do. A rosiness spread across her face at her own narcissistic thoughts.

She turned to the myriad of dresses. Every morning, for the past six years, she woke up knowing what to wear. Looking at the thousands of dresses, she had no clue. It was great. She never had so many possibilities, and it was exciting.

She walked through the maze, picking out as many dresses as she could hold and brought them back to the mirror. She pressed different colour dresses against herself, contemplating what suited her.

Then a small piece of blue fabric caught her eye from across the room. It was a unique kind of blue she had only seen once before – Alex's eyes. She dropped the gold dress she held in her hands to the floor and scurried down the corridor of racks, spreading apart the dresses next to it so she could get a better look.

Her mouth gaped in wonder. The dress was striking and unlike any dress she had ever seen before. It was a cerulean blue silk taffeta brocaded with silver thread appliqués. Large trumpet sleeves layered with lace pieces trimmed the cuffs, and the petticoat was blue taffeta with a black lace overlay and silver thread detail. The neck was embellished with lace. Giddy, she went back to the full-length mirror and pressed the dress against herself. The colour complimented her eyes and black hair and was just her size. It looked like it had never been worn. It was though it had been in the closet waiting for her.

With a goofy grin, she stared into the mirror. She frowned, noticing her foolish expression. It was silly what she was doing. Not that she had spent the whole day readying herself for no occasion, but she fell in love with a dress the colour of the King's eyes! She felt ridiculous. Deep down she knew she wanted to spend a night looking like a queen with him. She needed to forget about what happened in the Throne Room. He was probably just a frustrated, horny king that needed a fix. She just happened to be there.

She put the rest of the dresses back and took one last look at her dream dress then looked at her uniform. A feeling of repulsion and anger overtook her upon seeing her uniform. *What is wrong with me playing dress up?* she thought. *No one owns these dresses. Besides, noble women do it every day.* She deserved this.

She began putting it on, and with no assistance, it was challenging. Almost impossible. The laces to the stays were frustrating. She was forced to tie them by using the mirror to see what she was doing. It took forty-five minutes before she was finally in the dress, but she did not care. Living out her fantasy of being in a gorgeous gown was worth the aggravation.

Once she finished putting on the dress, she took one final look in the mirror. She looked like a young, fresh debutante, ready for her first ball. She traced her fingers down the detail of the dress. *All that trouble, I should be going to a ball,* she thought.

The bedroom was so large, it could work as a ballroom. She walked to the closet door and looked into the bedroom. She wondered if she should announce herself at her own ball. She laughed aloud. She thought the whole announcing name and title bit was quite pretentious. This was her ball, and she could make the rules. She walked into the room, head held high greeting her imaginary guests. Unexpectedly, the King asked her to dance, and she accepted. She began circling around the room, clueless how to dance in a gown. She tripped and fell to the floor and rolled about laughing. She had never been to a more delightful ball. She stood up again and continued dancing about the room.

Just then she stopped and stared at the wall. There was something strange about it. It was beginning to move. In a panic, she lifted her gown in her hands and scurried behind one the canopy bed's large curtains. She pulled at her skirts, holding her breath, hoping she would not be seen. Then there was a long silence as she waited to hear the door close. Instead, she heard footsteps enter the room.

"Oh, Miss Blaaack … come out and play."

10

SWEPT OFF HER FEET

Alex stepped into the Mistresses' Chambers from a secret passageway, smiling to himself, he called again, "Miss Blllaaaacckk?"

Behind the curtain, her heart began to pound. Being found playing dress up would be humiliating. She felt like a small child as she stood breathing shakily, his footsteps coming closer. He drew the curtain back, and they stood face to face. His jaw dropped as he stared, transfixed by her beauty. She swallowed hard looking down.

"Your Majesty," she choked and curtsied uneasily.

He raised her chin with his hand, "You look stunning tonight, Miss Black," he said, his tepid eyes heavy with lust. He glanced down at the hillocks of her smooth chest.

"You're forgetting something though," he said as he took her hand. She held her breath not knowing what to expect. He led her in front of a sconce on the wall, next to the bed and pulled at one of its vines. The wall cracked open an inch, revealing a secret door. He pulled the door wide open and she looked in. It was pitch-black and cold. Taking her hand, he guided her into the darkness. Then, he stepped away, leaving her blind in the middle of the room.

"Don't move," he said as he walked away from her. As she looked about, she could see glints of something around the room. She heard him fiddling with something and then the room lit up. Breathtaking tiara's, bracelets, necklaces, earrings, hair adornments and rings with sparkling diamonds and gems surrounded her on mirrored shelves. As she moved closer to him, the light hit the jewels at different angles, and they sparkled and flickered.

"What would Miss Black like to wear tonight?"

She gasped. Was he really going to allow her to wear royal jewellery? She looked at him in disbelief.

"Go on Miss Black, choose something,"

All the pieces were magnificent, some with overwhelmingly large stones complimented with smaller ones; others with delicate designs and an ungodly amount of small stones. One tiara caught her eye. It was embellished with smaller white diamonds, with little swirled designs that were like lace.

"Oh you like that one," he said, watching her green eyes. He took it from its stand and fixed it to her head. Beaming she looked about at the other treasures in the room. A large sapphire stone necklace with smaller white diamonds sat next to a similar necklace with rubies. She walked over to the necklaces looking from one to the other trying to pick. Behind her, he reached out and grabbed a necklace with emeralds.

"This will compliment your eyes," he said placing the emeralds around her neck and attaching the clasps. *He's right,* she thought. A light smile touched Madeline's lips as she gazed at her reflection in the mirrored shelf. She took the matching dangling earrings and placed them in her ears.

Alex took Madeline's hand and placed a tennis bracelet on it. She continued to look in the mirror, in awe.

"All right, now you're ready for the ball," he said.

She blushed and he took her hand in his and led her back to the Mistresses' Chambers, closing the secret room behind them.

Turning to her he bowed. Flushed, she curtsied. He took her in his arms, and he led her in a waltz. Holding her hand close to his chest and leading her by the small of her back, his touch was electrifying. It was as though she swayed into a fantasy. There with the King, she felt like the most desirable woman in the world.

He pulled her closer to him, and she rested her head on his chest. He breathed her in, smelling the rosewater she put in her hair.

"You're so naturally beautiful, you're perfect," he whispered.

She looked up at him through hooded eyes. His were closed, an incredibly sweet expression on his face. She wanted to kiss him, but was too intimidated to. She knew his intentions with her were physical, but she still questioned if it was proper for her as a commoner to act on her impulses. Ladies and princesses threw themselves at him. But from what she gathered, he didn't like that. Maybe he found it improper. On the other hand, Miss Hampton was extremely forward. Maybe he did like that. She stared off in thought when he unexpectedly swirled her about. Startled, she gripped him. He snickered, "You've got something on your mind, Miss Black?"

"No," she said, ignoring his eyes.

"Good, I'd hate to think anything was worrying your pretty head." He twirled her again and dipped her. She squealed, but he pressed his lips against hers, quieting her. She responded moving her

146

lips along with his. Intertwined, they explored each other for a few blissful moments. She wrapped her arms around him, murmuring. He raised her back to her feet, touching his forehead against hers.

"That's not fair," he murmured.

"What?"

"You know you're driving me crazy," he began speaking between kisses. "Everything you do … when you … fanny about with tea …" He began pushing her backward towards the bed. "When you … bend down … and wash my floor … and when you're up to something naughty."

She was startled by his words. How could he like watching her do boring things like pouring tea? Why would he want a woman that stole his things and played dress up? He kissed her again, backing her into the bedpost.

"That's when I want you most – when you're doing something you shouldn't," he removed the tiara from her head and tossed it on the bed. "Come to that, who said you could wear those clothes?" he asked sternly.

"I did," she said grinning, wondering if she'd get the same punishment she got a couple of nights ago. A grin crossed his face.

He wrapped his arms around her tightly pulling her close to him, kissing her hard. His desire for her was growing by the second. He caressed her face. Intuitively, he knew this would be her first time. He knew he should be gentle, despite his urges to play rough and naughty.

She could feel her centre beating in her ears as she moved her lips along with his. She breathed heavily, she knew where this was going to lead. Her movements became unsteady along with her nerves. As he kissed her, he moved his hand over her chest, feeling the warm beating beneath his palm. She looked down at his hand, feeling her own palms go clammy. Her eyes gleamed with the realization of what was about to happen.

Embracing her in his arms, he set her onto the bed delicately as if she were a porcelain doll. Taking off his coat, he casually dropped it to the floor.

"Tonight, we're going to find out what kinds of things Miss Black enjoys." He got on his knees, lifted the huge gown and disappeared beneath it. As he spread her legs, she began to feel the warm brush of his wet lips, against her skin. She then remembered how he had tried to do this to Miss Hampton. She promptly snapped her legs shut, mortified by the idea of him so intimately close to her sex.

Alex lifted the gown over his head onto her belly, a disappointed expression on his face, "Madeline, you want this, I know you do," he said coaxingly. She did. But she felt weird by the idea of him being there. It was so improper. No one did it. It was considered 'dirty'.

"Well, maybe we shouldn't be doing this?" she said shyly looking away, thinking he would accept her refusal as he did Miss Hampton's. But he didn't. He got up, looking at her in disbelief. It made no sense to him. The other night she had no problem licking and sucking at his cock. She swallowed his cum. Now she was refusing to allow him the pleasure of licking and sucking at her. He put both hands on either side of her, cornering her, he looked straight into her eyes.

"Don't tease me," he whispered, "I don't like to be teased. I may have to punish you and it'll be more than just a book this time."

She could feel her bottom and pussy tingle as he spoke. The idea of being 'punished' by him enticed her. Biting her lip, she slowly

148

spread her legs. Alex gave his devilish smile and got back on his knees. He began kissing her thighs again, his lips and warm breath inching closer to her sex.

Her muscles tensed as she looked up at the canopy of the bed, waiting for the instant his lips would press against her pussy. For a moment, she felt nothing. She looked down to see his eyes closed as he inhaled. He slowly opened his eyes into her. It reminded her of the moment back at the manor when he smelled the flowers, and she went scarlet. He parted her folds with his fingers and she held her breath as he stared at her for a few long moments. His gaze burned into her pussy, making her feel tingly and hot.

"Beautiful," he whispered to himself, then he slowly stroked his tongue over her pussy.

"Alllex!!!" Madeline whimpered, feeling his wetness upon her sensitive sex for the first time. No man had ever been so intimate with her. Her fingers curled into the blankets.

He began expertly slithering his it around her clitoris. Madeline grew wetter, her breath catching in her lungs from every rush of pleasure she felt at the movement of his tongue and the nibbling of his thick lips. He went on taking his time kissing, licking and circling about her. She tasted exquisitely sweet, and he didn't want to part himself from her. He greedily lapped up her juices, then slowly thrust his tongue inside her, pushing against her hot, velvety tunnel.

"'UUUnnnggghh!" she cried out, feeling it darting inside of her. Jolts of ecstasy began to course through her body like waves crashing on an ocean shore. She involuntarily lifted her leg and slammed it back down as she moaned. Enjoying every drop she gave him, Alex firmly took hold of her as he continued probing his tongue inside her. She began moaning more and more loudly, between her chest heaving. Feeling the heat of her, he knew she was at her brink.

He enveloped her clitoris with his lips, and began paying attention to her bud, while reaching inside her with his finger, pumping rapidly. Her pussy clenched his fingers as she felt a rush of wet heat through her, unlike anything she had ever felt before. She arched her back and grasped his thick black mane between her fingers, screaming as she came.

"Aaaahhh!! Alex! Ooooohhhh! Oh, GOOOODDDD!"

Alex continued fingering her, his mouth fixed on her. She squealed across the room again, cumming again into Alex's fervent mouth. Orgasm after orgasm began happening, with Alex tonguing every inch of Madeline's sex. She writhed and squirmed about and Alex had difficulty keeping his lips upon her. After her third orgasm, he pinned her hips down with both hands, looking directly into her eyes. He had an intense stern glare, and Madeline knew he wouldn't tolerate her wriggling about anymore. She held the bedsheets tightly, trying to keep herself grounded. It felt like his mouth had fused to her. He flicked her with his tongue and this sent Madeline over the edge again, a hot stream of her juices flowed. Alex lapped her slowly, knowing she was probably now raw and sensitive. She dropped her head back onto the bed, feeling disoriented, ready to pass out. He continued to lick her delicious nook gently, between soft kisses, before finally coming up and kissing her neck, "You okay?"

"Mmm?" she replied in a daze, her eyes feeling heavy as she panted. Miss Hampton was an idiot for refusing that. Alex pressed his forehead against hers. She closed her eyes drifting off.

"Don't you fall asleep on me now Madeline," he said, as he brushed her cheek with his hand.

Madeline opened her eyes to see the ravenous expression on his face. He sat up on the edge of the bed, then grabbed Madeline and propped her on top of his lap facing him. In a frenzy, he began unpinning her dress, throwing her gown off. He stared at her. Waiting.

She hesitantly began unbuttoning his shirt uncovering his chest. He smiled as he watched her. She sighed uncovering his perfectly sculpted muscles for the first time. He was stunning. She traced her fingers down his smooth tanned abs in awe as he loosened the laces to the back of her stay.

He stood up bringing Madeline onto her feet. He took her face into his hands, forcing her green eyes to met his azure ones. He lowered his lips to hers and slowly massaged her tongue with his, squeezing her tightly in his arms. Madeline purred, and he sucked and kissed her bottom lip. He moved to her cheek, down her neck and began kissing the hillocks of her bust, pushing the supple mounds above the edge of her corset.

"Mmm," he growled and pushed her onto the bed. He lunged for her smothering his face into her chest. He started kissing and sucking as he pulled and tugged on her corset until her ample breasts bounced forth. He grasped a handful and suckled on her small hard pink nipple, gently biting them and rolling his tongue over it as he worked the other nipple between his fingers. She crooned softly as he teased, tugged and tongued. Soon, she quivered with anticipation, in the depths of her she ached for him.

"Mmm, now."

"Now what?" he teased as he continued playing with her hard peaks.

"You know what," she said in her sweetest tone.

"Ask me, Madeline," he mumbled.

"Take me."

He rose from her, softly chuckling. Madeline felt ridiculous but looked at him imploringly. His expression turned to lust. He stood up at the edge of the bed and tore off her petticoat. Stunned, she questioned if she should run in the other direction. Then he started undoing his trousers. She forgot about the petticoat and watched him undress. He was fast. Within a matter of seconds, the King was standing naked in front of her. She gaped at him.

"Oooohhhh!" she murmured. It was as though Michelangelo's David broke through his marble and came to life, but hard and massive.

"Come here," he said gruffly as he grabbed her and pulled her by the hips to the edge of the bed. She looked down at him and for the first time truly appreciated his breadth. It was one thing to wrap her lips around it, another to be impaled by it. She reached out toward him, all inhibitions forgotten and grasped her hand around him. He was already wet, and her hand slid up and down his prick effortlessly.

"Mmm, Madeline," he said exultingly, as he closed his eyes back into his head.

Madeline felt empowered – and hungry with desire. She moved toward him quickly and wrapped her thick luscious lips around his cock.

"Ahhhhh," Alex opened his eyes when he felt her wet lips on his head. She began bobbing up and down his shaft, at a slow pace. He murmured, happy with the thought that she wanted it as much as he did. She began to quicken her pace as he drifted off in pleasure, his sex tingling and hot, "Ahhhh!!!" he groaned, "Madeline you know how to please a king."

He watched her amazed. Other than some lovely French courtiers he had met when he was nineteen, most women didn't want to do this. Some were disgusted by the idea of it. Most women that did this didn't do it voluntarily. It took a number of sweet gestures and persuading. Beads of sweat perspired from his forehead, aroused by her eagerness for it. Madeline's lips glided up and down his sex, her tongue swirled and slid smoothly about his cock in a smooth motion. He could feel his balls churn ready to explode. But he wanted to please her in other ways. "God, huh, stop," he growled, gently pulling her off.

She tried to grasp it and stay on. He was desperate to put himself in her warm sopping pussy. Madeline giggled as she withdrew and saw his cock covered with her red lipstick.

"Think that's funny, huh?" he smiled.

Madeline friskily crawled up the bed. He followed her onto the bed and smacked her bottom lightly. She gave him a sultry smile. He wrestled her down playfully, and she giggled nervously, excited. She was about to lose her virginity to King Alexander. It was like she stumbled into some alternate universe.

He tugged off her stay and threw it off the side of the bed, leaving her in nothing but his opulent jewellery. He pinned her arms above her head onto the mountain of silk pillows and began kissing her, gently sliding his tongue inside her mouth. She murmured between kisses, her sounds resonating through their bodies.

He put one of his hands on her hips, pinning her arms above her head with the other. Spreading her legs, she wrapped them around Alex as he began rubbing his prick into her pink muff. She pushed her bottom forward wanting him inside her.

"Quite eager, Miss Black?" he said between kisses, knowing her pussy was growing wetter with anticipation.

But he could no longer hold back himself. Slowly he entered her yearning sex, grunting as he appreciated its tight envelope.

153

"Mmhh! Uuunnnggghhhh! It hurts!!!!" she cried, her body ablaze, feeling her pussy slowly filling with cock for the first time.

"Shh, it's okay, it's okay," he whispered reassuringly, as he felt himself break through her innocence. He softly brushed her cheek with his hand, pecking tenderly up her jawbone to her ear, "I promise it will feel good soon. I'll make sure of that."

Alex lingered soft kisses on Madeline's lips. He took her hand into his, then slowly pushed forward. His soft eyes watching hers he slowly thrust into her whispering, "You're so beautiful … .so gorgeous." He kissed her softly, "In a room full of noble women, even in a maid's uniform, I only notice you."

She became wetter with his words and he began to slowly pace himself inside her. Her whimpers soon turned into moans of pleasure. She began to move rhythmically with every thrust wanting him in her innermost depths. Though it was clear that she wanted him to push harder, he restrained himself and continued pushing gently, discovering her sex. It was warm and taut, he inhaled the scent of her in the air as he explored her.

"Mmm, there, yes there," she whimpered. Realizing he had found a sensitive spot, she grasped onto him tightly.

Alex smiled winningly, "You want that?" he said pushing against her again.

"MMMM! Yes!" she moaned.

"Maybe you want this," he said as he put one of her legs up on his shoulder. Then, he reached down and began to rub her love button with his thumb.

Madeline's body shuddered, "Uuuhhhh!"

Alex began to simultaneously massage and slowly plunge into Madeline. She began to writhe beneath him squealing, "Oh Alex, oh

GOD!" She could feel herself building ready to release. She fought to meet his thrusts, "There! There! There!"

Her pussy clenched at Alex's cock. Then she came, her wails echoing across the room, her juices gushing around him and onto his balls.

"AHH! Oh! Ma-de-line! Yes!" he praised hoping she had more to give, he kept thrusting.

She didn't disappoint, still squirming beneath him, she began cumming again, "ALEX! ALEX! MMMMMM!"

Another wave of hot pussy nectar washed over Alex's sex and onto the sheets. He couldn't take it anymore, "FUCK! YOU MAKE ME SO AHHH!" he yelled shooting hot cum inside her. Madeline felt the hot spurts of his manhood, feeling a sense of triumph she gripped onto him, wanting every drop of him inside her. After he finished, he slowly withdrew, collapsing onto the pillows next to Madeline panting. He slowly mustered the strength to grab hold of her, resting her head on his chest.

"You all right?" he asked breathing hard.

"Mmm," she said exhausted, faintly, nodding her head.

She could hear his heart racing through his chest; along with her own, that beat into her throat. Her eyes were heavy with the desire to sleep, but Alex returned to kissing and nibbling at her neck.

"When you're ready, I could go again," he whispered.

"Alex," she sighed, closing her eyes, "I'll need a minute, I could fall asleep right here."

There was no way Alex would let that happen. He rose, working his way down her body from her neck to her chest. Her small pink nipples became erect and he began sucking and softly biting them.

"Ooooh!" she crooned, "That feels good."

"Tell me what feels good Madeline."

He continued sucking her nipples as he moved his hand down to her pussy. He tenderly began to finger her softly pushing against her wet velvet, caressing her bud with his thumb again. She murmured. "You like that?" he said. She ran her fingers through his black hair and nodded dreamily.

"How about this?"

He sat up brought her knees up so they pointed at the ceiling, he continued slowly thrusting his fingers into her and she sighed in pleasure.

"That's nice."

Alex laughed, "It should be more than 'nice', Miss Black."

He lips curved. Most ladies that liked it hard, fast and deep did not want to admit it. He had enough experiences with noble women and ladies-in-waiting in other European countries to know that. After fingering her in the Throne Room, he knew that Madeline would enjoy rougher sex. It was a matter of getting her to admit that. Alex understood it was not ladylike for women to want hard sex. On the other hand, Madeline seemed to revel in sucking cock. He figured she might be more willing to admit to dirtier sex. He slammed his fingers into her at a fast pace and Madeline immediately reacted.

"Yes! Oooh! Alex! I love that!" she said twisting her hips, rubbing his arm in encouragement.

Alex continued ploughing into her with his fingers and she moaned and grew more slippery each time he rammed them in. Her blood boiled with pleasure building in her body, as she grew hotter, Madeline knew her orgasm was looming. He could hear it in her moans that she was seconds from her release. But he abruptly stopped, withdrawing his fingers from her.

"Mmm Alex, don't stop!" she gasped trying to grab his arm.

Alex shifted onto his knees between her legs. Madeline realized what he was about to do and wriggled her hips in excitement. But he waited, his massive length solid at her entrance.

"Alex," she whimpered pawing at his hips trying to push him into her. He resisted.

"How do you want it, Madeline? Soft and slow or hard, fast and deep?"

Madeline looked down blushing. She did not know how to answer him. What did he expect her to say? Prostitutes liked it rough.

"Soft and slow. Like before," she lied.

"But you don't like it slow, you like it fast, hard and deep. You seem to really like it when I finger you hard," he whispered, his crystal blue eyes staring dominantly into hers.

Madeline ignored his eyes and turned her head, but Alex took hold of her chin and turned her head back.

"How do you want me to fuck you, Madeline?" he asked as he rubbed the tip of his cock about her wet sex, teasing her.

"Hard," she whispered embarrassed, "do it hard."

A wave of pleasure hit Alex upon hearing those words, and he kissed Madeline firmly on the forehead.

"If we do, I'm going to have my way with you in manners that may be considered 'improper' to most."

With that he took both her legs and put her feet at each of his shoulders, her bottom lifted upward. Madeline knew that this kind of sexual act was considered dirty, but she did not care. She was drunk with sex; Alex could have asked anything of her and she would have given in. He forced himself inside and Madeline's body shuddered.

"Uuuuhhhh," she moaned as Alex reached the deepest recesses of her pussy.

It felt incredible, filled again with his manhood. He slipped up and down her canal slowly at first but then, he bear down on her fast with all his force.

"OOOHHHH! ALEX! FASTER!" she screamed the harder he pounded.

He continued giving into her desires as she thrashed beneath him wailing. Soon her steamy channel became tighter and she flooded onto his sex.

"Oh God," he muttered in disbelief.

It was hot to see her give in, but as much as Alex wanted to give into his urges, he wouldn't. He wanted to see Madeline lose herself again, and wanted to see it again before the night was through. After she finished cumming, he withdrew. Quickly, Madeline sat up and nuzzled into his neck.

"More," she begged trying to catch her breath, "I like it like that."

"You'll get what you want," he said as he lay back. His member was rigid at his abdomen, his abs glistening with sweat. Madeline looked at them a moment admiring his beautiful abs and tanned skin that defined them. He held her chin directing it from his stomach to his face. Madeline blushed.

"Get on me. I want you to cum all over me," he commanded.

Madeline stared at him for a moment, shocked at the indecency of it. Let alone the fact she would be sitting higher than the King. But then a naughty smile grew on her face. All the dirty things they had been doing had made her hot. Why wouldn't this? She crawled onto him and positioned herself above him. He raised his cock upright. Their sexes lightly kissed, as she took hold and guided him into her wet twat.

"Ohh," Alex said groaning as he watched her come into her own.

"Mmm," Madeline murmured as she edged down every inch of him.

"Move up and down me," he said as he guiding her hips with his hands. Madeline obeyed, and he sighed, shutting his eyes, "Awww, yes, just like that."

Being on top was empowering, Madeline realized she was in control of her orgasm. She began moving up and down his sex, starting slowly then faster and faster. Watching Madeline was an erotic experience for Alex; her charging down on his sex relentlessly, her perfect breasts bouncing, her screams and sighs of delight. She came several times. Shrieking without any worry or care of who might hear her. The intensity of it was too much for Alex to bear. He stormed into her and the oversized headboard of the bed began slamming into the wall. The two moaned and wailed grinding into one another.

"ALLEEXXX! OH, GOD! OH, GOD! ALEX! HARDER! UH! OH!"

"Cum for me Madeline," Alex demanded hoarsely, "CUM!!!"

Hot as fire, Madeline clenched down on him like a vice. He pushed one hard final thrust and felt as though he broke a dam. She flowed onto him. He grabbed hold of her hips and moaning loudly, came deep inside her. It felt like a wetland between their sexes. He dropped back onto the pillows and looked up at Madeline noticing the sheen of her moist skin. He pulled her down to him and pressed a hard kiss onto her lips.

"God. I never, uhh," he trailed off, closing his eyes, ready to fall asleep.

Madeline climbed off him and nuzzled at his side. Wrapping his arms around her, he lightly grazed her cheek with his fingertips.

"I enjoyed that," she said when she finally finished heaving.

"I enjoyed you."

He pressed a kiss to her forehead. Her eyes grew heavy, and after several minutes in his warm embrace, she drifted off to sleep.

Several hours later, she still lied asleep, nestled at his chest. Not wanting to fall asleep himself, he had watched her the entire time. He softly graced his fingertips up and down her back. Then he sat up, noticing the scars on her back for the first time. He gently rocked her awake.

"Madeline, what happened to your back?" he asked concerned.

She bolted up realizing she had completely forgotten the scars. Pulling the sheets to her chest, she quickly turned to him, "It's nothing," she said quickly and tried to change the subject. "Do I need to leave? I mean I should go to the servants' quarters before someone spots me absent."

"No, you do not have to leave. You can sleep in this bed tonight," he said grabbing her shoulders and pulling her back down. She bit her lip, she was afraid he might say that. "Who did this to you Madeline?" he pressed, "Was it Lord Watson?"

"No. Lady Watson, it was years ago. I broke a figurine of hers," she said, knowing this was a secret he would not let her keep. She explained how she broke it, and that Lady Watson whipped her because she felt the horseman was not doing a good job. His temper piqued.

"What happened the night of their anniversary party then? Did she sell you at the market because you forgot to curtsy?!"

"No," she said, "Lord Watson, um, I was serving him tea and ... well ..." She looked away, but he knew.

"Did he touch you? Did he hurt you?"

"No. Lady Watson came in as it was happening. She was angry with me."

"She blamed you?" he asked, his voice rising as he clenched his fists.

"Alex?" she said putting her hand on his arm, calling him back. He looked over at her, and he bowed his head.

"It's all right," she said as she cuddled up to him. He embraced her in his arms kissing her head, combing her hair with his fingers.

"It's not Madeline. That's sick. All of it. It's wrong."

But you own me, she thought, ready to argue with him, but she stopped herself. It was not fair to compare her stay at Buckingham to the Watsons'. He would not do anything that would hurt her. He would never leave her out on the streets with nothing either. Now that she thought of it, he never did ask for the money back for the vase. She wondered why as she nestled up to his chest and drifted off again in his arms.

He let Madeline rest as he combed her hair with his fingers, thinking to himself. Just after midnight, he slowly eased her onto the pillows and crept out of the bed. He looked back at her admiring her beauty.

She looks so beautiful and peaceful, it looks like the whole world should sleep with her, he thought. He tucked her hair behind her ear and pulled the blankets around her. He got dressed and slipped out of the room through the secret passageways. He had business to take care of.

11

A PICNIC

"This is ridiculous," Marie complained to some of the other servants as they ate their breakfast together. "He wants to throw a party for no specific occasion in two days?"

Madeline entered the kitchen, dressed in her uniform, ready to start her day.

"Where have you been?" asked Marie, "I was really worried when I woke up in the middle of the night, and your bed was empty."

She knew Marie would ask about her whereabouts and had prepared an answer. She sat next to her and they spoke in hushed tones, "Can you keep a secret?"

"Sure."

"I ended up falling asleep on the bed in the Mistresses' Chambers."

"That's bold. You didn't get caught?"

"No," she replied.

She felt no guilt, she had told her the truth, she just left Alex out of it.

"So where are you working today?" Madeline asked, picking up an apple from one of the fruit baskets on the kitchen counter. "I haven't checked where I'll be working just yet, but wouldn't it be nice if we worked together?"

"We might be. I'm decorating the ballroom for this little party King Alex has decided to have."

"What? What party?"

"You haven't heard? So, the King comes out of his private chambers in the middle of the night, and decides that he would like to have a party. A formal party with invitations, a seven-course meal, all the trimmings and he'd like to do it this Sunday."

"But today's Friday. That's not enough time."

"I know, but I suppose his Majesty doesn't realize how much work this is. They already have several calligraphers writing the invitations as we speak. They've been working through the wee hours of morning."

"Is this a special occasion?"

"No reason was given. Maybe he had a dream or something. Woke up and thought he'd make our lives hell for the next two days."

Madeline laughed, "Oh I don't think the King is intentionally trying to make things difficult for us."

"You wouldn't, you've got eyes for him."

"What?!" She gave an uneasy titter. "What makes you think I fancy him?"

"Oh, please. The way you look at him. You're always asking questions about him."

"Well, I was curious about him."

"Don't feel so embarrassed, Madeline. You're not the only servant here who is curious about him."

The next two days were gruelling for the servants. Along with the invitations and decorations, a seven-course meal (including palate cleansers between courses), seating plans and entertainment had to be arranged. Madeline was impressed with how organized the servants were. There was little time to plan the event, but they remained focused and calm throughout, and everything seemed to fall into place.

Taking care of the decorations in the ballroom was easy. Nothing needed to be ordered or bought except for flowers. Buckingham had already had mountains of decorations for holidays, debutante parties, coronations and other celebrations tucked away in storage.

She was thankful that Saturday was her day off. Finally, she could sneak away to see the horse stables again. After breakfast with a jealous Marie, -who had to continue decorating the ballroom- Madeline slipped out to the Royal Mews.

She cautiously walked into the stables, unsure if she was allowed to be there. Marie went often, but it seemed that she knew everyone in the castle. She wondered if any of the horsemen would have a problem with her. She walked between the spotless stalls nervously, looking about. She turned a corner and saw a strapping fellow washing a horse.

"Excuse me?" she began timidly, "I was wondering if I could look at the horses."

He turned around, combing through his blond hair with his hand. He was tall and handsome. She understood Susanna Bathory's fascination with the horsemen of the guard. Except for the blond hair and pale skin, his muscles were almost as defined as Alex's.

"You weren't planning to steal one Miss?"

"Black," she answered. "Why? Do you think it's possible?"

He shook his head, grinning. But she went on, "Well, if I can't have a horse, perhaps you can take me for a ride on one?"

"Sorry, Miss Black," he said grabbing the horse's straps. "No man here would risk taking a lady riding. No matter how striking she is."

She frowned as he led the wet horse down the aisle of stalls and turned the corner out of view.

"Maybe he wouldn't, but I would."

Madeline whirled about. It was Alex. He strolled over to her, a trace of a smile on his lips.

"Miss Black, why is it whenever I see you, you're up to no good? First you take my vase, then you wear my clothes, and now you're trying to play with my horses."

She stuttered, "I-I- didn't know I wasn't supposed to."

"Right," he scoffed.

She smiled, looking down bashfully. She saw a picnic basket in his hand.

"It's okay, though," he said, his eyes devouring her, "I like the look on your face when you're doing something naughty."

She shyly rubbed her foot to the floor. She had the feeling he was referring to something other than dresses, horses and vases.

"I was about to go out for a picnic," he said swinging the basket lightly. "But it would be lovely to have some company. You're not busy, are you Miss Black?"

She looked up at him. "So let's see if I understand this. You had planned to go on a picnic by yourself, but then you happened to see me, and figured you should have some company?"

"Something like that," he said. He took a beautiful embroidered silk cloak out of the basket and tossed it to her. "So are you coming?"

"Do I have a choice?"

"Yes."

"What if I say no?" she challenged.

"I'll be delighted to persuade you to say yes," he drew close to her, and whispered, "I think I can be persuasive."

"I'll come on one condition," she teased. "You let me ride on one of your horses."

"That shouldn't be a problem. Wait outside of the stable. Put the cloak on and I'll be out with a horse for you."

She stepped out of the mews, and put the cloak on. She put the hood up and covered her uniform, hoping none of the horsemen would ride by. Within a few minutes, he came around on an impressive horse. Just one. It had a sheen golden coat and a slender body with almond shape eyes. She had never seen a horse like it.

"Where's my horse?" she asked, her hands on her hips.

"This is it. You're riding with me gorgeous," he said extending his hand. She had thought she would ride her own horse, but she liked the idea of riding with him more. Placing her foot in the saddle's stirrup, she took his hand, and he heaved her onto the horse. They rode off into the meadow heading towards a forest. Laying against his chest, cradled in his arms, felt like she was walking on air.

"It's a beautiful horse," she said, breaking the silence.

"She's my favourite," he said patting the horse.

"What kind of horse is it?"

"An Akhal-Teke. Her name is Princess."

"Why did you name her that?" she asked.

"Kind of a joke between Greg and me. He said I should name her that, because that way, I could say I was involved with a princess."

"Suppose she will be the only princess you ever ride?" she replied without thinking. Immediately, she put her hand to her mouth, embarrassed.

But he smirked. "It's funny you say that. Greg said that too."

Some time later they reached the woods, and Alex took Princess down a trail. They stopped at a small brook with lush green grass and tall green trees with large trunks next to it. He dismounted and helped her off. He gave the picnic basket to her and tied Princess to a nearby tree.

Madeline put her hand inside the basket fumbling around finding a blanket. She pulled it out, but as she did, he quickly grabbed it from her and lifted it in the air, placing it on the grass. He took the basket from her, kneeled down on the blanket, and began rummaging through it pulling out a set of wine glasses. She sat next him blushing at the idea that the King wanted to serve her.

"Have you ever had wine before Miss Black?" he said with a seductive voice.

"Yes, I used to drink some of Lady Watson's on occasion when she had guests."

"Now why doesn't that surprise me?" he said raising his brow. "Tell me something, did Lady Watson ever know you were taking things from the house?"

"Clueless."

"That doesn't surprise me either," he chuckled warmly. "She's not bright is she?" He took some food and wine out of the basket and put it next to them on the blanket.

"No, I stole lots of things from Lady Watson," she said feeling a little remorse. "I know I shouldn't have. But I she had once left a servant she owned out in the streets after thirty-five years of service. The woman was very old. I guess I didn't want that to be me."

"Why did you steal from me then?" he asked, wedging the corkscrew into the stopper and popping it off.

"Oh is that a fondue set? I've never had fondue," she said, ignoring the question.

He shook his head as he poured the wine. "Don't try to change the subject."

"I suppose because of the fear that might still happen to me. Being kicked out with nothing." She crossed her arms, "That, and you made some dumb comment about me not knowing anything about war because I'm a woman." He set the wine down on the basket.

"I made that dumb comment," he said caressing her face, "so you could stay in the room and I could keep my eye on you." He slowly leaned toward her and kissed her deeply. She surrendered, locking lips with his. She had been longing for his touch since last seeing him and needed to quench her desire. She slid her fingers up through his black, soft, tousled hair and stroked his body feeling his sculpted muscles over his thin linen shirt.

He pulled back, "You drive me crazy," he said in a low husky voice. "Here I try to be a gentleman and take you out on a picnic, and you try to take advantage of me."

"You kissed me!"

"I wouldn't have to kiss you if you weren't so desirable."

"What is it? The uniform?" she teased.

"I don't know. I guess there are too many irresistible things about you to name just one."

"And what are they?" she asked smirking.

"I can't tell you."

"Why not?"

"Then you'll know what my weaknesses are. Knowing you, you'll probably use them against me," he laughed.

As he set up the fondue set, he encouraged her to indulged herself with the food and wine. Many of the things he brought she had never tried. Devilled eggs, canapés, apple puffs and a dried kind of meat Alex called prosciutto. There were also fruits, breads and an assortment of cheeses. She watched quietly as he lit the burner and put some chocolate into the pot. She watched, a feeling of excitement welling inside her, "Can I ask you something?" she asked, eating a devilled egg.

"Sure."

"Why would you spend your time with a servant when you could be spending time with a lady or a princess?"

"Because they bore me. I mean come on, you served Lady Watson tea for years, I'm sure. You must have overheard some of the conversation they make."

It was true. Some of the most boring times in her life were just standing around pouring tea and listening to noble women talk about what was proper, or who had bought the latest fashion in Paris. In spring, they spoke about how the flowers were blooming. In winter, they talked about soup recipes. In the fall how the leaves turned colour.

"You're right," Madeline said and took a bite into one of the apple puffs. "I remember Lady Watson once talking for an hour about how she preferred being called 'Miss' instead of Lady Watson." She gave a high pitch giggle and playfully hit him. "I'm sure as a king, you always hear mindless conversation like that!" she said grabbing some cheese. "So why haven't you become a runaway?"

"I'm a king," he said briskly stealing her cheese, "I can't be a runaway, no matter how badly I wanted to leave."

She grabbed another cheese, sensing that maybe being royalty wasn't the ideal life people thought it was. She tried to make light of it, "You could always step down, have someone else take over. How about Sir Gregory Umbridge?"

He laughed a little then calmly said, "Can't do that."

"Why not?"

"It's complicated."

An awkward feeling had taken over the two. A frown drew across her face as she was reminded of when she first met him and told him that she was owned by the Watsons'.

"Besides," he said breaking the tension as he placed his prosciutto on a thin slice of bread. "You must be insane if you think Greg Umbridge could be a king."

"Yeah there'd be nothing but wild drunken parties and a naked king running about."

He chuckled, "That's what I like about you. You say what you think, do what you feel. Greg was the same. Still is."

"What do you mean?"

"I didn't grow up in Buckingham with my father. I grew up in Windsor Castle. When I met Greg, he was seven, and I was six. He was a common boy sent from a village nearby to see me every day so I would have someone to play with. While I took my lessons, Greg was told to play outside."

"Oh," she said, thinking that must have been hard for Greg.

He continued, "Every day while I was taking my lessons, I'd look out the window, and he'd be outside showing off. You know, making faces, doing dances and cartwheels. He tried to make it look like he was having a good time. They changed the room in which I studied, but then he'd just wait to do it in the hallway next to the room I was in."

She laughed, picturing a younger Greg, getting on the nerves of all of Alex's tutors.

"So it bothered him? You were being educated, and he wasn't."

"You bet it did," he said as he began dipping fruit into the fondue and putting the pieces on the plates. "He only did that to distract me from my lessons. He knew if he did it long enough, Sir Ashton would eventually have him take lessons with me. But that's just the thing you see. Greg didn't realize what he was doing was improper. He was never trained to act a certain way. He felt cheated, so he did something about it."

He handed her a plate full of chocolate fondue dipped fruits. She took it, grinning. "Wait a minute. Greg's a commoner, he must have been offered some sort of payment for playing with you."

"Once we became friends, he refused it."

"Wow," she said slowly in awe. She contemplated what Greg had done and had a new-found respect for him. "I feel kind of bad. Since meeting him, I've been kind of thinking he was the unofficial court jester."

He chuckled, "He kind of is, but he's also the most amazing friend a king could have."

As he talked about Greg, Madeline continued to eat. She finished her fruit quickly. She grabbed a fondue skewer and speared a strawberry. He watched as she slowly dipped it in the chocolate, and the strawberry fell into the pot.

"Oh, blast!" she said stabbing at the strawberry with her skewer.

"No, no, no, Miss Black," he said stopping her. "You just dropped food in the fondue pot."

"So?"

He gave his devilish smile, showing off his perfect teeth, "You know it's tradition that if a lady drops a piece of food in the pot, she has to kiss someone at the party?"

"I've never heard of that."

The truth was, she had heard of that tradition, but the thought of initiating the first move with him was intimidating. It wasn't just because he was a king and she was a servant; it was also because he was the most handsome man she had ever laid eyes on. His sculpted body, his bright blue eyes, his warm tan skin, his sweet smelling hair and breath; he was so perfect, he seemed inhuman.

"Should I command you to kiss me?" he asked.

"Fine," she said standing and putting her hands on her hips, "I'll kiss someone."

Lifting her skirts, she walked through the tall green grass over to Princess and planted a kiss on her snout. She walked back holding her head high with a goofy grin. As she stepped over his feet, he grabbed her legs, and she tumbled onto him. He pulled her face close to his.

"Kiss me, Miss Black."

She hesitated.

"Madeline, I ask-" Interrupting him with a soft kiss, her heart accelerating, he hummed as he kissed her back.

"I haven't been able to stop thinking about you since Thursday night," he said as he nibbled into the nook of her neck, sending sparks through her body. "I hope you don't think I'm being too forward," he continued.

He carefully unfastened her cloak and loosened the laces at the back of her servants' dress. She consented, slowly tugging at her dress sleeves, revealing her breasts to him. He embraced her and began kissing her, his warm breaths tingling her wet lips. She felt small tremors through her body, nervous and thrilled all at once.

He swiftly wrenched the dress off. She lay down in front of him, bare and vulnerable as she separated her legs, overwhelmed with the desire to be taken by him again. A knowing smile fell on his face, "Now, now, slow down," he said running his hand up her inner thigh. She breathed uneasily her body charged with excitement.

She giggled, "Me slow down? You're the one pulling off my clothes!"

"Come now Miss Black, we've done this before," he teased. He started kissing her delicate frame, her skin rising with goosebumps, at the soft blows and brushes of his lips against her silky skin. He grabbed the fondue pot and straddled over her. Curious, she opened her mouth to speak, but he pressed his finger to her lips, "Shhh."

Cupping her breast with one hand and taking the fondue pot with the other, he began to pour drops of warm almost hot chocolate onto her hard nipples and breasts. Shivers ran through her.

"Alex, mmmm... Oh! Oh!" she crooned, as drops of chocolate landed on her hard peaks.

It felt as wonderful as the warm wax she had put on her legs in the Mistress Chambers. But her body began spasming, her sensitive nipple reacting to each warm droplet.

"Huuhhuhhh!" her voice trembling from the affect. "More," she muttered beneath her breath. Alex continued, letting it drizzle across her breast to the other hard nipple. "Mmmm," she moaned bucking forward.

He took both breasts and he began licking off the chocolate in short, teasing strokes. As he did, the chocolate melted into her milky skin. He tongued over her nipples, devouring them as he nibbled, sucked and gently pulled them with his teeth. She responded with a chain of moans and sighs. She closed her eyes, feeling herself growing wetter with each tug and bite. A familiar feeling began spreading through her body, her eyes shot open. Was that even possible? She groaned, "Alex?! Allhhuh!"

He didn't pull away, he continued and moments later, Madeline found herself moaning and cumming onto the blanket. She giggled, "Did I just?"

"Sounds like it," he said and leaned down near her sex, breathing in her scent "Mmm..." He gave her a soft lick, tasting her sweetness. "Yes, you did."

He grabbed the fondue pot and stood above her. He quickly undid his trousers and pulled out his solid prick. Madeline rose up from the ground, and her eyes greedily ate up the sight of him pouring the fondue on his hard, red cock.

"Suck it clean," he said simply.

She eagerly crawled over on her knees. She couldn't think of anything more delicious. Little by little, she took him into her mouth. Like her breasts, the chocolate melted onto his shaft making it difficult to lick it 'clean.' Not that she minded, the chocolate was mouth-watering and so was he. She eased worked his shaft. Feeling his length harden he gasped, "I swear you get better at this every time."

The pleasure of it was so enticing, it brought him to his knees. Her mouth clung to him as he went down.

"That's it, suck ... suck," he said encouragingly as he slowly rose to his feet. Again, her mouth never left him. Alex watched, astonished at her and combed her hair with is fingers. He was hot, his body sweating as he watched her. Gradually, she took in his massive length so her nose was almost touching his abdomen, his cock deep in her throat.

"MADELINE!" he yelped fighting his urge to explode in her mouth. He tried to pull back, but she grabbed his backside with her hands and began guiding him in. She wanted him to let go, as he had in the Throne Room – on her terms. She thirsted for a taste of him again, and she was disappointed when it did not happen in the Mistress Chambers. Alex groaned. He felt conflicted. Looking down into Madeline's eyes he could see she wanted him to fuck her mouth. It was a turn on. It was the dirtiest request he had ever had. On the other hand, he did not want to hurt her. He wasn't entirely sure that he wouldn't get carried away with it. He tried withdrawing again, but she pulled him by his buttocks once more, pushing him further into her mouth, trying to entice him gyrate into her.

"Madeline," he groaned, "I don't want to hurt you."

Her lips wrapped around his cock, she looked up gave him a protesting look with her green eyes. He chuckled. "All right, but if this hurts, you pinch me and I'll stop."

Madeline nodded and Alex gently held her head and slowly delved into her mouth and throat, exploring her in new ways. Madeline kept her hands on his backside guiding him.

Beneath his breath, he mumbled a score of obscenities that put his good breeding into question. Quickly, his cock grew harder, twitching between her lips. No longer thrusting, he had become near paralyzed with pleasure. Realizing this, Madeline took over, grasping his behind clenching his cheeks and pulled forward into her mouth. She sucked hard her cheeks sunken.

"JESUS! MADELINE FUCK! FUCK! UUUGGGHHH!"

He liberated himself deep in her throat and she swallowed him. She released him and laid back onto the blanket, pleased with herself.

He looked ready to fall over. He stumbled through the thick grass to the banks of the brook and fell to his knees. Taking a white handkerchief from inside his coat pocket, he dipped it in the water and began washing his face with it. Breathing heavily, he looked back at Madeline. She sat on the blanket, a triumphant expression on her face.

Once he caught his breath, he stood up and stripped off his trousers and shirt and threw them onto the blanket next to her. He looked down at her, still sprawled naked, her legs spread wide.

"I hope you're ready for a little payback."

He got to his knees and threw back her legs looking greedily down at her sex, noticing the glistening wetness on her pink slit.

"Look at you, pretty angel. You're all hot and wet because you sucked me?"

"No, I'm hot and wet because I want you," she said trying to reach for his cock which was already at attention. He pushed her hand away. Lying down, he parted her folds and leaned in kissing and licking her and her bud.

"Oooohhhhh!" she moaned, her pussy moistening at his touch.

She saw the fondue pot in the corner of her eye, grasped it in her hand and raised it above her belly. She motioned Alex's head back, but he refused to part his lips from her. Pushing the fondue pot away with his hand, a muffled 'no' escaped from his lips as he lapped her juices hungrily. As his tongue rapidly brushed back and forth over her sensitive flesh, she squirmed, squeezing his head with her thighs.

"Alex! Alex!"

His tongue darted inside her wet chink, she grasped the picnic blanket, her toes curling. She could feel herself on the verge, Alex could feel it too.

"I'm so close," she exhaled, "more!"

Desperate to see her in an exhausted heap on the blanket, he quickly adjusted himself. Still pivoting and sliding his tongue into her now dripping hole, he placed his thumb onto her love button and began simultaneously stimulating her. It had an immediate effect, and she flailed about, Alex held his lips to her.

"Mmm, oooohhhhh, AAAHHHHH!" she screamed her fingers grasping at his hair. After she finished, he held his tongue flat against her. She gently pushed against it feeling several more jolts before her orgasm ebbed away. He sat up looking down at her tired form, her chest heaving, her hair moist with sweat.

"You're not done yet."

"Yes, I am," she giggled breathlessly.

She sat up and wrapping her hand around his thick member, eagerly wanting to put it back in her mouth. Desiring to drain her so she hadn't enough energy to lift a finger, Alex gently guided her back onto the blanket.

"You're not done until I say." He turned her over adding, "Come on, I want to play with your arse." Madeline grew excited, thinking of the throne room and how he had smacked her bottom. She got up on her knees, presenting herself to him and he smiled.

"Not exactly what I had in mind Miss Black, but I like to satisfy." He raised his hand and smacked her arse with his palm.

"A little harder," she said cocking her head back, a coquettish grin on her face.

He slapped her, she shrieked pleasure by every stinging slap.

This is dirty, why does this feel so good? she wondered.

"Mmmm fuck," he grunted amazed, noticing her twat trickling with cum. He began licking her eagerly and her body began to tremble again. He pulled back and reached inside her with his fingers and she began writhing as he held her. She shrieked as an earth shattering orgasm overtook her.

"ALLLEEEXXXX! OOOHHHH DAMN!"

She came, soaking his hand and the blanket beneath. She collapsed onto the blanket, heaving as though she'd run forever. Laying on her belly, she was ready to fall into a deep sleep, but Alex was far from finished with her. He looked down at her, and combed her hair behind her ear and kissed her cheek. He stared down at her perfect ass, now red and began to softly caress it. Madeline murmured. He let out a long deep breath. What he wanted to do was lewd. Something he had never dared with a woman, and he did not want her to freak out. He slowly parted her white fleshy globes, and Madeline's breath hitched. She knew he was about to do something dirty. Most likely obscene. Despite not knowing what it was, she objected.

"Alex I hope-"

"Madeline," he interrupted in a smooth tone, "I'm used to getting what I want. Besides, if you protest too much, you're not going to know what kind of pleasure I'm capable of giving you."

He stared longingly at her fleshy hole, for a moment. She did not protest again, so he began to slowly rub it with his thumb. She crooned and he leaned in taking small licks of her arse. Madeline's eyes widened and her mouth gaped open releasing a yelp of desire.

"Uuuhhhh."

Oh my GOD! she thought, disgusted by her own gratification. It was titillating, she could not help but enjoy the salaciousness of it. She murmured moving her hands down to her cheeks parting them, surrendering herself to him.

Alex's cock grew solid from her approval and he lifted her hips bringing her up on her knees. He continued eating out her ass and pussy, alternating between circling his tongue around them, and giving long licks. She grew light headed and dizzy, intoxicated with sensation.

"Mmm," she mumbled her orgasm building.

"Just like that," she whispered hoping he'd keep the motion going. He didn't disappoint, in moments she erupted screaming, "OOoooohhhhh! OHHHHH!"

She released her cheeks and stabled herself on her elbows as she cried out a torrent of hot fuck streamed out of her. A confusion of sensations and urges took over her body and she craved him inside her.

"Insi-" she began to demand, but before she could finish, he had already shoved his hard prick into her.

"YES!" she shrieked exulting him, "HARD!" she commanded, slapping her hand to the ground as her animalistic urges took over. Alex ploughed into her sopping sex, groaning as he did.

"Geez Madeline, you get so wet!" he grabbed her breasts and slammed harder into her. Madeline could feel her thick wet canal tighten, as her body convulsed in an eruption of pleasure. "OOOOOHHHHH!" she shrieked as another stream of juice flowed from her onto his balls. "More, yes, more!" he cried, as he plunged faster, knowing he was seconds away, but she freed herself from him.

"MADELINE!" he cried in anguish, knowing he was seconds away.

His carnal urges nearly took over, as he was about to grab her and finish what he had started. But he stopped, as she crawled close to him, her mouth wide open.

"Oh God," he whispered to himself, realizing what she was about to do. She took quick little licks at his glistening cock. She firmly wrapped her hand around it and looking up at him with her emerald eyes, took it in. He let out a deep groan. She began bobbing her head up and down his wet shaft. He moaned, his knees buckling from the intensity of it. She continued like this for some time, but every time he was edged orgasm she would switch her movement, teasing him.

"Madeline, please, no more," he begged. "I need to cum."

She smiled naughtily then held his balls in the palm of her hand, massaging them gently as she continued sucking his cock. If he was going to insist on wearing her out, she was going to do the same.

"Madeline, please," he begged again, nearly dropping to his knees.

Just then Madeline did something Alex had never imagined a girl doing, she gently began sucking on his balls. It was dirty and she knew it would get to him; his prick stiffened and there was no turning back. She tightly wrapped her lips around his tip and his hot cum spurted into her mouth. She swallowed eagerly as he came. When he finished, he flopped onto the blanket next to her.

"Good Lord," Alex gasped between deep breaths, staring up at the trees and clouds above him.

Madeline lay her head down on his chest, tracing his chiselled muscles.

"Miss Black, I think our exertions this afternoon warrant the need for a little bath," he said in his gentlemanly accent.

He handed her the bottle of oil and cloak and she held it at her abdomen. He put his arm around her and scooped her up in his arms. He carried her through the thick blades of tall grass to the edge of the brook and followed it up to a small waterfall.

"That's pretty," she said.

The water sprayed off into a soft white mist, and the brook was pristine, so clear she could see the stones and rough sand on the brook floor. A healthy green moss grew on the rocks surrounding the waterfall. He dropped the cloak onto the grass and began to walk into the water, taking her in with him.

"Blast! That's cold!" she whimpered, the moment the water touched her bottom.

"You need to clean up," he grinned and stepped deeper into the water. She held up the bottle of oil not letting it touch the water. He reached a rock beneath the water next to the falls and sat on it, settling her on his lap. Shivering, she nuzzled closely to him.

"Let's get that chocolate off," he said rubbing her breast.

"I think you're just looking for excuses to play with my breasts again."

"So, what's your point?"

She playfully pushed him.

"Here, give me that bottle of oil," he said.

She gave it to him, he leaned down to his side and scooped up some sand from the bottom of the brook. He poured the oil onto the sand in his hand, rubbed his hands together. He massaged the oily sand onto her leg, and she stretched it out in the air, giggling, "What are you doing?"

"It's a natural bath scrub. Dip your leg in the water."

She put her leg back down in the water and rubbed the sand and oil off. It felt incredible, like silk. She didn't know her leg could feel so smooth, even after she waxed it, it wasn't that satiny. He continued to rub the sand and oil onto the rest of her body, washing her back last, and tenderly washing her scars. She closed her eyes sleepily, purring.

"Does it bother you?" she whispered.

"It only bothers me that I can't wash them away," he said.

She turned to him and pressed her lips hard against his. She began nibbling his lower lip, waiting for entry. He opened his mouth slightly, and she glided her tongue to meet his, flitting about each other. They parted, their eyes melding into one another's.

She took the bottle of oil out of his hand, and he gave her a handful of sand. She mixed the two together and began smearing it onto his pecks and abs feeling the ridges of his muscles. Rubbing the scrub about his body, she appreciated his perfection. His glistening tan skin made him look as smooth as marble. This man could have any woman that walked the earth, she wondered why he wanted to be with her.

"When I hold you, I feel like the world is mine," he murmured into her ear.

184

She melted into his arms. If he felt, that way, then she wanted him to hold her forever. But another part of her worried that maybe he was only charming her for a short while. He had a reputation for that.

12

A PARTY

As the sun began to set, Alex carried Madeline back to the picnic site, wrapped up in the cloak.

"You're not cold, are you?"

"A little," she admitted.

He sat her back on the blanket. He pressed his bare chest against her body, rubbing her legs and feet, warming her. The cold tension within her muscles drifted away. He lowered his mouth to hers, kissing her gently while exploring her with his hands. She wrapped his arms around his neck, willing to be taken again. He pressed one more kiss onto her forehead, then pulled away, "I can't keep you here 'till dark. We should be heading back."

He rose from the ground and found her uniform and began dressing her. When he finished, she began packing everything in the picnic basket as he clothed himself. The blanket was covered in chocolate with a few clean patches. She held it up and shrugged, wondering if they should bring it back.

"There are plenty of blankets at the castle," he said in a light-hearted tone.

He snatched the blanket from her and threw it into a nearby brush. She waited by Princess petting her snout. He smiled, "It's unusual that she has taken to you. Princess is fairly loyal to me. She doesn't like other people often."

"Maybe she's grown tired of you."

"Or perhaps you've grown tired because of me," he said winking.

She blushed and said nothing. He untied Princess and mounted himself on her back. He turned to her offering his hand. "Let's go dolcezza."

That was the third time he called her that. He said it the night in the Mistress Chambers and he said it during their picnic.

"Why do you keep calling me 'dolcezza'?" she asked.

"It's Italian. It means sweetness ... You are very sweet," he said a sultry smile on his face.

She bit her bottom lip, suppressing a titter. She grabbed his hand and hoisted herself next to him. They said nothing to one another on the ride back. Cradled between his arms and resting against his chest she found herself at peace as she watched the scenic English countryside at dusk.

Buckingham's hustle and bustle the morning of the ball had Madeline watching dumbstruck. She had never seen a staff be so efficient. The morning flew by with all the last minute preparations, but everyone knew their duties and how to do them properly.

Her job for the evening was to stand at the perimeter of the Dining Hall and serve food and assist guests in any way they might need. She went into to the Dining Hall with the other servants and stood in a daze, surveying her surroundings. The table was a masterpiece. A dish service of gold and turquoise with beautifully detailed painted flowers in its centre. The centrepieces were cherub and angel statues of salt on circular gold platforms, with colourful fresh flowers underneath them. Each dish, sparkling glass, and red velvet chair was placed symmetrically to the one across from it. The servants must have used measuring sticks to place each setting just so. The cutlery was polished to a shine, and the crisp, clean napkins with Alex's emblem were folded into a Dutch bonnet.

Marie popped in front of her, awakening her from her reverie. "I think I need to train you on a few things about royal dinners at Buckingham."

"Oh," Madeline said knowing this would be a much more labour intense affair than her party at the Watsons'.

"First of all, when the guests come in, they won't be seated right away. They'll just be standing behind their chairs until the King comes, once he takes his seat, so will everyone else."

"All right so no adjusting anyone's chair before he sits," she said, taking a mental note.

"No, the footmen will be taking care of that," Marie said. "Next, it's considered rude for the guests to ask anyone to pass anything down the table. But that doesn't mean you go over picking up dishes if you see a guest eyeing it."

"So tough luck if it's not next to you?"

"Exactly. Also, if a guest drops a piece of food, they are not going to pick it up, so just go over and discreetly get it with a napkin."

"Right."

"And most importantly, when the King finishes a course, you take everyone's plate because they are finished too."

"What? Even if they are in the middle of eating it?" she asked, incredulously.

"Yes, don't feel sorry about it. It's not rude for you to do it. They expect that you will."

Madeline nodded her head in a nervous kind of twitch.

Marie grinned, "Don't worry about it Madeline, you'll be fine. You just need to remember those things."

"I'm supposed to be in the Ballroom later, is there anything I need to know for that?"

"No, not really. Just try to be invisible, and assist when needed. I'm sure you've done this sort of thing before."

"Yes," she said softly.

Marie walked off to her post in the front entrance while Madeline stood twiddling her thumbs behind her back waiting.

After several minutes, guests were being received and led into the Dining Hall. Their names were announced as they entered and were led to their seats. Lady Watson came, without the company of Lord Watson and Madeline figured he went back to the Caribbean early. Lord Watson had intended to stay a month, but after what had happened after the party, he likely decided to leave earlier. That, or

189

she ordered her husband to leave. She tried to avoid looking at Lady Watson, even a simple pleasantry would have been awkward.

It took a long time, but by quarter after four all the guests were ready by their seats, waiting for Alex. Finally, after a long silent wait that felt like hours, the King's presence was announced and he entered the room at four thirty on the dot.

As he swept past her to his seat, she got a better look at him. He was wearing an ivory coat lined with gold embroidery. It looked gorgeous against his natural tan face. She began to wonder how he was so lucky to have such a flawless complexion. He walked over to his seat with two footmen at his heels. They pulled out his chair, and he stood in front of it. His guests followed suit, watching him closely waiting for the moment he sat down. He moved down slowly and his footmen tucked the chair beneath him. The guests sat down, then Buckingham's footmen immediately entered the room with carts of food.

She and the other maids helped the footmen place the dishes on the table. The dishes amazed her. Marie had told her the night before that they had a dozen chefs on staff for the occasion, but she could have sworn there must have been more.

The dinner wore on for hours. Each course had a couple of dishes within it, and Madeline often wondered how they could eat so much. Though she did notice that whenever she took away a plate, there was plenty of food left on it.

As more and more courses were served, she began to feel somewhat embarrassed with how she handled the Watsons' reception. She wondered if she should have told Sissy and the rest of the girls to take away the plates when Alex had finished his. Was it a major faux pas? If it was, then it reflected badly on Lady Watson. On the other hand, Lady Watson would have been angry with wasting so much food.

It was difficult to stand there for so long, smelling the aromas of all the dishes and seeing all the delicacies made her hungry and tired. She decided that the last full plate she took, which would probably be full of food, she'd snatch a bite into a napkin and put it in her pocket to eat later.

Luckily for her, a better opportunity presented itself when she was told to push one of the carts to the kitchen at the end of the service. When she got there, she found some of the chef's eating from a tray of stuffed chicken they had made for themselves.

"Would you like one Miss?" said one of them, as he noticed her eyeing the food.

"Yes," she said excitedly. "The food looked so good. I'm absolutely famished. Thank you."

He grabbed a plate and served her, a huge grin on his face.

"How come she gets one Kenneth?" Marie asked as she came into the kitchen. "Warming up to the new girl as soon as you lay eyes on her?"

Kenneth rubbed the back of his neck, "Would you like one too?" He began making Marie a plate as she sat next to Madeline.

"Bullocks. You're lucky Kenneth only offered you chicken," said one of the valets to Madeline. "From what I hear there are a few male servants around here that would like to offer you more than that."

Marie gazed hard at the valet, "Move along, Jack. Miss Black doesn't want a dirty boy like you!"

Madeline ignored the banter. "We better be quick; we need to get down to the Ballroom."

"I don't think so," said Marie. "A few of the girls have already gone down. I'd prefer to stay her and enjoy my meal. We'll be there in good time."

Once they finished, they went down to the Ballroom together. Madeline looked into the large room, overwhelmed with all the people there. The party held for the Watsons did not hold a candle to this. There were at least one hundred musicians playing on a range of instruments. It was a full symphony, but it wasn't a lavish occasion. It was Sunday. All around the Ballroom there was other sources of entertainment other than dancing and music. There were card tables and other games people could place bets on, along with some billiards set up around the room.

"Maids usually stay behind the buffet table and serve punch," said Marie simply.

They moved between guests, trying to get to the drinks table to serve, but as Madeline did she could feel eyes upon her. Looking to her side, she could see the Duke of Axford at one of the tables, playing pharo with Sir Gregory Umbridge. There was something odd about the way he looked at her. It seemed as though he was ready to go up to her and have a conversation with her as if they were old friends. He continued to watch Madeline as she served punch, and absentmindedly set down a card. Sir Gregory Umbridge jumped up and snapped his fingers at the Duke of Axford.

"I WON! EVERYONE! I WON AGAINST THE BEST GAMBLER IN ENGLAND! AGAIN! PAY UP DUKIE!" he bellowed.

The Duke of Axford calmly rose from his seat and shook Greg's hand with a smile. But instead of taking it, Greg grabbed both of duke's arms and whirled him about. Greg let go and pranced about the room whooping, grabbing a glass of wine from one of the footman's trays. Madeline's eyes widened.

"Sir Gregory has had a bit much … yet again," said Marie chuckling.

Lord Bathory looked on with Lord Kinney as Sir Gregory danced and spilt his drink about the floor, "What kind of king would allow for such an indiscretion at his own royal residence? I didn't like my Uncle Charlie, but his son is a far worse ruler. Alex has no clue what it means to be royal. He shouldn't associate himself with that countryside filth. It's disgusting to think that a man of no privilege has a permanent home with the King of England."

"Does it really surprise you?" began Lord Kinney, swirling his wine in his glass. "He defended a maid when she didn't know who the Duke of Axford was in the House of Commons. But, fear not. Several of my friends, and I have thought through several ideas to rid this country of leaders that buy into this 'Enlightenment', or 'Age of Reason' ridiculousness."

"The boy is more of a libertine if you ask me."

Lord Kinney chortled, "Wouldn't you be a skirt chaser if you were the most eligible man in Europe? I can't fault a man on something I know I would take advantage of if I had that kind of power and good looks. The women find him brilliant as well."

"Go on, Kinney. Are you going to tell me he's gifted and perceptive too? I'm tired of hearing the hype."

"You can't deny he has something Bathory. He's been onto you since he was a young boy."

Lord Bathory took a sip of champagne, "I'd like to hear this new set of ideas you have. Perhaps one will finally work?"

"I'm confident that this one will, now that things may not look so good with Napoleon taking over so much of Europe. Come with me to the Library."

The men nonchalantly stepped away from the crowd through the Ballroom doors, as the eyes of Greg Umbridge followed them.

Just then, Alex entered the room and all eyes were on him. Everyone cleared the floor, making a large circle. He looked amongst the ladies and stepped toward Lady Watson extending his hand. Disgusted, Madeline almost couldn't look. She clenched her hands into fists. Why he would choose to dance with Lady Watson after knowing all that woman had put her through? The normally sour faced witch beamed and took his hand. He led her out onto the dance floor and the two began waltzing.

Madeline's mouth dropped open. He had waltzed with her the other night in the Mistresses' Chambers. She didn't know what he was playing at, but every eye in the room was glued to the pair as they swept across the floor.

Lady Watson was in all her glory, looking at the faces of the court as she swayed past them with the Alex. She wanted to punch her face, she couldn't stand to see that smile. Abruptly he stopped and moved closer to her, whispering something in her. Her face contorted into an evil grin and he led her out the hall. Madeline stopped serving punch and turned to the housemaid next to her, "I'll be back in a moment, I must use the lavatory." She sped out into the hallway before the girl could reply.

The pair were along further down the hall and Madeline watched them, keeping at a distance. He had his arms around her embracing her, touching her cheek and at one point tickling her. Baffled at his sudden interest in Lady Watson, Madeline moved closer hiding behind the knights statues that lined the corridor.

Alex grabbed Lady Watson's hand and pulled her outside to the terrace, she gave a high-pitched giggle as he did.

Madeline could no longer see them. She crossed the hall and looked out the French doors. There Alex was, his arm circled around Lady Watson as he pointed at the stars in the night sky. Madeline's eyes began to well up, and she felt foolish. She knew what kind of man he was. Again and again in the marketplace, she heard of all his affairs. He escorted Lady Watson down the steps to the grass.

Madeline crept out the French doors to the terrace. She walked up to the banister by the stairs and saw them romping hand in hand across the grounds towards the mews. Soon they went inside, and her heart sank, she felt sick. She sat on the banister for a while, looking at the palace grounds wondering how she could have been so stupid to fall for a king. He'd been toying with her; he had just run off with a woman who whipped and abused her. It was a game to him.

Tears began streaming down her cheeks. She hated to admit it, but in the past week, she'd fallen for him. He was a sadistic jerk that wanted to keep her about Buckingham to use whenever he wished. He would never leave his empire and title for a life with her. She sank to the stone floor beneath her and had a good cry.

13

JUST DESSERTS

Madeline sat on the terrace for some time, wiping away her tears. Her miserable thoughts were interrupted by Lady Watson. The witch staggered across the grass, but Alex was not with her. Madeline looked on with a raised eyebrow. Could Lady Watson not handle him? She folded her arms and decided not to assist her. Lady Watson was a wretch, and Madeline's days serving her were over.

Lady Watson struggled up the terrace stairs, and grasping onto the banister, groaning with each step she took. As she approached, the light from the windows fell on her, and Madeline could see her clearly. Her lipstick was smeared, her wig was in a disarray.

"Oh, Madeline," she said in a raspy voice, "I need your help. I must be going home."

Madeline watched in shock, Lady Watson looked as though she had been crying. She looked pale, almost sick.

"Would you like your coat?" Madeline asked, confused.

"Yes. Bring it out here," she said between laboured breaths.

"Why don't we go inside and I'll get you your coach and —"

"NO MADELINE!" she shrieked, slapping her hand to her thigh. "BRING IT HERE! NOW!"

It was probably because she still feared Lady Watson after all those years with her that Madeline jumped and scurried into Buckingham. Some time later, she returned with the coat, and Lady Watson held out her arms.

As Madeline put the coat on, she noticed Lady Watson was shaking, her eyes staring into the midnight air, not blinking. Her water filled eyes almost shed a tear as Madeline buttoned the coat. Lady Watson gazed back at her, opened her mouth to speak, but then said nothing. Turning on her heel, she tore away from Madeline and went back inside Buckingham.

On the terrace Madeline stood alone. What had Alex done? She had never seen her former mistress so disturbed. Just then, Alex walked up the steps, a solemn expression on his face. She confronted him, "What happened? Lady Watson left here a frightful mess."

"What? "he asked, feigning surprise.

"I'm no fool Alex. You did something."

"I did nothing," he said, as a cheeky smile grew on his face.

She glared at him, her hands on her hips, "What did you do?"

"All right. I took her into the mews, where she immediately stripped off her clothes, and I tied her up."

"You what?"

"We didn't do anything. After I tied her up, I left."

"Why would you do that?"

"Well, I had told Mr. Ackers that he could draw some pictures of the horses of the Royal Mews."

Madeline furrowed her brow, "Who is Mr. Ackers?"

"He's an illustrator for The Society Pages."

She realized then that the entire party was a ploy. Lady Watson's naked arse would now be in the most prestigious publication in the country and that would ruin her reputation. Lord and Lady Watson would never be able to climb into higher aristocracy. They'd never live this down.

"I can't believe you'd do that," she said despite trying to hold back a grin. "Why?"

"There were several reasons why I did that. She's an awful woman. She abuses her servants for no good reason."

Madeline thought of Sissy and all the punishments they unfairly endured, but she still countered, "Maybe. But that's not your business."

"You're right," he said slowly. "That's not my business. But whenever I see your back, it kills me to know what she did to you. That is my business. Every time I see your scars, I'll be reminded of what she's put you through. I'm sure it was more than whips. But you'll never tell me about those things, will you?"

Madeline shook her head, trying to fight her tears. It was humiliating to think that he perceived what she had been through, and felt sympathy for her.

Frustrated, he went on, "The day she whipped you, she wasn't just punishing you. Lady Watson envies any woman younger and more beautiful than her. I'm sure the first moment she saw you, she was looking for a reason to whip you. She was trying to remove any confidence or dignity you had for yourself. If this were true justice, I'd have whipped her."

It was true, and Madeline knew it. Other than whipping, Lady Watson had other kinds of tortures for servants, many of them so degrading some of the housemaids refused to talk about it. Other than solitude with no food or water, there were times she forced the housemaids to sleep in the men's quarters naked. Luckily for them, none of the men had never taken advantage, though everyone knew that's what Lady Watson had in mind. Strangulation was another common punishment, at times girls would pass out from it. Although whipping happened to be the only punishment that left permanent scars.

Madeline felt guilty for that part of her that was secretly rejoicing. Finally, Lady Watson would know what real humiliation was. Though Madeline was speechless, Alex could read her thoughts.

"Don't feel bad. You've done nothing wrong." He brushed her cheek with his hand, kissed her slowly. She kissed him back, grasping his shiny black hair between her fingers. She inhaled the familiar scent of sandalwood.

"Besides," he whispered with a sexy smile. "Nobody fucks with you but me."

She blushed, and he took her face in his hands again kissing her tenderly letting his lips linger about hers.

"We should be getting back," he said as he pulled away.

"Yes," she said. She wished she had the courage to ask him why he even bothered with her when there was no future for them.

Seeing him with Lady Watson made her realize just how ridiculous it was that they had ever been together. She opened her mouth to speak but stopped herself. Whatever this was she wanted it to last as long as possible. He led her by the small of her back to the doors. "'Till next time, Miss Black."

She curtsied.

He bowed and took her hand and kissed it, "Back to the masquerade."

She gave him an odd look. The ball was not a masquerade. He turned and opened the door and when he walked through it. It was then she saw a kind of change take place in him. He carried himself in a regal kind of way and for the first time she understood that there were two sides of King Alex. She was getting the privilege to know the man behind the mask.

She went back inside Buckingham. He was already down the hall, several paces ahead of her. Deep in thought again, she began to think of all the times he had defended her. When he kissed her hand instead of Lady Watson's, when she stole the vase, the time Lord Bathory insulted her for not knowing everyone at tea time, and just now he sought revenge for her. While she was unsure of whether he loved her, she believed he respected and cared for her.

Greg Umbridge brushed past her, rushing towards Alex, "I need to talk to you, Alex."

"Is it important Greg? I really need to tend to my guests."

"The guests can wait."

They looked hard at one another. Without another word the two walked briskly down the hall. Madeline went back to the Ballroom, wondering what they were talking about. She observed the guests dancing and soon noticed that some of the Lords were no longer present in the room. Lord Bathory, Lord Kinney and Lord Kensington were gone. Maybe Alex was in some sort of secret meeting with them?

The night wore on, and eventually the Lords came back along with Sir Gregory Umbridge. Alex never did though, and this caused her to worry. What if it had something to do with Lady Watson? Could he be in any kind of trouble for what he had done?

Around one in the morning the guests were gone. Alex made an appearance at the entrance to see them off, but as soon the last of his company left, he quickly disappeared again. Madeline, along with the rest of the servants, worked until the wee hours of the morning cleaning the Ballroom and the Dining Hall.

Once they finished, Madeline and Marie set off to the servants' quarters. "Did you see what the Honorable Miss Susanna Bathory was wearing?" Marie asked.

"Mmm?" Madeline replied, still lost in her thoughts of Alex.

"You've been acting a bit strange tonight. Every time I talk to you, it's like I'm talking to a brick wall."

"Sorry. I've just had a few things on my mind."

"Right. Well, what is it, Madeline?"

She did not expect Marie to ask that. Until coming to Buckingham Palace, Sissy had always been her confidante. She had never really thought of anyone replacing that friendship. Sissy knew almost everything there was to know about her. She even knew of Madeline's habit of stealing things, though she had not the courage to try herself. The only thing Sissy didn't know was her family history. She and Marie were becoming close friends, but as she thought of her and Alex, she knew that was a secret she wouldn't share with anyone. She felt horrible, but she knew she had to keep her and Alex a secret.

"I don't know," said Madeline. "Maybe I'm a little homesick. I'm used to Watson Manor."

"Watson Manor? Why would you miss being there? You said it was awful."

"I know, but I did have some friends there."

"That's a shame," said Marie, "I wasn't going to say anything, but I've heard about the Watsons in the marketplace. No one should work there."

"I know. I just hope my friend Sissy is all right."

Then, out of the corner of her eye, Madeline saw Alex sitting at a table, poring over a stack of books as they went past the large library doors. She wanted to sneak in to see him, but abandoning Marie to chat with him was out of the question. She continued down the halls with her until they reached the entrance of the servants' quarters.

"You know what, I've just realized I've left something of mine in the Dining Hall," Madeline fibbed. "I really should go get it."

Marie gave her a suspicious look. "What did you leave down there?"

"My handkerchief."

"I can go with you."

"No, no. You've already had a long night, and I don't want to keep you."

"Right," Marie said reluctantly. "Come back as quick as you can. I really was worried the night you slept in the Mistresses' Chambers." She paused. "You're not napping in there, are you?"

"No," Madeline laughed. "Just getting the handkerchief."

Doubtful, Marie nodded, and they headed their separate ways. Marie was not like Sissy, Madeline mused while she walked through the picture gallery. Had she told Sissy that excuse, Sissy would have believed it without a second thought. She would have to be careful with Marie. She wasn't as naive or innocent.

Thankfully, the hall to the library was abandoned, and Madeline felt confident that mostly everyone was in bed. Nonetheless, when she entered the library she closed the doors behind her. Alex looked up startled.

"Mmm, dolcezza," he said sleepily.

She looked over to a gargantuan clock on the wall. "Your Majesty," she began in a coquettish tone. "What are you doing up so late, or should I say early?"

"Trying to better understand something," he replied in a serious tone.

"I wished you'd tell me," she said concerned walking to the table he sat at. "You suddenly took off with Sir Gregory. I thought you were going to see your guests."

He considered her for a moment, took off his glasses and rested them on top of the books. "Come here."

She walked over and sat in a chair next to him.

"Lord Bathory is my cousin, and the next in line to be king."

She nodded, then a puzzled expression came over her, "Wait a minute, if Lord Bathory is your cousin, isn't he a prince, not just a duke?"

"He was a prince. My father and Bathory did not see eye to eye on many things. Often in the House of Lords he would publicly question my father and argue with him. You see, Lord Bathory always saw himself as becoming King of England because he didn't think my father would have an heir. After I was born, tensions between them got worse. My father took away his title as prince."

"Blast," she said, even royalty had family drama.

"He's been trying to usurp me since the time my father passed."

"What has he done?"

He sighed not really wanting to tell her.

"He's made assassination attempts?" she asked aghast.

"Several, I think."

"Why don't you just execute him for treason?"

"Well, there's not much evidence. Just one witness and lots of theorizing. If I do execute him, he has supporters, some of whom are more power hungry than him. They would try killing me as well."

"Why don't you just kill his supporters?" she asked.

"Not easy. We don't know who supports him and his politics. I don't want to take the lives of innocent people."

"Wait a minute," she said startled by all the information, "how did he get so many supporters?"

"It started years ago, during my father's time on the throne. My father, during his reign, spent money where he shouldn't have. Mostly on himself, building other royal residences and other extravagant things like gardens and ships. The renovations that we are finishing up on Buckingham Palace were started before his death. The nobility was disgusted and started encouraging Bathory to usurp him and take the throne. It's ironic because as much as my father spent, Bathory would spend more. He lives in luxury in a home close to the size of a palace, and he has quite a gambling problem."

"If he spends a lot, why would the nobility want him to be king?"

"Well, I think the real reason is that many of the nobles do not like this rise of the middle-class. It used to be the poor and the rich. But now there are folks coming from poor homes getting jobs in factories or getting an education and making something of themselves. Bathory is against the idea of a middle class. He believes people should be born into privilege or poverty."

"What a pompous arse," she said as she rose, putting her hands on her hips. "That explains why Susanna only wants to be referred to by her full title and called 'Lady'. I used to see her shopping quite often. She refused to acknowledge anyone that wasn't nobility – except her chaperone."

"Susanna learned that kind of thinking from her father," he said in contempt. "Anyway, when the Irish uprisings happened, my father went to battle but became ill. Sir Ashton took Greg and me to visit him. But he passed away one night while I was at camp with him. I was expected to lead the troops to the battle the next day. But the night before, Sir Ashton was walking through a forest near the camp and overheard a group of men talking. They were plotting to kill me on the battlefield the next day. It was dark, so Sir Ashton couldn't see their faces, but he suspected it was Bathory."

"How did you escape?"

"Greg saved me that day. He disguised himself as me. When Bathory went to the battlefield and found Greg and not me, he did not dare touch him. Killing the King's best mate would have got him executed."

Her mouth fell open impressed by Greg's bravery. Alex continued, "I went into the town earlier that day and sneaked into the rebel fortress. I killed the rebel leaders, which ended the uprising."

"Oh yes, I heard about that. You fought eight men at once with your sword?"

"Now Miss Black," he started shaking his head, "Don't try to make me sound like a hero. You –"

"But you killed them," she said cutting him short. He looked away. "I'm sure that's why Bathory doesn't want a sword fight with you?" she said putting her arms around his neck.

"Yes, that could be it," he said taking her into his arms and settling her on his lap.

"He's up to something," Alex said shaking his head. "Greg overheard Kinney, Bathory and Kensington talking in the library tonight about voting for something tomorrow in the House of Lords meeting. It's great that he overheard them plotting. Other than Sir Ashton possibly overhearing him plot to kill me the night of my father's death, I haven't any other witnesses to his plotting. Just suspicions."

"How did Greg overhear that? This room is huge, was he hiding between the book shelves?" she asked baffled.

"No. Greg has my permission to use the secret passageways whenever he sees fit. See that painting over there?"

She looked over to a painting of a king in hunting attire with his dog. "There are holes in that painting?"

"It's also has a thin canvas, so it's not difficult to hear what is going on."

Madeline pressed on about the Lords. "If they can vote for something in a meeting, can they force you to do things you don't want to do?"

"Not exactly. Lately, Bathory's trying to make me lose credibility. You know, make me look like a weak king to gain himself more supporters."

"You must be worried they'll find out about me, then?"

He bit his lip.

She folded her arms. It was an unspoken rule that she wasn't supposed to tell anyone about what had conspired between them. She had assumed it was because the nobility wouldn't approve, and other servants at Buckingham Palace might make her life difficult. She didn't think he could lose the monarchy over it. "I thought the reason why you didn't want anyone to know was because —"

"Because I want to protect you," he interrupted, his blue eyes absorbing hers. "Yes, I would lose my sovereignty, but you could lose your life."

She laughed, "How would I lose my life? Will the noble women tear me apart for getting my claws into you?"

He gave a crooked smile. "No, but people might hurt you to hurt me." He rubbed the nape of his neck, "Madeline, I've been so drawn to you that I haven't had my head on straight. What happened tonight made me wonder if it's safe for us to see one another. I care for you and I don't want to see anything bad happen to you."

She put her finger to his lips. "I don't care about the risks. This ends when I say it does." She kissed him gently, and he surrendered. He stood up slowly guiding her up onto the table, his lips still moving against hers. She pushed the books off the table to the ground, and quickly undid his trousers.

"Madeline," he protested, "we are in the library. If someone catches us —"

"I'll take off my clothes. If they don't see the uniform or my face, we'll be fine."

"Madeline —"

"Honestly, if they see you're busy, they'll just walk out."

He grinned. She was right. "You're irresistible," he admitted looking her up and down.

He withdrew a dagger from out his coat. Twirling the dagger about his hand, he abruptly put it at her back, his eyes piercing hers. He slowly weaved the dagger up between the laces of her uniform, and she could feel the cold metal send shivers up her spine. Once it was weaved into the laces, he flicked his wrist, slicing through them. She could feel her breasts relax, freed from their restraint.

"Show them to me," he commanded, tossing the dagger to the ground.

She pulled down the corset exposing her white fleshy tits, their pink nipples soft. She leaned toward him, pushing out her bust between her upper arms, offering them to him. He rolled her nipples between his fingertips and they became hard with his touch.

He covered her nipples with his full lips, sucking and circling his tongue around each of them. She murmured his name softly between her lips which had gone dry from her panting. He gently began biting them and she could feel herself grow wetter.

He squeezed them together and began biting and sucking them simultaneously.

"Oh, that's it. Mmmm," she praised as he squeezed and sucked.

Reaching down between her legs, he began rubbing her through the fabric of her uniform. She shuddered, clenching his soft black hair between her fingers as she crooned. He began sucking them really hard. She bucked, the intensity of it almost more than she could take.

"Uuuuhhh," she whimpered, feeling a small gentle wave of pleasure run through her. After she had calmed, he rose from her breasts, "I've wanted to eat your pussy since I last took my lips off it."

Madeline's eyes widened. He was so vulgar sometimes. "Alex!" she giggled nervously.

He laughed and held her chin, "I like hearing you moan and scream."

She felt a rush of heat run through her body at his words. Sitting on the table, she timidly parted her legs and gathered her skirts around her hips. He removed his coat and wrapped it around her then eased her down onto the table, giving his devilish smile. She edged her bottom to the end of the table. But Alex didn't assume his position in the chair.

"You like serving your King, don't you?" he asked his eyes roaming over her pussy.

She looked away nervously, hoping he'd start kissing her sex. Despite enjoying him go down on her several times, she still found it 'dirty', and was a little embarrassed by wanting to do it.

"I honestly couldn't think of a more luscious dessert," he continued, ignoring the flushed expression on her face, his eyes feasting on her pussy. "And considering all the delicacies I've had, and that's saying something."

She shuffled uncomfortably on the table. He knew his words made her feel awkward, but he continued to ignore it. He knew she loved sucking his cock and him smacking her arse, but for some reason, his desire to eat her out was taboo to her. Last time he had, she tried to pour chocolate over herself.

"Alex," she whined impatiently, eagerly wishing for his tongue to bury itself inside her. "Please do it."

"What Madeline?" he asked seductively, knowing what the problem was.

"Please don't talk about it. Just ... you know," she said her voice trailing off, an innocent simper on her face.

"I can't wait to. It's just there's something we need to talk about," he teased. "I was just wondering if you like serving your King ... you know?" His eyes dropped down at her cunt again. She exhaled. She understood he wasn't going to touch her until asked him to.

"Yes, I like serving my King," she said her face beet red.

"Now tell me, what do you like serving your King?"

She looked at him, stunned. He couldn't be serious. He didn't really want her to say that word. He caressed his fingers against her sex, his eyes meeting hers. Yes, he did.

"What pretty little dish do you like to serve your King, Madeline?" he pressed.

Humiliated but wanting his kisses down low, she answered, "I like serving my …"

She trailed off again, then rose from the table, leaning toward him. Her soft lips and warm breath brushed the word against his ear and a naughty smile formed on his face. He knew she was too bashful to say the word aloud. For now. He put his hand on the nape of her neck and drew her mouth to his.

She began to slowly lean back down onto the table. Alex's lips followed hers. Their lips and tongues gingerly touched, meeting and parting as she rested her body on the table. He gave her one last passionate kiss before he sat back down in his chair. After placing each of her legs onto an arm of his chair, he lifted her dress up to her hips. Grabbing her calve he began kissing up to her knee. Gooseflesh ran up and down her as she watched him, wishing he were naked so she could feel him skin to skin and adore his sculpted body.

"I wish you'd take off your shirt," she said startling herself with her own words. His eyes watched hers for a moment, then he whipped his shirt over his head adding, "I can take my trousers off too if you wish." Before Madeline opened her mouth to speak, he was tearing through the buttons. She smiled.

"I know, you're too shy to ask," he said kicking his trousers across the floor.

She looked at his god-like perfection and sighed. She was damn lucky and she knew it. Not only was he a divine piece of work, but a King that cared little about social status or social convention. If he cared for either, her pussy wouldn't be feasted on by his gorgeous mouth. He stared at her sex longingly, a lustful look on his face. Her clit was engorged and pulsating, ready to be savoured. *Mmm,* he thought, as he softly touched it with his fingertip. He knew it wouldn't take long for her to cum.

She questioned whether he enjoyed giving as much as she liked receiving. The ravenous expression on his face made her quite sure that he liked it more. She splayed her legs wider finding herself becoming wetter with his locked gaze. She was getting anxious wanting his lips fused to her twat. She reached her hand down to herself and spread her labia apart, giving him the most explicit visual. He grunted, "I'm going to lick and nibble each one of your lips, then I'm going to suck your little button and make you cum everywhere."

He delved between her thighs and swept his tongue between the folds in a smooth, languid motion. She shivered, her bottom rising from the table. He eased her hips back down pinning her. He began to swirl his tongue about her clit. Madeline felt the spasms shooting from the tip of his tongue, surrounding every muscle in her body with a sweltering heat. Taking short sharp breaths, Madeline tried her hardest not to wail.

"Ugh!" she bit down on her bottom lip, fearing being caught.

"Let it out Madeline," he demanded between feverish whirls of his tongue.

"Huh, what if, huh, someone huh, huh ugh hears?"

Alex moaned loudly into her muff, signifying that he didn't care how loud she became. The vibrations of it sent chills up her spine, she arched her back and released her lip from her teeth, moaning. She could feel nothing but sensation build inside her as the movement of his tongue became more intense. Her moans became louder and louder and Alex found himself pinning her down, forcing her to feel every fiery stroke. He pressed her clit between his lips in a grinding motion, spinning her out of orbit. She lurched up from the table, grabbing his head, holding his mouth to her.

"AAAHHHH! I'M CUMMING! I'M CUMMING!"

She gyrated her twat into him as he continued the onslaught, his senses filling with her smell and his mouth filling with her taste. As the last jolts of pleasure dwindled from her, she released his head.

He looked up at her. "Do you want more?" he asked breathlessly, knowing she did.

Madeline's eyes rolled back in pleasure, smiling. She refocused them on the painting she saw earlier. She was almost certain she saw something move in the King's eyes. But she did not care. She did not want Alex to stop.

He carefully touched her hot quivering pussy and he slowly pushed his finger inside her. She gave a little jump. His tongue glided up her wet slit. As he stroked his finger inside of her, he noticed her moans become more audible. Her body trembling, he knew she was ready for more than a finger and a lick.

He withdrew his finger.

"Alex," she whined, "don't stop."

He moved to her neck slowly nibbling up to her lips. "No, I want to be inside you," he murmured.

"You will be," she said coyly.

He shook his head, "Right now Miss Black," he said teasingly, "you want it, you just don't know yet."

"Aren't we a little cocky, your Majesty? Thinking you know what I need."

His eyes locked with hers as he lifted her off the table, and sat back down with her straddling his lap.

"Thirty seconds, that's all you'll need," he said positioning his twitching girth at her entrance. His eyes glued to hers, he grasped her hips and plunged himself into her sopping sex.

"Uugh!" she murmured on receiving him. She clasped on his shoulders as he began grinding into her. She gasped, feeling the familiar sensation of her orgasm building. She grazed her hand down his perfectly sculpted chest and surrendered resting her head on his shoulder, panting as he went onwards and upwards. He grabbed her bottom, and pulled her back onto the table, "This is a royal command," he grunted, "don't take your eyes off mine."

She obeyed.

He slammed himself into her eagerly feeling her walls tightening around him.

"Oh Madeline," he groaned in gratification. He smiled with a naughty twinkle in his eye. He rammed harder and faster, knowing she wasn't far from cumming. She immediately moaned with every thrust, feeling his hot sweaty, shimmering skin slapping against hers. His stare piercing her emerald eyes, the hot smell of sex in the air.

"Oh GOD," she yelled between clenched teeth. The intensity of it all was too much, she came screaming. Alex quickly put his mouth to hers, her wailing muffled as her scream resonating into his mouth. His mouth pressed to hers, she came again harder, her toes curling as she slapped her hand against his hard chest.

Alex groaned in response, his body quaking as he erupted inside her. But he kept pumping still inflamed with desire for her, he could go again.

"AAHHHHH!" Madeline screamed parting her lips from him, cumming so hard Alex could feel her exploding onto his thighs. Tears streamed down her cheeks, and she collapsed on his chest. Alex pounded harder, spurting inside her again, grunting as he did.

"Fuck," he whispered when he finished. She didn't respond, he gently took her face in his hand and raised her head. She had passed out. He tenderly put her head back down to his chest and let out a long deep breath.

After several minutes, she came to. Her eyes drifted about sleepily as he pressed soft kisses on her head, tucking her hair behind her ear. She nestled closely to his neck, pecking him softly. She shut her eyes again, sighing in the afterglow of carnal nirvana.

14

THE MURDER OF THE SWANS

In the wee hours of morning, Alex leaned back in his chair yawning as he closed his eyes. Neither had tried to get up to go to bed. It felt like they had melted into one another, it was unthinkable to part. Madeline awoke, her tired eyes dropped to the floor, where a book lay open to a picture of a beautiful noble girl. She had the long black hair, plump red lips, and the glowing complexion Marie managed to capture in her drawing. Madeline was sure it was her mother, Miss Elizabeth Swan. She wore a gorgeous plum dress with a beautiful silver tiara full of diamonds and royal blue feathers.

"Who's that?" she asked, as she went to the floor, picking up the book, setting it on the table.

He opened one of his big blue eyes, "That's Miss Elizabeth Swan."

She knew it was her mother, but wanted to know why he was looking at the book. "Why would you be interested in Miss Swan?"

He let out a big yawn and stretched before she sat back on his lap.

"All these books I have here are books of the peerage in the last fifty years. I find that often political views run through families. My father wrote down names of people that supported Bathory in his journals. I'm trying to make connections."

"And is Miss Swan a supporter?" she giggled.

"Far from it. Miss Swan is no longer with us. Her entire family is gone."

"Oh," she said. No one had ever told Madeline that her grandparents were dead. She reckoned because she was a bastard child, they wanted nothing to do with her.

"I'm guessing you've never heard of the Swans?" he asked.

"Well, Marie has a drawing of Miss Swan on our dormitory wall," she paused and looked at him. "How did the Swans die?"

"You don't want to know that. It sounds like a ghost story. I swear noble women must tell their daughters of Miss Swan just so they remain obedient to their parents. They tell young girls that Miss Swan haunts Swan Manor, regretting betraying her family. What happened is quite grotesque. You don't want to hear about it just before going to sleep."

She sniffed, "I'm not a child Alex, you can tell me." She crossed her arms.

He hesitated, "Well, Miss Swan was a beautiful girl. The most beautiful in London and all the Lords and Dukes wanted to marry her. I think at one point even Lord Bathory tried for her hand. Anyway, the Duke of Axford gets Lord Swan's permission to marry her, except she runs off with some actor she met at court during a play put on for my father."

"Oh, so they would never have met if your father didn't have that play?"

"Absolutely not, which of course my father always regretted. He loved Miss Swan. He thought she was the most delightful girl in London. My father once said that if he had a daughter, he'd want her to be like Miss Swan. See that hair tiara she's wearing?" he said as he pointed to the picture. "My father gave that to her. Apparently she wore it quite often."

"Did you know her?" she asked curiously.

"Not well. I remember seeing her once when I was a boy. She was the vivacious sort of girl that would light up a room when she walked in."

Her lips curved into a smile. She often heard about how beautiful her mother was, but nothing about her personality. It was comforting to hear she was 'delightful' and 'vivacious'. He continued, "Anyway, she made some bad choices and ran off with the actor and had a bastard. No one really knows what exactly happened after that. But one morning, the servants of the Swan residence went inside the manor and found a bloody massacre in the parlour. The strange thing is, there were no bodies."

She stared at him in shock. Her voice trembled, "Did they ever find their bodies?"

"No. They searched the manor top to bottom, the slave quarters and the woods nearby but never found a trace. There are all sorts of wild theories of what happened. Some people say the Duke of Axford grew jealous, trapped them in the manor and killed them. Others say it was the servants. But the Swans were known for treating their servants well. They treated them so well that many of the servants left to build lives of their own."

"What do you think?" she asked, thinking he might have a reasonable explanation for the mystery.

"Oh dolcezza, who knows? I mean it's just awful the whole thing. It wouldn't surprise me if Axford had something to do with it. But I wouldn't think he would act alone, probably conspired with some other nobles. He's one of the men I'm trying to figure out. I don't know where his loyalties lie. I need to know. He has many powerful connections. It wouldn't surprise me if he did kill the Swans. He's a man who knows how to get what he wants."

She wondered if she should tell him who she really was, but decided against it. It was embarrassing being in his company as a servant. Revealing she was the Swan bastard would be beyond humiliating. "Whatever happened to the actor and the bastard?" she asked, wondering how he would answer.

"You know what the sad thing is? No one really knows because no one cares. The baby was the biggest victim of all of this, and yet its whereabouts are as unknown as the location of those bodies."

"Sad really," she said slowly.

He nodded in agreement. She looked away from him, her eyes were pained with tears she wouldn't allow herself to release. Her mother was thought of as the most beautiful, delightful girl in all of London. Everybody knew Elizabeth Swan. But Madeline was thought of as a bastard. People didn't even know her name. She sniffed and swallowed hard.

"It's all right," he said as he cuddled her. "It happened so long ago; it's history now."

Yes, my history, thought Madeline. He brushed her hair softly with his fingers, pecking her forehead with soft kisses. She snuggled close to his chest. There was a part of her that wanted to tell him, but she still had questions of her own. He seemed to know more about her family than she did. She pushed on, curious of everything no one told her. "Who lives in Swan Manor now?"

"No one. What happened to the Swans still bothers people, so it was boarded up and abandoned."

"But who owns it now?"

"In situations like that the crown escheats the land," he said in an even tone.

"You own it?" she said in disgust. "Why should you own it?"

"Don't be angry with me, Madeline. It's the law. I didn't steal it from anyone, I acquired it through the law."

"I think the bastard should own it," she said, pulling away from his chest.

"Unfortunately, Elizabeth never married the actor, so the bastard has no legal right to it. This world is cruel."

"Not to you."

"You've stolen things from people, myself included," he smirked as he held her face. "Please don't judge me for something I have no control over."

"I should get going to the dormitories. You should get going too. You need your rest," she said taking his hand off her face.

He looked at her puzzled. His owning the Swan residence seemed to bother her to the point of rejecting him. She left without kissing him good night and walked back to the servants' quarters in a daze.

Their brutal killing, the bodies that were never found; what had happened to Madeline's family was disturbing. She had assumed her entire life that her mother died of some illness, and her grandparents wanted nothing to do with her. Now she knew the truth, and if her grandparents were the type of people that treated their servants well, maybe they would have accepted her.

It probably was the Duke of Axford with a few conspirators like Alex had said. It would explain why the first time she served him tea he stared at her like she was a ghost and asked for her name again. *Would that mean the Duke of Axford knows I'm the daughter of Elizabeth?* she cringed. If he knew, he had not said anything yet.

She had to admit, as much as she fancied Alex it irked her that he owned Swan Manor. He had his fair share of wealth and real estate. But, she knew he wasn't to blame. It was just the way things were. Madeline could not be the legal heir of the title or the land because she was a bastard. It was unlikely that the House of Lords would allow Alex to give away Swan Manor to a poor bastard woman. It would look suspicious.

She crawled into her bed, Marie sleeping soundlessly across from her. She lay awake for some time staring up at the ceiling. It seemed that her mother had a perfect life; a nice family that treated their servants fairly, King Charles' favour, Lords and Dukes seeking her hand. Why did she leave it all for Isaac Black? She had always thought that what her mother did was foolish. But, if the Duke was some kind of love-crazed killer, maybe Isaac Black was an escape. Maybe the Duke was jealous of the attention she got from other men and was abusive towards her.

All her life Madeline had judged her mother harshly without knowing much about her. What Alex had told her was the most she had ever heard of her mother. Her father always dismissed any questions she had. The only thing he ever said of Elizabeth was, "She's dead, the whore."

In fact, she did not know that her mother was a noble until several years ago, just before she had begun working for the Watsons. Mr. Sheffield unknowingly told her as he recounted the story of how they met. Madeline began to wonder, who was Elizabeth Swan?

15

A SYMPHONY

Madeline woke up the next day to find a small note on top of her dresser. It was a simple love note that read "… your secret admirer." She was puzzled, there was nothing there. She looked around the dresser and the room but found nothing. She turned to Marie.

"Do you know anything about this?" she asked, waving the note.

"What is it?"

"A note. It says 'your secret admirer'. Did you see anyone come in the room?"

"No," Marie beamed. "You have a secret admirer?" She snatched the note and looked at it. She cocked her head.

"Well," Madeline laughed. "Whatever the gift was, it seems someone took it."

Madeline turned about and opened her dresser drawer. Her uniform was not there, though. A soft lilac dress with sheer fabrics and an empire waist was in its place. It was rather simplistic in its beauty. No frilly bows.

"Oh! Madeline, that's beautiful." Marie said as she grabbed it from her inspecting its quality. "He must really like you." She grinned, "Is he the reason you've been acting so funny?"

"Really Marie, I have no idea who gave that to me."

"You know," she said holding the dress against her, "this kind of style is very fashionable in France."

"It is?"

"Oh yes," she said grazing her fingers across the fabric. "I have a rather wealthy uncle that's a merchant there. Every five years or so he visits. He came last summer with my cousin, and she wore dresses similar to this."

Obviously, Alex had thought his gift giving thoroughly. Nothing nobility would wear, but fashionable. It was sweet. It was the first dress she got since being sold into service. She watched as Marie spun around, the dress pressed against her.

Madeline went back to the dresser and opened the drawer beneath but saw a soft periwinkle fabric. She quickly shut the drawer before Marie could see. Apparently, Alex had become a little too sweet and forgotten that a footman could hardly afford one dress, let alone two. She opened the bottom and final drawer. There was another dress, ivory in colour. Next to it were three pairs of shoes and a packet of seeds.

Madeline turned to Marie, who was now admiring herself in the mirror with the lilac dress pressed against her. She slowly pulled out the seeds to inspect them. Queen Anne's Lace. Birth control.

She quickly tossed it to the back of the drawer, hoping Marie hadn't seen it.

Where's my uniform? Madeline thought, panicking for a split second. She pulled back the ivory material and the uniforms lay beneath. She breathed a sigh of relief, smiling to herself. She never thought she would panic over not finding her uniform.

"Can I borrow this dress Mad?" Marie asked timidly, "I'm going with Harold Vallant – he's a footman – to the market on my day off."

She grinned, "Is that a date, Miss Greenwood? Without a chaperone?"

"It might be."

"Sure. Anytime."

Marie shrieked, "Oh I knew when we met I'd like you Madeline Black, but I didn't know I would ADORE you!"

"I'm sure you would do the same for me."

The two got ready and after breakfast and checked their daily schedules.

"That's strange," said Madeline looking up at the board. "I have tea today. Monday is Cecilia's day for tea."

"Maybe she's not well?" offered Marie, as she tied her apron on.

"Hm," said Madeline thinking of what Alex told her last night. It looked like she would see what Bathory was up to. The rest of her day she was scheduled to clean the Music Room.

"Oh lucky!" said Marie, seeing her schedule. "You've had lots of good news today. Dresses, tea time, and the Music Room. It's not even noon yet!"

Madeline reached the Music Room by nine. It was fascinating, but not circular in shape as Marie had said. It was a 'U' shaped room with a domed ceiling. It had large windows with green marble pillars on the curved end and all sorts of musical instruments on shelves on the other. There were large paintings above the shelves of the room. Each painting showed groups of people playing instruments together. Around the windows of the room were couches and other pieces of furniture and in the centre of them was a grand piano.

Despite her wonderment, there was something unusual about the room. It was clean. She tapped her finger to her lip and smirked. She sat at the piano and lifted its cover off the keys. It was a Schweighofer. Her eyebrows raised, impressed. But it didn't surprise her that Alex had the best brand instruments.

She lightly pressed her fingers to the keys and a clear sound vibrated from its body. She pulled some music notation from out of the bench and placed it on the book rest. Sitting on the bench and squinting her eyes at the notes, she became conscious of her inability to read music. She grasped the book in her hands, confused. It was like learning a new language. There were hardly any hints of what key was which. The notes mentioned the music being in D Major. But what did that mean?

She didn't care. She threw the paper to the ground and began to press down on the keys. It sounded horrible, but it was still fun, and she continued playing until she saw something glaring by the shelves across the room. She was shocked she did not notice it before. A beautiful gilded harp stood next to the corner window. She released the keys on the piano and stood up. But then she heard clapping behind her.

"Lovely, Miss Black."

It was Alex. He turned and closed the door behind him.

"Your Majesty," she began. "You're late for your morning meetings."

His lips curved, "I've cancelled the morning meetings. I'm sure everyone is still recovering from last night, myself included."

"Why aren't you in your bed recovering then? What are you doing here so early?"

He walked over to the piano. "Well, I fancied playing some music, but you beat me to it." He stood next to her and placed his hand on the small of her back.   She paused and glanced up at him, "Thank you for the dresses, they are absolutely gorgeous."

"I'm glad you like them," he said, combing her hair back with his hand. "Have a seat."

The two of them sat down together on the piano bench. She watched as his long fingers lightly graced the keys. "What kind of song would you like to hear Miss Black?"

She had no idea how to answer this. She did not know many composers' names.   "Uh, how about something classical?" she suggested.

"All right. I have this amazing piece that a German composer gave me. He's going deaf, but he's brilliant." Alex walked over to a writing desk just across from them.   "Now I promised him I wouldn't play it for anyone. He hasn't quite finished the symphony, but he played the second movement for me when he visited recently. I requested a copy of it." He sat down again, "But I suppose I could break that promise for you."

"Well, that's a little dishonest, your Majesty," she said cheekily. "You're not supposed to play this piece for anyone."

"Would you like to hear it or not Miss Black?"

She nuzzled her head to his shoulder and looked up at him, a sweet simper on her face.

"Good," he said and rested his fingers on the keys and began to play. His fingers and feet moved gracefully, keeping to the beat. Madeline watched on in awe. The song was sombre but moving, and he had talent, the sound that came from the piano was crisp and clean, like morning air. He was doing more than just playing the music. It inspired him so strongly, she could feel his connection with it.

He finished the piece then stopped and turned to her. She kissed his lips softly.

"I've never heard anything so heartbreakingly beautiful," she admitted.

"I know it's an incredible piece of work."

"No. It's not just the music. It's you," she said in awe. "It's the way you play. You feel the music."

"Thank you."

"I wish I had that kind of talent."

"What instrument would you like to play?"

She smiled, "Just as you came in, I was eyeing that harp over there."

"Oh you mean the only instrument in this room painted in gold?" he said winking.

"Oh shut up."

He laughed heartily. He moved off the bench and took her hand. "Come, I'll teach you."

They walked hand in hand to the harp. He pulled a red velvet upholstered bench from the nearby window and set it next to the harp. He straddled it and sat down. He adjusted the pedals at the bottom of the harp with his feet, then shifted back so she could sit with him.

"Sit here," he said patting the velvet in front of him. She sat down between him and the harp, at the edge of the bench.

"No, you need to straddle the bench, like me," he said. "You'll find it easier to play."

"I can't do that I'm wearing a dress!"

"Then lift your skirts," he said as he pulled her skirts up to her lap.

"I'm sure there's no need to lift my dress. That's not appropriate your Majesty," she teased.

"I'll decide what's appropriate, Miss Black."

He grazed his lips across her neck sending shivers down her back. He squeezed her shoulders with his hands and continued kissing her.

"Mmmm Alex," she said breathlessly.

"I'm sorry, but you're distracting. How am I supposed to teach you how to play the harp?"

His hands moved down her arms to her hands guiding her to the harp's strings. He raised his right arm and put it in the curve at the top of it body, tipping the harp, so it leaned softly against her shoulder. He moved his hand back to hers again.

"Don't ever hunch over the harp. Bring it to you and hold your hands like this," he instructed as he began molding her hands with his.

"Your thumb needs to be higher than your finger," he said brushing his lips against her ear. He plucked a few strings to demonstrate. She followed his form and was filled with delight.

"I'm playing!" she giggled.

He laughed warmly, "You plucked a few strings. Let's learn to play a song."

He played several notes. "All right, now you play those strings."

She repeated them. He showed her several chords, repeating them several times. "All right, now play all those notes together, Madeline."

She began to play stumbling a little with the strings, but she could hear a familiar song. Not the entire song, just the first few bars.

"That's Twinkle, Twinkle Little Star," she grinned, "I thought you'd teach me to play classical music. That's a lullaby."

"Few are naturals," he said as he brushed the tip of his nose up her neck, her body quivered. "But you're doing quite well for your first time."

"You're a good teacher."

"Well, you're an excellent pupil," he necked her with his thick lips, and she melted back into his arms. He pulled her dress and chemise further up her legs and rubbed her thigh.

"When I had lessons, I was always rewarded when I did a good job," he whispered.

He slid his hand to her crotch and started massaging her. She exhaled slowly, his sensuality was something beyond imagination. She realized she would never get used to it. He'd always do something to leave her breathless. He kissed her neck as he rubbed her with one hand, cupping as squeezing her breast with the other.

He lifted her from the seat and kissed her passionately. "I'm dying to do something to you," he said huskily.

"What's that?" she asked in a sexy whisper.

"Do you trust me?"

She nodded.

"Take off your dress."

She did not question him and began stripping. He moved the bench behind her perpendicular to the harp.

She stood stark naked her dress at her feet. Alex was eyeing the curves of her body in a way that made her feel vulnerable.

"What are you going to do with me?" she asked, full of anticipation.

"Sit on the bench and lay back. You're about to find out."

Alex walked over to one of the cupboards in the room and pulled out a small stack of folded silky cloths.

"What are those?" she asked cocking her head.

"They are cleaning cloths for the instruments. Put your wrists together underneath the bench, dolcezza."

She did as she was told. He began wrapping and tying her wrists together.

"What are you doing?" she questioned.

"Madeline, I would never do anything you weren't okay with," he said earnestly. But he could see that it had already begun to make her uncomfortable. He tried to convince her, "Have I ever done anything you did not like? If I do, tell me to stop and I will."

She had to admit, she was curious to know what he had in mind. She liked being spanked and had longed for it since the night in the Throne Room.

"Have you done this before?" she asked.

"No."

She bit her lip, as she learned that they were experimenting together. "Okay," she said timidly "but if I ask you to, stop."

"I will," he promised.

He carried on with tying her wrists together, then got up to his feet. He picked up her right leg and lifted it to the harp, so her ankle was cradled in its curve. He restrained her with a silk cloth, caring little for the craftsmanship of the harp. Madeline squirmed with excitement. He was going to fuck her hard. But he didn't. He looked around the room as though he had forgotten something. He sauntered over to the shelves and opened one of the cases. He pulled out a trumpet and began piecing it together.

"No, Alex," said Madeline. "Don't you dare come near me with that thing."

Alex ignored her and blew out the trumpet. An odd expression grew on her face. He walked over and placed the bell of the trumpet inches away from her pussy. She began to laugh.

"What do you think you're doing?" she asked rolling her eyes. He ignored her, putting his lips to the mouthpiece. He blew into it and she yelped, "BLAST! UH!"

The sound waves hit her pussy and Madeline wriggled beneath the vibrations. The feeling was indescribable. Like small shocks, buzzing on her skin. He played another note and the sensation heightened, as the sound waves stronger than the last. She wiggled her hips into the bench.

"Mmmm!!! More!" she demanded.

Alex continued blowing and the waves hit her one after another, making her feel torn. She did not want him to stop. But she also knew his dick was probably solid, and ready to ravage her. She let him blow for a while longer as she exhausted herself and her muscles tensing, she sighed, "Alex now, I want you now."

"I don't think so."

"What?!! Why not?!" she thrashed about, trying to wriggle free from the silk bindings.

"Because I have you tied up, which means I have you at my will."

These words made Madeline hot and she murmured. He smiled and tossed the trumpet to the floor. He began softly kissing her and tonguing her pussy. He enveloped her with his mouth and penetrated his tongue inside. He began slithering it in and out of her, as she moaned and sighed. He pulled back and slid two fingers into her now slippery velvet.

"Blast Alex," she said wantonly, as he massaged his fingers back and forth inside her wetness. Timidly, he reached between her cheeks with his ring finger and began circling her rosebud, then squeezed his finger into the tight orifice. Her eyes jolted open. It was crude and improper. He crossed too many lines. Every time she was with him he always did dirtier things. She hadn't really cared when he licked her there the other day, but having his finger inside of her, felt odd.

She was about to object, but as Alex pushed all his fingers forward, she paused. It felt so incredible. An insatiable urge overcame her, and she knew she couldn't protest. The strange feeling had quickly turned into an exotic one as he continued to slowly penetrate her, letting her fill with the new sensation. It was a full feeling, the pressure pushing intensely on all her secret places, she surrendered closing her eyes.

"Yes, Alex yes," she whispered approvingly.

He forced his fingers forward more forcefully and Madeline exhaled. He brought his lips back down to her sex and began licking, then engulfing her into his mouth, he pressed all his fingers onward and upwards.

"Ahhh, Ahhh!" Madeline moaned.

"I'm going to make you cum everywhere, Madeline," he said heavily between licks and small sucks on her nub. "After you go, I'm going to fuck you until you go numb."

"Ahh!"

Madeline slammed her free foot to the floor, wriggling from the pleasure of having her arse, pussy and clit being played with at once. Soon her moans grew louder and she came all over his hand and face, her juices dripping onto the carpet. He felt his balls churn as her sweetness flowed onto him, his mouth devouring what it could.

After she finished, he sighed as he withdrew. Feeling dizzy, he was sure there was no blood in his body except for in his erection. He stood up, cleaned his face with his hand and licked the fingers that were in her pussy. She watched him, her interest piqued as to why he enjoyed that was beyond her.

When he finished devouring her taste, he tore off his clothes and threw them to the floor. He stood before her naked as Madeline scanned his perfectly chiselled muscles and his big, hard, red prick.

She knew what was to come, he was going to fuck her until she was numb. She was delighted that he was a man of his word.

He shoved himself inside her. Gripping the leg that was tied to the harp and the bench at her side, he began slamming himself inside of her. She immediately bucked and twisted to the onslaught.

"Oh! Oh! Uh! Alex!!! OOoooohhhhhh!"

"Fuck yes," he grunted, his hunger finally soothed.

Alex pushed onwards as Madeline met his thrusts and the two fell in motion together. He charged into her feeling her juices flow around his cock. There was no greater pleasure than this. Bound to the bench submissive to his every thrust, she squirmed to meet him, wanting him in the deepest recesses of her pussy. "Harder!" she panted.

Beads of sweat grew on his forehead, dripping off his face and onto her chest and stomach. Madeline smiled triumphantly, he sweat to please her. She could feel herself rounding her orgasm, but held back. She wasn't quite 'numb' as he had promised.

"Madeline," he said while he huffed, "give it to me. Cum."

"No. I'm not numb yet," she heaved, teasingly.

He smiled, "Fine. Have it your way then."

He pulled himself out, grabbed her free leg and tossed it on his broad shoulder. Lifting her arse into the air, he put his hands on her arse and hip. With her own hands still tied around the bench, Madeline had no control. She could barely squirm. He entered her again, this time more deeply. *Oh, fuck!* she thought seeing the insatiable look on his face. He meant 'business'.

Pistoning inside her wet chink, Alex began to lose himself, listening to Madeline wailing. He could feel the intense heat of his sex and could barely stand it. She too could no longer try to hold back. He seemed to have control over her muscles. She could barely move as he relentlessly pounded the deepest part of her.

"UH! MADELINE," he growled. He lightly smacked her arse gripping her skin between his fingers. This sent her over the edge.

"OOooooooohhhhhh! Yesss!"

He pulled himself out and her fuck juice flowed everywhere. He untied her leg from the harp and gently set them both to the floor. She sighed, as her body melted into the bench. She looked up at Alex, who stood before her his prick still rigid. He reached around her and untied her hands, then helped her up from the bench.

"Come," he said. He sat on the floor in front of the bench, resting his head back on the bench seat. He looked up, his eyes grazing over her creamy white flesh before meeting her emerald eyes.

"Have a seat, Miss Black," he said with a wink and looked down at his length.

Madeline gave him a sultry glance and positioned herself above him, her feet flat on the floor. She bent her knees and slowly inched herself down his cock.

He sighed, kissing her shoulder. She began to move up and down his erection.

"Not yet," he said and grabbed her hand and tied it to the leg of the bench. Then, he tied the other hand to the other bench leg. "Now, Madeline."

Alex stabled her with his strong arms. Madeline climbed up and down his hard shaft, her hot sex tightening around him. Alex groaned and panted, "I'm not untying you, Miss Black. Not until you make me cum."

Madeline smiled. She was hoping he'd put her up to that. She continued gliding up and down his trembling length as he groaned, falling into rhythm with her. As the passion heightened she charged up and down him frantically, slapping her creamy white bottom against his abs. Alex tried to meet her pumping with quick hard thrusts. But soon it became challenging for her. Mixed with her gratification, she could feel the muscles in her thighs and arms tense up in agonizing pain. But stopping was out of the question. Not just for his pleasure, but for her own.

She could feel his cock head poking against the deepest recesses of her, and she became wetter with every penetration of him. He groaned repeatedly, refusing to release, enjoying her unbridled, relentless charge on his length. His breath heaving, he watched their intimate contact, fully understanding the phrase 'going at it like rabbits'.

Madeline kept up her pace, then her strained muscles began to give way to a new sensation. As she came closer to her brink, her thighs became like a white fire spreading heat into the rest of her body, the intensity of it was overwhelming. Each muscle tightened, she jerked and squeezed down on his swollen cock so hard, Alex let out a loud cry as a hot stream of semen spurted inside her.

"MMMMMMMAAADDDD! UGH!" he yelled, his voice straining.

Madeline fell apart on him, crying out and convulsing as she came again and again. Finishing, she plopped back on him and they both heaved exhaustion.

"My God," he whispered to himself in disbelief.

He untied her hands and wrapped his arms around her and pulled her face closely to his. She gazed at him wantonly. She could not believe herself, but she wanted more of him. She playfully stroked his cock with her hand.

Alex shook his head, "Madeline," he kissed her softly, "I think you just drained me."

Madeline, got on her knees and slowly began licking at him, hoping he would spring back up.

Alex picked her up from off the ground, and though he was ready to drop, he sat on the bench and placed Madeline over his knees. Believing that a woman should never leave unsatisfied, he was determined to finish her off again. Alex began fingering her and she murmured happily. He raised his hand.

SMACK

"OOOOHHHHH!!!! YESSS!" She wriggled her bottom wanting more. She had been fantasizing about this.

He slammed his finger hard into her and Madeline rubbed herself against him in response, eager for another spank.

SMACK

"YESSSS! MMMOORRREEE," she begged.

Alex continued to ram his fingers up inside her pulsing hot twat, motivated to make her shriek, cum and turn to a weak, sweaty body on his lap. She began to tremble and seized his fingers, she knew she was moments away. He began to repeatedly smack her arse and she erupted, bucking against him shrieking.

Cradling her lithe body in his arms, he pecked the top of her head several times as she rested against his pectorals. He said nothing as he listened to her pant, her hot breath warming his skin.

When she finally caught her breath, he helped her to her feet and casually picked up the clothes off the floor. He handed her uniform and threw his clothes onto the bench. He helped her into her dress, tightening the laces in the back.

"Your hair is quite dishevelled Miss Black," he teased, pressing a kiss on the side of her neck. "Whose fault is that?"

"You're not suggesting it's mine?" he asked a mischievous twinkle in his eye.

"Well, you're standing here naked as the day you were born," she said her eyes roaming over his chiselled figure. "If anyone were to walk into this room, they'd think you were the guilty one."

He laughed and began to put his clothes back on. "That's what is great about being a man. I can walk out of this room, and no one suspects a thing. Nor does anyone care. But the moment you walk out of this room, your hair, and that cute little smile on your face says everything."

"Well, I can do something about the hair. But I can't do anything about the smile."

"Nor will I," he grinned. "I'll see you at tea time then?"

"How did you know I was serving tea?"

"I know your schedule everyday dolcezza," he said as he raised her hand to his lips and kissed it. "See you later."

She gave him a face and playfully pushed him. He pulled her close to him and kissed her. Despite her exhausted body, she could still feel tingles race through her.

"Bye, dolcezza," he whispered.

He left her in the Music Room. After she fixed her hair, she played around with the instruments until she had to prepare for tea. Unfortunately, she could not find anything as moving as Alex's instrument playing.

After their tryst, Alex went to his private library. He hadn't been able to piece last night together. Greg had found Lord Kinney and Lord Bathory acting peculiar before they stepped out of the Ballroom. Throughout dinner, Greg noticed the pair talking to one another in hushed voices.

The Duke of Axford was and always had been a confusing piece of the political puzzle. He, like Lord Bathory was a Duke, and like Lord Bathory had been a cousin to a king (Alex's father, King Charles). Alex was always unsure of him. Besides the fact that he was guilty of killing the Swans, he had a reputation for being impulsive and was an avid gambler. Many nobles were indebted to the Duke of Axford, and because of this, Alex felt weary of him. He was not certain what his politics were, for all he knew he might have ambitions for the throne himself. If he had any kind of political ambition or bias, he could quickly find support amongst the nobles.

Nonetheless, the Duke having ambitions for the throne did not make much sense. He had never married. After the murder of the Swans and of Elizabeth, he did not show any interest in another woman. If he wished to be a king, he would most likely want an heir.

Alex thought of each Lord and what he knew of them and their family. Just then, Sir Ashton Giles entered the library.

"Your Majesty," he said bowing deeply. "Where did you go after breakfast this morning? I've searched for you everywhere."

"Oh, sorry Ashton," he said grinning to himself as he turned the page of his book, "I was just playing in the Music Room."

"His Majesty King Fernando of Spain and his family have had to flee the country," Sir Ashton presented Alex with a letter, "Napoleon and his armies have now taken over."

"Could this war get any worse?"

"In this letter, King Fernando has asked for refuge for himself and his family, your Majesty."

Alex paused a moment and looked up from his book, his breath caught in his chest. King Fernando's daughter was around eighteen. He knew where this was leading. Now that King Fernando had lost everything, he was going to use his daughter to secure his future.

He wished he could say 'no'. The only problem was, Spain was an ally of England and given that Napoleon had occupied most of Europe, he was not in a position to turn them away. His Lords and Parliament would question why he would.

Alex pressed his finger to his lips. His fun with Madeline was over. He couldn't play host to the Spanish royals and see her at the same time. He'd be a laughing stock to his country if they found out what he'd been doing the past several days. If he messed up political

241

negotiations with an ally because of a servant girl, his country would hate him. Bathory would have no difficulty rallying supporters behind him.

"We will entertain them won't we your Majesty?" asked Sir Ashton taking him out of his reverie.

"Yes, yes, of course," he answered slowly.

"Excellent. I will inform all the head butlers and housekeepers. Will you be announcing this in today's House of Lords meeting, your Majesty?"

"Suppose I'll have to," he said in a downhearted tone.

Sir Ashton bowed before exiting the library.

Alex let out a frustrated groan. He knew his fun with Madeline was too good to last. There was no way he could see her now.

16

UNFORTUNATE MESSENGER

Madeline pushed her tea cart down the halls of Westminster to the entrance door of the House of Lords. When the clock struck two, she headed in and found herself walking onto a yelling battlefield. All the Lords were yelling at one another across the benches. She pushed forward timidly as her ears took the assault.

Alex remained composed sitting at the pulpit observing the scene. The men did not stop arguing. As she reached him, she began to register what they were arguing about.

"… but it's a way to motivate the troops!" roared Lord Kinney, "These men have to believe –"

"What sense does that make? Our last King died in the last war!" Lord Davis yelled.

This was unusual. Lord Davis had a calm demeanour and never raised his voice.

"Our last King did not die in battle! He died of old age!" Bathory boomed. "The troops need the motivation."

"Yes," agreed Lord Kinney. "If the King cannot back his troops he looks weak! If other European countries think our King is scared to defend his country it looks —"

"AFRAID TO DEFEND HIS COUNTRY?!" Lord Davis shouted. "You're talking about a man that killed eight men by sword for his country."

"That's quite enough," said Alex calmly.

The arguing stopped abruptly, and the Lords collected themselves and took their seats.

"While you make a compelling proposal Lord Bathory, I'm afraid it is too late," said Alex.

"How is that your Majesty?" Lord Bathory said through gritted teeth.

"Well, I've just received word this morning that the King of Spain and his family would like to seek refuge here, and I have consented. It should be good for political relations that they stay here. For the good of my country, I should not leave."

Madeline stopped pouring Alex's tea and looked at him, stunned. He didn't tell her anything about the Spanish royals coming. She stirred honey into his cup, wondering why he hadn't said anything.

"That makes sense," said the Duke of Axford, "Princess Sofia is of a ripe age, and may be a good match for the King."

"REALLY?" screeched Bathory. "The King should leave the duty of serving his country for his love life?"

Madeline nearly tipped the cup, her face turning red with anger. Alex casually took the cup and saucer from her hand, ignoring her glare.

"That is not what this is about, and you know it Lord Bathory!" started Sir Ashton Giles. "After this war is over, it would be good for the country to look forward to relations with Spain. Considering all other political options across Europe, Spain makes sense."

"What's done is done," said Alex. "They are coming, and I believe my duty as king is to stay here in my country, looking after its political interests."

Political interests? Marrying the Princess of Spain was a duty? Madeline's eyes stung as she stared at Alex. He continued to ignore her presence. She wanted to ask him why he didn't tell her, but she knew why. He wanted sex.

"If all works according to plan, we may be able to work out several treaties with Spain that could be in our favour," Alex went on. As he spoke, she turned and stomped down the steps, back to her cart. All the Lords seemed to agree with Alex, and nodded their heads in unison, except for Lord Bathory, who along with Madeline, had a sour look on his face. She served the tea, listening in to the conversation.

"Perhaps the Spanish royals and the King should stay at Windsor Castle," Greg Umbridge piped up, "Buckingham Palace with its renovations, is not a place to receive such guests."

Angrily, she trod across the floor with the Duke of Axford's tray. She wanted to throw something. That was not Greg Umbridge speaking. Alex told him to say that. Greg barely uttered a word during these meetings, except to ask for his special tea. She poured the Duke's tea, while the Duke gave her an odd look. She glared back at him. Angry, she tipped the cup with its hot liquid onto the Duke's lap.

"Argh!" he yelped in pain as he jumped up.

"Oh dear," she said in a sarcastic tone. "I'm sorry, your Grace."

"Quite all right dear, quite all right," he said, as she passed him a small towel.

"Miss Black," started Alex, "you need to focus on what you're doing. You could have burned his Grace."

"Better him than you, your Majesty."

All the Lords began to laugh, including the Duke of Axford. The Duke gave Madeline a warm smile, looking into her eyes. But he didn't see Madeline, his mind was in a different time and place. Seeing his dreamy expression, she edged away to her cart glancing back at the Duke, who was still adrift in another world.

Madeline finished her tea service, purposely serving Greg Umbridge an empty teapot. Before she left, she learned that the Spanish royals would arrive in only a couple weeks and Alex would leave for Windsor Castle in four days. She arrived in the kitchen with the cart, livid. She went about her work forcefully, slamming the cart about as she wiped it down, throwing her towels to the side. She wanted to give Alex a good smack in the face; she was sure she would next time they were alone together. She sat down on a stool and cried. She knew it wouldn't last, she just did not think it would end as abruptly as it did.

Over the next several days, Alex ignored Madeline. She went on pretending to clean already clean rooms as she had before, without any visits from him, but looked for opportunities to talk with him. It was near impossible. It seemed that he had planned his own schedule and hers making sure they did not cross paths. Frustrated, she decided to use her duty in the House of Lord as her opportunity to give him a piece of her mind. The next time she did the tea service she left a little card on his tray that read:

You owe me an explanation, you dolt.

He did not seem to notice it at first, but as she made her rounds with the tea, she kept glancing up waiting for his reaction. Just then, amongst a conversation the Lords were having, an expression of disgust grew on his face. He looked down directly at Madeline, glowering. She held her head high with a huge grin from ear to ear and finished her service. But as she walked out of the House of Lords and the huge doors shut behind her, a dark feeling overcame her. Something told her she would regret leaving that note.

The next few days were long. She couldn't focus on anything. She no longer worked in clean rooms and was doing a shoddy job of cleaning. Unfortunately, every room she worked in, she worked alone. Left by her lonesome, she began over-analysing what she had done. Calling him a dolt was harsh. She couldn't deny wanting to be with him, and wondered if she had taken things too far. She figured she must have, she was now cleaning dirty rooms. He was treating her like any other servant.

One morning, during breakfast, Marie sat next to her, a big grin on her face as she slammed The Society Pages down on the table in front of Madeline. "Did you see this?" she squealed.

"What?"

"Lady Watson! She was found naked in the Royal Mews the night of the party. One of the artists for the pages found her and drew her, then published it."

Madeline took the paper up in her hands to see the familiar derrière of Lady Watson.

"And that's not the worst of it," Marie continued, "Harold heard from some of the valets this morning that Lord Watson has lost his position overseas. Apparently, several Lords sought his Majesty and demanded he be relieved of his position, so he can stay home and keep his wife from acting like a prostitute."

"Really?" she said complacent and put the paper back on the table.

"Yes. They probably won't be invited to court for some time either."

"Hm."

Marie was put out by Madeline's passive response. "What's eating you?" she asked, in concern. "You've looked depressed these past few days. I thought this would get a reaction from you."

"I suppose I've been feeling a little peaky lately," she said in a sad tone, pushing her eggs across her plate. "Perhaps that's why I looked depressed. I've just been under the weather, that's all."

Sceptical, Marie didn't press the matter. It was obvious that Madeline wasn't going to share, and she didn't want to make things worse by asking more questions.

On Tuesday, Madeline was scheduled to clean another room alone. But she noticed something odd. It was already clean. She wondered if Alex wanted to visit her again. She was happy. He probably wanted to resolve everything. She calmly waited on a chair for him to come. A few hours past, then quite unexpectedly, Greg

Umbridge walked through the door. Madeline immediately stood up, humiliated that she had been caught lounging about. However, he said nothing and sat down across from her in another chair.

"Sit back down, Miss Black."

She could smell brandy on him as she took a seat. "Where's Alex?"

"He would have come, but he has other meetings to attend today." He shifted about uncomfortably in his seat. "He apologizes that he didn't come himself."

She felt insulted, "What kind of meetings?"

He pursed his lips, "Meetings to discuss how we will accommodate the Spanish royals."

She crossed her arms, "Well, I hope he has fun planning his little welcoming party" she said with heavy sarcasm.

He ignored it and continued, "These meetings are actually why I came down to see you. Alex wanted me to tell you that we will not need your services today for the House of Lords. The meetings have been cancelled. He also told me to tell you that if you no longer want to do the meetings, he'll understand."

She stood up, "I'm going to keep doing them Sir Gregory. He won't be getting off that easy."

A smirk grew on his face, "Excellent, then I'll see you Thursday. Oh, and if you wouldn't mind, a little whisky in my teapot, love?" he said getting up from his seat, heading for the door. "Your little lovers quarrel has nothing to do with me and my need for a stiff drink during those stupid meetings."

"I'm sorry," she said, knowing what she had done to him was unfair. "But really Sir Gregory, perhaps you shouldn't drink so much."

He laughed heartily, "Right. Well, I'll see you Thursday then, Miss Black." He left the room leaving her alone with her agonizing thoughts of Alex. She was disappointed that she wouldn't see Alex, and sending her to a room that had been already cleaned gave her high hopes. It seemed as though his Majesty was playing head games. Or maybe she was thinking about it a little too much.

Thursday finally came, and Madeline knew it would be her last chance to do anything. She wrote another small message and set it on his tea tray.

When she set the tray down next to him, there was a note already there. She picked it up.

I'm a king. I'm truly sorry, but you knew this wouldn't last.

I owe you nothing.

Despite this, she did not take the note she wrote him off his tray. She still wanted him to read it. But he did not pick it up. As she served the tea, she watched him closely. He ignored it and the tea she had served him. When she finished, she left with a miserable expression on her face.

Once she was gone, Alex looked down at his tray debating whether he should read her note. He tapped his fingers on the pulpit. Whatever she wrote would not matter, he reasoned. It would change nothing. He figured he should read it just so he wouldn't wonder what she had written. He discreetly opened the small envelope as the Lords discussed amongst themselves.

I suppose with all the treaties and wealth she has to offer, she's

the better deal. Have fun with your fairy tale life.

It felt like a thousand daggers stabbing his heart. The possibility that he would have to marry Princess Sofia was not a 'fairytale' as she thought. Given the political state of Europe, it was an expectation.

He read the note again and again, losing his focus on the discussion going on around him. He said nothing else for the rest of the meeting. When it ended, several men walked up to the pulpit to address him on different matters. But he was short with them, "Gentlemen, I've had a long week planning for Princess Sofia and the Spanish royals' arrival. Any issues or concerns you have will have to be dealt with at the next meeting."

All the Lords left, except Greg, who climbed up the pulpit stairs. "So I see you read the note. I thought you said you weren't going to take any drama from her."

"If I don't read it, I'll always wonder what she wrote. I know I won't stop thinking about it until I know."

"Right," Greg said giving an eye roll. "I think you're thinking with the head in your trousers, not the one on your shoulders. God knows how many love notes you've ignored by other women. Were you hoping for an invite, Alex?"

"An invite?"

"You know, one last round in the Music Room, Mistresses' Chambers or wherever the hell else you do it."

"I'm not in the mood for jokes."

"Want a game of tennis or go hunting or something?"

"Let's head to the Billiards Room."

They set off and Alex explaining what the note had said. Once they reached the Billiards Room, Greg began setting up the balls while Alex found the cues.

"I can't do this," Alex said handing Greg his cue. "I can't leave here without her understanding it's nothing personal."

"You should have spoken to her alone after she gave you that first note."

"What difference would that make? Telling her that I care for her, but will eventually marry someone else. She knew it would have to end. She knew I would have to marry some noble woman or princess. She knew that."

"I'm sure she knew that, but I think she just feels insulted about the way she found out. You should have told her. Using the House of Lords as a way to communicate the fact that you were no longer going to be with her was a wanker thing to do. Especially considering that you fucked her that morning."

Alex stared, slack-jawed, "How did you know that?"

"Bloody hell Alex, Sir Ashton had me looking about for you. I walked by the Music Room. She's a loud little thing isn't she?"

He blushed. "Never mind that. Besides, it wasn't a wanker thing to do. I mean, it wasn't intentional. I got word of the Spanish coming after seeing her that morning."

"She doesn't know that."

Greg was usually so out of touch with women. It was strange, what he was saying made sense. "I think what's actually upsetting her is how you're casting her aside like you didn't fancy her at all."

"I don't fancy Madeline," Alex corrected, "I care for her, but I don't fancy her."

Greg scoffed, "Bullocks your Majesty. You were rearranging your schedule and hers so you could spend time with her. These past ten days you've looked for every opportunity to be with her —"

"Never mind that!" he said in frustration, pacing about the billiards table. "I don't want to leave here ..." He trailed off, then stopped tapping his fingers on the side of the table. "I should take a few servants with me to Windsor Castle."

Greg gave him a dark look, "Oh God, then what? Have her witness the whole courtship? You must be out of your mind."

"Plenty of men have mistresses. Why can't I?"

"Well first off," he began trying to speak some sense to him, "most men don't have mistresses that share the same home as the wife, mate. Princess Sofia will find out."

"I know. But I'm not ready to let go of Madeline just yet."

"Oi! So, you do fancy her?"

"Yes," he admitted, the tension in his body releasing. "I think I love her but —Greg," he hesitated before continuing, "go down to the servants' quarters this evening and pick about eight servants to come with us to Windsor Castle. Make sure she comes. If she refuses to go, release her from service."

"You mean from ownership?"

"Yes."

17

WINDSOR

Several hours later, Madeline sat in a rocking chair in the servants' parlour, her needlework in hand. She hated herself for falling in love with him. She could not stop thinking of his last words, 'I owe you nothing'. The words ran through her mind repeatedly, trampling any hope of being with him again. It was over. Done. She decided she would run away from Buckingham Palace after he left for Windsor Castle tomorrow. She doubted he would fuss over her running away, given the circumstances.

She rocked herself in a chair next to Marie, who was staring at her. Madeline shook her head, coming back from the trance she was in.

"Why are you looking at me?" she asked.

"I've been watching you the last few minutes Madeline. You've been staring at nothing. You haven't done any needlework since you sat down," she said gesturing to her fabric.

Madeline looked at her blank canvas. "Well, I expect I'm not really in the mood for needlework," she said, trying to sound casual, setting it down on the table next to her.

"Something is bothering you. You've been avoiding telling me. But I might be able to help you. What is it?"

"Nothing."

"Madeline —"

Just then Greg Umbridge entered the room. "Excuse me everyone," he said loudly getting everyone's attention. He eyed Madeline in her chair. "The King has come to realize that we are somewhat short staffed at Windsor Castle. We will be having the Spanish royals coming so we will need eight servants to join us temporarily there. Are there any volunteers?"

Marie's hand along with several others shot up in the air, "Oh! It would be exciting to go to Windsor Castle!" she gushed.

Greg looked over at Madeline, who quickly picked up her needle and fabric and acted as though she heard nothing. He let out a long deep breath as he looked at all the raised hands. He began to stall on picking servants, and soon Madeline realized the real reason Greg was choosing volunteers. He looked in her direction, an imploring expression on his face. She stubbornly refused to raise her hand. If this was Alex's way of making amends, she thought it was pathetic. She continued with her needlework, looking in every direction but Greg Umbridge's.

"Anyone else?" he said slowly. "Right. Fine then."

He began picking people hesitantly, looking at Madeline from time to time. After some time, he was searching the room for the last volunteer. Her mind began to race; she knew she was punishing Alex. She hated to admit it, but by hurting him, she was hurting herself. Deep down, she knew she had never been so miserable. She regretted calling him a dolt; she knew she would regret not going to Windsor Castle too. She timidly raised her hand, as Greg was about to point at Emma, to name her the last volunteer. "Miss —"

Madeline coughed loudly. He looked back at her, "Miss Black."

Marie cocked her head, "So I sit here waving my hand for a good fifteen minutes, you barely have your hand up three seconds, and you're going to Windsor Castle?"

"Well, you wouldn't want to leave Harold here would you?"

"Huh. I suppose not."

Early the next morning, a queue of coaches lined the horseshoe drive outside Buckingham Palace. Each carriage was black, with lacquered finish, had Alex's emblem inlaid in several places, and had gilt leaves on its edges and corners. There were red velvet and gold trimmed curtains in each window. The drivers wore red coats with gold trim. Most of the carriages had two horses, except Alex's, his had four. The royal coach made the others look plain. It was black with a lacquered finish, but it had decorative inlaid panelling, gold gilt on each spoke of the wheels, and the windows were adorned with gold silk curtains.

Madeline had packed her bags the night before, along with the new dresses Alex had given her. She stood in line along with the rest of the servants outside. Alex's entourage of valets were also there with Sir Ashton, waiting next to the carriages. Madeline watched as the footmen packed the coaches with luggage. She glanced at the entrance door of Buckingham Palace, every so often, waiting for Alex.

Greg Umbridge walked up behind her and spoke in a soft voice, "Miss Black get in the second last coach right now."

She looked quizzically at him. "Shouldn't I be staying out here with the rest of the servants?"

"Make my life easy for once love. Just do it."

She discreetly walked over to the second-last coach, the royal coach just behind it and let herself in. She sat waiting, looking out the window as the other servants scurried about the coaches. Soon, Alex came out, and everyone bowed and curtsied. Greg walked up, and the two exchanged words, and then Greg walked over to her carriage and climbed inside.

"All right Miss Black," he said as he settled into the seat across from her. "The King wants you to take this door and sneak into the royal carriage," he said as he pointed to the other door not facing the servants.

"Make sure no one sees you," he said offhandedly. He began closing all the red velvet curtains in the coach.

She folded her arms and crossed her legs, "What if I decide I'd like to stay here?"

"I don't think the King would be too pleased."

"Then I'll stay here."

"I'm not good company to keep love," he said hoping he could persuade her to see Alex. "If you spend time with an arse like me, you do as I do." He pulled a bottle of whisky from under the seat and waved it about.

She bit her lip. She did not enjoy drinking very much, her father's alcoholism made her wary of it. But drinking with Greg Umbridge was more enticing than talking with Alex. Her forgiveness wasn't going to come easy and she wanted him to know it.

Soon the coaches were packed, and everyone climbed into the carriages. Alex sat in the royal coach wondering why Madeline had not come. As all the coaches lurched forward and began the journey to Windsor Castle, he soon realized that she did not want to see him. He sat, his muscles tensing. He needed to talk to her, and sitting alone in the coach made him anxious. He felt a hole in the pit of his stomach and wondered if he should stop the coaches and somehow force her inside his. But how?

Meanwhile, Greg Umbridge had found two tumblers in the coach and began pouring the whisky into each. It intrigued him to be spending time with Madeline. She was the only girl that Alex ever had any heartache for, and that was saying something, considering his past.

"Here you are Miss Black," he said passing her a tumbler. "To drinking!" he said clinking her glass with his. He threw his drink back. She laughed and threw back hers.

"Have another, have another," he said, pouring more whisky in their glasses. "So Madeline, can I call you that?"

"Sure."

"More about you now, where are you from?" he said gulping some more whisky.

"I'm from London."

"Right. Okay, so how is it you came to Buckingham Palace anyway?" he said throwing the rest back and pouring himself some more.

"I was bought at the market."

"Bloody hell?! Bought at the market?"

"Yes, my father sold me to Madam Ravine when I was around fourteen."

"Your father sold you into that kind of life? So, before Buckingham, you were a whore?" He covered his mouth with his hand, stopping himself. "Not that I have anything against ladies of pleasure, I mean what man does?"

She started laughing. It did not take long for him to get tipsy. She corrected him. "No, I was never a lady of pleasure. Luckily. Mr. Sheffield, a man my mother once knew persuaded Lady Watson to buy me from Madam Ravine."

He blew a raspberry. "I can't stand Lady Watson. She fancies Alex something fierce. It's disgusting to watch an older married woman fall all over herself for him. Quite pitiful, really."

"At least you've never had to live with her."

"No worries over the old bitch then. What about your mother?" he asked, pouring another glass.

"I don't know very much about my mother. She died when I was a baby."

"Oh, I'm sorry."

An awkward moment fell over them. She broke the silence. "So what about you, Greg. Can I call you that?" He nodded, and she continued, "Alex told me you are a commoner, but now you live with him, what's happened to your family?"

"Alex has been extremely kind to my family. After I had come to live in Windsor Castle with him, he insisted that my family be taken care of. They own some land in Aylesbury Vale. It's in Buckinghamshire. They rent out small farms there."

260

"That's lovely!" she said taking another sip of whisky. She and Sissy used to talk about running away to the countryside and buying a small farm. She tipped to her side a bit and steadied herself with her arm. The whisky was getting to her. "Have you any brothers or sisters?"

"I've got six sisters; I'm a middle child. But, I don't go home much."

In an instant, the coach halted and they both spilt some of their drinks. A muffled commotion was taking place outside their carriage, and they looked at each other wide-eyed.

"You're not wanted for some crime are you, Sir Gregory?" she said giggling, taking another sip. "Is this whisky stolen from the King?"

"It always is."

The door flew open, and Alex climbed in and sat down next to her, a worried look on his face. "Madeline, why did you not come to my coach?"

"Ooohhh! Someone is in trouble now!" she said pointing at Greg as she toppled about.

"You got her drunk?" said Alex aghast.

"She didn't want to see you, so we had a few drinks. What of it?"

"Greg," Alex said exasperated as he began to strip off his coat and hat, "put these on, and go to the royal coach, please."

"Always ruining a good time!" Greg huffed as he took off his coat and put on Alex's. He left the coach, leaving them alone.

"I don't want to talk to you," she said shifting to the other bench.

"I'm sorry for what I've done," Alex said sincerely. He sat next to her and tried to embrace her. She pushed him away, folding her arms she turned and looked out the window. He closed the velvet curtains. She scowled at him.

"I care for you, but you must understand; either I stay here misleading Bathory and everyone else that I'm going to marry the Princess, or I go out to the battlefield where Bathory will find a way to kill me."

She turned her back to him, "So you are not going to marry Princess Sofia?"

He took her in his arms. "That's never really been my intention. I'll entertain her while she's here and once things calm with the war, they'll go back to Spain. I won't make any proposals or any kind of treaties. They most likely won't propose anything unless I do. Once they've left, we can go back to the way things were."

She looked into his crystal eyes. She wanted to be with him, forgive him completely, but a part of her felt unsure.

"Madeline, please forgive me. I'm sorry." He brought his hand to her cheek, and she knew she was on the edge of surrender. She had not planned to let him off that easily. He knew by her loss of words that she had relented. He leaned in and kissed her, taking her hand in his. As he wrapped his other arm around her, she softened and went adrift, his lips melting into hers. He kissed her tenderly. Releasing her hand, he began unbuttoning his trousers and she look at him in disbelief.

"Just like that you expect me be that forgiving?" She turned again so that she was facing the window.

He rubbed her thigh, "I just want to kiss and make up, please don't be angry with me."

"How could I not be?"

"Would it make you feel better if I made it up to you first?"

"What did you have in mind?"

"What would you like?"

She thought about it for a few long moments, he grew impatient and began lifting her skirts.

"ALEX!" she said giggling.

"Well, if you can't think of a way I can make it up to you, can I propose one?" He quickly got to his knees, threw up her skirt and kissed her thigh. "Please Madeline," he begged. "I swear if you came into my carriage earlier, I would have licked and nibbled you all the way to Windsor."

"It sounds like you want it more than I do," she said, lightly pushing his shoulder.

"I do."

"I just forgave you, to be honest with you Alex, I'm not so sure we should do this just yet. I'd feel kind of cheap."

He flashed a sexy smile, "Normally, I would do the kingly thing – which is the gentlemanly thing – and leave you be. But, you drive me crazy, so don't expect me to sit here and be good."

"So what are you saying? I'm not going to allow you to make me feel cheap."

"I'm trying to make some kind of deal with you. One where we both get what we want."

"I might be agreeable to letting you put your head between my legs, but nothing further than that, your Majesty."

"That's all I need."

He began kissing her thighs again, but she pulled his head back.

"We haven't discussed what I'll be getting yet."

"What would you like?"

"I want my freedom."

"You're free to leave the castle whenever you wish," he said quickly moving towards her, she pushed him back.

"No, I want to be free from your ownership."

He paused for a moment, looking up at her face. He reached out and gently pulled her face close to his. "I've never considered you a person I own Madeline. You're not property to me. So if you want me to tear up the ownership papers, I'll do it. But, I've left them at Buckingham Palace."

"When we get back, I want to tear them up," said Madeline.

"Fine."

He nuzzled his way to her sex. He pressed soft kisses into her thigh trailing up to her pussy. It tickled as he came closer to her. She held her breath, inflamed with the thought of what was to come. But he moved to her other thigh, giving her a soft massage with his lips. He moved up to her knee and back down again. Then he softly kissed her sex, and she jumped the moment his lips touched her pink, fleshy skin. He breathed a breath of warm air onto her that sent tingles through her body. She moaned, she knew she got the better deal. Alex breathed another warm breath across her pussy lips and Madeline began to tremble with desire.

"Mmm, lick me Alex," she muttered wriggling her hips, "I want it now."

"But I like teasing you," he said between soft kisses on her sex.

"Eat it, lick it! Please!!" moaned Madeline surprised at her own words.

At a slow pace, Alex slid his tongue down her slit, tasting her exquisite sweetness. "Mmm," he muttered. "I could swear you were made to be eaten Madeline."

He put his lips to her sex slowly sucking on her labia, she squeezed his head between her thighs and pushed his mouth down to her hard. Smiling to herself, she thought there had to be some sort of 'punishment' for what he had done. He could barely breathe, but he read Madeline's mind. It was payback. Not that he minded. It just meant he was going to have to endure the 'suffering'. He entered his tongue inside her. Madeline lessened her grip, groaning as he enjoyed her taste. Her body quivered. He spread her lip with his fingers and started stroking her clit with his tongue, moaning as he did.

She could feel the sensations, a kind of humming enter her body. It was almost like the trumpet in the Music Room. She began convulsing, "Oooohhhh! Pleeeease!"

Between the moaning and her thighs trembling around his head, he knew she was ready. He reached up and began tweaking her hard nipples. It was more than she could take, she hurtled forward screaming, "AAAAHHHHH!"

Throwing themselves into a passionate heat of kisses they put their hands all over one another. Madeline could not help herself, she began feeling through his already loose trousers and grasped onto his pulsating dick.

"You want that now?" he asked. Madeline nodded as she stared down wantonly. Alex undid the last few buttons of his trousers, and Madeline got to her knees, her hand still firmly holding his cock.

"There you go," said Alex as he watched Madeline guide it into her mouth. She sucked gingerly on his tip, looking into his baby blue eyes with her green ones. She took in his taste, licking off the pre-cum that Alex gave her. Tasting him, she grew excited and sucked hungrily, wanting more. Seeing her desire, Alex gently took her head in his hand, and combed through her hair with his fingers as she went up and down his length. He felt guilty, knowing he was supposed to be pleasuring her. He guided her off and leaned toward her. She pushed him back, pouting, "It's my turn."

"I believe I have to fulfill my part of the deal first Miss Black," he said coming toward her again. But she moved quickly. Grabbing his cock, she ran her warm wet tongue up the underside of him, from the base to the tip. As she went, he felt each nerve awaken.

Unable to contain himself, Alex arched his back into his seat, "Aaahhhh!" he groaned, grasping the edge of the seat.

She ran her tongue up his length again, but a little more slowly. When she nearly reached his tip, he let out another long deep moan. She knew she hit a sensitive spot and began tapping and caressing her tongue against it.

"Oooohhhh fuck," his voice shuddered. "Madeline, huh – stop. I'll …"

She ignored him and continued brushing her tongue against his weak spot as she took him in her mouth again.

"Uuuuhhhh!"

She kept swirling her tongue about him. It was a pleasurable torture. Alex thrust his hips forward, squeezing his muscles wanting more. He began gyrating his hips. It did not take long, after sliding several times into her mouth, Madeline took hold of him, and he began fucking her mouth. As he watched her, he shook his head in disbelief. "Maadelinne" he moaned in a shaky, exhausting tone.

He reached his apex, and came hard. She could feel him sputter at the back of her throat. She hungrily swallowed what he gave her, spurt after spurt. Once he finished, she continued softly licking and sucking, hoping he would stir. She wanted him intimately, sliding back and forth inside of her. He lifted her from off the floor and set her on his lap. She wrapped her arms around him and nuzzled closely to him.

"Give it to me Alex," she whispered pleadingly.

"I would," he said his chest heaving, "but you need to learn to listen to a king's command. I said 'stop'. I'm drained now."

"Listen to a king's command!" she taunted. "I don't need to listen to you! You should be obeying my command right now." She crossed her arms and addressed him in the most demanding voice she could muster, "Give it to me, Alex."

No one ever commanded Alex, not even Greg had the nerve. He did not know why, but her attitude excited him.

"I'll give it to you Miss Black. Before I finish, you'll be begging me to stop."

"I doubt that," she replied challenging him.

He said nothing but began pulling at her the front of her dress, exposing her breasts. Cradling her in his arm he began twisting her nipples between his fingers. She twitched a little, enjoying the new sensation. He began nibbling on one nipple as he tweaked the other with his fingers. She wriggled her hips into his thighs, his cock was stiffening. She pulled up her skirts when Alex grasped her arm.

"You're not getting any of that until I'm through with your breasts."

She shook her head, "You can't suck and pinch them all day Alex."

"You're absolutely right Miss Black," he said in a dangerous tone, "but they need to be taken care of."

He reached behind her dress and began pulling at the corset's laces. She gave him a curious glance, puzzled by his actions. But, as he tightened the laces she saw her mounds pop forward and crush together, she understood. He smirked wickedly staring at the large soft orbs. He smacked them with his hand. The tight corset around her breasts intensified the shock that ran through her. Her jaw dropped, surprised by what he'd done. Her sulky eyes met his, but he made no apologies for it. Instead, a cocksure expression settled on his face. Her emotion softened, she couldn't help feeling aroused; resisting his confident domination was impossible for her. She slowly reached down rubbed her hand against his arm. Knowing he had won, he smacked them again.

"Mmm," she murmured, submitting to him.

He buried his face between them sucking and pulling at them with his lips. He smacked them again. He went like this for a while, biting, sucking, tweaking and smacking her breasts. She whimpered and moaned watching as her breast grew redder and felt her pussy glisten with the need to have him crushing himself inside her again.

As she squirmed about in his arms, he repeated the assault, her lips quivering and her moans growing louder with every suck, bite and slap. The coach abruptly ground to a halt, the horses whinnied, and they slid forward in the seat.

"Blast!" said Madeline knowing she had been too loud.

They could hear the coach driver climb down from his seat. Madeline panicked, she rose up from Alex put he pulled her back down and planted his face between her breasts. A knock came at the door. Madeline thanked God that Greg had closed the curtains earlier.

"Sir Gregory, are you quite all right?" asked the coach driver. Madeline worried that he would try to open the door.

"Quite fine," said Alex casually.

"I'm going to enter, Sir. I would just like to be certain." The door handle turned, and Madeline nestled her head down into Alex's hair, shoving his face into her breasts. Immediately she heard the door slam.

"Sir Gregory," he began in a humiliated tone, "I'm so –"

"Oi! Can't a man have some privacy?" Alex said pulling back from her. "Besides, I'm sure the King would like to make it to Windsor Castle eventually. Get back to your job and I'll get back to mine!" Alex yelled imitating Greg's brazen attitude.

"I'm so sorry Sir," the driver apologized. "I didn't mean to impose!"

Madeline could hear him bolt up the driver's steps and quickly take hold of the reins. The coach was propelled forward.

Alex started laughing.

"That wasn't very fair to him," she scolded. "He was only doing what was expected of him in that situation."

"Oh come on, that was funny."

"I suspect that you and Greg switch often?"

"You suspect correctly, Miss Black," he said touching her chin. He then looked down at her chest and noticed how fleshy pink her skin had become. "I think I went a little overboard with that?" he asked. She disagreed; she wouldn't have minded him going at her tits for longer. The only problem was she didn't want to get caught again. He pulled the curtain back and looked out of the window, surveying their surroundings.

"There's plenty of time," he whispered. He turned to her and began lifting her skirt.

"Alex I don't think that's a good idea, we almost got caught."

"He's going to think twice before coming back here, Madeline. He thinks he knows what's going on back here now."

He continued lifting her skirts and she giggled excitedly. He was finally going to give her what she yearned for – him pumping in and out of her as if the world was coming to an end. But instead, he got down on his knees, spreading her legs. Madeline grew frustrated. "I can't take this anymore! Give it to me!" she whispered harshly.

He ignored her and flipped her around onto her stomach. Spreading her cheeks, he slowly drifted his thumb over her rosebud, massaging it. Madeline breath quaked as she exhaled. He never held back. She began to wonder what he might do next. If it was what she thought it might be, she wouldn't be surprised.

Then she felt his warm tongue rimming her hole. He'd done it before, but she still found it startling that he did it. It was dirty, but like everything else dirty he wanted, she loved it. It was tantalizing, erotic, warm and wet. She just had a hard time not making a sound. She bit hard down on her lip as he continued swirling about with his tongue.

"Huuuhhhh," her breath quivered as his tongue entered her. "Alex!" she protested.

"Move then," he mumbled.

But she couldn't and he knew she wouldn't. His tongue slithering in and out of her like a snake felt too good. *Why does he do this to me?* she wondered. Why does he make me admit enjoying this? Even the humiliation of it was intriguing for her. She could feel her body respond though she was disgusted that it did. She became more aroused. Whimpering with every stroke and dart of his tongue, she could feel the ribbons of pleasure mounting and soon she came. He quickly turned her onto her back. As the hot flood of orgasm flowed from her, he lapped her greedily.

When she finished, he quickly stood up and entered her. Appreciating how dripping wet she was, her muscles still tense, he could feel them clench around his sex. Madeline sighed, satisfied at the feeling of his cock finally filling her. Knowing she was moments away from Alex fulfilling her needs again, he had seemed to take a burden off her chest. The last few days had been emotional and this was liberating.

He lifted her so her bottom was suspended, her shoulders on the carriage seat. He steadily began sliding back and forth and she twisted her hips in response. He began picking up his pace and soon was slamming himself into her. She moaned and arched he back into the seat, wanting him further inside her if it was possible.

"Deeper!" she whimpered. "I want you as far as you ca –"

SMACK

"OOOOOHHHHHH!" she moaned. Her eyes bulged feeling the burn of his bare palm against her bottom.

"AGAIN!" she begged wondering why he hadn't done this before. He buried himself deep in her.

SMACK

"UUGGHHH!"

SMACK

"UUGGHHHHHHH!"

A series of deep thrusts and slaps followed, with Madeline losing her breath as she moaned, her senses heightened. The sting of every slap, the pound of each deliberate stroke. She could feel electricity in waves across her skin as she lost her breath, her chest hurting, as she gasped repeatedly. She should have stopped, but her need for him was stronger than her desire for air. She screamed, soundlessly small squeaks coming from her voice box. She came again and again and it felt as though she'd never stop. Soon everything around her went fuzzy for several moments as he supported her lithe body, into his arms. She closed her eyes and the two exhaled in unison. The last few moments had been distorted. She looked up at him.

"Did you finish?" she asked curiously.

He laughed, "Are you kidding? I don't think I've ever gone so hard."

"Did I pass out?"

"Yes," he smiled and gave her a soft peck on her forehead.

"I've missed you," he sighed. "You have no idea how miserable I've been these past few days."

It was relieving to hear. For a while, Madeline thought he hadn't cared at all. She rose and pulled back the curtains. She rested back on his shoulder, gazing at the English countryside.

"Are you still mad at me?" he asked, his emotions hinging on her answer.

She blushed, "No. I don't think I could ever stay mad at you."

He smiled and wrapped his arm around her, but he worried. He knew that inviting her to come to Windsor Castle was only a temporary solution. One day he would have to marry someone else. He needed an heir to the throne that was not Bathory or Axford. He stared out the window pondering their future, then looked tenderly down at Madeline. She had drifted asleep in his arms and had a sweet simper on her face. He combed her hair with his fingertips, sighing. He knew their future would never have a fairy tale ending. If anything, it would be difficult, especially for her, who would have to share him with another woman. As he watched her sleep, he decided he would do everything possible to make their lives together normal as possible. Perhaps, after he married, he could hide her in a small estate, and visit her and their bastard children regularly. He buried his face in his hands. He felt ashamed for having these thoughts. Leading two separate lives felt wrong, but Madeline felt right. It angered him that someone that felt right for him came with so many complications and obstacles. It seemed unfair that the woman he wanted to be with seemed to be the only one he could not have. He never found it easy to be a king, but now he was beginning to resent it.

18

MISS TILLY SMITH

As they neared Windsor Castle, Greg stopped the coaches and they switched coats and carriages again.

Before leaving, Alex spoke to Madeline, "Be sure to get a tour of Windsor Castle, all right? It will be easier for us to meet up if you know where you're going."

He softly kissed her cheek. He turned to Greg, "Don't get my lady drunk again. The last thing I need is someone reprimanding her."

"Why worry your Majesty? I'm sure you could get her out of trouble."

"Shut up Greg."

Alex left the carriage, and Madeline's eyes followed him out the window.

"Awww, did you kiss and make up?" said Greg, noticing her gaze.

"Shut up Greg." Madeline said, biting her lip, trying not to giggle.

The rest of the ride Madeline nodded her head as Greg babbled on about Windsor Castle and the stuffy guards.

"I don't know about them," he said, "they seem suspicious of just about everything. Once I tried …"

But Madeline was no longer paying attention. Her thoughts were on Alex and wondering what would happen when Princess Sofia left. He wanted things to go back to the way they were before. In time, would he ignore all the social boundaries and laws of royal marriage and marry her anyway? Or would he go on being a bachelor king? Madeline mulled these thoughts over, but stopped as they pulled up to the castle.

"Wow," said Madeline, "it is huge!"

It was much larger than Buckingham. It looked like it could house a small town. Madeline wondered how many people worked within its walls. The carriage drove through the entrance gate and pulled to the front doors. As she stepped out of her carriage, the famed round tower soared high in the sky above her. She could see crenelated battlements and arrow shaped keystones. The castle had a medieval gothic motif with statues of knights and some very grotesque gargoyles. The carriages waited by the State Apartments' entrance on a reddish gravel path, which surrounded a square courtyard of perfectly manicured green grass.

As the rest of Alex's entourage stepped out of their carriages waiting for the King to make his entrance, plenty of guards marched around the gravel square. They wore the same type of uniform as the guards at Buckingham Palace. Alex stepped out, everyone bowing and curtsying to him, the guards saluted.

A man, dressed in similar attire to Sir Ashton Giles stood on the steps to the apartments. He bowed deeply, "Your Majesty," he said emphatically.

"Lord Cadogan," Alex greeted back, "it's good to be back at Windsor Castle."

"We have missed your presence, your Majesty."

Lord Cadogan escorted Alex into the State Apartments along with Greg. A few moments after they entered, several servants and footmen came out and directed everyone where to go.

"All right you Buckingham lot, I'm Mr. Tinney, come with me, I will take you to your quarters."

Greg walked up the steps, Alex pulled at his arm, "Make sure that Miss Black looks after tea at the House of Lords meetings," he whispered.

"Is that all you want her to be looking after your Majesty?" Greg teased.

"Hmph! Get going."

Alex then turned to Lord Cadogan. "Shall we Lord Cadogan? I'm sure there's much you want to share with me now that I'm here in person."

While King Alex was touring the castle, being informed of the most recent news of Windsor Castle, Madeline and the rest of the servants followed Mr. Tinney into the castle.

Mr. Tinney was a gangly, hollow-cheeked man with spectacles and a brown coat with long tails. His excellent posture had Madeline

276

thinking there was a stick shoved up his backside. He strode down the halls at a quick pace. The castle seemed quite similar to Buckingham Palace in taste but bigger; the paintings in the halls and the rooms themselves. When they reached the servants' quarters, the kitchen, the parlour and the dormitory were quite similar to Buckingham Palace's.

"All right, up on this chalkboard here, you will all find your name and room number," said Mr. Tinney. "Some of you will have your flatmate show you around the castle, others will come with me. All of your flatmates are waiting in their rooms to meet you."

Madeline found her room number and set off down the corridors to the dormitory. Entering her room, she did not find many differences between Buckingham Palace and Windsor Castle. Once again, she was provided with an armoire, dresser and a bed, but there were no pretty drawings posted on the walls, no character. Madeline realized her flatmate was probably not as bubbly and fun as Marie.

On the bed sat a young, slight blonde haired girl, brushing through her hair. She was around fourteen.

"So you're one of the servants from Buckingham Palace?" she asked as Madeline set her bag down. The girl had a high-pitched voice that irritated Madeline's ears. Madeline hoped she wasn't too talkative.

"Yes, I'm Madeline Black."

"Tilly Smith," she said, putting her brush down. She looked at Madeline for a long moment then added timidly, "Do you see much of the King at Buckingham Palace? We don't see much of him here."

"Well, not really, the King is a busy man."

"So you don't get a chance to talk to him much?"

"No," Madeline lied.

"Oh," she said looking disappointed.

"I imagine that the King will be busy here too. You know, entertaining the Spanish royals and all," Madeline said as she opened her bag and began arranging her clothes into the drawers.

"Oh my! What lovely dresses!" Tilly said noticing them as Madeline hung them in the armoire.

"Thank you."

"Where did you get them?"

"A friend of mine bought them for me," said Madeline casually.

"I would love to know your friend."

Madeline said nothing but continued to put her dresses in. Tilly watched and Madeline began to feel slightly annoyed; she wondered if Tilly would be the one to give her the tour of the castle. She hoped not.

"Is it true? Is he going to marry the Spanish Princess?"

Madeline scoffed, "I doubt that."

"That's exactly what I said to Jane, she's another servant here. I don't think the King will get married anytime soon. I think he's going to be one of those men that'll fancy much younger ladies."

Madeline held back her laughter, pressing her lips together. She was rooming with a young girl that had an infatuation with the King. Marie had once mentioned to her that there were plenty of maids with secret crushes on him. Madeline wondered how often Tilly would gush about the King, but then it started.

"Isn't the King gorgeous?"

"I suppose he is," said Madeline, a knowing little smile on her face as she pictured him naked.

"And he's such a gentleman! He spent last summer here with that vulgar Sir Gregory Umbridge. I was serving the two of them tea out on the terrace and Sir Gregory Umbridge started teasing me."

Madeline nodded. She could imagine Greg giving Tilly a hard time, "Why? What did he say?"

"He said that in a couple more years, the King would get so desperate for attention from ladies; he would probably chase after me!" A huge grin grew from ear to ear, a twinkle of hope in her eyes. "Can you believe that?"

Madeline sensed that though Tilly pretended to be humiliated by the situation, really she was excited about it. "Actually, I can. It is Sir Gregory," Madeline said simply.

"Then Sir Gregory became so vile," her voice came to a whisper, "he said, 'You'd probably fancy some Italian sausage, wouldn't you?'"

Madeline's jaw did drop at this. Only Greg would have that kind of audacity. But she was also surprised and curious about something.

"The King is Italian?"

"Of course," said Tilly matter-of-factly, "his mother was Italian. I thought everyone knew that. Anyway," she said returning to her story grinning again, "the King told Sir Gregory that he shouldn't make a lady feel so uncomfortable. He told him to apologize, and Sir Gregory did!"

"Wow Tilly, that was very sweet of him," she said earnestly. Madeline was sure Tilly had spent the last several months obsessing over it, telling everyone she met.

"I'm not going to be able to give you the tour today. I think Mr. Tinney is. You probably won't be working today either. The castle is quite big, over a thousand rooms, but you won't see them all."

"Are you not working today Tilly?"

"Nope, it's my day off. I think I'll go down and see the horses. Who knows, maybe I'll run into the King. He likes to go hunting when he's here."

"Well, I'll be off to find Mr. Tinney then," said Madeline. "Nice meeting you Tilly, I'll see you later?"

"At dinner I suppose, bye Madeline."

Madeline left and found Mr. Tinney standing in the parlour, speaking to all the other servants of Buckingham Palace, who were sitting around the room. Discreetly, Madeline walked in, but her entrance drew Mr. Tinney's attention and he stopped, "Miss Black I presume?"

Madeline nodded.

"Excellent. All right that's everyone then, come follow me," said Mr. Tinney. He got up from his seat and the maids followed him, down the hall and up the stairs.

Madeline realized quickly that the tour was going to be quite boring. Mr. Tinney seemed to have a monotone voice and droned at length about the castle's history. The castle used to be a military fortress before it was turned into a residence in the middle ages. As they walked from room to room, Mr. Tinney bored them with dates of wars and kings, while explaining the architecture and what rooms used to be. Her tour with Marie of Buckingham Palace was much more intriguing; whenever they went to a room Marie just allowed Madeline to look about, ask questions, and Marie had all sorts of funny anecdotes about the servants or Sir Gregory Umbridge. Mr. Tinney's tour was painful. He also talked about all the treasures in each room, which drove Madeline mad. Unfortunately, the castle had many more priceless antiques, paintings, sculptures and cultural artefacts than Buckingham Palace.

Many of the rooms reminded her of rooms at Buckingham Palace. They had decorative wall mouldings and ceilings, heaps of paintings and tapestries and fine furniture. The only design difference was some medieval weaponry in the stone hallways a gothic style chapel.

After a few hours of touring the castle, they entered the Green Drawing Room. Madeline finally saw something of interest. It was a doll's house, with replicas of some of the rooms in the castle. She felt the child inside her grow excited, even though she never had any dolls when she was little. The craftsmanship of this doll's house was outstanding, with tiny paintings on the walls, carpets and tiles on the floors and velvet and silk furniture. Madeline considered it a piece of art rather than a toy. She reached out and caressed the miniature silk furniture with her finger.

"Miss Black," Mr. Tinney said in a drawn out tone, "that belongs to his Majesty, keep your hands to yourself."

Madeline put her hands behind her back embarrassed. She heard some laughter out in the hall; she looked over to see Alex with several other men looking at her. Alex had the sexiest smirk on his face. He turned and walked down the hall, the rest of the gentlemen following in his wake. Mr. Tinney continued to go on about the architecture, and how they had to change it to accommodate the Green Drawing Room. Then they headed into the Crimson Drawing Room. It was much the same. Just red with larger windows.

Once they finished touring the staterooms, they were finally brought back to the servants' quarters. Mr. Tinney had the group sit down in the parlour.

"All right Buckingham," he said looking at the small crowd of servants, "are there any questions concerning the tour or the service here?"

Everyone was too exhausted to ask any questions, many of them were yawning, putting their feet up on ottomans or leaning their heads on their hands. They did not want to hear Mr. Tinney talk at length about some other insignificant detail. "No questions?" he said curiously, folding his hands together.

There was a dead silence. Madeline debated whether she should ask him something. He seemed put out that no one had any concerns. She raised her hand, he smiled broadly.

"Mr. Tinney, will the House of Lords be held here now that the King is living here?" she asked.

"Yes, but I don't think they will be having as many meetings now. I believe it may be Tuesday and Thursday – no wait Monday, Wednesday and Fridays. No, wait! They will be entertaining the Spanish royals, so perhaps it will only be Tuesday and Thursday." He stopped. "Sorry dear, I really don't know."

Madeline could tell he was desperate to tell her the correct answer, as he tapped his chin, deep in thought. He seemed to be a very organized man, the type that would be disgruntled if he was not on top of his duties. She wondered if she would still be doing tea, but did not question Mr. Tinney. If he did not know when the

House of Lords meetings would be taking place, she figured he probably had no idea of who was looking after tea.

"You know what Miss Black, I'll be sure to find out for you. I believe Lord Cadogan mentioned that you looked after tea in the meetings in Westminster. Yes dear, I'll be sure to find out for you."

Mr. Tinney dismissed the maids, and Madeline went back to her room. On the way, she saw a familiar face. Greg Umbridge stood in the hallway near her door. He stood stiff, which made him look awkward.

"Hello, Madeline. His Majesty was wondering if you could do the afternoon tea again for the House of Lords."

"Certainly," said Madeline. She looked up at Greg and found it rather odd that he seemed so serious. A couple of other maids moved past them to get to their rooms. He stared straight at Madeline. Looking frustrated, he tapped his foot.

"His Majesty also wants you to know that the House of Lords schedule has changed. It will be taking place every other day while we are here at Windsor. So, you'll be working Mondays, Wednesdays and Fridays."

Madeline looked down at his hands and saw a note between his fingers. She curtsied and discreetly took the note from his hand. Greg smiled, relieved.

"Oh parting is such sweet sorrow," he said dramatically bowing before he left.

Madeline went quietly to her room. Tilly was gone, so she unfolded the note:

I love the look on your face when you're doing something bad.

Meet me at the doll's house at nine.

19

A STOLEN SEASON

Madeline sat in her room until dinner, then went down to eat with the other servants. When she finished, she started freshening herself up for the evening. Doing hair and make-up was fairly easy. Marie had just bought her some cheap lipstick, blush and mascara to thank Madeline for lending her dress for her date with Harold. However, she had a difficult time deciding what to wear. She did not want to wear her uniform, but wearing one of the dresses Alex had given her might draw too much attention. She sat on the bed debating for some time before Tilly walked in.

"What are you doing Madeline? Why's your hair all done up?" she began in her high-pitched voice.

"I have to see someone about serving the tea in the House of Lords tomorrow."

"Really? You get to serve the King tea? Oh, I'd give anything to do it. I'd trade you my day off just to do it!"

It was disturbing to her that Tilly would give up her day off to spend a few moments in the presence of Alex.

"Sorry Tilly, but they won't let anyone else serve the tea. I was trained specially to do it."

"Do you think you could train me?"

"Um, no Tilly."

"Why not?" Her normally high squeak sounded deeper, more demanding, "How hard could it be?"

Madeline pretended to consider it. "Tell you what Tilly, if you get the approval of the King to do it, I'll train you."

Tilly folded her arms miffed, "And just how am I supposed to get his approval?"

"Well, why don't you just ask him?" she said shortly, knowing that Tilly wouldn't dare try.

"Hmph! You just don't want to give up tea time!"

With that, she blew a raspberry and left the dormitory room. Madeline shook her head. She opened the armoire and looked at the dresses, wondering which one she should meet Alex in. She'd give anything to wear the periwinkle coloured one. She pulled it out, admiring its colour and soft textured material. She looked back into the armoire and saw the cloak he had given her the day they went for a picnic. She felt stupid for not considering it before. She could put her hood up and use it to cover the dress. At half past eight, she got dressed and discreetly left the servants' quarters. Upon reaching the Green Drawing Room, she found him sitting on a silk green upholstered chair next to the doll's house.

"Good evening Miss Black," he said as a naughty smile danced across his face. She said nothing but smiled back. "Did you want to play with my doll's house?"

She walked over as he pulled up his chair and invited her onto his lap. She sat down and wrapped her arms around his neck.

"I swear Tinney leaves out all the interesting things about the castle," he said. "He probably did not tell you about the royal prisoners and ghosts we've had in Curfew Tower."

She gave him a frightened look. He laughed and pecked her cheek, "Don't worry in all my years here I've never seen a ghost. Take a look at this."

He drew her attention to the library in the doll's house; it had tiny books on bookshelves, a small writing drawer and several other pieces of furniture and objects. He opened the drawer, inside were miniature pencils and papers.

"That's so neat," she tittered.

He pulled one of the books from the tiny shelves and opened it. There was small printing on the inside. She squinted at the top of the page, "The Six Swans. This is a fairy tale," she said, "when I was little, there were some ladies in my neighbourhood that would look after me sometimes. They used to read me fairy tales."

"Madeline," he spoke timidly, "how is it you became a servant girl?"

She ignored his eyes, not wanting to tell him her father sold her to a brothel before Lady Watson bought her. He quickly sensed that his question made her uncomfortable. He knew he would not get an answer tonight. She quickly changed the subject, "How is it you have a doll's house, your Majesty? Did you play with dolls?" she joked.

The expression on his face became sad. "This doll's house was not meant for me. My mother had this built for the daughter she hoped to have."

"That's strange," she said raising her brow, "I thought all queens wanted males for heirs."

"Not my mother, after she had me, she told my father she gave England an heir, so he'd better give her a daughter."

She laughed. "Seems to be a fairly outspoken woman."

He shook his head, "No. She wasn't outspoken," he stared at the doll's house, "she was just bitter. She hated England. She spent most of her day in her room. She was a hermit."

"Was she homesick for Italy?"

"Yes," he said, still staring into the doll's house, "that and she never loved my father."

His gaze avoided hers, and she got the feeling that his mother never cared for him either.

"Want to see another interesting thing that I'm sure Mr. Tinney left out?" he said trying to lighten the mood.

"Sure," she said rising from his lap.

He took her hand and led her to another table that held a huge book on a stand. He slowly opened the book, and Madeline looked as he slowly turned the pages. Delicate drawings of a child in the womb, the human skull, and internal organs and systems graced the pages he turned.

"Leonardo Da Vinci's original work," he said.

"Wow," she said, her mouth dropped open in awe. She had never had much of an education, but she knew who Leonardo Da Vinci was.

"What kind of language is he writing in?" she asked curiously, moving in for a closer inspection.

"Italian. But he wrote everything backwards. He was left handed and felt this was easier, I suppose."

She looked at the drawings, and without thinking touched her finger to the page. She jolted her hand back realizing she should not have touched it.

"That's quite all right Madeline, you're in the King's favour you know. So much so that I have something else I want to show you. Follow me."

She walked several paces behind him as he led her through several other large rooms that led them down halls leading to other private rooms. Mr. Tinney did not take them to this part of the castle. As she looked about, she realized these were the apartments for foreign dignitaries. Princess Sofia most likely would stay here. The further they went the halls grew narrower, and the doors became smaller. She guessed that they were around the offices of Dukes and Lords. Sir Ashton Giles and the castle steward Lord Cadogan probably stayed in these parts.

There were fewer and fewer guards, and she figured that not many people came down these halls. She wondered if he was trying to sneak her into his bedroom through a passage. But she knew his apartments were in another part of the castle, far from where they were. Either way, it was intriguing. They came to a rather large tapestry and stood there for a moment as he looked around. He whispered back to her, "Do you see anyone?"

She looked behind her, "No."

"Come with me."

He lifted the tapestry, revealing a small door.

"This is it," he said as he turned the knob and opened the door to a very small room, an office. There was a desk, a few paintings, a couple of chairs and a small rug on the floor, but it was not as large or luxurious as the rest of the castle. He smiled at her and started stripping off his clothes. She watched bewildered. Not that she minded a naked Alex in front of her, but what did he expect of her? Noticing her confusion, he walked over to her and pressed his perfect sculpted body against her, closing his arms around her.

"You seem a little confused Miss Black," he laughed.

"Well, I –"

He walked over to the writing desk and opened one of the drawers. He pulled out some drab clothes a peasant would own. He threw them on along with a hat.

"You look ravishing in that dress. But I think you'll draw too much attention."

She was flattered. She knew she looked nice, but she did not think she drew attention.

"Here, put this on." He tossed her a drab black cloak. She took hers off and put it on. As she did so, he took a lantern from out the drawer and lit it with a match.

"Perfect. Let's go shall we?" He tossed up a corner of the rug and uncovered a door in the floor. He lifted it open, revealing a set of stairs, and began walking down the old cobblestone steps.

"Where are we going?"

"To the inn. Maybe we'll catch a show or something."

She grinned, excited. She followed him down the steps, holding his hand. They reached the bottom of the rundown steps and began walking down a huge arched corridor. It was cold, pitch dark and damp. He moved the lamp about to see.

She could hear droplets of water spilling onto the stones somewhere in the distance. She looked down to her servant's shoes and sighed in relief. They were still clean, there weren't puddles on the ground.

"This tunnel is huge," she said, she could not see the walls on either side of the lantern light.

"Yes, it was originally built so the royal garrison could leave the castle and fight enemies that were attacking Windsor. When the royal garrison would exit the tunnels, they would be directly behind the enemy for a surprise attack. There are several more tunnels, too. Brilliant isn't it?"

"Yes. Where does this lead?" she asked, gripping tightly to his hand.

"To a street outside in the town."

"And we are going to an inn? What if someone recognizes you?"

"Most of my subjects have never been face-to-face with me. Not the ones that fancy several drinks late on a Friday night anyway."

"I'm guessing you and Greg have done this quite a bit."

"Clever girl."

"But, for some reason I get the feeling that it was all your idea, sneaking out of the castle."

He laughed. "Very clever girl," he said turning back, "what made you guess that?"

"Surely Greg didn't even know about the stairs until you showed him. So, what was so tempting in town that you had to sneak out of the castle?" she asked nudging his side.

He looked back at her, not sure how to explain. "Well, when you're a fifteen-year-old boy, and all you do all day is take lessons and go to meetings, you have to have some kind of outlet. Anything outside the castle becomes more interesting than what's in it."

"Hmm, makes sense. Your meetings are pretty boring."

They reached another set of stairs.

"This is it." They walked up a huge staircase, and he took some old brass keys out of his pocket. "You wouldn't mind holding this a moment?"

He passed her the lantern. She took it and held it up as he fumbled with the keys. She could see that there were four locks he had to turn on the underside of a sewer cover. He turned the key in each lock and lifted the cover up slowly.

He peeked to see if anyone was near. He saw the shoes of some people passing by, and could hear their voices as they headed down the street.

After some time, the voices died away, and there was nothing but silence. He slowly lifted the sewer cover off, looking about. There was nothing but small dog running and barking down the street.

"All right, it's clear," he said as he pushed the cover away and climbed out. He sat on the street looking about and extended his hand out to help her. She blew out the lantern and left it on the last step. As she scrambled out, she lost her footing and fell into him.

291

He laughed, "Easy, Miss Black." He steadied her onto her feet, then bent over and covered the sewer passage, locking all four locks with the key. They began their journey down the streets of Windsor hand in hand.

She took it all in. Other than the castle, she had not seen the town of Windsor. Looking about, it seemed to be a quiet, quaint little town. The lamp lights were softened by the foggy air rising from the ground, and other than the dog barking in the distance, she could hear nothing and saw no one. As they walked down the street, she observed the old medieval style homes. Most of the windows of the homes and buildings were now dark. But then they came upon a small house, with a candle glowing in the front window. There was something odd, almost eerie about it.

"Alex am I mad or is that house … leaning?" she said raising her brow.

"Yes, everyone calls it the 'crooked house'. It looks like someone gave it a shove."

"Interesting. Is there anything else about Windsor that is strange as that?"

"Oh yes, there are a few. But for the most part, it's a sleepy little town."

They turned the corner, walking next to the crooked house, when they got to the next intersection, Madeline could see the castle just feet away from them. She shook her head looking at it, "Sad that you can't just walk through your front door."

"Small price to pay if I don't want people to stop and talk to me about country affairs. It's really not a safe thing for me to be out in public without some kind of protection or escort."

"Don't worry your Majesty, I can protect you," she joked.

"With what exactly?"

"Oh, I'm trained in combat. You didn't know?"

He laughed warmly, "Well done, Miss Black."

He led her down a narrow, cobblestone street called Church Street. "Here we are," he said, pointing at the inn's sign.

She looked up and read the sign, "Ye Olde King's Head? That's a dumb name!"

"Don't poke fun at my bar."

She chuckled, "I'm doubting this hole in the wall is a royal residence."

"With the amount of time I've spent here with Greg it could be," he winked and held the door open. He escorted her inside, his hand at the small of her back. She tingled with his touch, despite the state of the bar. It was dimly lit with thick dark wood tables and booths. It was dank with a funny smell in the air. She questioned the last time the place had been dusted. There were no men in uniform from the castle. Just peasants dressed in drab clothing, half drunk and loud or passed out on the bar. Most seemed to be regulars, familiar with the bartender and all the other patrons. They sat down across from one another in a booth. She rested her hands on the table, but after feeling the sticky surface placed them on her lap.

"What'd will it be?" asked a rather rough looking waitress.

"Two pints," Alex said harshly. He kept his eyes glued to the table, hiding his face with his hat.

The waitress, disgusted by his odd behaviour, placed her hands on her hips. "Fine, mate." She walked away mumbling something beneath her breath that neither of them could catch.

"So this is interesting," Madeline teased, "the wealthiest man in England takes me out to a dirty little inn."

He looked abashed, "Sorry dolcezza. I just wanted to be with you outside the walls."

"It's all right," she said giving him a light push. "I was only kidding."

He got up from his side of the booth and sat next to her. He had a kind of giddiness about him that she noticed despite his trying to be invisible to everyone else there. She watched him as he glanced up at her, beaming.

The waitress walked over and set down the mugs of beer. He placed some coins on the table. She scooped them up, shaking her head and went back to the bar to chat with some customers.

Madeline took a sip of her beer and he put his arm around her waist. He took a few gulps of beer, glancing at her as he did.

"There have been things I've been wondering about you, Madeline."

"Really?" she said nervously.

"Did you grow up in London?"

"Yes," she said shortly, fearing what other questions about her past he might ask.

"What did your parents do?"

She gave him a dark look.

"What's wrong?" he asked hurt. "My parents weren't the best parents either. I've already told you a bit about that."

"I don't want to talk about them," she said firmly. "Not ever. Promise me you'll never bring them up again."

He pulled her closely to him.

"You can tell me," he said his hand caressing her cheek. "You're not my slave you know. You're so much more to me than that. If you want me to, I'll –"

"There's nothing I want you to do. I never want to see or hear of my father or mother again. Understand?"

He nodded in understanding. Her family seemed to be a sensitive topic. After all they had been through in the past few days, he did not want to do anything that might upset her. "So what's the most intriguing thing in the castle you think?" he asked, changing the subject.

"The doll's house."

He laughed, "What? I have a book of Da Vinci's scientific discoveries, Curfew Tower, where some famous royal prisoners spent their last days, more royal mews, thousands of paintings and other priceless cultural relics, and you like a doll's house!"

"I never had a doll."

His expression softened, "My dolly has never had a doll of her own?"

She smiled, "No."

He kissed her passionately, purring, "I like that I can kiss you and no one cares." He pecked her softly on the temple, "It would be lovely if we could do it all the time."

She looked about the bar. No one was looking or suspecting anything. The patrons went about their drinking, mumbling incoherently, hollering loudly at times about different things. "Actually, there was something I found interesting in the castle," she said taking a sip from her mug.

"What's that?"

"Tilly."

He sniffed.

"I take you know Tilly, hm Alex?" she said playfully.

"Yes."

"She's um, fond of you," she said imitating Tilly's squeaky voice. But he did not laugh.

"Fond is putting it lightly. I know some of the maids enjoy, well, like me." A bashful look grew upon him. It was a modest sweet face that she wanted to kiss. "Some of the girls will go out of their way to find out where I am and what time of day I'm there. I think they just want to see me or something."

She shook her head, "That's strange."

"It's not terrible though. Tilly takes things a little too far. I've caught her in my private chambers on a few occasions."

She stared, her jaw dropping, "What is she doing in your chambers? I've never been in your chambers!"

"I'm not exactly sure. Once I caught her sleeping in my bed, the other time she was coming out of my closet."

"Sleeping in your bed? That's weird." She bit her lip. "What was she doing in your closet?"

"I'd rather not know," he chortled.

"It's not funny! You should be calling in your guards on something like that."

"Madeline," he began uncomfortably, "Tilly is just a fourteen-year-old girl. Completely harmless. If I fire that poor thing, God knows what her parents would do to her."

She rolled her eyes, his empathy was touching, but naive. This girl had issues. "She was in your chambers, in your closet. Why? Other than being obsessed with you?"

"Maybe she was watching me have sex with another girl," the corner of his lips curled to a smile, and he brought his beer to his lips his gaze piercing Madeline's.

"That's different," she said, embarrassed. "I didn't know that Miss Hampton was about to corner you in Lady Watson's room."

"I'm sorry Miss Black," he smiled, "I didn't realize you were having a little thieving spree."

They paused looking at one another and laughed.

"If I were to punish every maid or noble woman that did something that was inappropriate, I wouldn't be a gentleman," he said.

"You mean not many women would like you."

"Probably not," he said his eyes twinkling, "I'm glad I decided not to pull you out of the closet."

"Why didn't you pull me from the closet? You had good reason to."

He considered her for a moment. "I suppose I didn't want to make you feel ashamed or embarrassed. That, and I didn't want you to feel uncomfortable around me."

"Why? As far as you knew, that would be the only time we would have ever met. I mean, you didn't know I was going to work at Buckingham Palace."

"Even if it was only for one night. I still wanted you to like me. I doubt you would have thought fondly of me if I pulled you out of the closet."

A few moments of silence passed, he took another sip of his pint before speaking again, "You know, we won't have much time together once the Spanish royals come."

"I know," she said, frowning. She was hoping they wouldn't talk about them.

"I can't have anyone thinking that I'm not interested in Sofia. We need to keep the Princess here until after the war ends."

"That could be years," she said in annoyance.

"I know. In the meantime, we could look for other reasons for me to stay in England. If I keep refusing to go to war without a good cause, I will be seen as a weak leader, and if that happens, Bathory will take advantage. Could you imagine a country run by him? Then after he died, Susanna Bathory?"

She pressed her lips together. She had never thought of the 'Honourable' Susanna running the country. She barely knew her, but knew she was selfish and had some perverse beliefs about rank and status. Susanna would treat commoners like barnyard animals; their purpose would be to sacrifice for nobles. She shuddered at the thought. "What do you want from me, Alex?"

"Whatever you see, when I'm entertaining the Princess, don't forget it's an act. I'm not in love with her."

Strangely, when she first saw Alex with Miss Hampton, she was not seriously envious. Perhaps this was because Alex was not hers. Now that they were seeing each other, the idea of a princess coming and spending quality time with him bothered her. She couldn't have quality time with Alex whenever she wanted. They had to keep their relationship a secret. The sneaking around was exhausting. Just thinking about it made her feel jealous of how simple it was for Princess Sofia. The Princess could express her feelings for Alex and not be judged. Meanwhile, Madeline was expected to take orders from him. If she tried to have a personal relationship with him, even a friendship, people would be suspicious and disgusted.

He watched as the wheels turned in her head and saw the anger grow on her face. Her fingers began tapping the dirty table.

"Madeline, you should feel sorry for Sofia. I'm going to lead her on to think I'm going to marry her. Then I'll end up being a complete scoundrel."

She paid no attention to anything that he said, but started with on him with her fears, "Have you met her before?"

"No."

"Then how do you know you won't fall in love with her? How can you know?"

He held her close and cupped her face gently in his hands. "There's no room for her in my heart." He pulled her closely again, pressing his thick warm lips hard against hers. He swirled his tongue about hers gently exciting her. As his wet lips continued to entwine with hers, they drowned out the world around them, lost in their embrace. After several minutes of kissing, he let out a low groan, as exciting as it was a big part of him wished they were alone. He rocked her gently in his arms as they cuddled cheek to cheek.

20

DOLLED UP

The weeks leading up to the Spanish royals' visit went by quickly. Alex went out of his way to make time for Madeline. This included having Greg arrange her schedule again, and sneaking off to the inn with her in the night. He was also more amorous too, seducing her just about every day; she soon needed to be supplied with more Queen Anne's Lace. Not that she minded. She figured he was trying to make up for the situation they were in.

Most nights they went to the King's Head inn, Alex, of course, had his questions about her past and she'd always change the subject.

"What exactly is your and Miss Hampton's relationship?" she asked one night.

He shook his head, "I think because she is the Duke of Axford's goddaughter, people at court suspect that maybe one day she might become Queen of England."

"Aside from princesses, I suppose she'd be your best match. The Hamptons are very wealthy and have a clean reputation."

He chuckled, "No, they aren't as proper as they appear. Trust me when I say this, Miss Hampton is far from being a lady. She can be downright vicious and rude at times."

"Really? Then why were you in her company?" she asked with a mischievous grin.

"Back at Buckingham Palace, do you remember how I told you that I needed to know where the Duke of Axford's loyalties lay?"

"Yes."

"Miss Hampton might be the only person who knows the answer to that. The Duke doesn't spend much time in the company of others unless he is doing business. Miss Hampton is the only person he has afternoon tea with."

"Oh. So the night at the Watsons —"

"I was digging for information. She knew that."

Madeline nodded in understanding. She always felt that their relationship seemed very strange. But now it made sense. Miss Hampton was trading Alex information for sex. She certainly wasn't the sweet innocent lady The Society Pages had made her out to be.

Other than going to the King's Head with Alex, Madeline spent much of her time helping prepare for the Spanish royals. There was a welcoming banquet planned, which was more effort than the small party he threw a couple of weeks before. He also allowed the Spanish their own set of private apartments and chambers. The rooms had to be cleaned, and each royal would be assigned two servants to wait upon them. Madeline was not one of them, Alex had made sure of that.

Preparations aside, it was business as usual, and she continued to serve tea in the House of Lord that now convened in Windsor Castle. Bathory was irritated throughout most of the meetings, making snide remarks beneath his breath about all of Alex's decisions. Alex and the other Lords seemed to ignore his behaviour. He was a childish man, and Madeline wondered how he rallied any supporters behind him.

The night before the Princess was to arrive, Greg gave Madeline a note that instructed her to meet Alex in the small office at nine. She guessed he wanted to have one last night out together in Windsor, but he was late. She waited until nine thirty then began questioning whether she should leave.

Out of boredom, she began searching the office looking at the paintings on the walls, and through the writing desk. The writing desk had nothing of interest. Just a few scrap pieces of paper, some quills and peasants' clothes. The paintings on the walls were all beautiful scenes of royal families from years before. She closely inspected a huge painting of three little princesses playing together. The eldest was around seven or eight, the next was four or five and the last was a toddler. It was a sweet moment between the girls, and she stared wondering whom they were. She noticed the artist used a heavy amount of oil paint. There was so much there were globs of it dried to the canvas. She touched the paint softly.

CRASH

The painting fell from the wall to the floor, sitting on its edge. She gasped and looked about frantically, wondering if anyone heard. She quickly hid under the writing desk and waited.

No one came, so she came out of her hiding place and looked over at the painting. It had fallen so easily, and seeing the wall, she understood why. A painting was hidden behind it. A face of a young boy with smooth black hair and tan skin sat on a white horse,

302

brandishing his sword in the air. The horse stood on its hind legs leaning back, kicking its front feet into the air. Surrounding the horse were bodies of several dead men. She recognized him immediately. It was Alex, celebrating his victory against the Irish rebels.

"I hate that painting."

She turned stunned to see him at her side.

"Blast! You scared me," she said holding her hand to her chest. "I'm guessing that's why you hide it in this office?"

"I would destroy it, except the artist that did it still visits the castle from time to time."

She could understand why he hated it. It was grotesque, but she still wondered, "Do you feel guilty for killing them?"

"No. I did what any good soldier would do. I did what was best for my country."

"If you had to do it again, would you?"

"Yes," he said shortly.

"Why do you hide the picture then?"

"There is nothing to boast about in taking a man's life, even if there's just cause." He looked away somewhat irritated.

She nodded her head realizing the sensitivity of the matter. "Sorry, I shouldn't be asking these kinds of questions."

"Well," he sighed, "that day was the worst day of my life. Sorry, but I don't like to talk about it."

"Have you ever told anyone?"

"No one."

303

"Not even Greg?"

"Nope."

"What happened?"

He stared at her in surprise that she had the nerve to ask. "I'm sorry Madeline, that's just not something I share with people."

"Why?"

"Because what everyone believed to have happened, didn't really happen."

"But everyone says you're a war hero. Are you saying you're not?"

"Well —" he paused, going red. She was smart. Now he'd have to tell her; otherwise, she might assume he was a coward. "I did fight them, it's just not the sword wielding story everyone thinks it is."

"So you outsmarted them?"

He smiled, "I thought I had outsmarted everyone concerning this matter … until now."

She leaned on the desk, crossing her arms, "Let's hear it then."

He took a deep breath then, over the next half hour, he explained what had really happened. Once he finished, he surveyed the stunned expression on her face. He bit his lip.

"That doesn't make you any less of a hero, Alex," she said rubbing his arm. "Actually, I think you're the bravest person I've ever met."

"It wasn't about bravery. It was about survival."

She nodded feeling somewhat awkward, she then walked over to the painting of the princesses and tried to put it back up, but it was too heavy. He walked over, and together they hung it on the wall.

"By the way, I'm sorry I was late," he said. "I was waiting for something."

"It's all right. Let's get going."

He smiled, "No. I thought we'd stay here tonight. I have something for you."

He gave her a small box, and she opened it excitedly. No one had ever wrapped a gift for her. She took the lid off the box and beneath the wrappings, she found a breathtakingly beautiful porcelain doll. It had shiny black hair, green eyes and ruby red lips and wore an exquisite blue dress and an emerald necklace and earring set.

"Oh Alex," she gushed, pulling it out of its box. "She's gorgeous! My first doll!"

"I know," he grinned. "Who does she look like?"

She was tempted to say it looked like her mother, but stopped herself. "Me?" she asked.

"Yes," he laughed. "Smell her hair."

She brought the hair to her nose, "Rosewater," she said slowly.

He pulled a bottle from out of the wrappings, "Here," he said giving her a bottle of rosewater.

She looked at him overwhelmed by his gift. "Alex this is — she's perfect. I don't know what to say."

"You're right she is perfect," he said as he gently stroked her cheek.

Her cheeks flushed as he bent down to kiss her.

"So what do you want to do tonight, dolcezza?" he said embracing her.

She thought for a moment. There was not much they could do. They could not have dinner together, and it was too late to go horse riding. She realized what she wanted to do. "I want to sleep next to you, in your chambers tonight."

He turned away, knowing he should have expected that answer from her. "How about dinner? I could order some food to the chamber, whatever you like, and we could eat together."

She had never thought of that. But she wondered why he was ignoring her request of sleeping next to each other.

"Then we could sleep together," she added.

He gripped the back of the writing desk chair, "Yes, yes I suppose we could," he said hesitantly. "So what would you like for dinner?"

"What can I have?"

"Just about anything you could imagine."

She laughed, thinking he was joking. "I'll have lobster and caviar then!"

He considered her, realizing that she had probably never experienced fine dining on a royal scale. "Tell you what, I'll order some dishes and delicacies you've never tried. You'll eat like a queen."

She wriggled in excitement.

"Go to my chambers and I'll go and order someone to get the food."

21

PRIVATE DINNER

After putting away her new doll and rosewater in her dormitory, Madeline headed down to the Round Tower. She had never been in Alex's room before. Mr. Tinney had taken them to the Round Tower where he stayed, but they had never entered his apartments. Only his head servants, valets, guards and Sir Ashton Giles were allowed in. Greg Umbridge was most likely the only person who could enter at will.

When she finally reached the apartments, she noticed some guards at his apartments' entrance. She held her breath. Alex had forgotten about them. Both of them were tall, brawny and intimidating. The one on the left had a large gash across his cheek. She knew these men were experienced; otherwise, they wouldn't be where they were. She casually walked by them as though she were on her way to another part of the castle.

Both guards eyed one another as she walked by. It was odd that she was in this part of the castle, especially at this time of night. She sped faster down the hall, feeling their eyes watching her.

"Excuse me? Miss?" one of them called.

She hesitantly turned around to face them. "Yes, gentlemen?" she said in a girlish tone.

"What do you think you're doing up and about the castle this time of night?"

"Well, I was, um I was –" her voice trailed off. She couldn't think of a quick lie. They stared at her suspiciously.

"Perhaps we should find Mr. Tinney or Lord Cadogan," began the one with the gash. "We can't have people wandering about the King's Apartments thinking nothing of it."

"Miss Black!" said a familiar voice. Madeline turned to see Greg Umbridge turn the corner of the hall, walking towards them. "These are not my chambers," he continued. "They are the King's Apartments. Must I have to run around the castle to be sure I get some tea?"

The guards gave one another a strange look.

"Greg Umbridge wanting a spot of tea rather than his usually night cap?" asked the guard with the gash.

"Not bloody likely," said the other.

She could not believe the audacity of the men. That they spoke to the King's most trusted friend that way, was appalling. She realized why he disliked the guards at Windsor Castle so much. Nonetheless, Greg held his own.

"Yes, I suppose that is true. But while you'll be watching over a grown man tonight, I'll be spending my evening with stiff drinks, chasing this cute maid about the castle. Does your night end in a wonderful drunken stupor with a beautiful woman? I think not."

She stood staring in disgust at what he was suggesting, but given her situation, there wasn't much she could say.

"You think we'll believe that you will be with this woman tonight?!" The one with the gash asked. They both howled in laughter stomping their feet on the ground, holding their bellies howling. Though she'd never dream of spending the night with Greg, she felt sorry for him. Greg said nothing but confidently wrapped his arm around her. She gave a weak smile.

"Come with me darling. I'll see you later, gentlemen."

Their laughter was replaced with dumbfounded expressions. Greg led her down the hall, a triumphant grin on his face. At the corner, they turned out of sight down another hall, filled with statues of knights in armour. "Thank you, Madeline."

"I'd prefer you not tell Alex about this."

He laughed, "Alex sent me here after he had realized he sent you down here to deal with the guards."

She smiled, "I owe you, Greg."

"You and Alex both," he said. "Follow me."

They set off down the hall. After they had passed the third knight in armour, he directed her to the wall, "Behind this painting is a secret passage to Alex's Drawing Room." He reached behind the knight and pulled a lever. The painting moved forward from the wall, revealing a door. She pulled the heavy painting and stepped inside. "How do I get there?"

"Are you serious?" he said laughing. "Just go back the way we came of course."

"But where is the door?"

"You'll see it."

She gave him a curious look as she peeked into the dark passage. Reading her mind, Greg reached inside of the hole in the wall and pulled out a small oil lamp and match. He lit the lamp and handed it to her. "Right. This is all new to you I suppose."

He closed the painting door behind her. She lifted the lamp as she walked down the passageway. The walls were decorated with paintings and blue damask wallpaper. She moved through the passage turning around the corner. She came to a door, outlined with a huge decorative gold gilt frame and laughed inwardly. The guards were just on the other side of the wall. Little did they know she was about to break into the King's Apartments.

She turned the handle, pushed the enormous door open and spilled out into the King's Drawing Room. She closed the door behind her and surveyed the room. The room was immense, with a large, vaulted ceiling painted with a scene of Greek gods, floating amongst the clouds in the heavens. Alcoves housed beautiful Grecian statues, each between huge oil paintings of other Kings and Queens of England. The walls were also lined with silk chairs and half-moon marble tables. There was a huge window on the opposite end of the entrance, and to her right she could see another door, which must have led to the King's Bedchamber.

In the centre of the room, in front of the fireplace, were two large sofas and two winged backed chairs. She sat down on one of the sofas. As she waited, she felt something drip down from the ceiling. She looked about and saw a droplet of wax onto a crystal ice bucket on the table beside her. She looked up at a large chandelier. It held hundreds of candles some of which were dripping wax. Fear came over her as she realized that someone might come in at any moment to check and relight them since some of them were reaching their ends.

Just then, the door opened. She jumped up startled. To her relief it was Alex. He quickly shut the door, "Sorry, did I scare you?"

She shook her head chortling at herself, "Yes. I was just thinking that maybe someone might come in here to light the candles."

"Don't worry about that. They won't come until tomorrow afternoon to replace and relight the candles." He walked toward her, took both her hands in his and kissed them. "It'll be a while, you can't rush gourmet food."

They sat on the sofa, he reached his arm around her. They were silent for a few long minutes, both rattled by the thoughts of Princess Sofia.

"They are coming tomorrow," he said, breaking the tension. "Are you worried?"

"I know you will tell me not to be," she began, relieved that he was willing to talk about it. "I just can't help it though. What if she is an incredible girl? What if you fall in love with her?" She broke down weeping.

He held her closely, "I've met princesses all over Europe. None of them have impressed me. They all seem to think and act like every other princess. Besides, whoever I marry will have to be able to tolerate the rudest person in the world."

She gave him an odd look as she wiped away her tears. He was never rude. He was always chivalrous. She had once noticed that he had an endearing habit of always standing at attention, with his hands behind his back, whenever she entered a room. She wasn't sure if he did this for the rest of the maids. But she knew Greg Umbridge would never think to be so gentlemanly.

"Oh," she said as it dawned on her, "you mean Greg."

311

He laughed, "I could never get rid of him. No matter what princess came along." A concerned expression fell on his face. "You don't have any problems with him, do you?"

She giggled, "Of course not. He's a bit of a rogue as you say, but he means well."

He smiled, "I'm glad you feel that way."

"What are princesses like? You say none impress you, why?"

"You'll find out soon enough dolcezza. They are demanding, nag constantly, and they count on daddy to give them everything they ask for. Marrying a woman like that means that someday you'll have to take daddy's place, and give her everything she asks for. I won't do that. It's hard to keep someone like that happy."

She knew of the kind of woman he described. Lady Watson was a demanding nag. Lord Watson hated her for it because she offered nothing in return. Not love, nurturing or kindness. She was selfish from the day she was born, and she probably would be until the day she died.

"But you know," she began, deciding to play devil's advocate. "By law, wives are considered the property of the husband. I wouldn't want a man that considered me his property."

"I don't consider you property. You know that. I'll tear up the ownership papers when we get back to Buckingham Palace."

"Oh really? You can tear up the papers your Majesty," she said in a flirty tone, "but I still believe you see me as property."

"Hmm, what can I do to convince you that I don't?"

"Give me whatever I ask for."

"All right, I'll give you whatever you ask for," he whispered softly in her ear.

"You're willing to give me whatever I ask for? I thought that you wouldn't do that for any woman?" she asked as she light-heartedly pushed him in the chest.

"Yes, but you're the only exception to my rule."

He kissed her softly across her shoulder and neck, and she could feel her skin tingle with his warm breath. She thought of the first time they had met, and he told Lady Watson that 'exceptions could be made'. Her cheeks became rosy at the thought.

"So I'm your exception?" she whispered, a hint of girlish excitement in her voice.

"My only exception."

Just then there was a tapping at the door.

"Must be the food. Go and hide in the Bedchamber," he said quickly.

"Your only exception has to go hide in your Bedchamber?"

The servant at the door pounded harder.

"Stay then. Should be interesting to see what would happen."

She shook her head, "We can't do that," she scurried over to the Bedchamber and hid inside.

"Enter," he called.

As Alex received the dinner, Madeline surveyed his Bedchamber. It didn't have the Greek theme like his Drawing Room. The colours were that of royalty. The walls were covered in crimson silk and had several large tapestries of people, each framed

313

with thick gold gilt. His bed had a canopy of dark purple and green fabric. A towering gold painted crown at the top of the canopy, swept all the material into loose drapes, each finished with gold fringes.

There were two large fireplaces with white marble mantles mounted around them. A gigantic window on the other side of the room had a striking view of the moon and stars. She looked up at the ceiling and saw another painting similar to the one in his Drawing Room, except it showed the gods at night; floating amongst the clouds, sleeping and yawning. Goddesses read stories to young children. Elaborate woodcarvings of cherubs holding swags of fruit and flowers framed the ceiling like crown moulding. Two large chandeliers kept the room dimly lit. Across from her, there was a smaller door, and she figured it was his closet. She cocked her head, wondering how Tilly managed to get inside without getting caught. She walked past his bed and one of the fireplaces, to the large window and gazed up at the night sky.

Alex walked in, pulling in a cart full of food. "Are you ready to dine like royalty, Miss Black?"

She grinned almost jumping in excitement. She didn't want to seem ridiculous, but other than the little picnic he had treated her to, she hadn't tried many delicacies. "Can we eat next to the window, under the stars?"

"Of course," he rolled the cart next to the window. He walked over to the wall and pulled out two red and gold chairs and placed them by the window.

"There's no table Alex, perhaps we should just eat on the floor?"

"You're not eating on the floor." He walked to the opposite corner of the room, next to his closet door, where a large round black and gold table stood. He heaved it up with both arms.

"Alex! That's too heavy! Put that down."

He said nothing but she heard him breathe as he brought it over and set it down. He set the chairs next to it and pulled one out for her, gesturing her to have a seat. "Votre chaise, Mademoiselle Black."

She sat down, and he tucked her in. She flushed, giddy. Something was sexy about his being able to speak French.

"Mademoiselle means 'Miss', doesn't it?" she asked.

"Mademoiselle Black means Miss Black."

He took one of the silver domes off the cart and set it in the middle of the table. Then he took out two bone china plates and some silver forks and knives and set them down. He placed a napkin across her lap and winked at her.

"You're supposed to set out the plates and cutlery first your Majesty," she teased.

"You'd think after years of being served I'd know that," he said as he took out a bottle of wine and poured them each a glass.

"Oh! Wine?! What kind is it?"

"Romanee-Conti."

She gave a baffled expression.

"It's a French Vintage. Very famous. Very expensive." He removed the silver dome from the first plate.

"What's this?" she asked looking at the dish curiously. "Asparagus?"

"Yes, I thought we'd start with some simple food first. This is poached asparagus with orange sauce."

He sat down and placed his napkin around his collar. She put down her fork realizing she had not put her napkin on her lap, and she was eating with a king. Embarrassed, she set it back in its place, unfolded her napkin and placed it on her lap. He served some asparagus to her. She waited for him to eat his first.

"Go on, eat," he said as he served himself.

She speared the asparagus and took a bite. "Mmm, this is delicious."

"I'm glad you think so."

They ate, and though she did her best to try to be a lady, she found it difficult. It was too good to put her fork down and have a polite conversation, which he did from time to time. She nodded as she listened to him tell her about his day. She finished her plate and looked over at his half-full plate. Somewhat embarrassed, she put down her fork and continued listening to his story of how Greg was trying to cheat at chess.

"After years of playing with him, he still thinks he can move the pieces while my back is turned. I only talked to Ashton for ten seconds, and he thinks he can pull the wool over my eyes."

"Has he ever beaten you by cheating?"

"No."

"Maybe you should let him win for a change."

"What's the point in that?" he asked dumbfounded.

"Maybe he'll think he could win and stop trying to cheat."

He laughed, "No I doubt that. Greg would dance like a fool around me then tell me he never wants to play a game of chess again."

"Alex, that's ridiculous. I'm sure he wouldn't do that."

"He usually does it if he beats one of the Lords at cards. He did beat me at cards once. We haven't played cards since," said Alex looking peeved.

She rolled her eyes, "How long ago was that?"

"I was nineteen. He was twenty."

"Tell me something, do you win at mostly everything?"

"Well yes," he began a little abashed. "But —"

"Let him have it."

"If I let him win at something out of sympathy, I don't think I could consider myself a gentleman. Gentlemen are honest in these types of matters."

"Gentlemen are honest?" she replied giving him a look. "No. You just hate losing."

"I —," he noticed her empty plate. "Here," he said as he passed the next dish. "These are devilled quail eggs with caviar."

"Don't you go trying to change the subject with good food your Majesty."

"I wasn't doing that!" he said chortling.

"Oh, and now you're lying. That's not a gentlemanly thing to do."

"Fine. All right. I'm a sore loser. But that's only because I don't lose."

"Aren't we cocky?"

"Sorry if I sound cocky, but other than that card game, I can't think of any other game I've lost to him."

"Is Greg better than you at anything?" she asked, amazed that Alex barely lost at anything. He thought for a few moments.

"He can handle more alcohol than me. But I'm not much of a drinker so —"

"Do you play drinking games?" she asked taking a bite of one of her quail eggs.

"No."

"Oh, this is excellent," she said tasting the egg. She looked at him, a miffed expression on her face. She understood why he set the quail eggs in front of her before he finished his asparagus; to distract her. She persisted, "So you only play games that you win at?"

"Well, no."

"Yes, you do. Otherwise, by now the two of you would have played a drinking game, and Greg would have won."

He was speechless. There was some truth to what she was saying. He was amazed he lost an argument to her. "Drinking isn't a game or sport," he said, after a minute.

"Depends whom you ask. My father made a regular game of it." She stopped talking, realizing that she had brought up her father. She looked down, wondering if he would ask more questions about him. To her surprise he did not, and asked her what she thought of the quail eggs instead.

They continued chatting, and she asked him more about his childhood and growing up in Windsor Castle. He tried to ask her about her upbringing. But she ignored the questions by changing the subject or asking something about him. This worried him, and he began to wonder if she was ever going to let him into her past.

Alex kept bringing out dishes, each one more impressive than the last. After the quail eggs and caviar, there was tonnarelli pasta with sea urchin eggs, saffron and mussels. The pasta was divine like all the others dishes, but nothing could have prepared her for the dish afterward.

"This is one of the most interesting dishes you'll ever eat," he said taking off the silver dome. Underneath the dome was lobster.

She grew excited. "Lobster! I've always wanted to try it," she said excitedly. She grabbed her fork and lunged for the plate.

"Ah, ah, ah, Miss Black," he said, pulling away the plate. "You forgot your manners. Besides, this just isn't any kind of lobster. I want you to know what it is you're eating."

She gave him a look, but he continued, "This is a Scottish lobster, with white truffle, caviar and abalone."

"Abalone? What's that?"

"Sea snail."

"Yuck!"

"It's on the plate because it's delicious. It also has gold leaf sprinkled all about," he said pointing to the gold flakes.

"What does that mean? I'm eating gold?" she asked astounded.

"Precisely, Miss Black," he smiled.

She gaped at him, "How much do you think it cost to make that?"

"You don't want to know. Just enjoy."

She was flattered that he was treating her to the best of what his kitchen had to offer. But she was beginning to have a hard time accepting it. "That's a little extravagant don't you think? I mean all this for —"

"Madeline," he interrupted, "if you can't be my Queen, at least let me treat you like one."

Her cheeks turned a rosy pink. Alex had never said that he loved her, but if he wished her to be his Queen, there was a chance he did. Looking at the lobster in front of her, she speared it with her fork deciding it was okay to be extravagant sometimes. The lobster shell had been cracked and opened, so Madeline did not have too much difficulty eating it. Though, Alex had to teach her how to open the claws.

Dessert was just as extravagant as the course before it. He set something before her that she'd heard of but never seen, "Is that ice cream?" she asked, hopeful.

"Yes," he said simply.

Her jaw dropped. Royalty or the extremely wealthy ate ice cream. She'd remembered Michel, attempt to make it for Lady Watson, several times. Unfortunately for him, he always failed. She brought a spoonful up to her lips and the cold cream melted in her mouth. "Mmm, is this vanilla?"

"Yes, it was made with vanilla beans from Africa, I believe. I think the chocolate bits are from Belgium."

She said nothing, dumbstruck as she savoured every spoonful. As she did, she wondered how Alex had become such a level headed person. It did not seem as though he was denied anything, even when it came to food. Yet, he wasn't demanding or spoiled, not like many aristocrats of his court.

After they finished, the cart full of dirty plates, and their bellies full, they went to work on finishing off the bottle of wine. Though she was wary of drinking too much, she couldn't help herself. It was a delicious wine. As they talked, she could feel herself become tipsy. She fell about the table, giggling at Alex's retelling of the kind of mischief he and Greg used to get into when they were younger.

"Madeline you have fantastic breasts," he smiled swirling his wine in his glass, "take them out I want to see them."

She tried to laugh it off, then noticed the serious look on his face and stopped.

"Don't make me wait. Those pretty apples are one of the first things I ever noticed about you. Take off your dress and play with them."

Flushing she looked down to the floor. Stripping down in front of him completely, him talking dirty to her gave her second thoughts. She could not help but wonder how many other gorgeous noble women and princesses he had done this with. How many nasty words of praise he had given them. She didn't want him to start asking that she talk dirty too, then she'd sound like a common prostitute. She had wanted their last night to be a gentle, intimate evening.

"You treat me like I'm your whore sometimes. Don't talk to me that way," she said softly.

He sat in silence for a moment, dumbfounded before he finally spoke, "I don't understand. You're willing to —"

"All right, I've done things with you. But I'm not going to talk dirty to you. Forget it."

"Why?" he asked calmly.

"I'm not comfortable with that."

He couldn't help but to laugh, "I have talked dirty to you before, dolcezza. You've never had a problem with it. What's wrong now?" He held her cheek, a naughty smile on his face.

"Maybe I should get going," she said turning on her heel, heading toward his Drawing Room. She didn't want to tell him why it made her uneasy. The explanation in itself was embarrassing.

"I'm sorry if I said something that's upset you. Please come back." But she continued walking. He ran toward the door blocking her, "If you want to leave that's fine, but at least tell me why you're not comfortable with it."

She folded her arms, glaring at him but knew he would not let her pass without an explanation. She decided to deliver the truth, thinking it would shut him up and make him realize how ridiculous he was being.

"You are going to tell me how perfect every body part is? How excited you are to see me? Alex, please. You've probably been with half the ladies of your court. Ladies like Miss Hampton or Miss Cavendish, who have the silkiest hands and not a hair out of place. I love being with you, but honestly, sometimes the dirty and sweet nothings that come out of your mouth humiliate me. I have a maid's rough hands and scars across my back. I don't have servants apply creams, doing my hair, and dressing me to make me look like a porcelain doll." She rolled her eyes as she pushed past him. But he scooped her up and threw her over his shoulder.

"Let me down!" she cried out. She wriggled about throwing her fists onto his back. Despite this, he effortless carried her into his closet where there were mirrors all about the room. He planted her in front of one. "Look," he commanded.

She looked up into the mirror, then turned away shaking her head. He clasped his palms on each side of her jaw. "Look," he repeated more sternly.

She stared into the mirror at her emerald eyes, her black tresses between his fingers.

"You're right Madeline, I've been with some pretty noble girls. But you must be blind if you think they hold a candle to you. Be honest, have you ever seen a girl with sparkling green eyes and black as night hair like yours? I know I haven't, and I've been all over Europe."

Not used to compliments, she forced her eyes to the floor, "You've seen girls with green eyes and black hair before, I'm sure."

"Yes, but they don't have a pretty chisel face with a cute nose and a naturally creamy soft complexion. Honestly, I've never known a woman with such natural beauty. You turn heads. You walk into a House of Lords meeting, and suddenly, the Duke of Axford wakes up from the stupor he's been in for years. Hell, so do the rest of the men. As soon as you enter, all of them start paying attention because they'd all hate to look foolish in front of the cute, sexy maid. Say whatever you'd like about all the other women I've known. If they didn't have their maids dolling them up every morning, most of them wouldn't turn heads."

"Tsk! The Lords look at me?" she asked incredulously, "I think all that is in your head."

"I know those men. I've sat through meetings with them for the last twelve years. You've made an impression on them ... and me."

He wrapped his arms around her waist, kissing her shoulder and neck, leading back up to her ear. She closed her eyes, melting into his hard body. He could feel her relenting her objections, believing his words.

"All the ladies I have ever known want a crown," he whispered, "I will never tire of you. You know how to thrill me. You damn well know you could have me on my knees begging for you. No woman will ever compare to you." He got down to his knees, "Madeline Black if you don't allow me the pleasure of telling you how much I love every piece of you, I'll go to sleep heartbroken." The sweetest pout spread across his mouth as he took her hands in his.

Through the corner of her eye, she could see the reflection of them in the mirror; him, in his expensive tailored clothes, on his knees in front of her. The sight of it made her well up in tears. No one had ever made her feel so desirable. She gave in. "We'll try it. But if I want it to stop, we stop."

"Yes," he said as he rose from the floor. He scooped her into his arms, carrying her over the threshold as they reentered his bedroom. He set her down on his bed and kissed her slowly. A fluttering began inside of her, knowing how he felt about her. The idea of him watching and commenting on her body made her hot. She held his face with both her hands consuming every movement of his lips and tongue. He pulled back, "Now, take off your dress."

The sexual tension crawled through her nerves like electricity, and she could feel her skin shiver. She reached back and slowly undid the lace to her stays. Slipping off the bed, she let the dress drop to her ankles. Her soft breasts bounced out.

"Beautiful. Just beautiful," he said with a light smile tracing his lips as he stared at her chest. "You have a perfect set of tits. Touch them for me. Make those sweet pink nipples nice and hard."

It was lewd but arousing. She looked at him and surrendered, pinching her nipples and squeezing her breasts. She sighed. It was erotic, him watching. She continued massaging her breasts and playing with her nipples. His eyes absorbed her every twist, mutter and shudder, "God, you make my blood hot, I'm so hard."

He began to touch his cock through the material of his trousers. "Keep touching them," he said watching as he groaned rubbing the bulge.

Her eyes glowed with lust as she watched him, the material becoming wet with his arousal. She salivated at the thought of him taking it out and stroking it skin on skin in front of her. "Say it Madeline. Ask me to take it out."

"Take it out," she muttered.

"Take what out Miss Black?" he said his voice smooth as wine.

She opened her mouth to speak, but her mouth became dry and her head blank.

"Cat got your tongue?" he said knowingly. "He won't come out to play unless you ask ... nicely."

She shook her head, "You can't keep him in your trousers."

Alex said nothing but walked toward her embracing her with a soft kiss. "We'll see about that won't we?" he said staring at her lips. He then reached around her placing both palms on her bottom squeezing her cheeks hard. "You have a sweet little tush." He intertwined his lips with hers, caressing her tongue with his.

He lowered down to his knees, leaving a trail of kisses between her breasts and down her stomach. She giggled excitedly, as he kissed her body. Then he grabbed her hips and whirled her around so that her arse was in his face. He feverishly kissed her cheeks grabbing and squeezing her.

"Alex!" she wailed as she lost balance and nearly tumbled onto the bed. She planted her palms first, locking her elbows so she didn't fall flat on her face. Alex watched, bemused, her small frame leaning over his bed.

"I love it when you bend over naked. Then I can see your pretty cunt next to your cute derriere," he grunted as he moved to her on his knees.

She gasped, stunned by his vulgarity.

"Aw, did those dirty little words scare you?" he teased as he placed his hands on her. "But that's what it is, isn't it? A Gorgeous. Slippery. Cunt." His breathing hard, he kissed and sucked her flesh, "Your skin is so creamy and supple," he mumbled between kisses, "it drives me wild."

"Alex," she sighed, enjoying his attention. He spread her fleshy orbs apart, Madeline could feel his eyes upon her and she could feel every hair on her skin rise.

"Tell me you're beautiful Madeline."

"What?" she asked confused.

"I'm going to sit here with your cheeks spread and stare at your sweet arse and cunt until you admit to me that you think you're gorgeous."

"What? Alex!" she said cocking her head back. "Don't be absurd."

She tried to break free of him, but his strength held her in place.

"I'm not being absurd. You've had the King of England get on his knees kissing your arse just for the sheer pleasure of it. I could have any woman's arse. But I want yours. There must be a part of you that knows you're beautiful?"

His words made her hot and he watched as her pussy began to glisten with need for him.

"If you want me to lick that pretty little cunt, you'd better tell me you're beautiful."

She whimpered at his dirty words, tantalized by them. He smacked her arse, commanding her again.

Her knees buckled, her emotions overwhelmed, her sex swollen and teeming wet with longing. "I'm beautiful," she cried.

"Tell me you're gorgeous. Tell me you're the sexiest woman to walk this earth — because you are."

He smacked her again and she cried the words out. She jumped as she felt his tongue, flat against her pussy licking all the way to her asshole. Her elbows gave way and she crashed onto the mattress, moaning. Alex quickly began flicking his tongue between her wet slit and hood. Her body, already wracked with desire for him, came hard. "Uuuhhhh! Oh, I'm cumming! Huh! AAAAAAAAAAHHHHHHHHHH!"

His fingers dug into her bottom as he lapped her up. When he finished, he gracefully traced his fingertips up her back, across her scars, and wrapped his arms around her convulsing frame.

"I swear I can barely control myself around you. I want to hear you moan and scream a thousand times over — then a thousand times more."

"Take it out," she said grabbing at his trousers.

Alex restrained her, holding her arms down. "Tell me how badly you want it."

"Mm Alex," she looked away mortified. She wriggled her hips, yearning for him to be inside her. "Please, Alex," she begged pouting.

He was tempted to give in, but he pressed her, "Do you want my prick or not? I think if you want it badly enough, you'll say just about anything to get it."

"You want it just as badly as I do," Madeline countered.

"It won't be easy, but I'll restrain myself. How else will I ever see you act and talk in the way I like? Besides, deep down, you know you like it too," he smiled with a carnivorous expression on his face.

She sighed. Not only was he right, but her sexual frustration was growing by the second. She could feel her need for him radiate from her sex to every part of her being. "Take it out Alex, take your cock out of your trousers."

"Why should I?" he asked suggestively.

"Because I want to see it. I want to see you," she paused. "I want to see your big hard cock," she finished, her voice trembling.

With a triumphant look on his face, Alex dropped his trousers and taking her in his arms, began kissing her.

Madeline pushed him back, smiling. "Stroke your cock Alex," she said wondering if it would mortify him as much as it did her. "I want to see you play with your big dick," she giggled.

Alex did not laugh or show any sign of humiliation. He stepped out of his trousers and stripped himself as he casually walked over to the table next to the fire. He grabbed a chair and dragged it next to the bed. "Lie on the bed and spread your thighs. I want to watch your pussy while I do this."

She crawled up onto the bed, grabbing some pillows to prop herself up. She wanted to watch him. She lay on the bed the pillows beneath her head, her knees still touching.

"I need you to spread your legs nice and wide," he demanded. She obeyed. Alex sat in his chair staring at her pussy, his hand grasping around his sex. He grunted, "I can see why men call it a flower," he said staring at her, parting her gently with his fingers. "It's delicate," he breathed her in, taking in her scent. "I want to watch you play with yourself." He took her soft hand and placed it on her sex, "Show me what you like."

"Like you don't already know."

He laughed, "Educate me anyway."

She hesitated, she had never masturbated in front of anyone. She felt awkward even when she did it alone. But she paused as she saw him, confident in his skin as he pleasured himself, his normally large hand looking small against his cock. She bit her lip, feeling tempted to ravage him. "God that's such a hot sweet little cunt," he began as he gawked at her wet pussy. "Honestly, I've never seen a girl cum like you do," he encouraged, as he stroked himself. "Please do us both a favour and shove a few fingers up there. I want to watch you cum everywhere."

Madeline obediently massaged and fingered her pussy, and she found it gave her some relief from her urge to jump him. She reamed into herself, trying to satisfy her need. Watching her, Alex was beside himself and soon began groaning, feeling an intoxicating heat spin the room around him. As he rubbed his red, swollen prick harder and faster, she could see a bead of pre-cum drip from his tip

"Oh Alex," she moaned, her eyes glued to him. "I'll cum for you," she promised, knowing he was close to his peak. Quickening the pace of her fingers, her legs began twitching.

"Oh fuck," Alex cried, trying to keep himself together. She shrieked as she came onto the bed, calling his name, begging for him. Alex bolted from his chair standing over her, his cock eager and angry from being denied her so long.

"Where do you want it?" he grunted. "Here," she said touching her pussy lips, "Or here," he said kissing her mouth. Madeline was torn and did not answer. She wanted him in both places. Alex could see her frustration and without another word, barged himself into her hot pussy.

"Oooohhhh Alex yes! Fuck my cunt!"

"That's. My. Dirty. Girl," he yelled thrusting between each word, Madeline whimpered in pleasure. Alex clutched her arse with his hands, filling her to the hilt as he moved deeply inside the velvety flesh. She wriggled her hips matching his every thrust, their bodies slapping against one another in a frenzied yearning. In their rhythm they found themselves lost in a sea of lust, their surroundings a blur, the room spinning. A harmony to their senses was the raw smell of sex and the sight of their bodies bounding against one another.

Soon Madeline climaxed, screaming between clenched teeth. Alex moved onward and upward inside of her releasing wave after wave of gratification from her.

He could feel the trickle of her hot sex down his thigh, "Oh God Madeline," he murmured, he withdrew himself from her. Then, quickly, he scrambled onto the bed and lay on his back. She took her cue, climbed on top of him, and began sliding up and down his prick. She whimpered in delight, as he began praising her with more salacious words. Madeline could feel her pussy muscles seize his

330

cock, her body afire with his words. She shrieked, pounding her fists down to his abs.

Alex moaned as he felt a torrent of her sex juice gush about his abdomen and sides. "Madeline!" he shouted, edging on his release. She swiftly moved off him and took his cock into her mouth, bobbing up and down his shaft. She slowly inched her mouth down his length, he could feel his tip nudge the back of her throat. "Shit! Mmm!!!! AAAHHHH!!!"

He held her head with both hands and released himself into her mouth. She swallowed as he came, spurting more and more into her mouth. After he finished, she casually sucked, licking at his erection, tasting him as the last throbs of orgasm coursed through his body.

Alex watched her for a while. Then pulling her into his arms, he rested her head onto his chest. He graced her cheek and kissed her on the head.

"Go to sleep dolcezza," he whispered.

She quickly drifted off. He combed through her soft tresses of hair between his fingers, his eyes were heavy with the urge to sleep. But he couldn't. He did not want to frighten her in the middle of the night. Trying to resist, he kept opening his eyes wide for some time, but the comfort of Madeline's presence and his tired body gave way to slumber.

22

STABLE BEHAVIOUR

Madeline awoke in her King's arms, hearing some scurrying about in the room next to them. "Alex!" she gasped trying to shake him awake.

"Mmm," he grunted, his eyes fluttering, "Madeline" he smiled.

"I think I hear someone in the room next to us."

Just then, Greg Umbridge burst through the double doors closing them behind him. "I thought I'd find you here. There's a bunch of servants looking for you, Madeline."

"Oh!" she said, popping up forgetting she was naked. Alex quickly grabbed the covers, pulling her face down to his chest. He covered her back and bottom. Greg laughed. Usually, Alex did not care what he saw.

"A little possessive, Alex?"

"Never mind," he said annoyed. "We need to make excuses for her."

"If you'd like I could tell Mr. Tinney she was in my chambers last night," Greg said.

"Yeah do that," Alex said quickly.

"What?" she stammered.

"Madeline," Alex began in a serious tone, "It's ten o'clock. By now they've searched the castle looking for you, so we can't say you fell asleep somewhere."

"Why don't we say I fell asleep in one of the haystacks in the mews?" Madeline offered.

Alex gave her a forbidding look, "Those men have been in there since five this morning. You would not have gone unnoticed if you had slept there."

"What about the Mistresses' Chambers?" she said.

"They'll reprimand you for that," said Alex worriedly.

"What's the worst they'll do?" said Madeline throwing up her hands.

"Mr. Tinney is pretty harsh with punishments," said Alex shaking his head. "He might make you clean an extra couple of rooms."

"Hey, what's wrong with saying you slept with me? I'm not a bad looking bloke," said Greg, insulted. "Besides, I think the guards in front of Alex's chambers already think we slept together."

A confused expression came over Alex's face as he looked over to her. Nonetheless, he quickly made the connection. Alex had asked Greg to get her into his room safely, she had forgotten to tell

333

him how Greg managed. As Madeline sat, swaddled in the covers, a dark cloud came over her; if the guards thought she had slept with Greg, then soon the rest of the servants would know. Alex took her out of her reverie, "Madeline please, I hate the idea of you getting punished for this." He grazed the scars on her back with his fingertips.

"You don't think Mr. Tinney would —" she began fearful looking into Alex's eyes.

"No," he whispered. "But what kind of man would I be if I allowed him to punish you? Please just say you slept with him."

"What if everyone else in the castle finds out?"

"Doesn't matter. We know the truth."

She backed down, "Fine."

"Greg take her to Mr. Tinney. Explain to him what happened. But do not allow him to punish her. If he tries, tell him he will have to deal with me."

She sat up, holding the covers around her. Greg stayed in the room, not taking the hint to leave.

"Uh, Greg, a little privacy for the lady?"

"Right," said Greg laughing, he threw up his arms. "Sorry love, I can be a little thick sometimes."

"I wonder," said Alex raising his brow.

He exited into Alex's Drawing Room, shutting the doors behind him. Alex got up and began to search around the bed.

"Here," he said handing the dress to her. "Don't forget what I said. Everything you see between Princess Sofia and me, it's just an act. Who knows, she might have a lover too?"

She gave him a look. Any princess that had a lover would quickly drop him for Alex. She put on her dress, and they embraced one last time, his fingers running through her hair, he pressed his lips softly to hers. "You should get going. Before they start searching my chambers."

"Bye," she pecked him one last time and left the room, joining Greg in the Drawing Room.

"Have fun last night?" he asked daringly.

"Shut up Greg."

Greg escorted her down to the servants' parlour, where Mr. Tinney was delegating work to several servants.

"Madeline Black!" Mr. Tinney yelled, storming towards her. "Where have you been?"

It was the first time she heard Mr. Tinney speak without his monotone voice. It was alarming, and she worried that, despite Alex's instructions to Greg, she would be reprimanded anyway.

"Mr. Tinney, I have collected Miss Black," Greg said, in an authoritative tone.

"That's good Sir Gregory. I will have a word with Miss Black and give her a fair punishment."

"That won't be necessary."

"Surely it is. She has been missing for hours. Not only have we not had her help with the preparations for the Spanish royals, but we also did not get the help of the servants that went searching for her!"

"Last night Miss Black was tending to my needs," Greg said suggestively. "I kept her till morning."

335

Greg smiled from ear to ear. She did not know whether she wanted to slap him, or hide beneath a rock. Mr. Tinney gave them an abashed look of understanding.

"I see Sir Gregory. Ahem," he turned to her, not making eye contact, "Miss Black tend to your duties then."

"Yes sir, Mr. Tinney," said Madeline abashed. She went to the chalkboard to see where she would be for the day. She was to help with decorations, and oversee the dinner and the ball, just as she had for the last party. She was relieved that she did not have to attend to any of the royals. She went down to her room, to get her uniform and start her work, but to her surprise found Tilly waiting there. She felt uncomfortable.

"Hello Madeline," she said innocently. "Where have you been? I was up all night worried."

"I was busy," she said flatly.

"The question is where do you go? You've been gone quite a few evenings, not coming in until the early hours of morning."

"It's not your business Tilly. Why aren't you working?"

"You've been up to something. Spending time with someone."

Madeline swallowed hard. She knew that Tilly had a habit of going to the King's Apartments. She wondered if she had been snooping about the castle, seeing them together. There was only one thing she could do. Lie. "Well if you must know, I'm seeing that man you call vile."

"Sir Gregory Umbridge?" Tilly asked, giving her an odd look.

"Yes, he's not all bad. He's quite kind."

"Oh, but this must mean you've been spending time with the King," she said excitedly. "He's gone missing an awful lot."

"How would you know that?" Madeline asked, disgusted by Tilly's obsession.

"It's just, I haven't seen him about as much."

"Don't lie Tilly, I know about your little closet escapades in the King's Bedchambers," she said through gritted teeth.

"Bugger off, Madeline. I'm not there to watch him, I'm there to protect him."

"Protect him? From what?"

"Well, that Lord Bathory," Tilly said putting her hands on her hips, "I've overheard him saying he'd like to off 'em in the halls and rooms of this castle."

"THEN WHY HAVEN'T YOU SAID ANYTHING?" yelled Madeline.

"The King is quite smart you know. He knows I'm sure. But he needs someone to look out for him. I think I could save him."

Madeline watched as a smile grew on Tilly's mousy face. "How many times have you been in the King's Apartments, Tilly?"

"Quite a few times, while he slept. I'd watch him from the closet."

"Do you realize the King is trained to know when someone is in the room with him —"

Tilly laughed, waving her hand. "Not while he sleeps. I wait till he sleeps."

Madeline could not believe what she was hearing, "Were you there last night?"

"No, I think he may have been entertaining someone last night. I've been wondering who," she said as she eyed Madeline.

"The King has no interest in a servant. Especially when his best friend has an interest in me," Madeline said.

Realizing that it was stupid to tell Madeline all that she had, Tilly began to panic, "Promise me you won't tell the King I've been watching him sleep. He might get the wrong idea. I just want to protect him." She grasped Madeline's arm, with desperate eyes. "Please say nothing to the King. He needs someone to watch him. He has awful dreams at night."

"Awful dreams?"

"Yes, he often wakes up yelling. He's usually babbling on about that Irish uprising years ago."

Madeline wondered why he had not done that the night before, "How often does he do that?"

"Every night, I've watched him."

"I won't say anything," said Madeline. "But what you are doing isn't right, Tilly. You need to stop before he catches you."

Tilly nodded casually, but Madeline knew the delusional girl would go back. "Tilly, what use is it going to the King's Apartments anyway? You can't have any kind of relationship with the King, not even a friendship. Going there is asking for trouble."

"What do you know about it?" Tilly shrieked, anger contorting her face, she stormed out of the room.

Madeline sat on her bed, shaken by Tilly's behaviour. She was beginning to scare her. It wasn't safe for Alex to be around someone like Tilly. She would have to talk Greg into arranging Tilly's schedule so she would not be around him.

The servants were asked to arrange themselves in the courtyard next to the vestibule by one in the afternoon to greet the Spanish royals as they walked in.

Madeline arrived half an hour early, curious of what Princess Sofia would be like. Mr. Tinney darted about, checking over all the servants, making sure their uniforms were clean and worn properly. Though Madeline knew she was supposed to stay in the courtyard, she edged toward the Garter Throne Room entrance door where she knew Alex would be waiting to receive his guests.

She peeked through the window as Alex entered the room, sweeping up the aisle as Greg, Sir Ashton Giles, Lord Cadogan and several others followed. He stood in front of his throne and waited. He looked absolutely divine, wearing a red coat with gold embroidery. She sighed. It didn't matter what kind of woman Sofia was, he was irresistible. There would be no better match for her in all of Europe. As she was about to turn her attentions back to the courtyard, she took notice of Greg standing next to him. He was wearing a blue coat with silver embroidery. He looked well-groomed for a change. His hair was neatly in place, and his clothes were clean, not wrinkled.

One o'clock finally came. Trumpets began to play, and King Fernando and Queen Isabelle of Spain were announced at the entrance of the courtyard. She stood upright and put her hands behind her back. The Spanish King was a stout man, with thick curly hair and a beard. His wife was very thin, with brown, curly hair.

They then announced Princess Sofia. Madeline was disgusted. The Spanish royals had two children, but Princess Sofia was the only one there. They weren't coming for refuge. They were here to play matchmaker. She watched as Princess Sofia joined her parents. Led by several footmen and Mr. Tinney, they brushed past Madeline to the Garter Throne room entrance. She curtsied as they went by, her head down, lifting her eyes.

As Sofia passed, she got a better look. She was stunningly beautiful, with long luxurious soft brown curly hair and a curvy bottom. She wore a soft red empire waist dress with gold embroidery around its sleeves, chest and skirts. Lace gloves covered her dainty hands, and a crown of diamonds sat on her curls. She had a sort of confidence about her as she walked. With her head held high, it was as though she floated across the room. Madeline looked down, her stomach doing flip flops. She had a feeling despite everything Alex said to her, he would fall in love with this adorable creature.

She watched as the Princess entered the Garter Throne Room with its royal blue carpeting, gold guilt and wood walls, and gargantuan oil paintings of kings and queens, Princess Sofia stood out, capturing the eyes of her company.

"Your Majesty," Sofia said curtsying as she lifted her hand.

"Princess Sofia," he said and kissed her hand.

Sofia stood back up, smiling into his crystal blue eyes. Her cheeks burned up, she waved back and forth and began to teeter over. Greg Umbridge reached out to grab her before she hit the ground.

Madeline tried to contain her laughter outside in the courtyard as she looked into the window. Princess Sofia was obviously trying to get Alex's attention, hoping he'd catch her. But strangely, she did not wake as Greg Umbridge gently shook her in his arms. Madeline watched him call to her several times as he gently rocked her. Alex reached out and put his hand to her forehead, checking her temperature. He turned to King Fernando and said something she couldn't hear.

It was then Madeline saw King Fernando, who had his face in his hands, shaking his head. The Queen seemed to be trying consoling him, patting him on the back. It was too good to miss, Madeline silently opened the door to the Garter Throne Room and hid in the doorway alcove, where no one could see her.

"Perhaps you should take her to her room, Greg," said Alex, "I don't think she's feeling well."

Greg scooped Sofia up in his arms.

"Princess Sofia's personal maids step forward please," said Lord Cadogan.

Tilly and two other maids stepped forward. Madeline gasped.

"Ladies, please help the Princess get settled in her private apartments," said Lord Cadogan.

Tilly and the maids followed Greg with the unconscious Sofia, who was limp in his arms. Madeline could hear King Fernando grumbling in Spanish as he shook his head.

"It's quite all right Fernando," said Alex. "How about I give the family a tour of the castle, and when the Princess is feeling better, I can take her tomorrow."

Fernando seemed enthusiastic at this and stopped grumbling. Alex led them out of the front entrance and began taking them about the castle.

Mr. Tinney began to make his way toward the courtyard door. Madeline quickly slipped outside before he saw her. He entered the courtyard a serious expression on his gaunt face, "Good job everyone. Back to your posts. We need to be ready for this evening's dinner and ball."

The next several hours were long, and Madeline wondered what the evening would bring. She ate dinner in the servants' quarters, then made her way to the State Dining Room, where Alex and the Spanish royals were having dinner. When Mr. Tinney had given them the tour, he explained that they used the State Dining Room for special guests, but he never mentioned the elaborate tableware and centrepieces. She stood in awe staring at the table. Down the centre of it was a long silver centrepiece holding several flower arrangements. Two huge flower arrangements were at its centre, each of them surrounded by several smaller arrangements. In the two huge arrangements, there were hundreds of red carnations surrounded by some beautiful greenery. The smaller arrangements were filled with cream carnations. There were also some magnificent candelabras placed between the two large arrangements and on either side of them.

Several footmen and maids, Madeline included, began checking over the table. Looking for any slight imperfections, they nudged seats into their proper positions, straightened crooked utensils and refolded any napkins that did not resemble an impeccable Dutch bonnet.

Madeline busied herself with some other servants, wiping the already clean mirrors behind the buffet tables. The mirrors reflected the huge arched windows opposite them and made the room look much larger than it was. After she finished the mirrors, she adjusted the large ropes to the red velvet drapes, making sure the gold fringe tassels were in their proper position.

When they were done, the footmen and maids left the room and headed down to the Great Kitchen. She had only been down there once before, when Mr. Tinney had given them the tour. Moments before they crossed the threshold, she could hear the clanging of pots and pans echoing across the stone walls, and chefs yelling to their assistants who scurried about the hubbub of heat and delicious aromas. Carts were lined up against the wall next to them, the footmen rushed each cart over to the chefs by the counters to load them up with large platters. She walked alongside one of the carts making sure none of the dishes fell off. Not that she needed to worry; like the centrepiece, all the dishes were made of silver. Each dish was majestic in size and gleamed under the chandeliers as they walked.

As the footmen with the food waited in a room next to the State Dining Room Madeline, along with several other maids, walked into the State Dining Room and stood next to the windows and walls, prepared to clear the plates.

There were not as many place settings as there were for the party at Buckingham Palace weeks before. Mr. Tinney had explained that this was because the King did not want to overwhelm his guests with all of the nobility during dinner. Instead, the court was invited to meet the Spanish royals at a ball held in their honour. As Madeline waited patiently, she scanned over her uniform, sweeping the wrinkles of her apron over with her hands.

Just then, they entered the room. Alex was arm in arm with Princess Sofia, escorting her to her chair. It felt like daggers speared into Madeline's chest. She looked down trying to hold back her emotions. He was going to marry her. He needed an heir.

Madeline spent the entire dinner staring at Alex, waiting for a smile or glance in her direction. But he didn't glance at her. It was as though she was invisible. He went on talking to King Fernando about the situation in Spain, and how he was forced to abdicate the throne to Napoleon's brother. Madeline understood how much King Fernando wanted Princess Sofia to marry Alex. To restore power over the throne in Spain, King Fernando would need support. If Sofia married Alex and the English won the European war, he would regain the throne. They spoke briefly about politics, then King Fernando pointed down to Princess Sofia.

"Sofia has never enjoyed Spain. She always took to other European cultures. She's barely seen this country, and she already thinks it's more beautiful than Spain." King Fernando chuckled.

"Really Sofia?" Alex asked intrigued, "What's wrong with Spain?"

The Princess was silent for a moment, "Nothing, I suppose."

Out of the corner of Madeline's eye, she could see King Fernando glare at his daughter.

"Well, I, uh," her gaze shifted about the room. "I don't really care for the music in Spain. I love Italian opera. Also the food, I prefer French and Italian cuisine."

"Anything else?" King Fernando pressed. She looked down shyly, her cheeks burning red, Madeline wondered if she would faint again.

"The men," she said taking a sip of her wine staring down into her plate. "The men are not gentlemen. Not like English gentlemen."

There was an awkward silence as Sofia, looked up from her plate to Alex with an innocent smile. He did not smile back and looked in another direction.

Greg immediately took his opportunity. "English gentlemen?" he laughed. "That's nonsense. English men aren't

344

always chivalrous. I should tell you about all the times I've pulled down my —"

"Sir Gregory," Alex interrupted, wanting to avoid speaking of all the times Greg took off his trousers in front of the servants. "What are you doing tomorrow?"

"I'm, uh, not exactly sure," said Greg.

"Excellent, then you can come with Princess Sofia and me," Alex continued. "She hasn't seen the castle yet, and I imagine you could tell her more about English gentlemen later."

Greg said nothing, but looked pleased as he went back to the food on his plate. Alex turned his attention to King Fernando again.

Meanwhile, Greg began to make funny faces at Princess Sofia. She tried hard not to laugh, but soon gave in to a fit of giggles. King Fernando gave her a forbidding look. She immediately stopped, humiliated, her lips trembled as she stared down at her lap. Then, Madeline saw something she thought she would never see — a look of guilt on Greg Umbridge's face.

After dessert was served, Alex along with the entourage of advisors led the Spanish royals to St. George's Hall. Madeline along with the rest of the servants followed in their wake, preparing themselves for the next part of their service.

As they walked down the halls and galleries filled with suits of armour and huge paintings, someone crept out from behind one of the knights. Tilly.

"Oi," Tilly whispered as she came out of her hiding place. Several of the other servants muttered under their breaths and grunted at her presence.

"Tilly," Madeline responded shortly. "What are you doing here?"

"Oh, I was just curious how the dinner went," Tilly said casually as she walked alongside her.

"It was fine," Madeline said before sighing.

"That Princess Sofia is annoying isn't she?" she whispered, then bopped her head up, catching a view of Alex ahead of them. "I don't know if he'll ever see anything in her."

"Probably not. Aren't you supposed to be somewhere else?"

"Oh yes, the Great Kitchen, but Mr. Tinney never notices me missing."

This did not surprise Madeline. Tilly was a young girl and Mr. Tinney would be unsuspecting of her. He probably thought Tilly did not understand where she was supposed to be and what she was supposed to do. When they reached St. George's Hall, Madeline could hear Alex's name and title being announced, then the Spanish royals were introduced. The servants discreetly went into the hall and Madeline picked up a tray of canapés and began circulating the hall.

St. George's Hall was unlike any other room in Buckingham Palace or Windsor Castle. All down one wall, it had large circular windows above tall arched ones. Black and white marble tiles outlined the floors. The vaulted ceiling had several murals of Greek gods on chariots surrounded by huge oval mouldings carved with laurel leafs and cherubs. On the walls opposite the huge windows were massive tapestries and columns. When she had first stepped into the hall on the tour, she thought she had stepped into a fantasy world. She had never seen anything so grand. Not an inch of the walls or ceiling was untouched; either carvings, gilded moulding, a painting or panelling. Though most rooms of the castle were this way, St. George's Hall was more detailed than the rest of them. She imagined it had taken years for the artisans to paint the murals and weave the tapestries.

There were no gambling tables set up like there had been the night of the party at Buckingham Palace. She supposed this was probably because they had wanted to make a dignified impression. Gambling tables, alcohol and Sir Gregory Umbridge were a recipe for disaster.

As she walked about she saw two familiar faces standing next to her, Lady and Lord Watson. Her heart missed a beat. She thought Lord Watson had gone back to the Caribbean. She turned away trying to avoid them.

"Over here girl," Lady Watson called, "I'd like to have a canapé."

Nervously, Madeline turned about and came face to face with the pair.

"Lord and Lady Watson," she smiled faintly, trying to be casual.

"Madeline," said Lady Watson in surprise, taking a canapé. "I thought you worked at Buckingham Palace."

"Yes, but they needed extra help here," she said quickly. She turned to walk away, but Lord Watson grabbed her by the arm. She wanted to pull away, but his grip was strong, "Madeline, you work for the King. Do you think we are no longer in his favour?"

"I don't know who the King favours," Madeline shrugged. "The only man I can think of is Greg Umbridge."

"Well, you see," said Lady Watson, "we believe we are no longer in his favour. Recently Lord Watson was relieved of his post in the Caribbean."

"I'm sorry to hear that Lord Watson," she lied. "No, I wouldn't know anything of whom the King favours and whom he doesn't. Perhaps he has something in mind for you closer to home? All this business with the Spanish, I'm sure there will be more responsibilities and posts here."

Tapping her chin, Lady Watson turned to her husband, "Yes that could be it. Don't be surprised if you get a different job or promotion soon. Maybe he's thinking of appointing you to a more important job in one of the royal residences. A post like Lord Cadogan's? You may sit in the House of Lords meetings."

Madeline's tense muscles relaxed. For a second, she worried that Lady Watson suspected that Alex knew about the abuse happening in the Watson household. But that wouldn't make sense. The King shouldn't care about how his servants were treated by other masters.

She walked away, surprised at what Alex had done. Lord Watson losing his station was not a coincidence. It was Alex's clever way of punishing him for attacking her. It was cruel too; nothing would drive them crazier than questioning where they stood socially. Reputation meant everything to the Watsons.

As she weaved through the crowd, Madeline could see a man sitting on a bench watching the guests in the hall. He had some paper and conté and was drawing the scene around him feverishly. She immediately knew it was Mr. Ackers reporting for The Society Pages.

Madeline was brought out her reverie as the guests began to form a circle around Alex and Sofia. They began to dance together in the middle of the hall. Madeline looked on as Alex twirled Sofia across the floor. He flashed his perfect smile at her, and her cheeks went rosy. He whorled her again, and she began to giggle as he took her back into his arms.

Cross, Madeline clenched her hands into fists. She took a deep breath, reminding herself of the promises that Alex had made to her. But he looked delighted with Sofia. If it was all an act as he said, then he was quite the actor. He kept his gaze on the Princess, it seemed there was no one else in the hall but them.

Unable to watch, Madeline side stepped towards one of the exits into the Guard Chamber, and ran down the Grand Staircase with tears streaming down her face. She crossed paths with several guests and other servants, but looked off into another direction so they could not see her pain. Once she was alone, she sat next to a life-sized vase and cried quietly.

"You can't take that seriously," said a familiar voice. She looked up her eyes puffy and red. Greg Umbridge was looking down at her, a tumbler of brandy in his hand. He sat down next to her, "You think he's in love with her? After one evening?"

"Probably not," Madeline admitted. "But she's beautiful, and she seems sweet. A life with her would be simple. He'll realize that soon."

"Be reasonable," said Greg waving his hand dismissively. "Alex's life will never be simple, I should know."

Madeline sniffed, wiping her nose with her hand and gave a small chortle. He slumped next to her, offering his tumbler. She turned it down.

"He is a man of his word," he went on, "he's not going to abandon you for her."

"But if he falls for her," she said, gasping between tears. "He can't change that. I could see him falling for her, she's perfect. She's every bit a lady."

He shook his head, "Are you serious? She fainted the second she saw him."

"That doesn't mean she's not a lady."

"She's not perfect either. If anything, I feel sorry for her. Did you see the pressure her father put on her to talk about her love for English men?"

"She likes him already, you can see it in her face. I mean she did faint."

"She barely knows him," Greg reasoned. "If she's falling for him it's because it's what is expected of her. Maybe she fainted because of all the pressure she felt."

"Either way, it doesn't really matter," she said downcast. "He is going to find being with me and pretending with her exhausting."

"I've known him since we were children. He can handle it," he said confidently.

"I'm sorry Greg, but I think I need to be alone." She rose from the floor and walked away leaving him debating whether he should follow her. She wandered outside aimlessly on the grounds but eventually found herself in Windsor Castle's stables.

She wandered down its corridors looking at all the extravagant horses. Some of them had come from Buckingham Palace. She came across the King's horse, Princess.

"Hello Princess," Madeline said happy to see her, despite currently hating princesses. She checked to see the corridors were clear. The grooms were finished for the day, so she opened the stall gate and walked in. Princess was somewhat startled by the visitor, she balked, stepping back with her hind legs. She remembered that Princess had a special bond with Alex and normally did not take to other people. Nonetheless, she boldly grabbed Princess' muzzle and

350

pulled her close. Strangely, Princess didn't panic but stayed in her embrace, softly neighing.

Madeline picked a carrot from the floor, and offered it to her. Princess slowly took a small bite of the carrot and Madeline pet her snout as she ate.

"I'm sorry. I know this is hard for you."

Madeline whirled around, surprised to see Alex standing by the stall door. "You have no idea," she said feeding Princess the last bite. She turned away from him.

"Please don't be angry with me. I left that party just to see that you were all right."

"How-huh- could I- huh- be-okay?" she stammered. He took her in his arms, pecking her cheek as she held back her tears. She breathed in the familiar scent of sandalwood as she rested her head against his chest. She resented that Princess Sofia had smelt it all day.

"Don't think this is easy for me either – pretending to care for someone else," he said.

"Is this difficult for you? Do you love me?"

He looked deeply into her eyes, "Yes Madeline, I love you."

"I love you too," she confessed cupping his face with her hands. He leaned down and kissed her, lingering his soft lips on hers. He slipped his tongue between her lips and moved it slowly about hers. He picked her up, his lips not leaving hers. Cradling and kissing her in his arms he carried her out of Princess' stall to an empty one and set her down on a clean pile of soft hay. He moved his lips down to her neck softly kissing, blowing on her skin. She murmured, feeling the shivers run up and down her spine. He pressed his thick lips into her neck hard, and she could feel her nerves spark.

"Huuuhhhh," her voice shuddered aloud as her body trembled.

"Are we going to get a little noisy again, Miss Black?" he asked seductively, combing her hair with his fingers. She opened her eyes into his, her breath going shallow, excited for what was to come.

He stood up, walked over to the stall door and slid it closed. He turned and began unbuttoning his trousers. She watched intrigued, his confidence was arousing. He stripped down completely naked, without any hesitation, standing before her in the bright light of the lamps about the stall walls.

"Are you blushing Miss Black?" he asked as he noticed her absorbing every part of his being.

"No," she said smirking, her eyes roaming around the floor.

"Right," he said moving towards her. Straddling her on his knees, he leaned down his nose brushing against hers. He gazed at her with adoring eyes softly caressing her cheek, "You set a fire in me. You give my senses no rest."

He closed his eyes and pressed his lips tenderly against hers. As their lips danced, she became inflamed. Holding his face, she kissed him more intensely, sucking on his bottom lip. He could feel his cock twitching, and sighed deeply.

Instinctively, she grabbed his hot sex with her hand and began rubbing up and down his length.

He wrenched her skirts up to her belly, revealing her soft, moist mound. He looked down lustily, he began to lean toward her womanhood, but she pushed him back.

"Quite eager your Majesty?" she teased.

"I'm always eager to taste you. You're the sweetest thing that's ever been in my mouth."

Madeline pulled him toward her and kissed him hard. He took his coat from the floor, and rested it behind her head. She leaned back on it as Alex spread her legs wide and stared at her. He wet his fingers and slowly reached inside her, pulling them back out and licked off her nectar. He did this a few times and she revelled in him taking his time tasting her. He drew his mouth to her lips and began kissing her as he fingered her hard. She sighed and moaned as his thick lips moved about hers. "Do you like that?" he asked between soft kisses, his eyes smouldering.

"Mmmm," Madeline moaned in approval, heaving deep breaths.

"I just want to please you dolcezza," he continued whispering between kisses and the slamming of his fingers. "I love you. I need to hear you moan and cum. I need to taste you."

At these words and his deep thrusts Madeline could feel her body begin to grow tense and quake, she rode his hand, grinding down hard.

"Allleexxxx!" she cried out, and her juice swept about his fingers. But Alex kept probing with his fingers, ramming them against her most sensitive area. Madeline's moans became louder and louder again.

"Cum, cum. I want more."

"AAHHHH!" The cum trickled down his hand.

"Yes," he whispered, "more."

She came again onto his hand and Alex could see her dripping onto the hay. He withdrew his fingers licking his hand.

She looked up moaning, the last throbs of pleasure ebbing away through her. She saw a black riding crop on the wall and dirty thoughts raced through her head. Alex looked down to Madeline; seeing her gaze, he followed it up to the wall, smiling as he noticed the riding crop. He chuckled softly, "Is that what my dolcezza wants?"

She whimpered. He stood up walked over to the riding crop, his tanned and chiselled body in her view. Her eyes followed his godly perfection as he stood behind her, riding crop in hand. She excitedly pulled up the hem of her skirts, a sultry smile on her face.

"Oh no. Take off your dress. Get on your hands and knees and spread your legs."

She did so obediently. She stripped off her uniform and tossed it onto the hay. Then she got on her hands and knees and stared back at her King. She knew he was in command, and so did he.

"Part your cheeks for me. I want to see every little bit of you."

She placed one hand on each cheek and parted them. Alex groaned followed by a few moments of silence as he stared at her. She felt the leather tip of the crop touch her sex lightly and began parting her moist folds with it. Madeline sighed, the feeling was erotic and she felt a tingling sensation grow and flutter inside her. Alex continued using the leather tip to lightly stroke her skin and her entire body began to quiver. "Put your hands to your side."

Madeline obeyed, knowing what was to come next, he continued to stroke her skin lightly then She felt the sting of leather on her backside. "Uuuggghhh!" she whimpered confused by the pain and enjoyment of it.

He slapped her bottom again. Noticing a red mark across her white fleshy cheeks, he stopped a moment. He knew that she loved a slap on her arse but perhaps this was taking things too far. He was leaving marks. Nothing that would last, but he did not want to hurt her.

"Dolcezza, I don't know. I'm leaving marks —"

"I like it," she interjected, "It feels tingly and exciting. Don't stop."

He raised the crop several times as her orgasm began to rise in her loins. Soon he could see her pussy glistening as she twiddled with her hard pink nipples and begged for more. As her breath wails became sharper and short, he changed to short, fast stinging taps, which sent her into a screaming euphoria, "MMUUNNNGHH...OH GOD!" She came down her thighs and onto her uniform beneath her.

"Holy fuck," he whispered watching her. He got to his knees and licked her, groaning. It was so hot knowing her could make her cum by hardly touching her. He was ready to enter her when she turned.

"My breasts too," she whimpered.

"Your breasts?" he asked incredulously.

"Yes." She pressed them together; Alex watched feeling the heat rush to his groin.

"Whip them," she demanded seductively.

"I'll hit your fingers Miss Black."

She was about to protest, but then she noticed him rise and grab some straps that hung on the wall. Kneeling down next to her, he wrapped them about her chest, binding her breasts. She looked down at herself and smiled at him, "Where does the King get naughty ideas like this one?"

He looked into her eyes, "Looking at you gives me all kinds of naughty ideas."

As he stood up, she rubbed her nipples between her fingers. The sense was intensified and she could feel her nerve from her breasts to her cunt awaken.

"Miss Black," Alex teased, "you should be keeping your hands to yourself."

He grabbed another strap from the wall, knelt down and pulled her arms behind her back. He belted the strap at her elbows, pulling her shoulders back so her chest thrust forward. She got up onto her knees resting her bottom on her feet, excited for what was to come.

"Spread your knees apart," Alex commanded.

She did so, exposing her pussy to him. He exhaled shakily as he watched her. She was more vulnerable than she'd ever been, offering herself up to him with her eyes and body, begging for him. He was ready to come where he stood, but he restrained himself. Lifting the crop, he whipped it against her fleshy mounds.

"Ooooohhhhh … Aaahhh!"

He strapped them again, and the sensations radiated through her body like wildfire. Alex sent a barrage of short stinging slaps of the crop, lashing around her nipples. Abruptly, he stopped the short, sharp slaps on her breasts and began to hit her inner thighs. He alternated between her breasts and thighs and this sent Madeline spiralling into sheer ecstasy. Wailing uncontrollable she fell to her side, reaching her peak. As she trembled on the floor, he trailed the crop further up her thighs pushing it up against her love button, allowing the last torrents of pleasure to flow through her body. She lay there a few moments as he gawked in amazement.

Shakily she rose up and noticed his body trembling like a volcano ready to erupt. Watching his red prick which was dripping with pre-cum, she edged over to him on her knees opening her mouth.

"God," he groaned beneath his breath. He fed himself into her mouth and her mouth tightened around him as she began suckling and bobbing up and down his length.

"Don't take it out of that perfect mouth," he muttered. He held the crop behind the nape of her neck locking her in.

Mouth full of his sex she gazed up at him, startled by his sudden dominance. She continued moving up and down him, feeling the crop stick brushing against the back of her neck as she did. He sighed as he rolled his head back, gazing up at the ceiling. He knew it wouldn't be long. She pumped up and down him, a woman on a mission. He rolled his head back down his eyes falling to hers.

He released the riding crop and dropped it to the ground. But she continued, licking and sucking him clean. She dropped back onto the hay, her eyes glued to him. He was still erect, she tittered provocatively, happy that neither of them were finished with the other.

He stared at her sex, knowing after all they had done, it would be a tight, musty, inferno, ready for him. He removed the belt from her elbows and lifted her to her feet. Kissing her hard, he backed her into the wall between the hooks. He placed each of her hands on them, "Hold on," he said smoothly.

She grasped tightly onto the hooks next to her hips. He lifted her, wrapping her legs around his hips. Entering her sopping cunt, his lips descended on hers again. As he plunged into her she lightly

357

sucked on his bottom lip, he parted his lips surrendering to her. He moved onward and upwards inside her at a languid pace.

"Uhhh," he groaned feeling the warm of her twat.

"Mmm...faster...faster," she demanded.

"Ugh...faster?"

She nodded, murmuring.

"Let go of the hooks and put your arms around me," he instructed as he withdrew his length.

She released the hooks and wrapped her arms around his neck. He scooped her knees, so they rested in the crooks of his elbows. Then, he grasped both hooks on the wall with his hands. Her back resting against the wall, she traced her fingers down his sculpted chest and stomach. He held her there so effortlessly, she could not help but be amazed by his strength. She could feel his cock at the entrance of her sex. She called for him, whispering his name softly. He pushed himself inside, claiming her. He moved slowly at first discovering her, as she leaned forward and pressed her lips to his, their tongues wrestling in a fit of passion. Soon she was succumbing to harder faster, strokes, as his cock moved deeply inside her, nudging against her. Beads of sweat formed on his brow, dripping onto her breasts.

He pulled back from her mouth, to catch his breath. He could feel his thighs and arm muscles sear with pain, holding her there as he moved inside her. But he kept propelling himself inside her. His lips melted into hers again, his desire for her growing with every stroke. Nothing satisfied him more than being submerged in her, feeling her reel with every shift of his cock. It was addicting. Empowering. The ache he felt through his limbs would subside the moment she clenched her most intimate parts. She continued to whisper his name repeatedly, louder and louder. "Alex, Alex, ALEX, ALLLEEEXXX!"

He grunted loudly, gave one final thrust, sending himself spurting inside her. She watched him as he struggled to regain his breath, his eyes closed. He was spent. She touched his sweaty cheek and his eyes fluttered opened, sparkling up at her. He smiled. She released her hands from the hooks and he guided her down to the hay. "Dolcezza," he whispered softly.

Curled up in his arms, they relaxed in the hay awhile as he combed through her hair.

"There is something seriously wrong with us," he chuckled.

"Yes, I doubt any of your guests in the castle would even think of doing that."

"I should be more of gentleman," he said, feeling a twinge of guilt.

"Oh shut up. You liked it just as much as I did."

There was another long silence before he spoke again. "Madeline, I need to go," he said hesitantly. "I'm sure people are wondering where I went."

"No, no stay," she said sadly, gripping to his chest.

He continued to comb her hair with his fingertips, then he stopped. Someone was shuffling about with some steel pails in the stables.

"Damn it," he whispered beneath his breath. "I don't want to leave you."

He moved quickly darting about grabbing his clothes, putting them on hurriedly. She watched in awe at his speed, once he was ready, he bent down to kiss her. "It's just an act. Don't forget that."

He slid the door open quietly and looked in both directions, when he saw no one was there, he turned to her, looking at her fleshy red skin. "I want you to take the rest of the night off."

"But Al–"

"That's a command," he said sternly.

She needs rest, he thought. It had been a long emotional day for her. The thought of her watching him with Princess Sofia after their rendezvous made him sick. He left, shutting the door behind him.

She lay there, smiling to herself. He loved her.

23

SAD SONG

Eventually, Madeline sneaked out of the mews and went to the servants' quarters to get ready for bed. She tried not to think of Alex swaying Princess Sofia across the dance floor. She reminded herself that he loved her. She took the doll he had given her and cuddled with it in her bed. She drifted off to sleep, and a sweet simper lit her face.

Some hours later, she could hear Tilly come into the room, grumbling beneath her breath, "That annoying bitch."

Madeline roused from her sleep rubbing her eyes.

"Oh, sorry that I woke you," said Tilly, embarrassed. She began to undress out of her uniform. "What are you doing here already? Come to think of it, I haven't seen you for hours."

"The benefit of knowing the King's best friend," Madeline lied remembering that Tilly thought she was seeing Greg.

"You were with Sir Gregory Umbridge? So, you really do fancy him?"

"How was the rest of the night?" Madeline asked ignoring Tilly's question.

"The Princess couldn't keep her hands off the King. I think he got sick of it. At one point, he left. It was some time before he came back, too," she said with wide eyes.

"Really? So, what happened when he came back?"

"Oh, she went over to him of course, and he danced the night away with her."

Madeline's heart sank. She knew that he would be dancing with Sofia, but she had thought he would get in a dance or two with other ladies.

"There was not another lady he danced with?" Madeline pressed.

"Nope," Tilly said, getting into her nightgown. "Of course, the Princess was giddy as a child with a new toy before going to bed. She asked me all sorts of questions about him."

"Like what?"

"Oh you know, what he likes in a girl."

"What did you tell her?"

An evil grin lined her mouth, "Oh, nothing really."

"Tilly," she said, somewhat concerned, "what did you say?"

"Oh just that the King liked dirty things."

"What do you mean?"

"Oh you know, just that the King liked to share his women – with Sir Gregory," Tilly said with an evil grin.

"TILLY!"

"Sorry for bringing Sir Gregory into it, I know you fancy him."

"Tilly," Madeline began through gritted teeth, "if Princess Sofia believes that lie and leaves, so does the King."

"What? Why would he leave?" Tilly asked, furrowing her brow.

"Ugh. I serve tea in the House of Lords. If the King cannot keep Princess Sofia around, he'll be expected to go to war instead. Some of the Lords believe he should be fighting. They've talked about it during the meetings."

Tilly rolled her eyes dismissively, "Oh, don't be so dramatic. King Alex will not leave his country for some silly war."

Madeline rose from her bed and pushed Tilly down pinning her between her arms.

"Madeline!"

"Shut up, you stupid girl! You've overheard Lord Bathory plotting against him. You know he looking for ways to kill him. If he goes off to that war, Bathory will find a way to murder him somewhere on the battlefield."

Tilly went white. Her lips trembled as she spoke, "You don't think Princess Sofia will leave do you?"

"If she decides that she is no longer interested in him because she thinks he's some depraved sex addict, it will be your fault Tilly."

"Wha-what do I do?" she whimpered.

"Why don't you tell her you are obsessed with the King and you are jealous, so you told her a lie hoping she'd leave?"

"I can't tell her that!" Tilly said aghast.

"Well, you'd better think of something. Tomorrow, she may run off and tell Daddy that she refuses to marry him. I'm sure King Fernando won't be impressed with King Alexander after he hears what you told her."

She released Tilly and went back to her bed fuming. She pulled up the covers and stared at the ceiling. Though it was hard to watch Princess Sofia with Alex, it was better that than a murder overseas. Thoughts of him flooded her mind until the early hours of the morning. She felt stupid for not telling him what Tilly had been up to. She should have warned him in the mews how often she watched him and that Tilly herself had overheard Lord Bathory conspiring with other Lords. Madeline promised herself that the next time she was alone with him, she would not waste time whining about Princess Sofia and tell him what he needed to know.

Morning came and Madeline left her dormitory room earlier than usual. She was certain Tilly would ask for her advice and she didn't want to deal with her, so she quietly got dressed and went to the servants' kitchen. Some of the other staff were already eating breakfast. She sat down eating an apple, thinking of how to get a message to Alex about all the things Tilly had been up to. She was angry with herself that she hadn't told him that Tilly overheard Lord Bathory's machinations and was sneaking into his apartments regularly. Had she said something last night, Tilly would have been fired and Alex wouldn't have to deal with the outrageous lies she was telling the Princess.

Lost in thought, Madeline didn't notice that Tilly had sat next to her, eating some scrambled eggs. "All right, so I have a plan to fix all of this," Tilly started.

Madeline was annoyed. She turned her body in another direction, hoping that Tilly would get the hint. But Tilly went on, "I'll tell the Princess that the King and Sir Gregory Umbridge don't share women. That you're courting Sir Gregory and it was something you told me as a joke, but I took it seriously."

"WHAT?"

The rest of the servants looked in their direction.

"Makes sense, doesn't it?" said Tilly brightly. "I mean you and Sir Gregory are courting. I'll just say I thought you —"

"Stop Tilly. Don't you dare drag me into the mess you've created. You need to be honest." Madeline continued in a hushed tone, "If you dare, I will tell King Alex that you've been sneaking into his private rooms."

"Why are you so angry?"

"Why do you have to mention my name?" asked angrily. "Just say it was a rumour you once heard. I don't want this coming back on me."

"Fine." Tilly said shortly, got up with her plate and went to the other end of the table.

Madeline quickly ate and went to see where she would be for the day. As it turned out, she was scheduled to clean Windsor Castle's Music Room. As she went down, she realized that she'd have to write him a note and slip it to him during the next House of Lords meeting. Either that, or pass the message along to Greg.

Windsor Castle's Music Room was more simplistic than Buckingham Palace's. Unlike Buckingham's majestic circular room, Windsor Castle's room was much like a drawing room, with panelled walls, and crown molding around a coved ceiling with frescos. The panels had a sage green trim and were filled with a soft green colour. A large pipe organ stood between two doors. There were shelves of cased instruments on the other side of the room, as well as chairs and benches about the room. She ran her finger across the wood of the organ. Dust collected on her finger. She pouted. Now that Princess Sofia was here, she'd have to keep up appearances.

She set to work with a pail and cloth, and began to wipe down the organ, paying attention to the carved detail. It was difficult trying to dust every crevice and cranny, but she did her best to manipulate her cloth and her fingers. She went bug-eyed. It would take hours to clean it properly.

The door opened, and she turned to see Alex, Greg and Sofia come into the room. She gritted her teeth. This would not be easy to witness.

"Oh Alex, it's absolutely beautiful. Much nicer than the one at Madrid Palace. I adore playing music. Do you have a flute? I would love to play a song."

"Certainly Sofia, they're over here," Alex said and led her to the opposite side of the room. He opened a case and assembled the flute and handed it to her.

"Here," he said smiling with his sexy smile. "Don't hurt our ears."

She giggled flirtatiously. Madeline looked on, rolling her eyes. Greg stood next to her, "No worries Miss Black," he whispered, "I promise not to be impressed with her playing."

"Shut up Greg," Madeline said beneath her breath.

Alex and Sofia cocked their heads in their direction. Sofia bit her lip, her eyes still on Madeline.

"You do have some odd servants," said Sofia.

"How do you mean?" asked Alex.

"One of the girls looking after me, Tilly Smith, she told me some awfully odd things about you last night. But then this morning, she took it all back."

"I'm sure Miss Smith is just confused," said Alex trying to brush it off.

"Well, I think it's something you should be concerned about. Another servant named Miss Black told her that you...well, I won't say."

"Tell me," Alex insisted. "If it's something you're concerned about, I'd like to do my best to put your mind at ease Princess Sofia."

"Well, she told me that you and Sir Gregory ..." She trailed off and put her hands behind her back, like a shy toddler.

Alex looked at Madeline, irritated.

"Did she tell you that Sir Gregory Umbridge and King Alex share women, your Highness?" asked Madeline as she got off the floor, her hands clenched into fists.

"Yes," said the Princess embarrassed. "How did you know?"

"I'm Miss Black. Don't pay attention to anything Miss Smith says. She lies. A lot."

Alex turned and buried his face in his hand, hiding his mortification. He quickly regained his composure and turned around. "Miss Black, may I have a word with you?"

He motioned to the door, and Madeline followed him nervously. Once they reached outside the Music Room, he glared at her, "Tell me that you did not say that. Look me straight in my eyes

367

and tell me you didn't. I came down to the Music Room just to get a glimpse of you. Not to have this kind of drama play out. I understand you don't want Princess Sofia here, but without her, I'll be fighting on a battlefield."

"I never told Tilly that. She's obsessed with you and wants Princess Sofia to leave."

He shook his head, "Tilly is just a young girl with a crush. She has no reason to think that if Princess Sofia left, she might —"

"You have no idea, it's more than a crush," Madeline exclaimed. "She snoops about the castle all the time. You've found her in your chambers before."

"I haven't since."

"She waits until you fall asleep. She says she does it almost every night."

"I doubt that. Security in the castle — She couldn't get away with —"

"Tilly told me the other day that she had overheard Lord Bathory plotting to kill you in the hallways when you were here during the summer," Madeline said, desperate. "Now, she watches you sleep. She thinks she protecting you. She also said something about you having nightmares. She thinks you —"

"Madeline, Madeline. Stop," he said exasperated, no longer knowing what to believe. "If you knew this about Tilly, why didn't you tell me earlier? I mean if Tilly overheard anything Bathory said it's important. Damn it, I need to know."

"I'm sorry," she said, "I just, well, I meant to tell you yesterday, but —"

"Never mind," he said, his disappointment written on his face. "Don't talk to Tilly about anything again."

"What? She should be dismissed. Al—"

"And another thing," he said annoyed. "Don't speak to royalty without their permission. It's not customary. Sofia is probably wondering why I would allow you to speak so plainly to her."

Rage welled up in Madeline like it never had before, she quickly responded, "Can I give you some advice then your Majesty? Don't fuck your servants if you don't wish them to speak so plain."

Madeline turned on her heel and walked back into the Music Room without his permission. She grabbed the cloth by her bucket as he stood in the doorway angry. Greg looked between the two of them and shook his head. Alex re-entered the room, and immediately changed his disposition as he walked back in, all smiles for Princess Sofia. "Well, that's settled. Princess, will you play me a song on the flute?"

Sofia beamed as she brought the flute to her lips, and with perfect posture, began playing a beautiful, soft piece. Madeline pretended to dust the window sill while she listened in awe. Sofia was fairly talented. Madeline had a sideways view of Greg, who stood next to Sofia, and could see that even he was enraptured. She finished the song and Greg and Alex began clapping. Madeline felt a sinking feeling in the pit of her stomach. She thought of the day Alex showed her how to play the harp. It was hard to play a simple nursery rhyme. She would never be able to play the harp for him like Sofia played the flute.

"That was incredible Sofia," said Alex. "I'll play a song for you."

He went to the shelves and took out a large black case as Sofia sat down on a bench, and Greg joined her. He took a cello from out of the case, and her eyes brightened. "Oh, you play the cello!"

"He plays everything," said Greg sharply.

Madeline glanced over and wondered what their boyhood music lessons must have been like for Greg. If Alex was a gifted pupil as so many had said, it must have been challenging for Greg to impress their tutors.

Alex sat down on a bench, and held up the cello between his legs and wrapping his arm about its neck, he gently put his fingers to the strings and held up the bow. He whisked it to the strings and began playing, his long fingers pressing the strings artfully. The cello became like a woman he held in his arms and made love to. It was mesmerizing. Madeline wanted to storm out of the room in tears. That he played so magnificently for Princess Sofia bothered her. She was not sure if he was doing this to impress Sofia, or hurt her. Either way, she was jealous and angry. He had probably impressed all sorts of women this way.

He finally finished, and Sofia applauded. "Oh Alex, I had always heard you were quite the musician. But I'm still stunned. That was – I have no words to describe it."

"Thank you, Princess," he said a grinning from ear to ear.

"Shall I throw up in my bucket now or later?" Madeline whispered beneath her breath. The three looked over at her. She went on dusting as if she said nothing. In the corner of her eye, she could see that Greg had heard what she had said. He was trying to hold back his laughter, biting his fist. Sofia looked confused. Alex looked down at his cello and tapped the strings trying to figure out what Madeline said.

"I'd like to play something," Greg said. "Because even though I'm not so amazing that people from other countries know how gifted I am, I still like playing."

Sofia laughed heartily. Alex smiled shaking his head. Madeline grinned. Only Greg knew how to put Alex in his place. He even had the cheek to do it in front of company. She made a mental note to somehow thank him; she'd slip double the brandy into his teapot at the next House of Lords meeting.

Greg went over to the shelves and picked up a case. He opened it and pulled out a violin.

"Don't play on my Strads," said Alex. "You're rough with violins."

"What? You have seven of them. If I break one, I'm sure you could spare it."

"Spare a Stradivarius?" Alex said aghast. "Who would do that? Those violins are priceless and I don't want you ruining them. You can't ask the world's greatest violin maker to replace a violin when he's dead."

"Don't worry, I'm sure Stradivarius would come off his cloud in heaven just to replace it for you, your Majesty. You are the King of England after all."

Sofia softly giggled, then stopped, looking timidly at Alex, who was rolling his eyes. Greg held the violin at his chin and shoulder and began playing a slow piece. He was not as talented as Alex, but he played well. "Boring piece of classical," said Greg as he finished the piece. "Now, you're going to listen to some real music."

He started stomping his foot to the floor and started assaulting the strings with the bow. He was fiddling a kind of Irish folk song, and started dancing and stomping as he played. Madeline

371

looked up with a big smile on her face, she wished she could dance or clap.

"You're not a royal stiff like his Majesty, are you Princess?" he asked. "You're gonna dance, aren't you?"

Sofia nodded her head excitedly and grabbed Alex's hand and began dancing with him. Madeline watched the two of them and she noticed he was not as swift on his feet as he was with classical music. He looked cross to have to have to dance to it.

Greg danced about the room, continuing the assault on the violin. He neared where Madeline was, still dusting. "Come, Miss Black, dance with me," he said, stomping about her.

"I don't think so Sir Gregory," Madeline said, trying to busy herself with her work.

"Oh, don't break my heart Miss Black, please dance with me."

She paused for only a second before she threw her cloth back in its bucket. She danced about with him, tossing her hair back and giggling. She was thankful it was not a traditional classical dance. She did not know any traditional dances, but she did know how to jig.

"You're quite good Miss Black," Greg said, surprised. "See Princess, no one can resist an Irish jig."

Sofia clapped and giggled while she danced with Alex.

"You really do put poor Miss Black in awkward situations Sir Gregory," said Alex. He stopped dancing, his eyes narrowing on the pair. "This isn't the first time you've demanded a dance from her."

"And it won't be the last! Will it Miss Black?!" Greg said triumphantly.

"If we do nothing but jigs Sir Gregory, I'll gladly be your dance partner," Madeline laughed.

When Greg finished playing, Alex's lips tightened, "Thank you Sir Gregory. But we really should be moving on. There are other rooms in the castle the Princess has not seen."

The three of them put their instruments down and left the room. Alex did not glance in Madeline's direction before leaving. Instead, he took Sofia's arm. Greg followed at their heels, closing the door behind him, giving Madeline a wink. She smiled back faintly.

She knelt next to the organ and went back to cleaning it. As she tried to dust the detailed wood carved masterpiece, all she could think about was Alex's flirting with Sofia. She grew frustrated and stood up. "Why am I even going through all this trouble," she muttered, clenching her fists. "He's a cad anyway. Argh! Why should I clean his Music Room?"

She threw the cloth at the organ, then without a second thought picked up the pail of water and doused the organ.

"Easier this way anyway!" she cried angrily. Madeline grabbed some dry towels and began soaking up the water. There was a good chance she had damaged the organ, and they would have to send someone in to fix it. But at this point, she couldn't care less. If he really believed that she would try to sabotage him so that he would have to leave England and go to war, he didn't know how much she cared.

24

EVEN A KING

Shortly after Alex, Sofia and Greg finished the tour, Princess Sofia retired to her apartments to take a nap before dinner. The two friends left for the mews, to go hunting for quail. Alex had not said much to Greg as they prepared for the afternoon.

Alex wasn't in the mood to talk. Most of his conversation with Greg was short, one-word answers and he barely made eye contact while he spoke. When they finally arrived in the forest, all Greg could hear was the twigs breaking beneath his feet. Alex walked several paces ahead of him.

"So where do you want to head today? North or east? We had some luck heading east last time," Greg said, trying to break the tension.

"East."

"How many did you want to catch before heading back?"

"I don't know," Alex said flatly. He pushed forward, moving further into the forest with little care of where his friend was.

"So, do you really think Madeline told Tilly those things?" Greg asked casually, trying to figure out why Alex was giving him the cold shoulder.

Alex continued to step through the forest, trying to be careful of not frightening their prey. Despite his focus on hunting, he contemplated Greg's question. He didn't know how he felt about Madeline's involvement in the rumour. But something was irking him. "What was up with you? Showing me up in the Music Room?" Alex asked.

"Well, I thought that –"

"You clearly were trying to impress someone."

"Alex," Greg said, rubbing the back of his neck.

"Just be honest. You seem to want to be around her and comfort her whenever she's sad. Do you fancy Madeline?"

Greg looked at him, he put his hand on his forehead as he laughed. "Are you serious?"

"Explain getting drunk with her in the carriage, trying to console her at the ball and showing off and dancing in the Music Room," Alex grimaced.

"What were you playing at Alex? 'Oh Sofia,'" he said imitating Alex in a refined accent, "'that was incredible flute playing, can I play a song for you?'"

"So you admit it then? You want Madeline."

"What?! NO! But you're being a prat. Not just to Madeline, but to Sofia too. Like you really thought she was a magnificent flute player. She's no better than me," Greg said shaking his head.

"I was just being polite," Alex said sheepishly.

"Maybe. But, in the end, you don't care for her. Be fair and don't do things to make her fall in love with you. If you ask me, you deserved what you got in the Music Room. Serves you right for trying to use Sofia to make Madeline angry."

Alex stopped in mid-stride and put his gun at his side, a solemn look of disappointment of himself on his face. "You're right."

"I know."

He turned around to face his friend. "Sorry Greg. I know I've been difficult. It's just being me is difficult. I've always had to choose my countries needs over my own. But with Madeline, I don't know if I can. I'm jealous of you. If I were you, I'd be allowed to love whomever I wanted."

"I know," said Greg awkwardly.

Later, they headed back to the mews on their horses, and Alex went back to his apartments with Greg's words still in his mind. He knew that impressing Sofia to hurt Madeline was wrong, but he was angry. He figured Madeline had put Tilly up to telling lies to get rid of Sofia. Tilly was too young to understand what sharing women meant. A girl like Tilly would probably think sharing women meant sharing time. Greg was in his company often.

Nonetheless, he felt torn. Maybe it was because he loved Madeline, but he did not feel that she would do that to him. On the other hand, if Tilly invented the lie, why did she take it all back? He mulled over the situation, wondering if he should send Madeline back to Buckingham Palace. If her jealousy was getting the better of her already, it would only get worse.

He paced about his Bedchamber, then stopped. His eyes shifted slowly. He felt a presence, he heard a steady breathing. It wasn't heavy. It was soft and a little shallow. Whoever it was, they were small in stature. He unsheathed his dagger from under his coat, "Whoever is hiding under the bed, I'd suggest you reveal yourself. If you don't —"

He stopped mid-sentence as Tilly crawled out, her face white. She stood in front of him with her hands in her dress pockets and kept her eyes glued to the floor. He put away his dagger as he glared at her. "So, Madeline Black told you that I share women, hm?" He grabbed her by her arm and pushed her against the bedpost.

"Well, it was a bit of a misunderstanding your Majesty," she said, unable to look at him. "When she told me that, she was only joking, I took her seriously."

"You're an odd girl Tilly Smith. Why would you believe that from Madeline Black? Why do you think she knows anything personal about me?"

"She is seeing Sir Gregory Umbridge, isn't she?"

He tilted his head in confusion. For whatever reason, Tilly thought Madeline was with Greg, and if she believed that, whatever Madeline said about himself or Greg, Tilly would believe. He sighed. What he had feared had happened did; Madeline told lies to get rid of Sofia. He released Tilly from his grip.

"What are you doing in my room?" he asked.

She looked down sheepishly. "I wanted to ask you if I had ruined things between you and the Princess," she lied.

"No, Miss Smith," he said. He raised his brow, "Why didn't you just wait until the next time you saw the Princess and ask her instead of lurking in my private quarters?"

She shrugged a shoulder.

"Never mind. Tell me, what exactly did Miss Black say to you? When was your conversation with her?"

"The night of the ball. She was serving with me, I was telling her how lovely the Princess was. Then she told me she felt sorry for Princess Sofia. When I asked why, she said that Sir Gregory told her, well you know."

"Sir Gregory told her that we share women?" he said finishing for her.

Though everything Tilly said added up, he still had a feeling he couldn't shake. He didn't want it to be true.

"So will you be dismissing Miss Black?" asked Tilly.

"That's not your business. You should be leaving now."

Tilly didn't move. She held the bedpost.

"You're still here Miss Smith," he said annoyed.

"I know," she said slowly, "but I have to confess something."

"Go on."

"Miss Black has done something awful. I think she should be dismissed."

His heart sank, "What has she done?"

"She's been stealing things."

"Such as?"

"Nothing from you. But, she has been taking things from Princess Sofia."

"Mm? What did she take?"

"Some dresses. You'll find them in her drawers," said Tilly trying to sound helpful.

"Oh?" he said his curiosity piqued. "What do they look like?"

"Fashionable day dresses. One was ivory with gold lace, another was light purple and –"

"Hm," he interrupted. Tilly was describing the dresses he gave Madeline weeks ago. "So you were snooping about Miss Black's things?"

"No, no your Majesty," she said putting her hands behind her back. "Miss Black told me about them. She said she took them from the Princess and planned to sell them."

He furrowed his brow, "Stop Miss Smith. You've been lying to me."

"I'm sorry, your Majesty? Lying?" Tilly asked feigning innocence.

"I know the dresses you're talking about. Miss Black didn't steal them from the Princess."

She looked up at him fearfully, "I-I'm not lying."

"I know who gave Miss Black those dresses," he said firmly.

"Oh."

"You started the rumour that Sir Gregory and I share women, didn't you? Now, you're trying to get Miss Black dismissed so that the truth won't come out."

379

"No," said Tilly her hands quivering.

"Are you sure? I can always bring Sir Gregory and Miss Black here to sort this all out. After all, why would Miss Black tell you that rumour?" he asked angrily. "Even if it were true, which it isn't, why would she tell a young girl of such things?"

Tilly went slack-jawed unsure of what to say.

"I can't believe you'd be so foolish to tell so many lies," Alex went on. "You're lucky you're young. If you weren't, the punishment would be much more severe. I think I'll just send you back to your family."

"Oh your Majesty, King Alexander, please don't," she begged and got on her knees crying into his coat.

"Pack your things Miss Smith, you're leaving." He brushed her off and pointed at the door. "I want you gone by the evening."

Tilly got up and walked to the chamber door, crying quietly.

"Oh and Miss Smith, one more thing," Alex called across the room.

Tilly turned, her lips trembling.

"Apologize to Miss Black before you leave," he said. "You tried to get her dismissed today."

"Why should I?" Tilly spat back. She slammed the door snivelling as she left.

Alex grinned from ear to ear. He owed Madeline an apology. He left his chamber, and upon seeing a footman, he requested that he send Miss Black to serve him tea in the Weaponry Room. It was an odd request, but it was unlikely Princess Sofia would go there.

Madeline lay on her bed depressed, thinking of a way that she could convince Alex that Tilly was the one behind all the drama. She was angry that she had to convince him of anything. He should have believed her. If he loved her like he said he did, then why was it difficult for him to trust her? He did not know how crazy Tilly was. Madeline was going to give Tilly an earful next time she saw her. Just then, Tilly stormed into their dormitory room crying. She saw Madeline and began screaming, "YOU! IT'S YOUR FAULT!"

Tilly ran at Madeline. Madeline scrambled off the bed, and Tilly crashed onto it, missing her. "YOU SAID SOMETHING, DIDN'T YOU?" she screeched, jumping at Madeline.

Tilly tried wrapping her hands around Madeline's neck, but Madeline pulled her hair and smacked her face. "Are you mad, Tilly? You come in here and attack me? What have I done?"

Tilly got up, wide-eyed. Her body trembled as she tried to collect herself, "I've been sacked by the King himself." She began to weep. "I figure someone must have said something to him. Probably you. You're with Sir Gregory Umbridge."

"Tell me Tilly, what were you doing when the King sacked you? Were you in his chambers again?"

Tilly opened her mouth to speak then stopped, "What should that matter?"

"It should matter plenty if you've been spending time in places you shouldn't be," Madeline scolded. "Of course, the King is going to be suspicious of you. So, I suppose he knows now that **you** lied to the Princess?"

Tilly said nothing but stomped over to the armoire and pulled out her bag and began packing her things. Madeline discreetly moved to the door to exit.

"Where are you going?!" Tilly whimpered.

"I have things I need to take care of Tilly. Besides I'm —"

"I'm not done talking to you!" she snapped.

"What is it?" Madeline asked peeved.

"Well, I thought since you were such good friends with Sir Gregory Umbridge, maybe you could help me? King Alexander listens to just about everything he says. I'm sure you could help me."

Madeline folded her arms, disgusted. "Let me see if I understand this. You come in here yelling at me, saying I'm the reason you got sacked. You come running at me and try to attack me. Then you expect me to help you? PISS OFF!"

Madeline turned on her heel and walked down the dormitory corridors, leaving Tilly to pack her things. She joined some of the other servants in the parlour that had finished their work for the day. Plopping onto one of the sofas she sighed, she missed Marie and Sissy. She would never have had an experience like that with them. Then again, they were sane.

As she sat, she wondered what happened between Tilly and Alex, though, it didn't really matter. He knew the truth now and she expected more than an apology. She gazed at the other servants. She realized for the first time that she had spent so much time with Alex in the past couple weeks, she had barely gotten to know anyone, other than Tilly.

She was about to start a conversation with a group of them playing cards, when a tall, burly footman entered the room. "Are you Miss Black? The servant from Buckingham Palace?" he asked.

"Yes."

"The King has made a request that you serve him tea in the Weaponry Room in the Round Tower."

She beamed, "Really?"

"Uh … yes."

"Ahem," she said clearing her throat. "Well, I suppose I should be on my way then."

She got up from the sofa and began making her way out of the servants' quarters.

Once out of the parlour, she skipped through the galleries and halls. She knew that Alex did not want tea. He was going to give her an apology. Though she was happy, she had no intention of forgiving him quickly. He had to prove he was sorry first.

Alex waited alone in the Weaponry Room, trying to think of what to say and how to make it up to her. He paced about, nervous. He hoped she had not prepared tea before she came down. He heard some rustling of skirts and turned to see Madeline standing by the door. She looked about the room in awe.

It was unlike any other room in the castle. Instead of tapestries, paintings and wainscoting covering the walls, there were swords, arms, pistols and armour. All the arms were arranged in a way that they made designs on the wall; the swords weaved to make lattices, the pistols spooned one another to make circular spirals and there were bunches of spears. Large glass and oak hutches held more weaponry and armour. There were several red silk benches about the room, along with a torso of a wooden dummy which Madeline found a little strange. He stood in the middle of the room, his hand at his back, he gave a slight bow.

"Miss Black."

"I come here by command, not my free will," she said, trying to hide how relieved she was.

"I know," he said walking toward her.

"So what is it then? You're apologizing?" she scolded. "You're going to have to command forgiveness from me because I won't give it to you."

He looked at her tenderly. This is what he loved about her, what he loved about being with her – he was not some prize she was trying to win. Most women would have forgiven him the moment he showed regret, or gave a put-on apology. He was hers, and she knew it; without her he was a ship lost at sea. A small part of him wished it was as easy as giving her a gift. But she wasn't like the noble women or the princesses he knew. Any woman of good breeding would be delighted by that. But she couldn't be bought in a situation like this.

He looked up with a sad, helpless expression so sweet. She sighed, feeling her anger melt. Knowing she was moments from caving, she turned her head trying to ignore him. But then he dropped to his knees and grabbed her hand, "Madeline Black, I'm sorry for being such a prat. I shouldn't have doubted you and I definitely shouldn't have tried to make you jealous." He kissed her hands hard. "I know I can't buy your affections or forgiveness. All I have to offer you is my words, and to tell you how truly sorry I am. If that's not enough, tell me what is. It's yours."

Her lips trembled at his words. She looked deeply into his crystal blue eyes full of sincerity. He was right. She would have rejected any gift he gave. There, he was the King of England offering the only thing he had – himself. She thought of the time she begged for forgiveness when she had stolen the vase, and his special brand of discipline he gave her in the Throne Room. She thought of the last time she was angry with him, and the carriage ride to Windsor Castle. She smirked and drew close to him, reaching down his chest and abdomen, grasping the handle of his dagger in his coat. She unsheathed it, held it at his neck, a wicked grin on her face.

"Make it up to me," she said. She turned and headed toward one of the benches and sat down, spreading her legs.

"Gladly," he said with a devilish smile as he crawled over to her.

Alex lifted her skirts and leaned in, but she restrained him with the dagger at his neck again, "Alex."

"Yes?"

"This time, you're not done until I say. And you will do everything I say."

"Yes, Miss Black."

He slowly pushed the dagger away. He began massaging her with his fingers inside her, Madeline held the dagger against him once more,

"Ah, ah, your Majesty," she teased, "I want nothing but tongue. I'm not going to make this easy on you."

Alex nodded. She rested the dagger on the bench and he pecked a string of kisses up and down her thighs. She curled her toes, she loved the teasing, but it made her mental too. She grabbed his head with both her hands and forced his lips on hers. Alex grunted a muffled grunt between her thighs, surprised at her. He raised his eyes, giving her a look.

"What? You said you were going to make it up to me," she taunted.

Alex didn't protest. He nodded his head, brushing his tongue up and down her wet slit. She squeezed her eyes, biting her lip. Her eyes fell on the door and she realized couldn't make a sound. The door was open; the whole situation was reckless. Alex carried on, pushing his mouth and nose into her cunt, licking and sucking at her pussy lips, ignoring the risk along with her.

"Huuhhh," she whimpered softly.

He stopped his gazed fixed on her again.

"Keep going! You're supposed to –" She stopped talking as Alex gave her a long hard lick up her cunt. Madeline followed his lick with her hips, as she could feel he hot juice trickle around her sex.

He watched her as she purred contently, a sweet expression on her face. He smiled inwardly, she tasted more smooth and sweet than the honey he put in his tea. He couldn't really define this as a punishment or 'making it up' to her. He would do it anytime she asked, cancelling his parties, dinners, meetings, holidays. Whatever. If it meant he could have one of his heads between her legs, he didn't care. When he swallowed her nectar, he poked his tongue inside wanting more. Her thighs began trembling and she began to squirm. He moaned as his tongue took her flavour again.

She wriggled knowing what she needed next. "Suck on it."

Alex focused on her love button suckling on it softly.

"Harder Alex! Hard!"

He sucked back harder, brushing the tip of her clit with his tongue

"Yes! Huh yes, huh, so ... close .... Huh. Mmm ... ERRRR." She tried to let out a soundless scream, but it sounded more like a growl. She came into his mouth and he lapped her up furiously, which had her spinning. Grasping the bench with her

386

hand, she thrust her body forward, spurting into his mouth. She gushed like a waterfall, he could barely keep up with her.

When she stopped trembling, he stood up and looked down on her. She reached down and began to rub herself, pushing the last spasms of her peak coursing through her limbs. Not able to contain himself, he undid his trousers and let them drop to his ankles, revealing his hard sex. He took it into his hand and bent down positioning himself before her.

"I thought you were making things up to me your Majesty?"

"Fancy that," he said in disbelief, "you're going to try to tell me you don't need this right now?"

The corners of her lips curved into a smile. He was right. She gave in, and bent over the bench, her bottom in the air. He tossed up her skirts, throwing them over her hips. He moved closer to her and she could feel him, skin to skin. The tip of his head touched her labia then slowly slipped inside her. She murmured as she adjusted to his cock. He sighed as the warm wet velvet enveloped around him.

"Mmm," he muttered letting a long breath of air from his nose.

He started slowly probing into her wanton pussy filling his insatiable desire to have her. He could feel himself slick within her. He grasped on to her and pulled her toward him, crashing into her firm arse in a frenzy. Gasping, she buckled beneath his force, but brought herself up again. She squealed as she pressed her lips together, he was prodding just the right place. Several more pumps and she was sure she'd explode. But then he did something she didn't expect; he wrapped his arm around her and began pressing against her bud. She could no longer keep control, she slammed her head against the bench.

"AAHHH —" she screamed, cumming onto him. She bit down hard into the silk upholstered bench, ripping the silk, trying to muffle her sound. The bench slammed about the floor as her body shook and he continued ploughing into her. His body trembled, his need to cum grew, as his balls churned. Staring down at her perfect bottom, he grasped it firmly in frustration, and she crooned. He wanted to cum, he needed to cum, but he knew he was going to yell loudly if he did. He needed somewhere to plant his cry. Finally, he saw her soft, supple neck, he crashed into her, moaning into her as he released.

Madeline's body shivered as the vibrations of his pleasure crawled up and down her, gooseflesh covering every inch of her skin. She released her teeth from the silk and noticed two large punctures in the bench seat.

"Happy Miss Black?" he asked raising his brow, looking at the destroyed silk upholstery. He pulled his trousers back on and cradled her in his arms on the bench, kissing her. She could feel her skin tingle again.

"Did it hurt you? Me impressing Sofia?" he asked.

She nodded.

"Do you want me to impress you?"

"I thought you already did," she sighed.

"I have other talents." He stood up and walked over to a display of weapons. "I've been trained in every weapon in this room. See that dummy over there?" he said pointing to the wood torso. "I could obliterate it if you'd like."

She could care less that he could tear apart a dummy. But she was tickled with him trying to impress her. "Use one of the handguns or a rifle, I've never seen a gun go off."

He laughed, "That's a little too easy, dolcezza. Give me a challenge. Make me sweat."

"I thought I already did."

He blushed.

She walked about the room trying to decide. There were too many options. Swords, maces, axes, daggers, rifles, handguns, spears and crossbows and she wanted to give him a reasonable challenge. She soon came across a case of weapons from other cultures, and eras. There were sticks, samurai swords, sabres, twin hooks, balls and chains, claymores and hammers. It was difficult deciding. She was about to grab the ball and chain, "Too easy dolcezza," he said as he looked over her shoulder.

"Well, maybe it isn't."

"Fine."

He threw his coat onto the chair and took the ball and chain. She watched intrigued.

"Stand back, Madeline." He began swinging it, gathering momentum. He threw it at the dummy, taking off its head and hundreds of splinters of wood flew about. He swung it about himself and whipped it back hitting it again it the stomach, and more splinters flew, leaving a huge dent in the dummy. Her jaw dropped in amazement.

"I could destroy the rest of the torso easily, but you're supposed to challenge me, dolcezza." He put the ball in chain back in its display case. "Go on. Pick something else."

She grabbed a pair of axes and handed them to him.

He smiled. "A little more challenging than the ball and chain." He took the axes and walked away from the dummy, he then

389

turned and threw one of the axes in the middle of its chest. He ran towards it, stabbing the second axe into the chest, next to the first, taking out a huge chip of wood. He kept the two axes going taking out chips of wood, and he began to sweat a little. He stopped, breathing heavily, "Again, I could finish this off, or you could give me something more challenging."

She raised her brow, "How about I give you a bow or a spear ... or a wooden stick?"

He laughed, "Make it a fair challenge."

She looked over at the heavy claymores. "How much do those swords weigh?" she asked.

"Mmm, about ten stone."

"Use one of those swords."

He grabbed one knowing that because of its edge, it would not cut clear through the dummy the first few times. He grasped it in both hands and made a large cut into its side, a third of the way through the dummy. He dislodged it and cut another large cut into the other side. He tried to pull the sword back out, but it was wedged in the wood.

"I guess this is a challenge," she said, brightly.

He walked to her, and brushed his knuckles against her cheek, "This is a challenge, hm?"

She grinned and nodded.

He walked back to the dummy and stood in front of it evaluating the damage he had done. He yelled loudly, and kicked the top of the torso. It snapped in two, and the chest fell to the floor, along with the sword. She stood her mouth hanging open.

"I was also trained in martial arts. Impressed?"

Her face went a rosy hue. "Yes," she admitted.

"I'm glad I could finally impress you." He then looked back over at the display cases, "So you've never seen a gun go off?"

"No."

"Want to see?"

He picked up the chest of the wood torso and placed it back on top of the bottom half of the torso. "We'll shoot this off," he said.

She became nervous. "I don't think we should be using guns inside. Aren't you supposed to do target practice outside?"

"There are shields behind the dummy, what's the worst that could happen? Pick a gun."

She studied the guns. There were hundreds of them. They were made in all kinds of sizes and designs. Looking at them she realized she knew nothing about them, so she picked a wooden one with a steel barrel with decorative engravings that flared out at its end. She walked over to him, holding it out in front of her.

"A blunderbuss pistol? Huh. The choice of pirates and thieves. Interesting," he said in a suggestive tone.

"Oh shush, it looked pretty." She gave him the gun, and he walked back over to a hutch and opened one of the drawers. He prepared the gun with gunpowder, and some other kind of gravel like material.

"There," he said handing it back to her.

She looked down and looked back up at him wide-eyed.

"You're shooting," he said simply.

"What? No!" she exclaimed, pushing the gun into his hard chest. He grabbed the gun and wrapped his arm around her.

"Come on," he said pulling her to the centre of the room, several feet away from the dummy.

"I'll ruin something, I don't know how to shoot a gun, Alex."

"Dolcezza, really, it's not hard; just point and shoot."

He held her arm up with his and pointed the gun at the wooden chest. Her arm and hand quivered.

"Stop shaking your hand. Hold the gun straight and pull the trigger."

She tried, but could not stop her hand from shaking, "I don't want to pull the trigger, you do it."

He chortled, "It's not hard. I'm holding your arm, just relax your hand and shoot."

She closed her eyes and shot the pistol, her hand still trembling like a leaf. It shot upwards, missed the dummy, and hit a crossbow mounted above the shields. The crossbow fell to the floor with a loud clatter and smashed into several pieces. She gaped as he ran over to the pieces.

"Aw blast," he moaned falling to his knees. Just then, they could hear steps coming, and their eyes averted to one of the doors. "Go! Leave Madeline!"

She put the pistol on the floor and scurried out of the room, through another door. Tense, she knew that she must have destroyed something valuable.

His lips were quivering, he looked down at the pieces in disbelief. A guard ran in and quickly bowed.

"Your Majesty, is everything all right – OH NO! JOAN OF ARC'S CROSSBOW!"

"Can you see that this gets repaired, if possible?" Alex asked miserably.

"Yes, your Majesty," he collected the pieces of the crossbow and left the room.

Alex sighed as he got up from his knees. A priceless piece of history destroyed, all because he wanted to impress a girl. Shaking his head, he left the room to join the Spanish royals for dinner.

When he arrived at the King's State Dining Room, the Spanish royals, along with Sir Ashton Giles and Greg Umbridge were already there awaiting his arrival. Greg Umbridge, who was typically late for dinner, sat next to Sofia, and seemed to be immersed in conversation with her. As Alex arrived and his presence was announced, everyone but Greg stood up from the table. Upon seeing Sofia rise, Greg followed suit.

"Forgive me for being late," Alex apologized. "I was busy in the Weaponry Room, had little mishap there."

"What happened, your Majesty?" Sofia asked as everyone sat down.

"I accidentally destroyed a priceless piece of history. Joan of Arc's crossbow," he said with a grave expression.

Greg gave him an odd look, knowing there was more to the story.

"Good that you did," King Fernando said. "Women going to war. Nonsense. Women should be at home, looking after children. I raised Sofia to know what makes a woman a good one."

A meek smiled traced Sofia's lips as she gazed longingly at Alex.

Alex grinned, "So Sofia, what is it? What makes a woman a good one?"

There was an awkward silence, as everyone stared in her direction. Sofia stared down into her lap. Greg began to laugh, trying to take the attention off her. "I can only think of one thing that makes a woman a good one," he said, his eyes roaming about Sofia's body. "Oh all right, maybe two or three," he said looking directly down at her breasts.

King Fernando looked over enraged "Sir – that is – she is the Princess of Spain!" he bellowed slamming his fist on the table. "Do not look upon her as if you could own her. You common heathen!"

"Sorry, that he offended your family, Fernando," Alex broke in. "Sometimes Sir Gregory Umbridge forgets himself. Especially when he is in the presence of such beauty."

King Fernando calmed himself at these words. Sofia continued to gaze at her thighs, blushing as the servants began placing the first course on the table.

King Fernando began to speak politics again with Alex while Greg turned his attention to Sofia. "So tell me Princess, did you enjoy the tour about the castle?"

"I wish you didn't do that just now," she whispered ignoring eye contact.

"I'm sorry. I was just trying to get you out of an awkward situation," he whispered back.

394

"Well, I prefer you didn't. I'm supposed to be attracting the King. You're not helping."

"Oh yeah? So, what does make a good woman? I would love to hear your answer."

"I don't need to answer to you," she said through gritted teeth.

"You're right. You don't. But I could tell you if your answer would be a good one in Alex's eyes."

He piqued her interest. She turned to him and answered, "Well, I think what makes a good woman is one that can be supportive, loving, kind, and knows how to look after children."

"That's lovely if you're married to an average man, but being married to the King of England requires more than being supportive and loving."

"Really heathen?" she smiled. "What does the King of England need?"

"He needs a queen," he said assuredly. "A leader, someone that is strong and offers their opinions whether he wants to hear them or not. He also needs someone to look after him."

She began to laugh, "You have some silly ideas Sir Gregory. No man likes an opinionated woman. And what grown man needs a woman to look after him? That's ridiculous."

"Every man. Even a king."

25

TABLES TURNING

It was not until the next House of Lords meeting that Madeline saw Alex again. She felt sorry for the crossbow. She prepared his tray with an extra scone she made herself, and a note.

I'm sorry about the crossbow. I hope it wasn't too important.

I hope you like the raspberry scone. I made it myself.

He discreetly read the card with a smile. Beneath his breath he whispered, "Thank you, dolcezza. Don't worry about the crossbow."

She nodded and continued serving his tea, he softly brushed his fingers against her hand and murmured, "I'll arrange something for the two of us to be alone again."

"Don't keep me waiting too long."

"Never."

She walked down the pulpit stairs and made her way to Lord Bathory, but as she approached him, he abruptly stood up and yelled at Sir Ashton, who sat a few seats down from him.

"We are in the middle of war! The lower classes will simply have to understand that! Food prices will go up. We cannot freely give away food or start a kind of rationing program. They can learn to make do with what they have."

So selfish, Madeline thought. Lord Bathory never thought of anyone that wasn't a noble. She shook her head and rolled her eyes.

"I didn't ask for your opinion missy," Lord Bathory bellowed, annoyed by Madeline's reaction.

"I never gave it my Lord," she retorted as she poured tea from his pot to his cup.

"Oh yes you did!" he countered, "I saw the look you gave me. I know what you were thinking."

"My Lord, I assure you," she grinned cheekily, "if I gave you my opinion you wouldn't be yelling at me – you'd probably smack me."

The House of Lords fell into uproarious laughter, even Alex could not contain himself. Madeline turned to serve the Duke of Axford when Lord Bathory swung his hand out to smack her. Seeing his hand coming towards her, she jumped back. He missed her by an inch. The laughter dropped to a dead silence.

"Good God Bathory," cried the Duke of Axford, "be a gentleman! It was only a joke!"

"Is smacking a woman that has outwitted you the only defence you have?" Alex asked his blood boiling.

"She was out of line, and you know it. If you were any kind of king, if you were a true leader, you would be down here putting her in her place yourself! Hell, you don't do anything properly! We have gentlemen in here that aren't even Lords," Bathory said heatedly, pointing a Sir Ashton and Sir Gregory.

Tension filled the room, sending shivers down everyone's back. Realizing his stupidity, Lord Bathory froze. Alex looked down at him, with an icy glare. "That's disloyalty to your King, Bathory."

"No, your Majes –"

"You've been disloyal for quite some time – plotting. Don't think I don't know."

Gasps could be heard around the room.

"Your Majesty, where did you hear such things? I have –"

"Since my father's death, my advisors and I have been watching you. I have several witnesses to your offences. You're a fool. You even had the audacity and stupidity to plot in my castle. I was waiting to find out whom your other conspirators were and what you had planned. But I can't tolerate another day of having to look at you. Guards – take Lord Bathory and Lord Kinney to Curfew Tower under the charges of High Treason to the King. Once found guilty they will be stripped of their titles and estates and perhaps beheaded."

The blood drained from Lord Kinney's face. Whispers began to fill the room, words like, "Did you know this?"

"How long has this been going on?"

"Lord Kinney too?" As the guards circled about Lord Kinney and Lord Bathory.

Lord Bathory ran at Madeline and pushed her to the floor. "Dumb girl! This is your fault."

"GUARDS RESTRAIN THAT MAN!" Alex yelled.

The guards grabbed Lord Bathory and held his arms behind his back.

"Sir Gregory, please assist Miss Black," Alex commanded.

With a big grin, Greg moved over and helped Madeline up off the ground. She looked over to Alex, who looked angry as he contemplated something. The guards began to pull Lord Bathory away, but he stopped them.

"One moment." Alex descended the pulpit to the floor and stood in front of Lord Bathory. He clenched his hand into a fist and pounded his face.

"YES," yelled Greg Umbridge, punching his fist in the air. Lord Bathory wailed in agony, falling back into the guards. He regained his balance and took his hands from his face. His nose was gushing blood and his upper lip was cut.

"That was a cheap shot, your Majesty," he spat.

"Yes, it was … I'm glad I took it."

The guards pulled Lord Bathory and Lord Kinney out. Greg looked at his friend, "I would have gladly punched him for you, you know. No need to get your royal hands dirty."

"I know," Alex said as he grasped Madeline's shoulders. "Are you okay Miss Black?"

"I'm fine, your Majesty."

"Would you like a break? Perhaps lie down in your dormitory for a bit?"

"It's quite all right. I'll continue with tea."

"No. I think we are through with this meeting anyway," Alex said beneath his breath. He walked back up to his pulpit. "Given today's events, this meeting is adjourned."

Madeline shuffled out of the room with the Lords, leaving Alex with Sir Ashton and Greg. She headed to the Crimson Drawing Room. There wouldn't be much to clean. Other maids had also been assigned to the room and had probably done most of it, which was fine. She didn't want to lift a finger anyway. What happened at the meeting had shaken her.

As she entered the room, she looked down and traced the design on the parquet wood floor with her shoe. It was clean. She walked over and swept her finger across the black marble chimneypiece. Not a speck of dust. The crimson drapes with their gold fringes looked tidy. No cobwebs were in the crevices of the gold gilt ceiling either. She looked at the size of the room and realized it wasn't that it wasn't that big. Two maids could clean this room.

A smile crept on her face knowing Alex had looked after her. Scheduling too many servants for a room on a day she had to do tea time was the perfect way to get her out of work. The regular servants would suspect that it was some sort of mix-up since they would see on the schedule that she also had to do tea.

It was a relief. It gave her a moment alone to collect herself from the drama that happened earlier. She sat on one of the red couches, resting her head on one of the large pillows. She idly ran her fingers through a gold tassel.

"Hello, Miss Black. I've been looking for you." Madeline jumped up and whirled around. It was Princess Sofia.

"Your Royal Highness," Madeline said. She curtsied, humiliated that she had been caught resting when she should have been working.

"I was wondering if I could speak to you about something?" Princess Sofia asked ignoring Madeline's infraction.

"What can I help you with Princess Sofia?" Madeline asked, putting her hands behind her back. She wondered if it had something to do with Tilly.

"Well, I can't help but notice that Tilly Smith is not here anymore," she began innocently. "As you know she told me some odd things about the King. I was just curious if you could –"

"Explain?" Madeline said with attitude, putting her hands on her hips. Madeline sighed, knowing she had overstepped her boundary and Sofia didn't deserve it. She put her hands to her sides, "I'm sorry for that. I just don't like Tilly. The reason she told you those lies is because she loves the King."

Sofia laughed, "But she's just a girl!"

"Don't underestimate her. That girl used to sneak into the King's Apartments all the time. The King found her there the day she was ordered to leave the castle."

Sofia tapped her chin with her finger. "Why do you think she mentioned your name, Miss Black?"

"We shared a dormitory room together. I'm usually serving at Buckingham Palace. We weren't close, she needed someone to blame I suppose."

Sofia said nothing, but went over to the couch and sat down. Feeling awkward, Madeline went over to the tapestries and began cleaning them with a dry brush. But then Princess Sofia spoke, "Now that Tilly is gone, I need someone to replace her. The other woman that serves me is Dutch and doesn't know much English, Spanish or any other language I know."

Madeline could see where this was going, she quickly turned from the tapestry and interjected, "Well, I'm sure Mr. Tinney could recommend someone to you."

"Oh, I don't want to trouble him. You've been quite honest with me about the whole situation. When I asked his Majesty, he would not tell me much except to say that he had got rid of Tilly."

"The King is wise," she swallowed hard trying to change the subject. "When he was young –"

"Miss Black could you replace Miss Smith?" the Princess interrupted.

Madeline's breath was caught in her chest as she stopped brushing the tapestry. This was the last thing she wanted; to witness and hear everything that went on between Sofia and Alex. It would make things more complicated than they already were. She began to make excuses, "I have to do afternoon teas for the House of Lords, I'm not so sure the King wants me to stop that. He specifically requested that I do it."

"Oh, that's not a problem for me. I mean you only do it for a few hours a week. I won't mind. Besides, if he specifically asked for you, then I know you'll be an excellent replacement."

"Well, I don't know –"

"I'm sure the King won't mind. You are helping a guest."

Just then Alex entered the room his eyes glued to Madeline. He walked towards her, extending his arms when he stopped dead in his tracks noticing Princess Sofia.

"Your Majesty, I'm so glad you're here," Sofia beamed. "Miss Black has just agreed to be Miss Smith's replacement."

Bewildered, Alex addressed Madeline, "But Miss Black, I'll be needing you to take care of afternoon tea."

"That's quite all right," said Sofia. "Miss Black can still do that. So how was the meeting today?"

"Satisfactory," he said quickly adding, "I really don't think Miss Black is the proper replacement Sofia, she's more of a housemaid, not a personal servant."

"It's not that difficult, I'm sure she'll be fine." He opened his mouth to protest again, but Sofia interjected, "I feel I can trust Miss Black. I would be most comfortable with her."

He gave Madeline a helpless look. "All right Princess," he said.

Madeline pursed her lips. She wanted to object, but how could she to a king and a princess?

"Anyway Miss Black," Alex went on, "I wanted to ask if you are all right. I imagine what happened in the meeting was startling."

"As I told you earlier, I'm quite fine your Majesty," said Madeline.

The Princess gave a puzzled look. "Why should Miss Black be so startled? What happened in the meeting?"

"Well, Lord Bathory was sent to the Curfew Tower for high treason. He pushed Miss Black to the floor before leaving," Alex explained.

Sofia looked shocked, her usual sweet demeanour changed to a harsh one. "I asked you a moment ago how the meeting went, and you said it was 'satisfactory'."

"I'm sorry Sofia," Alex said, realizing his mistake. "I meant to tell you, I just well —"

"Meant to tell me? You told me after you checked on your servant?" Sofia stomped out of the room, her arms folded across her chest. Madeline watched in surprise at her sudden mood swing.

Alex turned to her, a sweet smile crept on his face before he took her into his arms. She could smell the familiar scent of sandalwood as she pushed her hands against his solid chest, "Alex," she giggled.

"What? She's gone now."

"This isn't smart."

He melded his lips to hers. She playfully tried to fend him off, but clasped between his hard muscles it was impossible. She gave in, melting her mouth to his, knowing she could never ignore his advances. She crooned as his lips tickled her neck and shoulder, and she kissed him back, enjoying the taste of his skin, wishing she could have him whenever she wanted.

He backed her down onto the couch as a thought came upon her. With Lord Bathory imprisoned, perhaps the Spanish royals could be sent back. The charade could end. None of the other Lords would propose the King go to war. She pushed him back, and he relented. "What is it?" he asked concerned.

"With Lord Bathory out of the House of Lords, you no longer have a need to court Princess Sofia."

"Well," he began hesitantly, "I can't ask them to leave. Besides, there is no guarantee that none of the other Lords would not suggest I go to war, now that the idea has been put in their heads. Don't forget, there are Lords that support Bathory and his vision. If I were to die now, Parliament would most likely take him from Curfew Tower and make him king. Right now, his supporters would be desperate to murder me themselves. I wouldn't be surprised if they are planning something now."

She stared at him, "So your life is endangered more now than it was before?"

"Well, for now, yes," he said quickly adding, "but once Bathory's trial is over, and he has been stripped of his titles, then I no longer have to worry about him or his supporters. A full investigation will take place, and we will learn who the conspirators were."

Her eyes began to well up. She wished she hadn't said what she did, Alex would not have reacted the way he had. Tears streamed down her face, having Princess Sofia come was to save him from a murder plot, now she had put him back in it.

"How long will it take for a trial?" she asked.

"Several weeks."

"But you're the King. You can't speed that up?" she asked getting up from the couch.

"I'm the King, but there are laws to be followed in these types of matters. This will all be over soon, I promise you," he said confidently. "Truthfully, I'm glad you did what you did in the meeting."

"I'm not, this is all my fault," she stammered. "If something happens to you —"

"Nothing will happen," he interjected. "I'll keep Princess Sofia in my company during the day."

She guffawed, "What good will that do?"

"The conspirators won't want to ruffle any feathers with the Spanish royals. Once they come back to power in Spain again, there will be tensions between them and Britain if they get Sofia involved in any way."

"Your life is too much politics."

He laughed.

"That's not funny," she said shaking her head. "I can't handle all this. Pretending with Princess Sofia, worrying about you … about us."

"I know," he said, understanding how exhausting it must be for her.

"So you're just going to continue to court Sofia then?"

"It won't be for too much longer. Once Bathory is found guilty, I will not have him imprisoned for life, I'll have him beheaded."

Her eyes widened, "Are you sure you want to do that? I mean, he is your cousin."

He stood up and wandered over to the fireplace. Resting his hand on the mantle, he stared down at the small fire. "When you're a king there isn't always room for leniency, especially when it comes to power hungry relatives. God knows how many men have become kings by murdering whoever was ruling."

Just then Sofia entered the room, she looked between the two curiously, then turned to Madeline. "If you are to wait upon me Miss Black you should be with me don't you think?"

"Yes, sorry your Highness," Madeline curtsied and followed her at her heels. She could tell by Princess Sofia's swift movements that she was annoyed. They had walked through several State Apartments and a hall before they reached her apartments.

"I need help getting prepared for dinner," Sofia said curtly as they entered her room. "Can you prepare a bath for me?"

Madeline looked about the room, it was beautifully decorated with a large king sized bed with a silk canopy of dark purple and blue. Silver fringes and tassels hung all around its seams. The vaulted ceiling had a painting of a seventeenth-century party with nobles dancing and singing.

"The closet is just over here," Sofia said her heels clacking against the hardwood floor as she moved to a set of huge cherry wood doors.

Madeline looked about, wondering if there were any secret passages leading to this room. She doubted it. It seemed as though there would be no space to do so, unless it was a trap door like the passageway in the office. She opened the large closet doors for Sofia and folded them back. It opened up to a large room, similar to the one in Buckingham Palace with rows of racks of dresses.

"Beautiful," Madeline commented, "are all these yours your Highness?"

"No," said Sofia downcast, "I had to leave all my dresses behind. The King has been so kind to allow me to use these dresses," she smiled. "He is sweet."

"Yes, he is a good king," Madeline agreed.

"Especially to your folk," said Sofia. "He told me about a food program he'd like to start for some of the commoners in England. That's quite kind of a king to his lower subjects."

"Yes. I heard him talk about it in the House of Lords meetings."

"What do you think of it?"

"It's good of him. But it's useless to the commoners."

The Princess gave her an odd look. She wasn't used to servants saying what they thought. "King Alex mentioned you were quite outspoken," she began, "I suppose it doesn't bother him. Then again, he's the type that regularly visits your kind."

"What do you mean?" Madeline stuttered, wondering if Alex had taken Princess Sofia out to the Olde King's Head bar.

"Oh, he speaks with his subjects about their concerns at his castle gates once every month. Odd thing for a king to personally do."

"I didn't know that King Alexander did that," Madeline said furrowing her brow.

Princess Sofia laughed, "You lived here and didn't know that your King does that? I suppose he would see no need for a common servant girl to know his schedule."

Madeline said nothing but was surprised that Marie and Tilly had never mentioned this to her. Was it common knowledge like his bravery at the Irish uprisings? She followed Sofia into the closet with all the elaborate dresses around them.

"All of these dresses are so gorgeous," began Sofia, "but I don't know what the King likes. Do you think he likes a more conservative woman or a more revealing woman?"

"I wouldn't know Princess," she said interlocking her fingers.

"He is handsome, gentlemanly and smart. I wish I could figure him out."

"What do you mean?" asked Madeline.

"Well, no woman, not even a well-bred one could be in a room alone with him without trying something. The other day I did. We were alone having tea in the Crimson Drawing Room, we were sitting on one of the couches, and I moved closer to him. I started rubbing his thigh, and I tried to kiss him, but he moved away."

"What's wrong with that? He's being a proper gentleman, you are a princess after all," Madeline reminded her.

"Being a gentleman? Do you know what kind of reputation this man has?" Sofia asked in disbelief. Madeline shrugged her shoulders pretending not to know. Sofia continued, "A few summers ago, we had some visitors from France. One day I overheard some of the ladies talking about him. It was all in French, and I didn't understand most of it, but he seemed to have made quite the impression on them."

"Why? What did they say?"

"I'm not exactly sure, but they were giggling a lot talking about how generous —" Sofia stopped mid-sentence, blushing. "Well, I should not be talking about such things."

Though her curiosity was killing her, Madeline said nothing. She began searching through the dresses, trying to find some suitable dinner attire, when Sofia broke the silence. "You don't think the King is into that sort of thing, do you?"

Madeline looked up from the dresses, "What sort of thing, your Highness?"

"You know …" she paused, her face beet red. "Three ladies were talking about him. You don't think he prefers to please more than one at a time?"

She looked at her in shock, realizing that Sofia and Tilly probably had a similar conversation. "I really wouldn't know."

"But you must know something. You work here. Servants talk."

Madeline did not know what to say. She didn't think Alex was that kind of man. "Well, perhaps they were talking about different things he did with them. I'm sure the King is a gentleman and wouldn't dream of insulting a lady by suggesting that a few other women join them."

Tapping her finger to her chin, Sofia smiled, "Yes, that makes sense. What kind of things do you think the King may be doing?"

"I really wouldn't know," she said innocently.

"You're just being polite. Or shy. Miss Smith was only fourteen and even she had some ideas."

"Perhaps he enjoys certain sexual acts," Madeline offered.

"Like what?"

"Maybe he likes it when a woman you know, um … sucks his …" She trailed off, biting her lip.

"Ugh. Here I am trying to guess what kind of lover the King is, and you're saying he might be a deviant," said Sofia frustrated. "No gentleman of good breeding would ever expect a lady, much less a princess to get down on her knees and do that."

How wrong she is, she thought with a smile, visualizing his trembling cock between her lips.

Sofia glanced at her, before her eyes fell to the floor, "Do peasant men enjoy when a woman does that?"

"Sorry, I wouldn't know."

"I wonder what those ladies were talking about," Sofia went on.

"Perhaps he was on his knees loving them?" Madeline suggested, knowing this might get another rise out of her.

"How do you mean?"

"You know … licking?"

"MISS BLACK!" Sofia yelped turning scarlet. "THAT'S DISGUSTING!"

"Well, it's a possibility. Either that or some unusual sex positions."

"No, that's not possible. The Church only approves five different sexual positions," she said matter-of-factly. "I'm sure the King is aware of them and would abide by them."

Madeline's lips trembled as she tried to hold back her laughter. Sofia had taken a strange stance on sex, and a weird view of Alex. Suggesting that he was a little more adventurous was something she refused to hear. She wondered if she should start sucking and riding Alex in front of Sofia to prove a point.

"I'm going to try wearing something a little more revealing tonight," said Sofia. "Something that will show off my bosom."

"How about this?" said Madeline pulling out a plum dress, it had a corset and was a little outdated, but would show her cleavage. Sofia scanned the dress. "Yes, I think he would like that. I think he might like breasts."

Madeline laughed, Sofia did not have much for breasts, "What makes you think this your Highness?"

"Miss Black, every man has a favourite body part; bottoms, breasts, legs. I notice that Alex looks at breasts a lot." She looked at Madeline's chest and pursed her lips.

At that moment, another maid walked into the room and looked between the two.

"Miss Van Gogh," Sofia called across the room, "this is my new maid, Miss Black. Do you know each other?"

They both shook their heads. Madeline surveyed Miss Van Gogh. She was a spindly woman in her mid-thirties with dark blonde hair and blue eyes.

"I'm Aletta Van Gogh," she said in her heavy Dutch accent.

"Madeline Black."

"I'm learn English."

Madeline nodded in understanding, "That's fine."

"I like the cut of the dress, I just don't like the colour," Sofia said, ending their conversation. "Can you find a similar dress in red and gold?"

Dazed, Madeline looked at the rack of dresses wondering where she should begin, she looked over to Aletta, who looked very confused. "Aletta," Madeline said and began enunciating her words, "This dress. But in red and gold."

Aletta seemed to understand this, and the two went searching through the racks while Princess Sofia sat at the huge mahogany dressing table in the closet and began looking through the drawers.

Madeline sorted through a few racks pulling the dresses back to get a good look at their cut. She noticed Aletta go back to the plum dress several times to check its design again. But Madeline had it memorized as she searched through the racks. There was so much boning in the plum dress it could make cleavage of the most unpromising chest.

As Madeline scanned she couldn't help but think that Sofia was an odd princess; she had intimate conversations with maids she barely knew, and asked them for advice on love. But though Sofia was strange, she seemed kind. It made her feel guilty. There would be more conversations about Alex. In time Sofia's confusion would only grow, and Madeline would know why. It sounded as though he was already unresponsive towards her.

A vibrant red and gold silk dress popped out at her. It was similar to what Sofia had in mind. She took it off the rack and made her way through the racks of dresses back to Sofia, who was staring at her lap. She walked up behind her, about to tap her on the back when she noticed what Sofia was actually doing. Staring down, the Princess pushed her breasts together with her hands, trying to create cleavage. She glanced back up at the mirror and saw Madeline in the reflection. Immediately she dropped her hands.

Madeline wanted to fall on the floor laughing. She was quirky. First her fainting when she first met Alex, her odd sexual conversations with servants and now this.

"I've got the dress I think," Madeline said, pretending she hadn't caught Sofia pushing up her breasts.

"Ahem, oh excellent. You've got a good eye, Miss Black. Miss Van Gogh?" she called, "Miss Black has found the dress I've been looking for."

413

Sofia sat down at the dressing table, and Madeline and Aletta began to touch up her make-up, presenting different shades of lipsticks, foundations and blushes. Once they had finished, they set to work putting on the dress and stepped back as Sofia gazed at herself in the mirror.

Madeline held her breath as she watched Sofia study herself. She hoped Sofia wasn't particular like Lady Watson. She hated when she had to readjust a dress or reapply make-up. Sofia cinched her waist with her hands and pouted, "There must be a way to make my waist look smaller and my breasts look bigger."

Aletta turned her head away and rolled her eyes. "Princess, you haven't big breasts," she began in her throaty Dutch accent. "That's fine. You're fine lady."

"It can be done Miss Van Gogh, you just need to find me a proper stay or corset," Sofia insisted.

Something told Madeline that this was not the first time Princess Sofia tried to find an outfit that would give her a bigger bust.

"There must be a solution," Sofia said stomping her foot to the ground. A large grin grew on her face as she eyed a basket full of accessories next to the full-length mirror. "Those handkerchiefs. I could stuff my stay with them."

It was too much. Both maids keeled over laughing.

Sofia scowled, "Don't laugh." She pointed at their chests. "It's so easy for the two of you to laugh, neither of you have this problem."

They stopped, looking down sheepishly.

"Especially you Miss Black," a smile grew on Sofia's face, "You could probably polish marble floors with those."

414

The three women laughed heartily and for quite some time. When they all finally regained themselves, Madeline asked, "Do you really want us to stuff your corset?"

"Couldn't hurt," said Sofia.

They fulfilled her odd request, as Sofia surveyed herself in the mirror, "The King's love is fickle," she said her eyes in a trance. "He's gorgeous, intelligent and has power beyond the average man. He doesn't have to be kind. He can give a glance or a smile and women will fall to their knees. Being by his side makes you the most powerful woman in the world. But the moment he tires of you, or you become an inconvenience, you are nothing, no one. I've heard of his reputation. He's left a trail of shattered hearts across Europe. If there will ever be a woman to win his heart, they'll need to know his mind first."

Sofia sounded cryptic, as though she feared what she needed to do. Madeline and Aletta said nothing and escorted her down to the State Dining Room.

26

MIND YOUR MANNERS

Greg Umbridge noticed Sofia the moment she entered the State Dining Room. He grinned to himself. It was going to be another night of her dolling herself up and throwing herself at Alex. He loved the fringe benefits of Alex not fancying her. It meant he did not feel guilty about owning her with his eyes and fantasies.

Madeline looked around as King Fernando and Queen Isabelle sat down. Unsure of what to do, she began helping the servants serving the dinner, while keeping a close eye on Sofia. Aletta stood next to Sofia, passing dishes and serving portions of food onto her plate. Greg looked over at King Fernando and began talking about the hunting around the castle.

"Don't be silly Sir Gregory, no one wants to talk about hunting," Sofia said, taking a sip of her drink. "I'd rather hear more about what happened in the House of Lords today."

"Nothing that would interest you," Greg chortled.

"Tsk. Were you even there Sir Gregory?" Sofia asked sarcastically. "A man was sent to prison."

Greg and Sir Ashton looked up at Alex curiously. King Fernando and Queen Isabelle looked stunned.

"Yes," said Alex uncomfortably moving positions in his seat, "Yes, Lord Bathory, he has been disloyal for some time. He became angry with one of my servants, lashed out and said some traitorous words."

"That's appalling. What did this servant do to make him react in such a fashion?" asked King Fernando.

"She rolled her eyes to a comment he made," Alex said, his eyes grazing over Madeline. "I'm quite glad she did it. It finally gave me an excuse to imprison the man."

"If this man was a traitor, then why hadn't you thrown him in jail earlier?" asked King Fernando

"We did not have much evidence, but his public display today was what we needed to convince other Lords that he may have committed high treason."

"It is rude for a servant to roll their eyes at a Lord. She had no place in doing so," Sofia said. "Why would she roll her eyes at him?"

"She didn't agree with something he was saying," said Greg simply.

"Rolling her eyes is still rude," Sofia countered. "What did he say?"

King Fernando glared at Sofia, "Subjects such as politics belong between men of class. Not women or servants."

Sofia dropped her eyes to her lap, humiliated.

"Sir Ashton has been proposing that we hand out food rations to the people of London," said Alex ignoring King Fernando's comment. "These Napoleonic wars have been difficult for them. Lord Bathory felt differently; he thought that the lower class had to make do with what little food they have."

"What do you think, your Majesty?" Sofia asked raising her head again.

"I agree with Sir Ashton. I do talk to some of the commoners at the castle gates from time to time. They don't have much, and yet some of our most patriotic subjects come from this class and have gone to other lands to fight for their King and country. I owe it to them to do what I can for them."

"Oh, that is an excellent idea. You are such a kind and brilliant king to your subjects," said Sofia emphatically.

Madeline rolled her eyes and shook her head. Alex noticed this and could not help himself. He was dying to know what was going on under that pretty black mane of hers. "Miss Black?" he said putting down his fork, "That's the second time you've rolled your eyes today. Now I must know what you are thinking. It always amuses me."

Madeline froze in shock. No one ever wondered what she was thinking. She looked over at Greg Umbridge. His lips were quivering – he was ready to fall over laughing.

"Yes, Miss Black," said Sir Ashton. "If you do have an opinion I'd love to hear it."

Madeline looked about anxiously, unsure if she should speak what she honestly thought. She began cautiously, "Well, it just seems to me, your Majesty, that it makes no sense to give the lower class rations. It will only cause more trouble. People will steal it from one another, use it for currency. Really, if you want to help the poor give them some seeds, dirt and planters and they can plant their own gardens on their rooftops and in their homes. That way they'll be dependent on themselves. If they have a green thumb and do well with their plants, they can sell food or herbs at the market."

Silence came over the room, as Alex was lost in thought. "Sensible. Give a man a fish ... teach a man to fish. That is an excellent idea, Miss Black. Perhaps I should give you the floor to speak in our meetings." He tore a piece of bread and dipped it into the oil.

The dinner conversation continued, and Madeline tried to disappear a few feet behind Sofia, who seemed to be having a one to one conversation with Greg.

"Tell me Sofia, how does it feel?" Greg asked.

"How does what feel?"

"Being upstaged by your servant? I told you Alex liked a woman with an opinion. Not one that agrees with him all the time."

"Tsk! That's what all men say. But you're all the same. I'm sure his Majesty would rather have a woman agree with him than one who will put him in his place and hurt his pride. You'll see, he'll punish Miss Black later."

"Yeah, I'm sure he will," Greg said chuckling. "You know Sofia, you're not the first princess to parade herself down these castle halls, dance and dine with the King and tell him he's brilliant. You're just like every other princess. Blank. No opinion."

Her jaw dropped aghast. She stared at him a few moments before finally speaking. "Fine! You want me to give an opinion?" she said through gritted teeth.

"Yeah, I'd love to hear it," he said, egging her on.

"Greg Umbridge, you are the most foul and simple man I've ever met. You parade yourself down these castle halls drunk off the King's best liquor and wine, and think the King needs you. The King has no use for a drunk that strips himself naked in front of the servants. I have no idea how you weaselled yourself behind these walls, but once I'm behind these walls for good, your drunken arse will be gone."

Greg calmly set down his fork and knife to his plate and turned to the Princess, grinning from ear to ear. "Suck. My. Dick. Princess," he whispered.

She stood up and raised her hand.

SMACK

"I'm the Princess of Spain, don't you ever say anything so vile to me again! I swear Greg Umbridge if you ever step foot on Spanish land your head will be in a noose."

She ran out of the room in tears of embarrassment. Madeline and Aletta were about to follow, when Greg stopped them, "No, Miss Black, Miss Van Gogh, I'll take care of this."

"Umbridge I would like to know how you insulted my daughter," began King Fernando, rising from his chair.

Alex put his hand on King Fernando's shoulder, "I think we can trust Sir Gregory to make a proper apology," he said hoping this would calm him. Fernando sat back down, and Greg left the room to find Sofia. He could hear her sobs and began to follow them. She led him down to the cloisters, where he saw her looking out of a window at the courtyard, wiping her eyes.

"I'm sorry, Sofia. I shouldn't have said that," said Greg.

"I'm sorry, your ROYAL HIGHNESS!" she yelled, turning to him.

"I'm sorry, your Royal Highness," he said.

But more tears fell from her cheeks, as she began breathing heavily. "He-he doesn't seem – interested in me –" she sniffled, "does he? Why isn't he here?"

Greg stood silent, not knowing what to say.

"He's polite and nice but ..." she trailed off. "I need him to love me," she cried and stomped her foot in frustration.

It relieved him that she seemed more perturbed about Alex having no interest in her than what he had said. He thought he would be on his knees begging for forgiveness. She paced about with her arms crossed. Words of anger and frustration about Alex came between sniffles and stutters.

Greg gazed at her sympathetically. He could understand why she was so confused. She was every bit the lady his friend should want. Greg thought she was stunning the first moment he laid eyes on her. She was even cute when she was angry. He stepped in front of her and brushed her cheek wiping her tears. "You're beautiful Princess. You're perfect."

He moved towards her and kissed her slowly. She tried to push him off, then slowly relented, taking him in. Her lips moved in unison with his, he pulled back, a smug smile on his face. "You liked that didn't you, your Royal Highness?" He moved in to kiss her again.

"Don't," she said pushing him away. She ran down the halls, through several state rooms, heading back to her room.

Alone, she sat on a large leather chesterfield next to the window and rested her chin on the edge of its back. She stared out

421

of the window as heavy rain fell across the castle grounds and trickled down the windows. Her face streak with tears, she wiped them with a handkerchief. She hated Greg Umbridge. Not just because he forced her to recognize Alex's disinterest. That he, a simple commoner, had the audacity to say such disgusting words to her and then kiss her. She blushed just thinking about it. Slowly a ghost of a smile grew on her face. She had to admit, he was delicious.

"No" she mumbled to herself. "It meant nothing. He's a wicked heathen. I'm supposed to be with Alex. He should have been the one who kissed me."

She gazed outside. Rain drenched the gardens, and there was a thundering in the distance. As she listened to the rain hitting the window glass, she meditated on the situation. Marrying the King of England was what was expected of her. Her father would be angry if she could not deliver. Besides, she and Alex made sense. He was a gentleman, handsome, polite, intelligent and considerate. Greg Umbridge though kind of ruggedly sexy with his tousled hair and devil-may-care attitude was hardly polite or considerate. Most importantly, he was not a man with power. He did not have any lands or money, just the favour of a king. There was only one thing she could do. She had to be more assertive with Alex; like Greg had been with her. She would have to corner Alex when they were alone and make an offer he would not refuse.

Greg had returned to the State Dining Room and found that King Fernando and Queen Isabelle had already left. Madeline and Aletta were there along with some other servants all of whom were busying themselves clearing the table and stacking the carts. Greg sat back down, rubbing his neck. "Everyone's left so early?"

"Does that come as a surprise?" Alex scoffed.

"I'm not in the mood for a lecture, your Majesty."

422

"Could you tell me what you said to Sofia? Why did she storm out of the room like that?"

With a guilty countenance on his face, Greg answered, "She said some nasty words, so I told her to suck my dick."

Alex jaw dropped, "GREG! You told a PRINCESS to ... oh GOD!" he buried his face in his hands.

Madeline could hear the servants around the room trying their hardest to contain themselves as they cleared the dishes. Recognizing their presence, Alex dismissed them, "All of you leave. Except you Miss Black, someone needs to clear this mess."

Aletta along with the rest of the footmen and servants exited the room shutting both sets of double doors behind them.

"You told her to suck you off? What the hell is wrong with you?" Alex said staring.

"She thinks you're attracted to women that have no opinion."

"It doesn't matter what she said. You don't talk to a woman like that," Alex exclaimed. "Besides, she's just playing a part. A well-bred woman is seen not heard. She's only doing what is expected of her! What you said upset her so much, it's not a wonder she reacted the way she did."

Madeline continued to clear the plates setting them onto a cart, saying nothing. She was a little self-conscious for expressing her thoughts earlier about the food rations. It proved that she was not a woman of good breeding.

"I can only imagine how angry King Fernando is with her for that public explosion," he continued. "No doubt he's giving her an earful. Why did you say that?"

A frown lined Greg's face as he thought of the lecture Sofia would get from her father. He didn't seem like the kind of man that would overlook his daughter's indiscretions. Nonetheless, he made excuses, "She overreacted," Greg said shrugging.

"Overreacted?"

"Yes."

"Really? Madeline, come here and have a seat in Sofia's chair, next to Greg," Alex requested.

Madeline walked over and sat down. She looked between the two curiously.

"Greg, I want you to say to Madeline exactly what you said to Sofia," Alex instructed. "Be honest. Say it with the same intonation. Madeline, after he says it, tell him how it made you feel."

"Fine," said Greg. "But Madeline's a relaxed kind of woman, I doubt she'll care."

"Do it," Alex insisted.

Madeline turned her attention to Greg. He hesitated, twiddling his fingers.

"Go on," Alex insisted.

"Suck. My. Dick Princess," he said imitating it the way he had said it earlier. Madeline said nothing but blinked, taken aback. He gave her a faint smile trying to make her laugh.

"Dolcezza, what are you thinking?" asked Alex.

She pursed her lips, "I think if any man were to say that to me in that crude manner, I'd be running to the Weaponry Room."

"You see Greg, a person doesn't have to have an education in manners to know what you said was inappropriate and offensive," Alex reasoned.

"I apologized," Greg offered, resting his face on his hand.

"I doubt that apology means much. You need to make this right. I want you to offer Princess Sofia more than an apology," said Alex.

Greg laughed heartily, "Right, mate. What can I give a princess?"

"Once you think of the right thing, you'll know," said Madeline.

"Couldn't you just tell me?" Greg asked. "I'd hate to give something she hated. Actually, I think I may have already done that."

"What did you give her?" Alex asked.

"A kiss."

Alex and Madeline stared, speechless.

"To be honest, I think she rather liked it," Greg grinned.

Madeline scoffed, "I wouldn't want a kiss from a man that spoke to me like that."

Greg looked defeated; he had hoped that maybe there was a part of Sofia that liked it. Alex turned to Greg, "Why did you kiss Sofia?"

"Why should you care?" Madeline asked. "It's not like you're going to marry her."

"We are trying to put up a façade," Alex reminded her. "Sofia and I are supposed to be courting one another. I don't need her to start feeling things for Greg."

"I doubt she ever would," Madeline mumbled.

"Forget doing any kind of gesture for her Greg," said Alex. "Honestly, I don't think anything could make up for your rudeness."

Humiliated and guilt-ridden, Greg stood up from his seat, "I should probably get going. I do have some business to discuss with Mr. Tinney and Lord Cadogan."

He walked to the door, but then he turned on his heel, realizing the irony of Alex criticizing him. "You know Alex, I feel terrible for what I said to Princess Sofia. But I suppose there are worse things I could do to a woman," he turned his head from one to the other. "Have a lovely evening with your princess, sorry no, your servant." He shut the doors to the State Dining Room, leaving the two alone. There was an awkward silence between them before Alex broke the tension.

"I'm sorry Madeline. He's only saying that because he's angry."

"But he's right," she said, feeling ashamed, "we are both leading Sofia to believe that you and she will be together."

"I admit it's ugly, but do we have any other choice?" he took her in his arms and sat her on his lap. They said nothing as they cuddled. She nestled to him, her lips brushing against his neck.

"Madeline," he said softly, giving her a kiss on the forehead. "You know how I mentioned that Bathory's followers might try to break into Curfew Tower or pay me a visit."

"You mean kill you?" she said bluntly.

"Yes. I don't think I'll be sleeping in my apartments very much over the next few weeks."

She tried to hold her composure, "I wish I hadn't provoked Lord Bathory. Now it's another thing you have to try to figure out."

"No, no," he reassured her, "this was bound to happen dolcezza. His temper and scheming led to the confrontation. Not you."

"But we went —" she spoke between gasps, wanting to cry, "through all this ... trouble. Pretending to court Sofia to see that you wouldn't go to war, to keep you safe and now ..." She took a deep breath, "Now I've put you —"

He combed his fingers through her hair and took her into his arms. "Don't blame yourself. My life has always been at risk. That's part of ruling a country." He wiped away her tears with his fingertips. "Besides," he continued, "once this trial is over, I will no longer have to deal with him anymore. I can finally be at ease. It's worth the risk. Anyway, I would feel more comfortable sleeping next to you in your dormitory than alone in my bed. At least until the trial and sentence are carried out."

A sultry simper fell on her face, "Oh. Is this your sneaky way of making love to me every night your Majesty?"

"It could be," he said his devilish smile lighting up his face. "Shall we go?"

"It's only eight o'clock. A little early, isn't it?"

"Dolcezza, it's never too early or too late." He winked.

She shook her head, grinning. "There are too many servants walking down the corridors of the dormitories. How can I sneak you in?"

"It'll be easy. Have I taught you nothing about disguises?"

He was right. It wasn't difficult to smuggle him in. There were plenty of spare Windsor Castle uniforms for her to take, along with one of the ridiculous looking white powdered wigs the guards traditionally wore. She brought them back to him in the State Dining Room. As he put it on, she guffawed. Wigs did not suit him.

"I finally know why you have such a reputation for being handsome," she said when she stopped laughing.

"And why is that?"

"You've avoided wigs all your life, it looks so unnatural on you."

"I think they look unnatural on everyone. I imagine a wig would do damage to your natural beauty."

Her face went hot and she rubbed her foot against the floor. He finished dressing, "Let's go."

"What about your face? Won't anyone notice?"

"Miss Black, didn't you hear? I burned my face in the kitchen," he said covering his face with his white gloved hand. "You're taking me down to the dormitories to treat me."

The journey down was not difficult, though Mr. Tinney had stopped them to ask what had happened. Madeline explained the lie Alex had come up with as he sobbed into his glove.

"Buck up man! You don't want the King to see you in this state," cried Mr. Tinney. "Could mean bad things for your career."

"Yes sir, Mr. Tinney," Alex mumbled with a rough accent.

As they walked away from Mr. Tinney, the two tried to hold back their laughter. But by the time they had reached her corridor, they were running hand in hand and howling through most of the dormitory.

When they reached her room, he shut the door behind them. She stood between the two beds, still giggling, nearly out of breath. She stopped and looked at him. He was no longer laughing; his demeanour changed. He looked at her like a tiger looking at its prey. "I'm going to give you a choice Miss Black, you can get on that bed, or I'll throw you on."

"You could do that," she began seductively, "or I could do this." She reached behind her back and pulled at the laces of her uniform. Her eyes melted to his. The dress slowly fell from her shoulders to her waist. She wriggled it down her hips, and it dropped on the floor. He stared speechless. First it was holding a dagger to his neck and demanding he go down on her, now this. He exhaled shakily, "I'm so hard."

Madeline stared down at the bulge under his thin material at his crotch. She had not stopped thinking about sucking Alex since her conversation with Sofia before dinner. Sofia's belief that Alex did not want to be 'loved in that manner', made her feel closer to him. She realized that Sofia did not have the first clue about how to please Alex. She knew. She reached down and began rubbing the lump through the thin material.

He murmured, pleasantly surprised by her initiating, she began peeling the Windsor Castle uniform off him, frantically kissing every inch of his skin moving her lips down his hard muscles. She came to her knees her face directly at the buttons of his trousers. Staring up at him innocently, she began stroking him again through his trousers. He grew harder and soon she could see pre-cum soak through, "Huuhhhh," he exhaled shakily. "Please, please."

"Ah, ah, ah, your Majesty," she said waving her finger. "That's not the magic words," she smiled naughtily.

To her surprise, he refused, "I'm not going to do that. No gentleman uses that kind of – Madeline, please."

She put her hands on her hips astonished, "So you ask me to say dirty words to you but –"

"It's different using those kinds of words and asking you to do me a favour," he said. "That's something Greg Umbridge would do."

"It's different between us," she reasoned. "I won't do it, then." She turned around on her knees, knowing what kind of reaction she'd get. He swung her back around, so she was facing his crotch again.

"Suck my cock, Miss Black. Now," he said sternly.

She began unbuttoning as quickly as she could, pulling down his trousers and pushing him on her bed.

"Ow!" he grumbled, smacking his head against the wall. "Careful. We can't be too loud here," he whispered.

But she didn't care. She drew her finger up and down his prick gently. As his blood pulsed through his veins, he knew she was going to tease him awhile. On she went brushing his cock with her fingers petting him gently.

"Suck it dolcezza please," he begged.

She ignored it, wanting to see how crazy he would get. Softly, she blew and kissed his thighs. Then traced his abs with her tongue, kissing between licks. His was warm and salty and the closer she got to his cock the hotter he was. Pre-cum began dripping from his length, "Please, please," his voice became gruff.

She slowly moved her lips down to his balls, massaging it with her tongue. He growled. Nuzzling her face close to him, she alternated between kissing his balls and gently sucking on them, "Oh. God. Huuhhh, Madeline …. huhh, you're going to make me cum."

She kissed his shaft, then took the wet head into her mouth tasting him. He groaned again, feeling the rush dance about his skin with every press of her tongue and suck of her mouth. She trailed it about her lips, setting every fibre of his being aflame.

"Put it all in your mouth," he said untangling her black tresses.

She happily obeyed and allowed him to slither into her, poking the back of her throat. She tenderly moved her head from side to side, his head rubbing deep in her throat. She was getting too good at this, he thought as he moaned. At a steady pace, she began bobbing up and down his cock. He arched his back, his hands grasping her hair. Leaving him at his brink, she was driving him insane. He groaned, it was so good, he wasn't sure if he wanted her to keep going or finish him off.

She knew he was nearing his peak, but held back. She was taking her time enjoying the way he tasted and smelled. Most of all she loved the way he looked. Watching his gorgeous body and his face contort into pleasure made her hot and wet. She gazed up at him with her big emerald eyes. He shuddered, gazing back at her, he held her face to hold her stare. "You're so beautiful," he murmured.

She felt his prick grow harder between her lips, as ribbons of cum filled her mouth. Swallowing greedily, she began gently massaged his head with her tongue, and more spilled in. After some time, she pulled off slowly licking every inch of his length. Alex put his face in his hand, uttering a long deep breath, "Whoa."

He threw his head back onto the bed. Still rock solid, he pulled her up onto the bed. She reached down and began stroking him again.

"Oh, no," he sighed. "I'm not quite ready."

"You look ready to me."

"You don't look ready to me," he said seductively.

"Believe me, I am."

"No, you're not. I want to see you sopping wet first."

He reached his hand down to her pussy and massaged it in a circular motion with his fingertips, feeling her moist lips. He brought his fingers to her mouth and lightly tapped on against her bottom lip. "Here, dolcezza."

She tasted herself, as he pressed his finger to her tongue. He then withdrew and licked his other fingers. "Mmmm." Kissing her again, he slid his hand back down and gently rubbed her, pushing two digits inside. He rammed them rapidly and soon he felt her twat pulsing against his fingers. She murmured and writhed on the bed and it began to creak. Their eyes darted toward one another.

"Don't stop," she whimpered.

He ignored the squeaking of the bed and continued thrusting into her warm wet cunt.

It didn't take long for the stimulation to build in her loins. Soon her pussy was grasping onto his fingers and clenching hard. It was getting difficult to move them inside her, but as she moaned louder, he knew he had to force them harder. She came wailing through gritted teeth, trying her damnedest. But between her and the bed she was certain a few servants could hear her.

Alex gently massaged her pussy as the last strokes of orgasmic pleasure coursed through her. Madeline lay with a gratified expression of her face.

"More, Miss Black?"

Madeline said nothing, light-headed, still adrift in satisfaction.

"Uuunngggghhh!" she cried out feeling his tongue, pressing across her pussy. "Alex, uuh, you ca-can't. Someone will hear us."

"Someone probably already has," he said half-joking, as he dove back to her.

She pushed him back. "Mr. Tinney might check in on me. No one can hear us."

"You're the loud one. Should I put a gag in your mouth?"

She shoved his chest playfully, "Not funny."

He stood up and swung her legs onto the bed, swivelling her about so that her head was on her pillow. He straddled over her, his hard cock dangled above her head, and she understood what kind of 'gag' he had in mind. He parted her legs and went down to her again. She grabbed him and drew him into her mouth. But she could hardly keep it in; between his size and his gifted mouth, she found herself murmuring aloud. "Oooh, Alex huh."

Alex laughed into her muff, and she arched her back. She knew he saw this as a little game, and she was losing. She grabbed his cock and began sucking it. He groaned, the vibrations sending tingles about her cunt, but she held her lips to him tightly, let him slip further down her throat. They moved in a rhythmic motion, licking, sucking each other their hunger for one another insatiable. Alex dove deeper into her twat fucking it with his tongue, swirling about her love button. It drove her to her brink and she came hard, screaming onto his cock.

433

"MADELINE," he yelled, feeling the sensation of her scream. He rose from her in an instant, and she was sure he was about to run out of the room. But he came back down to her plunging himself in her sopping cunt. He grunted as he felt her tighten around him. He wrapped his arms about her head and kissed her, she opened her lips allowing him entry. He murmured as he explored her mouth.

His time with her in the Weaponry Room wasn't enough for him. He ploughed into her, his mouth to hers. She murmured with each deliberate thrust, the bed creaked noisily, its legs screeching against the hardwood, and the headboard slapped against the wall, but neither wanted to stop.

Alex parted his lips from hers, his chest heaving. She looked up at him as his warm breath touched her skin and beads of sweat began to drip down his skin onto hers. She bit her lip while moaning, watching his gorgeous face determined to please her was arousing. She broke down reaching her apex, wave after wave of orgasms came over her. Each time she came, she screamed onto his chest and shoulder, digging into his back with her fingers leaving marks.

"Madeline," he whimpered softly.

She released him from her grip.

"I want you on top of me," he said. "I love watching you."

They shuffled positions and she straddled over him, grabbing his prick, impaling herself on it, sliding down to his balls, she exhaled, "Mmmmm."

She felt something she hadn't expected, his hands which had been on her bottom, were now tracing her rosebud. She said nothing but slid up and down his length. He shoved his finger inside her.

434

"Ooohhh," she muttered enjoying the new feeling of having her arse and pussy stretched and filled. It did not take long. As both his finger and cock penetrated her, she spun out of control. Moaning and whimpering, she began riding him at a frantic pace, excited by the intensity of it. The bed began to bounce and its legs crashed against the floor. Alex watched her as her breasts bounced about, a line of determination on her lips. Someone had to have heard this, and would walk in at any moment. But the emotion in her eyes told him that she wouldn't stop no matter what he said or who came in. He thanked God for that because he was enjoying it just as much if not more, despite his self-control.

He thrust his hips forward joining her in the hail of fuck, grunting as he did, "AAIIEEEEE."

She screamed coming, the magnitude of it so great it felt like she was split in two. He groaned, her teeming sex spilling all over him. He threw his body forward into her breasts, biting down on her nipple as he howled, cumming shot after shot into her cunt.

Finally, after she had climaxed several times, she collapsed onto him, too exhausted to move.

After several minutes, Alex looked about. "We've made quite a mess of this bed, let's move over to the other one," he said looking over to Tilly's vacant bed.

She murmured incoherently, and he knew her sex hazed brain hadn't heard what he said. He got up out of the bed and picked her up and tucked her into Tilly's bed. Lying next to her, he drew her close to his chest. She could hear his heart still racing. "Should you stay here? There are no guards to watch over you."

"I told you, I don't want to go back. I feel safest with you," he whispered, then drifted off to sleep.

435

It was early in the morning when Alex left Madeline's dormitory room to head back to his apartments. He woke around four in the morning, his body spooned about her. He slowly crept out of the bed, put on his servant's uniform and sneaked out of the dormitory. There were not many guards or servants wandering the halls and galleries, and though this was normal, Alex felt uneasy.

As he reached his Drawing Room doors, he found no guards. He looked about, searching further down the hall, between vases and knights' armour, but found no one. He wondered if they had gone into his room and discovered that he was not there. Either that or there was an intruder already in his room. He paced the halls a moment, questioning if he should enter his room, or call his guard. He paced about. If he called his guard and there was no one inside, he might look paranoid and weak. Also, if there was someone inside, they would be given a trial, most likely be found guilty, and hung. It was another matter he would have to deal with, along with everything else.

It was an easy decision for Alex, who preferred to do things on his own terms. He entered his Drawing Room and looked about. He slowly moved about the room, amongst the couches and tables. Tripping over something he stumbled forward. He looked back onto the ground. A bloodied hand peeked out from beneath the couch. Alex held his breath, lifting the skirts of the couch.

Suddenly, the body came to life, rolling from under the couch the man struggled to aim a pistol directly at Alex. Alex fought back knocking the pistol from out of his hand, onto the couch seat. The man wrapped his hands around Alex's neck, clenching his hands in an attempt to strangle him. Quickly Alex unsheathed his dagger from the Windsor uniform he wore, and stabbed the man in his ribs. The man cried out in agony, scrambling, trying to reach the pistol on the sofa. Alex snatched it off the couch and shot the man in the heart.

Hacking his last breaths, the man's eyes rolled back into his head and his body was still.

Alex didn't recognize the man and began searching for any evidence of who he was. He could not find any kind of clues, until saw a familiar family crest on his overcoat – Bathory's.

Alex continued to search his Drawing Room suspecting he would find his guards dead. He circled the room, looking around the furniture. He found one in a decorative armoire, and the other behind the drapes next to the window. He quickly examined their bodies. They had both been stabbed in the neck.

He looked about the room, thinking there was another killer. The assassin he had just killed did not have a knife. Strangely he did not feel the presence of anyone else in the room. He cautiously edged about the room, looking in vases and boxes around the room for the knife that killed his guards, but found nothing. Then it dawned on him that the second assassin was in his Bedchamber, not his Drawing Room. Alex crept towards the Bedchamber door and pressed his ear against it, but the wood of the doors were too thick for him to hear anything. He knew that behind the Bedchamber door, the killer was waiting for him. He pulled the Bedchamber door open.

Pitch black, the curtains were drawn to a close, but he could sense a presence. He quickly lit the sconce on the wall next to him and observed the room in the dim light. He stood still for a moment next to the sconce. He knew the moment he walked to the centre of the room, the killer would charge at him. He stood perfectly still waiting, listening for movement. Nothing. He stared at the window drapes for movement, scanned the bed curtains. But there was nothing. In the dead silence that sent chills up his spine, he thought over all the possibilities where the assassin might be. He gazed at the bed but knew it was a disadvantageous place for a man to attack him from. He noticed his armoire but remembered that he usually kept it locked most the time. There was a large chest next to his closet. Then there was his closet itself.

Considering everything, Alex began edging about the wall. He stopped. If the killer was in the closet, why hadn't he run out to attack him? He moved back next to the sconce in the wall. He was growing frustrated. Whoever it was in his room was wise enough not to give up his perfect hiding place unless he had a sure shot.

It then occurred to Alex that his killer was not going to kill him with a knife but a pistol. It was unlikely that anyone would hear a pistol go off. His guards were now dead and his Drawing Room next to his Bedchamber would deaden the sound of a gunshot. Wherever the killer was, he did not have a clear shot of Alex, if he did have a pistol, which would mean he was not behind the curtain or in the bed curtains. Under the bed would be impractical, unless the assassin would roll out from beneath. He scanned the room looking for items that may have been moved. Nothing. He realized he would have to check the closet.

He was about to cross the room when he noticed the fire in his mantelpiece was no longer burning. It was not unusual for that time in the morning, but he could not feel the heat off the embers. It was very cold. Someone put it out. He looked on the hearth next to the fireplace, where an unusually larger heap of ashes lay. It was a wise place to hide. He did have a large fireplace; two men could fit into it. He wondered if two men were there, but he knew that two men crunched in a fireplace would make no sense tactically.

Alex slowly and silently took off his shoes. Tip toeing so that he was a foot from the fireplace, he knelt on his knees, and placed his shoes on the hearth, revealing the toes of his shoes to the assassin and waited. Just then, a man rolled out onto the hearth shooting into the air, missing Alex by a foot. Alex raised his dagger, stabbing down missing the assassin's leg by inches. The man quickly sat up and pulled out another pistol. But Alex was quicker; raising his dagger, he stabbed the intruder in the heart. Alex twisted the knife. Wheezing and coughing blood, the man released the pistol from his hand and dropped dead to the floor.

Alex exhaled. He looked at the man's face, but again he did not recognize him. Falling to his knees he began to search the man, but found nothing that hinted who had sent him.

After that morning, security was tighter in the castle with more guards surrounding Alex's door. Lord Cadogan suggested Alex have one or two guards at his side at all times. Alex refused.

27

CLOSE CALL

The days following Greg and Sofia's row, things were awkward between them. Greg went everywhere with Alex and Sofia, and so did Madeline. They had been to see several places in London as well as the English countryside. It took a couple days each way, but they went to Stonehenge.

Madeline had never been to the site, and was taken aback when they got there. As she walked about the lush green grass, next to the gargantuan stones, she felt like an ant. She lightly grazed her fingers across the moss covered stones as a crisp wind blew through her hair. Looking across the land, she admired its earthly beauty. It was spiritual, almost magical.

As they walked around the ancient stones, Alex began to explain more about the site's history. Madeline was impressed with how much he knew. He explained several theories of what Stonehenge was used for, but Sofia was absolutely bored.

"They're just a bunch of rocks, I don't see how they're important," she said dismissively waving her hand. "Whether they were used for astrology or sacrificing virgins, really doesn't matter. They are still just rocks."

Greg howled in amusement as Alex gaped in disbelief, "Just rocks? People have theorized and speculated about these rocks for thousands of years."

Along with Alex, Madeline was fascinated, but she knew she was not supposed to speak. The reason she was there was to wait on the Princess, but she could not help herself, "Excuse me, your Majesty?"

"Yes, Miss Black?" he replied, holding his hand at his back.

"Who built Stonehenge?"

"No one knows. It's a mystery," he said enthusiastically. She could see the little boy in him grow excited. "There are all sorts of theories of that too. Some think it's the supernatural, there are folktales of Merlin and the devil, but no one knows for sure. Records of who built it have been lost." He went on, "Anyway, it was once a burial site —"

"Oi! Stop boring these ladies with rock history," Greg said, as he hopped down from one.

"Sorry, Greg. But Miss Black has an inquisitive nature."

"I'm sure she does," he retorted suggestively. "But she asked who built the rocks, not what different theories there were on the subject. So, the simple answer would be 'no one knows'."

"Yes. I was a little long winded with that, wasn't I?" Alex chuckled. "Ladies, if either of you have any more questions direct them to Sir Gregory Umbridge, he'll be able to give you a quick answer."

Greg looked sheepish.

Sofia gave an evil grin. "I like simple answers. Sir Gregory, King Alex was saying that this is a burial site. Who was buried here?"

"Many have been buried here Sofia. Probably thousands."

"I didn't ask how many Sir Gregory. I asked who," Sofia grinned.

"No one knows. Maybe it was a place they buried spoilt rich people, or maybe it's for common simpletons like me."

"Most likely royalty or the rich," Sofia said confidently, "only they would be buried in such style."

"It doesn't matter," Greg said, assuredly. "Bones are bones. At the end of the game, the king and the pawn go in the same box."

Sofia laughed, "What kind of nonsense is that? The king and the pawn go in the same box?"

"It's an Italian proverb," said Alex. "It means that we all die eventually, and we are all laid to rest in the earth."

"Oh," Sofia said embarrassed.

On another occasion, they went to Frogmore House. It was just a mile from Windsor Castle, so the carriage ride was quite short, just fifteen minutes away. As it turned out, it was another royal residence, quaint in comparison to Alex's other residences. Madeline began to wonder just how many homes he owned. Of course, she would have to keep her questions to herself as they toured the home.

It was a lavish manor, meant to be a retreat. As they rode up in the carriage, Sofia grew excited, "Oh Alex, it's beautiful. Such a lovely little country home, this would be a perfect place for children to grow up."

"I suppose it is," he said awkwardly.

Madeline glared at him. She could not believe how guiltlessly he mislead Sofia. He had no intention of marrying her, so why get her hopes up?

"Frogmore was recently renovated," he said to Sofia trying to ignore Madeline's hard gaze. "My mother liked to come here by herself quite often when she was alive."

"What she did with her time here, no one knows," said Greg guffawing. "Most likely locked herself in her room. That's what she did at Windsor Castle."

"Sir Gregory you truly do have the worst manners. To speak ill of the King's mother in front of the King himself," Sofia objected.

Alex shifted about uncomfortably. "It's quite all right, Greg didn't say anything I found offensive."

"Really," she said incredulously, "you don't find many things offensive, do you?"

Alex said nothing but looked over to Madeline, who pursed her lips and looked back out the window.

"Do you visit here often?" Sofia went on.

"Not really, I prefer Windsor Castle to here. Every time I've been here, I've been either dismissed or called back another residence to attend to business."

She raised her brow, "Who would dismiss you?"

"His mother," said Greg.

443

Not much else was said until they entered the manor and walked through several rooms.

"This isn't quite like any of your other residences," said Sofia, "it's a little more ... uh, understated."

"Well, yes Sofia," said Alex, "it is meant to be a place to get away from it all."

Though Frogmore House wasn't to Sofia's tastes, Madeline loved it. It was still richly decorated with beautiful carpets and paintings. But the ceilings and walls weren't ornate and high as the palaces and castle. They stood in a room covered in green silk wallpaper and red and gold drapes. There were no frescos on the ceiling, just some crown moulding. The paintings on the wall did have enormous gilt frames, but they weren't floor to ceiling like in the Buckingham and the Windsor.

"Please wait here Princess," Alex instructed. "Sir Gregory and I are going to speak with Mr. Barry. He oversees Frogmore."

The two left the room leaving Madeline with Sofia.

"What do you think Miss Black?"

"Pardon, your Highness? What do I think of what?" she asked.

"Well, do you think you could get used to living here?"

Madeline cocked her head, "Live here?"

Sofia looked at her and laughed. "You don't understand why he's taken me to here, do you?"

Madeline had a good idea of what Sofia was assuming, but she shrugged, pretending to not know.

"This home was his mother's retreat," Sofia explained. "It will be a wedding gift to me of course. You can come here and wait on me."

Madeline gawked in disbelief, "Did he propose to you?"

"Well, no, not yet. But, my parents are expecting it any day now. Why else would he take me here?"

"Perhaps he just wanted to –" she cut herself short, noticing an irritated expression on Sofia's face. "Yes, um I'm sure he would like to show you how lovely it could be to be the Queen of England."

Alex and Greg re-entered the room. "Ladies, come with me," Alex said taking Sofia's arm. Greg took Madeline's and they followed behind. Madeline looked down at her arm intertwined with Greg's and felt a little guilty. She wondered if he was doing it so she wouldn't be as hurt watching Alex attend to Sofia.

"Sir Gregory, don't feel you need to do this," Madeline said.

"I'm not doing this to make you feel good," he whispered. "I know his Majesty wishes he were me right now, I wouldn't miss this for all the whisky in Buckingham."

She smiled, "Always a pleasure, Sir Gregory."

The four walked through a beautifully decorated corridor with floor to ceiling windows. There was a view of a pond with some ducks floating across it. They reached a set of large glass doors, and went outside onto the grounds.

"I thought you might enjoy seeing the gardens first Sofia," Alex began, "acres of beautiful, lush scenery."

"I do love gardens," she said in a sweet, high-pitched voice that made Madeline want to gag. Greg noted the disgusted look on

445

her face and tugged her arm. Annoyed, Madeline stared hard at him, "What?"

"First of all Miss Black it's 'pardon'," Greg said in a fake haughty voice. "You know, she's only being polite. It's what's expected of her."

She knew this to be true. Sofia could have hated gardens, but she still would have been expected to say she loved them.

"Let's go to the conservatory," Alex said, as he stepped down the terrace steps with Sofia.

"Oh there's a music room out here?" Sofia asked surprised.

"Oh no, not that kind of conservatory."

They had walked down several stone paths before they came to a circular building made of glass. Inside, there were plenty of lush green plants and trees. "Oh, I've never seen anything like it!" Sofia exclaimed. "A building made of glass. That's extraordinary."

Greg tried to hold back his laughter, his hand over his mouth. Madeline tugged his arm. "She's only being polite!" she whispered in a haughty tone, "It's what's expected of her."

He fell into Madeline howling. Sofia turned and stomped her foot. "Sir Gregory have you no propriety? I'm a lady and a princess. Most your life you've been around royalty, you would think you would have learned what proper manners are."

Madeline gave Greg a sympathetic look, knowing that if she had said nothing, he would have been able to contain his laughter.

"As for you Miss Black, I don't know what's more foolish; that you poke fun or that you want to try to impress him," Sofia said pointing at Greg, her face full of contempt.

Madeline looked down at her feet, embarrassed, she curtsied. "I'm so sorry your Highness. It was extremely foolish of me. Please forgive me."

"That'll do Miss Black," said Alex trying to prevent Sofia from lecturing Madeline further.

Greg quickly bowed, "I, too am sorry your Highness,"

"I suppose that will have to do," Sofia said with her nose high in the air. She grasped Alex's arm, and they headed into the conservatory.

As they stepped inside, the smell, taste and touch of wet warm flowers filled their senses. The glasshouse was full of magnificent exotic succulents, flowering shrubs, trees and herbs. The plants surrounded them, and created different paths about the greenhouse. The heat of the room kept them in a constant damp summer. Water droplets raced down the window panes as gardeners sprayed the colourful flora and foliage with water. Water babbled in the distance, and Madeline wondered if there was a waterfall or fountain somewhere. She stretched up onto her tippy-toes to see further inside, but it was no use. The large leafy plants covered everything, some of them reaching almost as high as the glass ceiling.

"Are you looking for someone, Miss Black?" Alex said putting his hand at his back.

"No, your Majesty, I just thought I heard some water trickling."

"Yes, there is a pond with a small waterfall in the centre of the conservatory. We can go take a look," he said gesturing with his other hand.

"First I would like to know a bit about the plants we're seeing here," Sofia said, putting her hands on her hips.

"Certainly," he said realizing he was catering to Madeline. "What do you see that interests you, Sofia?"

She looked about frantically, and touched the closest tree to her, "This one here, it's quite beautiful."

"The palm tree?" Greg said furrowing his brow. "Don't they grow in Spain?"

"Yes, I was just curious if his Majesty knows that," she stammered.

"He has travelled all over Europe," said Greg. "I'm sure he knows what a palm tree is, love."

"Love? I'm the Princess of Spain. I'm not 'love'," she said clenching her fists at her side. The two went on bickering as Madeline moved away from the group noticing some interesting plants under some glass cloches. Underneath a tall and slender cloche, there was a flowering plant that sprawled along a thin pole with unique blooms. She ran her finger upon the glass, admiring it.

"It's called an orchid," said Alex, "Would you like to touch it?"

"Can I?" Madeline beamed.

"Of course, Miss Black."

He lifted the glass cloche off the plant. Sofia stopped squabbling with Greg, noticing the two. She watched as Alex took Madeline's hand in his and they touched the flower.

"It looks delicate," he said to her, "but it's stronger than it seems. It can handle your touch."

Sofia quickly dashed over to the pair and raised her arm between them, pointing at another cloche. "What kind of plant is that?"

"An African Violet," Alex said simply.

"Can I touch it?" Sofia asked eagerly, clasping her hands around the cloche.

"It's not a good idea to touch it. Touching it can stunt its growth."

"Touching an African Violet doesn't stunt its growth," Greg protested.

"Really, do you remember nothing from our tutor Lord Nash? He told us that the day it arrived from Kenya," Alex recollected.

Greg's eyes lit up remembering what had happened. "Oh, right," he said bright pink. "Sorry your Majesty, the only thing I remember from our agricultural lessons was the day I pushed you into the fountain."

The Princess and Madeline laughed.

"You should have seen him that day," Greg went on with a huge grin on his face. "Earlier, he had been invited to visit the royals of Austria. Being fifteen at the time, he was quite excited about meeting the princesses, of course. Wouldn't shut up about it."

Sofia smiled timidly at the idea of a young Alex excited to meet princesses. It gave Madeline, an uneasy feeling; she wondered if he harboured excitement for princesses now.

"Anyway," he continued, "after all his bragging, I asked him, 'Can a frog really turn to a prince when you kiss him?' and he looks at

449

me like this —" He impersonated Alex with a slack jaw. "That's when I pushed him into the pond and said, 'Let me know'."

Madeline roared with laughter, and Sofia bit her lip trying to contain herself.

Alex chuckled, "Falling into the pond was worth watching Sir Ashton throw you in the dungeon for the night, Greg."

"Wait a minute," asked Sofia, "Sir Ashton threw him in the dungeons?"

"Sir Ashton oversaw our educations, and he thought it was a good punishment," said Greg with a broad smile, half laughing. "I remember him telling me that if I didn't start 'acting like a gentleman' eventually Alex would throw me in a dungeon himself."

"Much good that did," said Alex, his blue eyes alight with the memory.

"Yeah, was it just before midnight you sneaked down to Curfew Tower and released me?"

Alex's eyes bulged at Greg, hoping he would not go much further.

"That was quite the wild night – ouch!"

Alex stepped firmly on Greg's foot, but he continued, "I don't think we got back until six – ouch! Oi! Why are you stepping on my foot?"

"Not in the presence of ladies," he said between his clenched pearly white teeth.

Greg looked back at the girls, realizing his idiocy. He ran his hand tensely through his tousled brown hair.

"Back from where?" asked Sofia, her arms folded.

"Back from, um uh —"

"The Billiards Room," Alex finished quickly.

Madeline looked away knowing he was lying. They had probably escaped through the hidden tunnel to the manhole in the street he had shown her. If Sofia found out about it, they would have to explain where they had gone and what they were doing. Madeline had a few ideas, but she knew she was better off not asking.

"You played billiards for six hours?" Sofia asked sceptically.

Alex flashed his perfect teeth, and he gazed at her tenderly with his eyes and placed his hands on her shoulder. "We did what all young boys our age do," he spoke sweetly, "we had a few drinks and threw a few fists for fun."

"You fought?"

"Well, we didn't bloody each other up," Alex explained, "but we'd try to pin each other down."

"You'd be surprised, Princess Sofia," Greg began, "his Majesty looks muscular, but I can take him."

"When have you ever?" Alex scoffed.

"Is that a challenge?" Greg goaded, playfully punching Alex in the shoulder. "Follow me to the pond and I will." Greg took off down one of the paths, cracking up with laughter as he did. Alex turned to Sofia and Madeline, "I don't think anyone should go anywhere near the pond today."

Alex took Sofia's arm again and began walking down a different path. She began pointing to random plants and trees around them as they walked, asking what they were. He answered them all, explaining where each plant had originated and which plant family they belonged to. It was amazing to Madeline that he had

451

absorbed so much when he had been tutored. He was a walking encyclopaedia.

Though the Princess asked many questions, Madeline could tell she was not really interested in plants; she yawned from time to time as he spoke, barely paying much attention. Instead, her eyes roamed his body, taking in its perfection.

Madeline watched, nauseated. She wanted to tear Sofia from his arm and throw her into a thorny rosebush they were passing by. Then, Sofia casually removed her left glove, and Madeline held her breath. Proper women didn't take off their gloves while outside, so Sofia was up to something. Unexpectedly, the Princess put her hand on Alex's chest and ran her fingers between the folds of his shirt. Him and her, skin to skin. Madeline's blood boiled watching as Sofia tittered, "It's so warm in here, are you sweating a little, Alex?"

"I suppose it's a little warm, but I'm not sweating," he replied, swallowing hard, looking to Madeline from the corner of his eye.

Sofia moved closer to him, looking up innocently with her chocolate brown eyes. Madeline could see it coming; Sofia was going to attempt to kiss him. Quickly, Madeline crouched down, grabbed some dirt in her hand and smeared it onto Sofia's dress.

"Oh, your Highness," she said as she began wiping the stain.

Sofia pulled away from him, scowling as she looked down, her moment ruined. "My dress," she cried, grasping the materials into her hand and stomping her foot. "Miss Black, go inside and get some soap and a cloth."

"Is that necessary Princess?" Alex asked, not wanting Madeline to leave them alone together.

"I can't walk around a frightful mess," she exclaimed.

Just then, Greg stepped out from around some trees and shrubs. "I see that we are a little afraid to go anywhere near the pond your Majesty?" he said, nudging Alex in the ribs.

"No, we were just enjoying the plants. Unfortunately, Sofia has got some dirt on her dress."

"There's a lemon tree back there," Greg said pointing in another direction. "I can get one. Miss Black can use it to clean your dress."

"Sir Gregory, you want to put LEMON on my silk dress to clean it?" screeched Sofia in shock.

Alex buried his hand in his face. Greg had good intentions, but he did not think before he spoke.

"Why not?" Greg asked. "It's a natural cleaner. It will clean as well as any soap."

"Sofia," Alex began trying to calm her, "it's all right. It's just a little dirt, and I'm sure that later when we get back to Windsor Castle, I can get one of my staff to clean the dress properly."

"It should be cleaned now, before it sets into the fabric," Sofia complained.

"Oh," he said slowly, "I was hoping to show you a little surprise today."

Sofia dropped her skirts, her eyes rising up from her stain. "A surprise?" she said, giving a crooked smile.

"Yes Sofia, there is something else here on Frogmore grounds that I wanted you to see after the conservatory."

Truth was, Alex had something he wanted to impress Madeline with. He did not care if Sofia enjoyed it or not.

"That will be lovely your Majesty," Sofia said with a flirty voice.

"I'll just take us through the rest of the conservatory," Alex said. "There's a door on the other side that will take us to where we are going." Alex took her arm again and they continued through.

Greg walked alongside Madeline. "Watching this must be tough for you," he commented.

"She won't be here forever," Madeline whispered.

Greg said nothing but looked toward the trees, a thoughtful expression on his face. Curiosity came over her and she wondered how Greg would feel once Sofia had left. Spending so much time with Alex, Sofia had also spent much of her time with Greg too. Though Sofia often criticized everything about him, he did not seem to hate her. Oddly, Madeline had from time to time thought that maybe he had a bit of a soft spot for her. Sofia allowed him to refer to her with her first name. She also occasionally laughed at his jokes. Few women did.

They came round the pond, and Madeline was amazed by the landscaping; small waterfalls, rocks, lily pads, tall green grasses and cattails enveloped the pond with a small bridge stretching across it. Surrounding the pond were different paths each led to other parts of the conservatory. Each path was covered with different vegetation, and had gardeners feeding the exotic plants. The only light that could be seen came from the glass roof above. A butterfly flew through the air and landed on Madeline's shoulder.

"Oh look," Madeline gushed, forgetting her manners as a servant. "Isn't this beautiful, your Highness?" she asked, hoping her indiscretion would be overlooked. Sofia said nothing but looked above at the sky, apprehensively grasping her skirts.

"That's a male Adonis Blue butterfly," said Alex, a dimple in his cheek watching Madeline's delight. *What a know it all,* Madeline thought smiling. His intelligence was sexy though. She'd never met anyone so cultured. She carefully placed her fingers on her shoulder, and the butterfly climbed onto her index finger. Her eyes lit up as she observed it as it slowly moved its wings up and down in contentment.

PLOP.

"What was that?" Sofia asked anxiously.

"Probably a turtle or a frog," said Greg. "Would you like to see Princess?" he said offering his hand.

"No, thank you," she said and clung to Alex, her gazed fixed on the birds flying above them as they squawked.

"Oh come Sofia," Greg said grabbing her hand. Sofia pulled away.

"I said no, Sir Gregory. Do you not know how to listen to a command?" she barked.

Silence.

"I'm sorry, your Royal Highness," Greg said, bowing. Sofia dismissed it and turned to Alex, "It's getting awfully boring in here. I would love to see the surprise you were talking about showing me earlier."

"Certainly," he said. They crossed the bridge and headed down another path on the other side of the pond. As they passed all the different plants, Madeline observed Sofia. She seemed off. She looked up in the air as though a tree was about to fall on her. She hardly said a word, and once they left the conservatory, she exhaled, clasping her chest.

455

"Are you okay Sofia?" Alex finally asked, patting her hand.

"Yes, I'm fine," she replied her voice cracking.

"Right," he said, sounding unsure as they went down a limestone path. He looked at her again, "I'm sorry Princess, it's just I can feel your heart beating a mile minute."

"How on earth could you feel that?"

"Through your wrist, your pulse. You look as though you've seen a ghost," said Alex casually.

"Ghost? No!" she wailed, her body shuddering, her face white. "Why would you bring up ghosts?"

"No reason," said Alex calmly. "It's an English phrase. When someone looks pale, we say it looks like they're scared, like they've seen a ghost."

"I think I need a seat," Sofia said as she headed towards a bench on the path. "All this walking. Miss Black, could you give me a fan."

Madeline pulled a fan from her pocket and handed it to Princess Sofia. She sat down and began fanning herself. Alex and Greg looked at one another puzzled.

"Will you be all right?" Alex asked as he sat next to her.

"I'll be fine," Sofia said shortly. "My, it's hot." She fanned herself rapidly, taking shallow breaths. No one said anything. The way Sofia was behaving, it seemed like the smallest thing could set her off. It wasn't hot. The sun was covered with clouds.

"Is there anything I can do or get for you your Highness?" asked Greg trying to be helpful.

"Don't start on me Sir Gregory. If I asked you to get a glass of water you'd come back with wine," Sofia said glaring.

"But that's just me Princess," he said falling to his knees jokingly. He gazed up at her like a puppy, "I always say or do the wrong thing."

Sofia could not stop herself from laughing. Only he would have that kind of nerve. How many times he had apologized to her was unknown. It happened many times a day. After some time on the bench, she began to feel better.

"Shall we go?" Alex asked.

"Yes, let's go," Sofia said, then she looked over to Greg and Madeline. "Do they need to come?"

"I can't see why not," Alex shrugged.

Sofia looked down into her lap disappointed. She abruptly stood up and shoved the fan into Madeline's chest.

Alex led them down the path where they came to a large, caged structure holding many kinds of exotic birds. Madeline beamed, she had never seen so many interesting looking birds. Sofia stopped dead in her tracks.

"This is my aviary," he said smoothly turning to Sofia.

"Aviary?" Sofia repeated. Her hands began to tremble, as droplets of sweat began appearing on her forehead. Madeline grabbed a handkerchief out of her servants' pocket and offered it to the Princess. She reached out her arm quivering, taking it then dropping it. Greg picked it up and offered it to her.

"Greg," Alex warned.

"You must be joking Sir Gregory if you think I'll pat my brow with that dirty thing! It fell to the ground."

Alex took his handkerchief from his breast pocket and handed it to Sofia, "There you are."

Sofia's expression softened as she gazed at him longingly. Abashed, Alex looked back over to Madeline, who was watching the birds in their cages in the distance. With the way Sofia was acting, Madeline had no idea if they were going to make it to the aviary. She was tempted to sneak over to it to get a better look.

"I'm sorry Sofia, are the birds bothering you?" Alex asked, trying to sound compassionate.

"Yes," she said giving a nervous chuckle, "I don't really enjoy the company of birds."

Madeline could have broken down in a fit of giggles, but Greg Umbridge beat her to it, hugging himself as he howled, "A phobia for birds? Why?"

"They're unnatural, everything about them!" she exclaimed. "The way they move! Their beaks! Their feathers and disease! Ugh!"

Greg doubled up in laughter, "You're afraid of feathers and beaks!"

Sofia ran off, crying, holding the handkerchief to her eyes.

Greg sighed. "I know, I know. I'll go apologize," he said. His lips curled as he chased after her.

Alex raised his brow. "I suppose that leaves just the two of us?" he said as Greg ran out of sight. He took Madeline's arm, and they strolled down the limestone path to the aviary.

"This is nice," she said gazing up at him.

"To be honest, the only reason why I took her here was because I thought you might like it."

"Did you know she was afraid of birds?" Madeline asked with a curious expression.

"Well, I didn't think she was that afraid. She acted kind of funny once when Greg and I brought some quail in from hunting. At first I thought it was the carcasses that scared her. But have you ever noticed that she never wears feathers? They're always in fashion. She also seems to keep her distance from feathers."

"So you did know?" she said, giving him a light shove.

"Only guessed. She went strange like that during the tour of Windsor Castle. I was talking about ghosts in Curfew Tower. She demanded that I stop."

He moved behind her wrapping his arms around her waist, he softly nibbled her neck, as she watched the birds. She inhaled his smell and smiled. "I've missed you," she confessed.

"I can't stop thinking about you. This is driving me insane. I can't stand being near you but being denied tasting and touching you."

She stroked his cheek with her hand and kissed him on the lips. He shuddered as their mouths met one another, the chaos around them melting away as they embraced. When they finally parted, he ran his fingers through his hair, looking over at the cage. "The Spanish departure couldn't come sooner."

She nodded. "We should worry about the possibility of another Spanish arrival. People expect you to marry and make an heir to the throne."

He glanced down the path, "Maybe they do. But for now, I'm going to take advantage of this moment. I'm not letting go."

Embracing, they watched the birds. The aviary was a circular building split in several sections. They stood in front of an odd-looking bird with bright green feathers, goggled eyes and owl-like face. It hopped about its cage on the floor.

"It's a Kakapo," he whispered nibbling her ear. "It's a kind of parrot from New Zealand."

"Are you always such a know it all?" she teased taking his hands in hers.

"I'm just trying to impress you. Is it working?"

She giggled.

"I wish it were just you and me today," he said. "It would be a dream if I could take you about, tour places with you. I'd love to see the world with you."

They watched the bird as it hopped about.

"Do the birds not fly because they are caged?" she asked.

"Well, most of my birds fly. The Kakapo can't fly though; his wings are too small for his body."

He put on a thick leather glove that hung on a hook on the aviary and unlocked the cage. The Kakapo waddled out like a chicken and flapped it wings as it circled about. Quickly he plucked the bird from the ground and put him on the sleeve of his glove.

"It's got soft feathers," he said as he took her hand and brought it up to the bird, brushing her fingers allowing her to feel the texture. Though she smiled, she felt sad for the bright bird; nature would not allow it to fly like the other birds.

"Alex, we should be careful, they could come back anytime."

"I doubt that, did you see how barmy she got? I don't think she would go anywhere near these creatures."

She caressed the feathers of the bird, knowing they were on borrowed time until Sofia became suspicious. "We should get going."

He set the Kakapo back in the cage, put the leather glove on its hook and turned to her. "I love being able to take you to places. It's a shame that it's under these circumstances though. You make my entire being restless."

"Not as restless as Sofia gets around birds," she chuckled.

He held her in his arms, not wanting their time to end. He stroked her cheek with his knuckles. "When I'm an old man and look back on this day, I won't think of Sofia and the birds. I'll think of your beautiful face the moment you discovered the orchids, the Blue Adonis on your finger and our kiss here, now."

His words were heart-achingly sweet, and they brought tears to her eyes. He brought his lips to hers again, and she could feel the pain slip away as their tongues did a rhythmic dance, exploring one another, as she softly ran her fingers through his hair. She pulled back looking deeply into his eyes, his fingers graced her chin.

"Not yet Madeline, I don't want this to end."

He crashed his mouth to hers again, and she did nothing to resist.

As they headed back to Frogmore House, Greg rushed up to them on the path out of breath. "I apologized. I think she's still a bit

461

angry though. She's in the manor, and some of the staff are serving her tea."

"Right. I'll go back to playing host," said Alex.

They returned and found Sofia sitting on the terrace, sipping her tea. She seemed in a cheery mood, a perky grin on her face, as one of the Frogmore maids adjusted her skirts. "Sir Gregory tells me that you were thinking of getting rid of the aviary your Majesty."

Alex scowled at his friend. "The thought has crossed my mind," Alex lied. "For now let's have lunch. It's been a busy morning. I'm sure you're famished Princess." He offered his hand and Sofia took it, standing up.

"Miss Black, could you please escort her Royal Highness inside?" asked Alex.

Princess Sofia and Madeline curtsied to him and went inside. Alex rounded on Greg, "Why would you tell her I'm getting rid of the aviary? I love my birds."

"Oh come on," he said folding his arms. "She was hysterical. Besides, you have no plans to marry her. I told her a little white lie, so what?"

"I'd prefer you didn't. Let's go inside."

After lunch, they headed back to Windsor Castle. On the journey, Alex began talking about other places they could visit, "We could go to the Tower of London," he suggested.

Madeline's eyes lit up. She'd never been there, but had heard it was an amazing place to tour. But Sofia was hesitant, "Oh, I was hoping that if we went to London again, maybe we could do some shopping."

"Shopping? Princess, there's so much to see at the Tower of London," said Alex. "There's the Crown Jewels and –"

"There's menagerie of rare animals there," Greg piped up, glaring hard at Alex.

"Rare animals?" Sofia repeated. "What kind?"

"All sorts, bears, tigers and birds. From all over the world. Oh, we also keep prisoners there."

"Prisoners?" she yelped.

Madeline could feel Sofia trembling next to her.

"There's not many," said Alex reassuringly. "They are kept in another part –"

"I think I'd rather go shopping," she said shortly and looked out of the window at the English countryside.

Alex gave Greg a look. He ignored it, looking out of the window along with Sofia, but then turned and whispered, "Who are you really trying to impress, your Majesty?"

Alex frowned. He knew what he was doing was wrong. But he'd never get the opportunity to escort Madeline anywhere. Other than the King's Head, this was the closest thing they'd have to proper courting.

As Greg gazed out the window, an idea began to form in his mind. He finally thought of a gift he knew Sofia would appreciate. He beamed as he glanced at her, eager to offer it to her then. But, he couldn't in front of Alex. He'd have to wait for a day when Alex was too busy with royal duties to entertain.

28

HEDGE MAZE

The following Wednesday, Alex had to meet with the Crown barrister to discuss the evidence against Lord Bathory. It did not require Greg's presence, so Greg searched the castle looking for Princess Sofia to offer his gift. He found her alone in the Crimson Drawing Room sitting by a window, reading a book.

"Hello your Royal Highness," Greg said bowing to her.

"Sir Gregory," she said stiffly. She inclined her head slightly in his direction, keeping her attention on her book.

"I have something for you, Princess," he said approaching her nervously.

She begrudgingly put her book down and looked up at him. He had his hair combed neatly, was clean shaven and his clothes were not askew. She hadn't seen him look so smart since the day she arrived. She reddened. "Well, what is it?" she said trying not to smile.

"I've noticed that all these historical sites that the King has been taking you to are not your cup of tea. So I've made some arrangements."

"If you think I would like to go to an English bar, you can forget it Sir Gregory."

He felt humiliated that a bar was the first place she would think he would want to go. "No, I remember you once saying that you like Italian opera. I thought maybe you would like to see an English play. Do you like the theatre?"

Without thinking, she jumped up from the couch, "I would love to!"

He beamed, satisfied with himself. But then she sat back down, dropping her smile. "It's not Italian opera, but I suppose it will have to do," she said in a cold tone, trying to hide her excitement. "So what will we be seeing?"

"They are showing 'Hamlet' at the new Drury Lane. Robert Ellison is playing Hamlet, he's a fabulous English actor, and the theatre was just rebuilt, so I think it'll be wonderful."

"Well, uh, thank you Sir Gregory. I'm sure his Majesty and I will enjoy it. It will be nice for the two of us to have an occasion without company."

Greg was at a loss for words for a moment before he regained his composure. "I don't know if it would be fitting for you and King Alexander to go to a play without a chaperone."

"Oh, I know Sir Gregory," she giggled, "You would be the last person I would suspect to give me a lesson on proper etiquette. Miss Black can be our chaperone."

"I don't think that Miss Black is a suitable chaperone."

"And you are?" Sofia asked.

Usually, he had a witty comment ready to answer a snide remark. He and Alex regularly mocked one another, but he knew she could not handle his jokes well. "Well, ahem, I hope you, the King and Miss Black enjoy your time at the theatre."

"I'm sure we will. We'll tell you all about it when we get back," she smiled, knowing her words were hurting him. He had never felt so rejected. Most times, he did not care what others people thought of him, but with her, it was different. Unlike all the other princesses that had fallen all over themselves to be Alex's Queen, Sofia had some self-respect. She had not tried to seduce Alex in his private apartments at night like so many did. She did not pretend to know things about hunting, politics, and history, though she tried to show some interest out of politeness. She also was not as demanding. Most that had visited felt they had the right to more than just the closets of clothes; they wanted access to royal jewels too. He gazed at her trying to think of a way to persuade her to allow him to go to Drury Lane.

"Shouldn't you be going now?" she said, wiping the blank expression off his face.

"I thought you might like some company," he said hopefully. "What are you reading?"

"I'm fine, thanks."

"Are you sure? I was thinking of playing some music, would you like to come join me?"

"No."

He turned to leave, but decided to make one last attempt, "Where are Miss Black and Miss Van Gogh?"

"Miss Black is attending King Alex's meeting and Miss Van Gogh is preparing things for me in my room."

"Hm," he said, tapping his finger to his chin. "Miss Black must be fairly loyal. Alex trusts her with so many of his personal affairs."

Sofia said nothing but opened her book, ignoring his presence. He left feeling irritated. He wondered if Sofia would ever realize that Alex was not for her.

Alex's meeting finished earlier than Madeline expected, but it wasn't surprising. He seemed to storm through all the pieces and statements of evidence quickly, explaining to the Crown barrister, Lord Winthrop, "Present the strongest evidence first. And explain it chronologically. I want the jury to see how he's been calculating for years. Motives are easy to prove, but we need a focus on proving mens rea too."

What 'mens rea' was, Madeline didn't know. But the way he was taking charge of the situation, was 'mens sexy'. It was like he was the barrister himself. As for Lord Winthrop, he said nothing but sat and took notes from Alex. Nodding, with the occasional 'Yes your Majesty.'

"Bathory has an extensive education in law himself. I imagine he will be representing himself. Knowing him, he will object as often as he can to interrupt any arguments we try to make. Be tactical when asking questions, so nothing too blunt. Build up to your points with every witness, save the blunt questions for when you think the jury may already be concluding the same suspicion ..."

Not much of what Alex said made any sense to her. One thing did make sense though – pushing him onto the table, ripping off his trousers and well … *blast this Crown barrister*, she thought. She gazed at him, desire in her eyes, but he ignored her stare.

"Are you getting much of this Miss Black?" he asked, his lips curling.

"Oh, um" she looked about startled, then looked down at her blank paper. "I've been trying to get it." She nervously tucked her soft black wisps of hair behind her ears and began writing frantically with her quill.

"That's quite all right Miss Black. This is not the kind of work you typically do I suppose. I guess I'll mentally have to keep the minutes of this meeting."

Alex knew it was odd to have her, a female servant, take notes in a meeting. Usually it would be a Lord, Greg, Ashton or one of his valets. But, he knew that Lord Winthrop would not question him. After an hour, he turned to Madeline, "I suppose that's all we have to go over today. Lord Winthrop, you can organize all the evidence, speak to the witnesses, and we'll speak again in the days leading up to the trial."

Lord Winthrop stood up and took all the papers and evidence and left the office.

Madeline looked over to Alex.

"Well, then Miss Black!" Alex teased, "Did you get all the information down?"

"For the most part," she said her voice cracking.

"Never mind, if you didn't. To be honest, I don't normally have people take minutes for these types of meetings. But I saw it as an opportunity."

"How do you mean?" she asked, setting down her quill, looking up innocently.

"You know, Sofia is not expecting me back for some time?"

"Is that so?"

"I thought we could have some time together."

"What if we get caught?" she asked coyly.

"Ah, ah, ah, Miss Black, I wasn't suggesting that. I would like to spend some time with you."

She was frustrated. She was flattered that he wanted to have quality time with her. But recently she had barely laid hands on him. They had had plenty of time together, going to Stonehenge, Frogmore and other places in London. Through all of this, she was busily waiting upon Sofia, listening to her chatter on about Alex, and it was emotionally exhausting. Especially when she was with both Alex and Sofia, she watched, wondered and worried. He was always a gentleman towards Sofia, she couldn't help but be envious. She had wondered if he was taking a liking to her.

"I thought we could walk the castle grounds together," he said. "There will be few beautiful days like this one before winter comes. Besides, I would love to get you out of work."

"What if someone sees us?"

"Just carry some parchment and a quill. If anyone asks, you are writing down a statement I have concerning the trial."

They went outside and wandered to the back of the castle into the gardens. The leaves had changed to bright oranges, reds and yellows. As they walked across the green grass and about the shrubs, he wrapped his arm around her waist. "It's almost like walking into a painting, isn't it?" he said.

469

"I love autumn, the colours are lovely."

They sat on a bench next to the pond. He watched her as she stared straight ahead at the fountain sitting in the middle of the pond. He tucked her hair behind her ear and gave her a soft kiss.

"We need to be careful," she reminded him.

"You worry too much. I'm frustrated with everything. Spending time with Sofia, the trial, having to sneak around to see you. Right now, I just don't care if someone sees us," he said leaning in to kiss her.

"Yes, you do," she said, pushing his chest.

"Is that an objection Miss Black?" he smirked. "Do you not want any kisses?"

She blushed, "I do, I just –"

"Then hush," he whispered and lightly pressed his lips against hers. She felt a shiver crawl up her spine. He began lifting her skirts.

"Alex really! Not here! Besides, I thought you just wanted to have some quality time together?"

"So you don't want to play?" he asked, giving her a seductive smile.

"Well ..." she said, giving him a provocative glance. She stood up and traipsed to the entrance of a nearby hedge maze. She peeped her head out from the large bush and raised her brows at him. An evil little smile grew on his face, his dimples showing. He quickly caught on that he was the hunter and she was the prey.

"If we're going to play that game dolcezza, I should warn you that once I have you in my arms, I'm going to do whatever I please ... understand?"

"Unless I get to the other end of the maze," she giggled as her heart beat into her throat, "then the game is over your Majesty, and I get to do whatever I please."

"All right," he said rising slowly. They both paused looking into one another. A teasing expression fell on her face, and she took off in the maze. But he didn't chase after her; he strolled into the maze, laughing inwardly. Little did she know that the entrance was also the exit.

"Dolcezza," he called as he walked between the hedges, "I hope you know that I'm a man of my word ... I am going to do whatever I please."

He heard her giggling and speeding off not too far from where he was. Nonetheless, he paced himself as he turned the corner and saw her scurry around another corner. "When I get my hands on you," he called, adding beneath his breath "you're going to get it so hard."

She continued through the corridors of the maze looking back occasionally for him. Though she had nothing to fear, she still found herself nervous, almost scared to be caught. Her palms grew sweaty, and she heaved as she darted through the maze, hearing him call to her now and again.

But it was strange. It didn't matter how far she ran into the maze, she felt his presence. She could hear him crushing the fall leaves as he walked. She came to the realization that there was no way she could win their little game. He was familiar with this maze; he grew up in the castle and knew its shortcuts. Not that she wanted to win, but him hunting for her gave her a bit of a rush. "Alex!" she called, "I thought you wanted to play? I haven't seen you once since coming in here. Some challenge you are."

She ran down another pathway, putting more space between them. He heard her, but said nothing and continued through the maze. She ran further and further into the labyrinth, and soon she could no longer hear him breaking the odd twig or crushing leaves. There was silence. A fear grew in Madeline, and she began to wonder if there was someone else in the maze. One of Lord Bathory's or Lord Kinney's footmen. She sank into the hedge next to her, and called back to him, hoping he would respond, "I didn't think it would take you this long to catch me." She laughed nervously, "I thought you were trained in combat. You should be able to find me."

"I like the anticipation," he said stepping out from the hedge next to her.

She gasped startled. She jumped up and punched his arm. "Don't scare me like that! You weren't supposed to walk through the hedges, that's against the rules."

"I'm sorry Miss Black, but what rules? All is fair in love and war."

"Which is it then, love or war?"

"You know which it is," he said resting his hand on her cheek.

"I could swear, sometimes I really don't know."

"We're in love, and we are in a war with the rest of the world who would disagree with it." His mouth warmed hers.

"Oh, are we?" she whispered, between his kisses. "Then where is your armour?"

"You're my rock, but right now I think you're trying to distract from my prize."

She giggled, "Prize? What prize?" she asked pretending to not know.

He smiled, "Don't tease me dolcezza. I don't like being teased."

She darted away from him. He did not run after her. Instead, he shook his head, "Madeline Black why don't you just get on your hands and knees, because let's face it, we both know that's where you want to be right now."

She stopped and turned to face him, "You bugger. You really are crass. What makes you think after a comment like that I'd be with you?"

He calmly moved toward her, "You stopped. If you really didn't want it, you'd keep running. You can stop with the little game, I may be crass at times, but you're my dirty, dirty girl."

She giggled and turned to run again, but he quickly tripped her with his feet and caught her in his arms. Her eyes stared deeply into his as she pulled him closer to her kissing him hard. He lowered her down, gently placing her on the grass.

His hand crept up her neck and into her soft tresses that smelled of rosewater. He purred as she surrendered to him, her mouth embracing his as he caressed her face with his fingertips. "I won Miss Black, I would like to collect my prize."

He continued to neck her, naughtily chuckling as his lips explored her. He popped up and looked down at her gently stroking her hair.

"I don't think this was a fair game," she began, "you know this maze much better than I do."

"You're the only woman I've ever enjoyed chasing," he said lightly touching her chin. "Now, I've caught you, but you continue to tease me. I don't think that's a fair game."

"But you're fun to tease," she said a coy smirk on her face.

They stared at one another for a long moment, their desire for one another burning in their loins. They went at each other, tearing off their clothes heatedly, Madeline barely tore off his trousers, as he loosened her corset and began lifting her skirt. She grasped his hard erection the second she freed it, grasped it, licking and sucking.

"Uh, Madeline," he sighed closing his eyes, "every time you do that, I could just, mmm ..." he trailed off. He gently took her face and began guiding it up and down his length at a steady pace.

She pulled back, looking up at him, "You may have won your Majesty, but I'll be receiving the prize whichever way I want."

He released his hands from her face and she began to bob up and down his shaft quickly. He could hardly keep up with her and his prick began to twitch already. He sighed in frustration, he couldn't come now. There was something he had wanted to do with her for some time. With the deal that he was allowed to do whatever he liked, he could only think of one place he hadn't gone. He had never tried it with any woman before. Not just because it was taboo, but also because it was against the law.

He knew she was the only woman he could try something so perverse with. If she didn't want to, it was fine. He considered himself lucky with all she permitted him to do anyway. But there was still the matter of introducing the idea. He pulled her off his swollen member. She whimpered.

"Madeline, I want to please you first."

"You were pleasing me," she said with her hands on her hips.

He kissed her and threw up her skirts.

He slowly moved up the slit of her bottom she murmured, and slowly worked his tongue up to her anus tantalizing her with every small lick. She began to squirm, rocking her bottom about, but Alex gripped her, forcing her to take the rush. She could feel it from her toes to the tips of her fingers, boiling bolts of ecstasy resonating through her. He pushed his tongue inside her.

"HOLY, Uuuhhh," she wailed. She grasped the grass about her between her fingers. She was on the edge of her apex. Then, he quickly descended on her sex, slithering his tongue between her lips, teasing her clitoris. She came, but still craved more. "Alex," she gasped. She kneaded her cunt into his cock. "Now. Do it," she ordered.

He wasted no time and slipped inside her, exhaling. "Whoa," he muttered as he pushed himself to the hilt. His vision met her hair, a mess as she looked forward on her hands and knees. He withdrew himself.

"Alex," she pleaded, her need growing stronger by the second, "what are you doing?"

"I want to see your beautiful face," he said with a hint of dissatisfaction. She softened at this, and assisted him in taking the dress off. She lay on the earth, next to the hedges.

"No, you come to me," he said as he stretched out on the grass. She raised her brow.

"I just don't think —" he stopped himself, "just come to me."

Madeline tried to hold back a giggle. She knew that the part of him that had been raised refined was telling him he shouldn't let a lady lay in the grass and dirt. Despite allowing her to do a number of

475

unladylike things, sometimes she noticed there were some things he couldn't allow. Crawling on top of him she cupped her face in his hand. She descended on his length, adjusting herself then slowly began fucking him.

He grasped her breasts in his hands as she rode him. She leaned down towards him and he took them into his mouth teasing her nipples. She whimpered and gasped from the stimulation. She soon found she was fighting for breath.

As his thighs were growing stiffer and he rammed himself inside her, she wondered how Alex could manage to have so much stamina. But she had to go on; despite the pain, she was so close to coming. Reading her exasperation, he released one of her breasts and circled her clitoris with a couple of fingers. This was her undoing and she began cumming down his shaft and balls. When her body released and the last throbs of orgasm whirled through her, she began charging again, wanting to see him as sated as herself. He stopped her, "I'll take care of it from here. Plant your feet on the ground and hold on."

She put her feet, squatting just over him as he positioned himself. He gyrated into her and she felt him hit her in the deepest reaches of her cunt.

"OH!" she cried, the impact taking her by surprise. She gripped his shoulders, trying to hold on to him. But, with each thrust, he directly hit her most sensitive spot. She moaned, digging in her fingernails into him.

As he went on, the birds chirping in the distance, the smells of the garden and shrubs around them were drowned out. The only thing they could sense was her. Every thrust radiated through him. Every moan was music to his ears. The smell of love and lust. He wanted to cum, but resisted. She came several times more, screaming each time she did.

Then finally, she collapsed onto him her sweaty body melting with his. When she caught her breath, she gazed at him, "Did you?"

"No."

"Why?" she asked.

"Believe me, I was about to."

She looked at him mystified.

"Madeline," he began. He stopped himself then coaxed her onto her hands and knees. He kissed her softly. He parted her cheeks again and breathed deeply looking at her rosebud. Instinct told her what was going to come next. She had suspected before that he wanted to do this, and it made her hot. Perhaps because it was against the law and the whole situation was beyond bold. The 'buggery' law had been around for centuries now, and here they were on royal grounds, moments away from breaking it. He sighed nervously, then slowly pushed his wet finger inside her to prepare her for his hard, pulsating cock that would soon come.

"Yes, Alex yes," she whispered exhorting him.

He groaned at her words. He pushed his finger in deeper.

"Mmm!" Madeline moaned.

He slowly began fingering her tight hole and she bit her lip from the mix of pain and pleasure from it. The more he pushed, the more her muscles relaxed, she began pushing against his fingers. He took his cue; she was ready for him. Withdrawing his finger, he placed his prick at her opening and began to push his head into the tight orifice.

"Uhmm!" Madeline wailed, the pain was hot and burning, but pleasing.

"Do you want me to stop?" he asked.

"No," she replied breathlessly.

"Breathe" he instructed softly.

Slowly, inch by inch she took him, until her hole was wrapped tightly around the base of his cock. He closed his eyes and sighed. He did not want to hurt her, he wanted her to want it again. Madeline turned her head back and looked at him. "Go on Alex."

In minute movements, Alex began thrusting, he could feel her grow hotter beneath him, and, slowly he quickened his pace. She murmured and moaned in approval, as she gave herself to him. Her deep hole grew wetter and she began meeting him with every thrust. Soon he was slamming into her as she became a tight, fierce inferno of lust, "OOooohhhh yes, Alex yes fuck! fuck!" shrieked Madeline feeling her muscles clench his cock like a vice.

"Oh God!" Alex gasped trying to keep himself together. "It's so tight!"

She cocked her head to watch the expressions on his face as he pushed himself in and out of her. He was in ecstasy, at his brink and she knew he was enjoying himself too much to let go.

"Go faster Alex," she pleaded, knowing it would feel more comfortable for her if he did. He pushed forward, his thighs slapping against her arse.

"Oh my GOD! Oh, Alex! Yes, do it! It feels good, ooohhh."

A strange something came over her, she was reaching her climax – in a way she never had before. Her muscles were tensing; some were even going numb. A cool, tingling sensation happened in the lower half of her body. As the new senses came over her and she began to rub her twat at a furious pace.

He cried aloud, "OH! FFFFUUUCCCCKKK!!" spurting his hot seed inside her.

Between that, her fingers and his pulsating thrusting cock, she had simultaneous orgasms; exploding like a supernova, screaming till she could no longer sound. Her vision blurred, she panted heavily, and dropped to the ground.

Alex looked down on her concerned; he propped her up in his arms. "Are you all right?"

She said nothing but huffed and puffed. Giving her a few seconds he brushed her messy mane from her face. She weakly raised her arm touching his.

"I think I'm going to be feeling this for the next day," she said when she finally caught her breath.

He laughed, "I'll tell Mr. Tinney that I found you to be quite peaky today and that you need a day off."

"I don't think I'll be able to make it back to the castle to enjoy it," she joked.

He grinned and helped her into her dress, tightened the laces as she sat wearily. He put his own clothes on as she watched him in awe of his sculpture like perfection.

"Can't make it back to the castle, hm?" he swooped down, scooping her into his arms. "I'll take you back." He began carrying her outside the maze.

"Someone will see us, you should put me down," she protested.

"But you're feeling peaky Miss Black," he winked.

She said nothing, though she knew how improper it was. She couldn't help but want him to hold her. They got several strange looks from some of the guards as they came to the doors, but Alex slyly brushed it off as if it were nothing, requesting a few maids come assist 'poor, tired Miss Black'.

29

DRURY LANE

Getting out of going to the Tower of London was a huge relief for Princess Sofia. She did not want another history lesson from Alex. Going to the Tower of London, he would probably tell her of ghost sightings and stories; she had heard there were many there. Along with the animals and prisoners, she couldn't bear it. He had done this while giving her a tour of Windsor Castle – until her fears got the better of her and she demanded that he stop. The Tower of London had housed so many prisoners over the centuries. She guessed there would be plenty of ghost stories that he would share. She had had enough of history. A play at Drury Lane was what she needed.

Madeline, on the other hand, was disappointed. Alex had a lively way of telling the history of places that she really enjoyed. Ghost sightings didn't disturb her. She wondered if the people reporting them really saw it, or it was something built up in their heads. Either way, it was fascinating.

Alex had one of his valets, Jack Caston come along to the theatre. He didn't sit in the carriage with the rest of them, he rode with the driver. When they got there, Jack entered the theatre to tell the theatre owner of their arrival.

When he came back, they got out of their coach. Immediately, Madeline noticed that the way to the theatre door was cleared for them. The theatre had also laid out a red carpet for Alex's entry. Alex walked out arm in arm with Sofia as Madeline and Greg followed at their heels. Madeline looked about at all the eyes upon them. There were hundreds of people of different classes waiting to enter the theatre bowing and curtsying as they passed. She noticed all the nobles were dressed in their best. She looked down at her uniform and felt foolish. The peasants and middle class would be sitting amongst their own. Madeline was going to sit amongst the best dressed; she wished she had worn one of the dresses Alex had given her. Even Jack looked dapper in his Windsor Castle uniform.

Once they entered the theatre, Jack escorted them up several flights of stairs and to their box. Jack held out chairs for Sofia and Alex. That's when Madeline noticed a fourth chair. She looked about curiously, thinking it couldn't be for her, she was supposed to wait on Sofia.

"Have a seat, Miss Black," said Alex, reading her thoughts. "Mr. Caston will take care of the food while you tend to the Princess."

Madeline sat down next to Sofia and adjusted her dress. When Madeline was finished, she surveyed her surroundings. It was the largest box the theatre had to offer. Several smaller ones surrounded them. Behind them were tall drapes that hung high from the ceiling. Behind the drapes, Madeline could see Jack next to a food table pouring glasses of champagne and arranging canapés, cheeses, crackers and several other finger foods on trays.

"Thank you so much, your Highness, for allowing me to attend," Greg said to Sofia as he took his seat next to Alex. "I really hope you enjoy tonight's show. Have you ever seen Hamlet?"

Sofia grimaced. It wasn't that she had allowed Greg to come. Alex had invited him. "You're welcome, and no, Sir Gregory I haven't. My English tutor had me read the play with him, but I feel there was so much I misunderstood."

"Should Miss Black and I switch seats?" Greg offered. "I can answer any questions you may have during the play."

"Don't be ridiculous Sir Gregory, it would be rude of me to ask questions during the play. Besides, I'm sitting next to the King, who has quite an extensive education himself. I'm sure that he could explain the play better than you."

Alex folded his arms, "Did I forget to tell you, Sofia? Sir Gregory and I have the same education, we took lessons together."

She was flabbergasted. "Is that so?" She rounded on Greg, "How is it that you got in on his lessons?"

"He has his charm," Alex answered giving Greg a meaningful look. Greg smiled back.

"Up then Miss Black, you and I need to switch seats," Greg demanded.

"Wait a minute," began Sofia, "I'd still prefer –."

"You would make the King of England explain things to you and miss the play himself?" asked Greg trying to make Sofia feel guilty.

"Well, I-I –"

"I'm sure Greg can explain Hamlet, Sofia. He loves the theatre more than myself," said Alex.

Madeline rose from her seat and sat next to Alex, her face beaming. Out of the corner of her eye, she could see his mouth curve slightly.

"Do you know much about Drury Lane, Princess?" asked Alex, staring out at the stage.

"What is there to know?" she asked her eyes twinkling.

"Plenty, really," said Alex clasping his hands on his lap.

"Your Majesty," Greg began, "the history of Drury Lane is hardly interesting."

"How could you say that Sir Gregory?" Alex jeered. "It's hundreds of years old, has burnt down several times and has ghosts."

Princess Sofia turned pale, "Nonsense."

"It's true," Alex insisted, "the actors here have reported many sightings."

"I don't like all this talk of ghosts," Sofia said trembling. "It'll put a damper on our evening."

Madeline raised an eyebrow. It was becoming obvious that Sofia had a fear of ghosts.

"I'm sure there will be no sightings of ghosts tonight Princess Sofia," said Greg reassuringly. "They don't want to hear his Majesty's boring history lessons either."

Sofia burst out laughing, but then tried to contain herself, giving Alex a guilty look.

"That's fine Sofia. Laugh. I can take a joke," Alex said. "Look whom I've spent most my life with."

Sofia gave a faint smile as the wheels turned in her head, wondering whether he was being truthful or polite. She tried to put it out of her mind as the theatre quieted, and everyone found their seats. Two actors walked onto the stage, and the production began.

In the dim light, Alex slowly moved his hand and found Madeline's, he rubbed it and caressed it with his fingers. Her breath was caught in her chest. She glanced at Sofia wondering if she had noticed. She hadn't. Her eyes were alight watching the stage. She leaned over to Greg and whispered something, he gave a broad smile as he leaned towards her, whispering back.

Madeline continued holding hands with Alex, watching the play from the box enraptured. She hadn't been to Drury Lane in years. The last time she went was before she had been sold by her father. When her father had work, he would take her with him to rehearsals and she could play around the theatre and try to steal any food left about by patrons or troupe.

The last time Isaac Black worked Drury Lane, the company was doing Henry IV, and he was Falstaff. She had never gone to a show. Isaac could have never provided the seats that they sat in — royal box seats. They were reserved for Alex and other royal dignitaries. If royalty did not come, no one would be allowed to sit in the seats.

She had to go to the washroom; as she looked from side to side, she realized that because it had burned down since she'd been there, she no longer knew where everything was.

"What is it Miss Black?" Alex whispered.

Embarrassed, she looked down. Servants were intended to serve; she should have discreetly left without saying anything. "I need to go to the lavatory," she whispered.

"You have my leave Miss Black, go on."

Madeline left the private box and looked about the corridors. It was beautifully decorated with mahogany wood panels, the stairway balustrades had cute gold painted little cherubs holding candelabra, their candles lit. She knew that quality of it was nothing like Alex's estates, but it was much more tasteful now than it was when her father worked there.

Some time later, she finally found the lavatory. But since she had taken a few wrong turns, she didn't know how to get back. She walked about looking for familiar paintings and stairways she had passed.

She was about to walk up a set of stairs when she was grabbed from behind and dragged beyond a set of curtains. She shrieked, but her the sound was quickly muffled by a hand over her mouth. "Calm down, Miss Black I haven't even started on you yet."

She whirled around. It was Alex.

"You scared me!" she said as she looked about the room. It looked like it used to be an old box seat, but was now storage for sets and props.

"Sorry," he said his voice sincere.

"Let's go, we're missing the play."

"Never mind that Miss Black, I never cared much for Hamlet's moping and griping about his miserable life anyway."

She gave him a light push, "That's an insult to the greatest playwright in history."

"Why don't we forget the play?" he suggested.

"We really shouldn't. What if we get caught?"

"By who? Who will come looking for us here? Luckily for us they have an orchestra for the play too. No one will hear."

He pulled her to him, crashing his lips to hers. *A little kissing wouldn't hurt*, she thought. Resisting his lips was harder than resisting all the delicacies in the royal kitchen. Her passion intertwined with his they explored one another, her hands rubbing against his chest, his caressing her face. He sucked her bottom lip, then manoeuvred his tongue into her mouth. They continued kissing awhile until he pulled back and stared into her eyes, his eyes begging for more.

"We should go before they start wondering where we went," she muttered, releasing her hands from him. Saying nothing, he took off his coat and began unbuttoning his shirt. Her eyes bulged. "No, no," she said as she walked back towards the curtains. He grabbed her arm and pulled her back into his embrace. She tried to pull away, but couldn't break free.

Watching her struggle, he chuckled. He squeezed her body against his, covering her forehead with soft pecks. "Madeline, you know just as well as I do that I'm going to be up your skirts and you'll be in my mouth in a matter of minutes, if not seconds."

He pressed his lips hard against hers before she could object. She turned to a puddle in his arms, her hands gracing the rises and falls of his sinewy muscles on his chest and stomach. She began undoing his trousers hastily as he kissed her. He pulled at the laces on the back of her dress. It slipped to her hips and he tugged it, dropping it to her ankles.

"Madeline," he muttered breathlessly. He nuzzled her leaving a trail of kisses down to her white mounds, he took them into his mouth, massaging the peaks with his tongue and sucking them hard.

She tittered softly, as he squeezed them, manipulating them between his fingers, tremors running through her limbs as he did.

He left a trail of kisses as he dropped onto his knees, nibbling and kissed at her thighs, she slowly spread her legs, and he softly licked her sex. "Mmm," he hummed, she could feel the vibrations and warmth as his mouth enclosed around her pussy.

"Hhhuuh," Madeline moaned as her body shuddered. She stepped back slightly leaning against the wall behind her. Alex flicked her clitoris with his tongue, as her knees grew weaker giving in to the pleasure. She pressed her lips together trying to suppress the moans. Alex slithered about her pussy masterfully and he began focusing on her secret place again.

"Ahh!"

"Did you hear that?" Sofia whispered to Greg as she looked about.

"No," Greg said quickly. *Alex has no problems playing with fire,* he thought as he looked at her.

Sofia shrugged and went back to watching the play. The ghost of Hamlet Senior re-entered the stage on a platform. She jumped, grabbing his thigh as Hamlet spoke to the spirit. He smiled, she had a phobia of ghosts, even people acting as them. She looked over humiliated noticing where she had touched him. She released him slowly and shakily brought her hand to her lap. Her body trembled as the characters spoke to one another. She stared down into her lap at her hands clenched together.

"It's all right Sofia," he said reaching out unclasping her grip. He took her hand and rubbed it. "You're okay."

Sofia knew she should pull away. She certainly did not want Alex to see the two of them holding hands. But she could not help it. His holding her hand soothed her fear.

"Oooohh!"

Sofia cocked her head from side to side. "Did you hear that Sir Gregory? Do you think it was a ghost?" she asked, her lips quivering.

It took every ounce of will he had to keep from laughing hysterically. "No, Sofia. I think it's just an impolite audience."

Madeline was now lying on the floor with her legs spread, her hand still clasped to her mouth. "Alex! Alex!" she heaved, fearing she might scream louder than she already had.

Lost in a wonderland of his own, he paid no attention and continued licking and massaging her with his tongue. He wriggled his tongue inside her tasting her.

"Ooooohhh!!" she moaned her hand still over her mouth, "I'm cuuummmmiiinng."

Alex delicately lapped her up. Hearing her, smelling her and tasting her were making him hotter and harder by the second. He could no longer keep himself together to bring her to orgasm with his tongue. "I can't take this!" he said harshly. He pushed himself up from her legs and pulled her close to him, positioning himself at the entrance of her cunt.

Madeline sat up and began stroking his hard length kissing his lips softly. "But it's my turn, Alex."

He looked into her eyes in the dim light, and gently pushed her onto her back, caressing her lips with his. "I would love to let you have your 'turn', but I need you badly. I'll make you cum hard I promise."

He lifted her leg, forcing her to lie on her side and placed it at his shoulder. They had never tried this position before, but she could already see that Alex was going to have no problems ramming himself into her. No sooner had she thought that, then he had already begun. She could feel him grinding, nudging deep inside her. Her already well-lubricated pussy welcoming him in, intensifying her nerves as he went. Her gratification instantly came to a boiling point.

"AAHH," she began screaming then quickly bit down on her lip. She whipped her head sideways, looking for something to scream into but finding nothing. Next to her she saw a pair of masks, some old chairs and another set of curtains. Just then, she realized where they were – in a vacant box. She put her hand over her mouth, as she bit down. But Alex continued fucking, sliding in and out of her, whirling her into a blissful state of multiple orgasms. She could do nothing but take him, shrieking again and again as she bit down harder. She could feel a few droplets of blood on her lip, but she didn't care. The risk and pain were worth the pleasure and seeing Alex fall to pieces.

His balls churned as he grew stiffer and she could feel his hot seed spurt into her, filling her, as his breath grew short he called to her, "Mmmaa-del-line." He was gasping, as more ribbons of cum shot into her.

He stood up, his cock still solid and she stared up at him hungrily. "You're still hard," she said softly.

"Come here," he said gruffly.

She shuffled over to him on her knees and he sat down on one of the old dilapidated chairs. She opened her mouth eagerly, ready to have him inside her.

"Don't you try that just yet." He leaned down so that their noses were touching. "I want it squeezed between those gorgeous breasts of yours." He looked directly at her breasts, her eyes followed his, she touched them softly, their nipples already erect. "Go on, squeeze them together."

Seductively, she brought her hands about them, but then he abruptly planted his face between them, she let out a squeal.

"I can help you," he said, between kissing and running his tongue across them. He became distracted sucking and nibbling them, she whimpered in delight as tingles ran from her chest down to her pussy.

He leaned back, placing her hands on them. She pressed them together and they protruded towards his cock. He slipped his hard length between the large orbs sighing, "Move them up and down." She did as he asked, pressing the rigid member between her soft mounds moving down, his cock touched her lips. She realized that she wouldn't be able to move her breasts down to the base of his sex without taking him into her mouth. She opened her mouth, humming happily as she took his already wet tip in.

"Uuuhh," he groaned. Gripping the edge of the chair, he began gyrating his hips. The chair squeaked as he leaned back on the back two legs of the chair. Under the pressure, it fell apart, and he crashed to the ground, grimacing as he suppressed a yelp of pain. Madeline's mouth descended on him and she continued sucking. He reacted, stretching out his toes his breath erratic.

"Fuck." He trembled as he hurled himself forward, placing his hands on her head, cumming into her mouth, "Uuh. Uh. Holy."

491

She tasted and devoured him as he came. He watched, uttering a small groan, as he rested back down on the pieces of the chair. "Whoa," she could hear him whisper to himself. She cleaned him off, enjoying his taste and scent, before she popped up and glanced over at him.

His eyes were heavy and he smiled dreamily at her. She loved that face; a mixture of satisfaction and weariness that only she ever saw. She never saw him tired otherwise. Breaking him down like that was such a turn on, and her private triumph. Knowing they couldn't rest for long, they got up and began putting on their clothes. Alex surveyed her as they walked out from behind the curtains.

"Madeline, uh, perhaps we should take a trip to the lavatory."

"Right."

The two went back to the lavatories, Alex a few paces ahead of her. When she finished cleaning up, she headed back, but didn't spot him on the way. He probably had finished before she had, she assumed. She retraced her steps in frustration. There had to be a quicker way to get there, she just didn't know it.

Several minutes later, she found the box just as Alex was taking his seat.

"I've missed your company your Majesty, where have you been?" asked Sofia as she pulled her hand away from Sir Gregory.

"Forgive me, Princess. I ran into Lord Nash, he wanted to speak about the war in Spain with me. Believes he knows of some men in our court that may be spies for Napoleon."

"Really?" she said an astonished look on her face. "And you Miss Black? Where were you?"

"Well, I got lost —" Madeline began, unsure of what to say next. Nobody could be lost for that long. The play was in the middle of the fourth act.

"Lucky for me, she did get lost," Alex said, rescuing her. "When I happened upon her she was with Lord Nash. She took down some of the names he mentioned."

Sofia nodded her head sheepishly, "Oh."

Madeline was impressed. She thought she was a good liar, but Alex was quite the weasel.

"What a magnificent play. Such a tragic ending," said Sofia as they exited the theatre on the red carpet.

"I don't understand why everyone had to die at the end," said Greg. "I mean, I wanted Hamlet to take over Denmark."

"Everyone dying is what makes the play the ultimate tragedy," said Alex.

A footman opened the door to the coach and Sofia stepped inside and sat down. Madeline sat next to her. Both Alex and Greg followed.

"Hamlet is an idiot really," said Greg dismissively.

"Yes, he should have taken his opportunity to kill Claudius when he had the chance," began Sofia. "Such a procrastinator."

Alex laughed, "Hamlet was not a procrastinator Sofia."

"If he wasn't a procrastinator he certainly was a coward," replied Sofia, as the carriage lurched forward.

Alex continued making his point, "No. He was a religious man,"

"Perfect. Here we go," Greg said annoyed.

"He has the opportunity several times to kill Claudius," Alex started, "once while he's praying –"

"But he doesn't," Sofia interjected.

"Yes Sofia, he doesn't because he figures that if Claudius is guilty of killing his father than he would not want to kill him while he prays. He knows killing him while he prays will send Claudius to heaven, and Claudius is undeserving. He wants to wait until after he's done something sinful before he exacts his revenge."

"Which makes him a procrastinator," Sofia said stubbornly.

"No, it doesn't. It makes him calculating. He over thinks and analyzes every aspect of his revenge. He goes so far as to put on a facade of being insane," he said matter-of-factly. "Hamlet isn't a procrastinator. He accidentally kills Polonius in the middle of the play thinking he is Claudius. Hamlet is a man waiting for the right reasons and the right time to strike."

"Then why did things end so terribly for him?" Madeline asked without thinking. "Sorry," she said looking down.

A warm smile flitted on Alex's face. "It's quite all right Miss Black," he said, "but to answer your question, I think there's a moral here. Perhaps, revenge is something no man should seek."

"I don't know Alex," Greg began, "it seems to me that sometimes revenge has to be sought for the greater good. Your cousin comes to mind."

"Yes," Alex sighed, a tired look on his face, "I know when I grow older there will be things that I will regret. There already are."

Madeline glanced up surprised at him. She wished she could say some words to comfort him, but she had no idea what the hardships of being royalty were.

"That's part of being a great leader, your Majesty," said Sofia as she smiled sweetly at him. "If it makes you feel better, people won't remember you for all your regrets. They'll try to remember the great things you did."

Alex said nothing. He looked over at Madeline as she smoothed out Princess Sofia's dress and skirt. He wondered what it would be like to be a lowly servant instead of a king. He envied her freedom of responsibility. Making heavy decisions for the country was something Madeline would never have to think about. She did not have to consider what others would think of her for her political decisions or what she wore. Her biggest worry was to see that the master she served was satisfied. *But it would depend on the master,* he thought. Lord and Lady Watson's ill-treatment would be a living hell. However, even under a good master, Madeline didn't have a voice. She had to apologize just for speaking in conversation. He exhaled. It was odd. They came from two very different worlds, but neither of them could freely be themselves.

30

AN UNEXPECTED GUEST

They arrived back at Windsor Castle, and for the next several days, there were no excursions. Sofia tried to plan several outings with Alex, mentioning other sights in London and England that she would like to see. But Greg Umbridge always invited himself along, and in an instant Sofia would change her mind about going. It was several quiet days at the castle, enjoying music, horse riding, reading and occasionally playing games at tea time.

All the while, Alex and Madeline gave each other secret glances and touches when Sofia wasn't looking. It made Madeline feel somewhat guilty. She tried to reason with herself she wasn't taking Alex from Sofia. If anything, Sofia was trying to take something that did not belong to her.

After several uneventful days, Alex announced that he was going to treat Sofia to an Italian dinner. Madeline grew envious. She knew that the dishes he would have requested would be some of the most delicious delicacies Italians would have to offer. She was frustrated that she would have to stand back as Sofia threw herself at him, complimenting every dish. However, on the night of the dinner, he dropped a bombshell on Sofia. As they walked into the King's Private Dining Room, there were five place settings on the table. Madeline began to question if Alex had invited Sofia's parents too.

"Oh, this is so LOVELY!" Sofia said excitedly as she squeezed his hand. "You've invited my father and my mother?"

Alex bit his lip, "Well, actually Sofia, I thought it was time we give Miss Black and Miss Van Gogh a break. After all, they have had quite a few full days without any rest. Especially Miss Black. She has gone on many excursions to accommodate your needs."

Sofia stared at him dismayed. Silence fell over the room as Madeline, Aletta, Greg and Alex looked at Sofia. "I suppose," Sofia said slowly, tapping her finger to her lip.

"Wonderful," he said giving her a small peck on the cheek. Her eyes lit up with a big smile. Somehow, it was all she needed to accept the idea of servants sharing a table with her.

"Gentlemen," he said to the footmen standing around the table, "assist Miss Black and Miss Van Gogh to their seats."

The footmen escorted Madeline and Aletta to their seats, pulling out their chairs and tucking them back in. Greg rushed ahead of Alex and pulled out Sofia's chair. A miffed expression, Sofia sat down and jerked her chair towards the table, releasing it from Greg's grip. Alex sat at the head of the table.

Madeline glowed. Though she did not get to sit next to Alex like Greg and Sofia, enjoying an Italian meal was more enjoyable than standing behind Sofia and waiting upon her. Several more footmen entered the room each carrying tureens and dishes for the first course.

She squirmed excitedly in her chair. She remembered the last time Alex had treated her to dinner. She knew this would be just as delicious. More footmen entered the room carrying with them golden tureens, baskets of warm breads, dishes of oils for the bread, along with plates of antipasto.

"You look quite excited Miss Black. Have you ever had Italian food?" Alex asked.

"No, your Majesty," she lied, remembering the prosciutto they had on their picnic.

He looked at her genially, "That's good that you'll get to enjoy some of my favourite dishes tonight. This first dish is my favourite soup."

The footmen began pouring ladles of soup from the tureens into their bowls.

"Oh is this Italian Wedding Soup?" asked Sofia, lightly touching his arm with a twinkle in her eye.

"No, actually I'm not really sure what it is called. As a boy, I would always call it 'zuppa'. Whenever I ask the kitchen staff for 'zuppa', they have always known which Italian soup I was talking about."

Madeline dipped her spoon into her soup picturing Alex as a little boy asking for 'zuppa', her heart melted at the thought. She could imagine servants being happy to fulfill his requests as a boy. She stirred the soup about with her spoon looking at the contents of the bowl. There was sausage, potato and some kind of green leafy vegetable. "Sorry your Majesty, but what is this?" Madeline said holding up the vegetable with her spoon.

Sofia was aghast at Madeline's improper manners, "Miss Black it's not appropriate to address the King in so blunt a fashion."

Madeline set the spoon back into her bowl and was about to apologize when, he answered her question.

"It's kale Miss Black. It's a kind of cabbage."

"Thank you, your Majesty," she said and put a spoonful in her mouth. It was a burst of flavour, she was eager for another taste.

He watched her as she enjoyed the soup, making sure not to devour his quickly. The moment he finished his bowl, the footmen would take away everyone's and start serving the next course. He wanted to make sure that she had finished the entire bowl of soup. He waited patiently between spoonfuls, trying to finish his bowl just after she did.

Greg looked between the two. He leaned toward Alex and whispered, "For years my food has been carried away by servants before I could finish. She dines with you one night and now you're willing to wait?"

"She pleases me, what do you do?" Alex whispered back.

"Where do I begin?"

Sofia looked at them curiously. It was rude to have private conversations like that at dinner. But Greg Umbridge seemed to have no problem starting little chats with anyone; herself, even the King. Once she became Queen of England, either Greg would be given leave or given proper lessons in manners, she promised herself.

The dinner went on with more Italian delicacies, and Madeline found each course more mouth-watering than the last. It was fun to be waited upon. But it was difficult to remember table manners. She watched Sofia and tried to follow suit; resting her hands in her lap as she was served, taking small bites, sitting up with good posture and trying to make polite conversation. It was not easy.

She noticed Aletta sitting next to Sofia, watching her every move as well.

By the time dessert came, Madeline needed to go to the lavatory. She knew it was bad manners to leave during the dinner service, on the other hand, she didn't get an opportunity to freshen up before dinner like Sofia had. As the dessert course was about to be served, she asked Alex's permission, and he excused her.

Sofia shook her head. She had never seen such a lack of etiquette at dinner in all her life. Worse, Alex didn't seem to care. Proper ladies did not leave the table while eating. As Madeline stepped out from her chair, Sofia couldn't restrain herself. Proper manners needed to be adhered to. "His Majesty is too kind," said Sofia.

"How so Sofia?" he asked.

"To let so many improper behaviours be observed, you truly are sweet," she said touching his arm.

Madeline looked at the two, her mouth gaping as she walked.

SMASH! THUD!

Distracted, Madeline had fallen to the floor, her uniform covered in tiramisu. She had collided with the footman taking out the dessert. She looked at him, breathing shakily, her eyes welled up with tears as she could hear a commotion go on about her; Greg's laughter and Sofia's gasp. She felt hands grasp her arms and lift her up to her feet.

"Are you all right Miss Black?" asked Alex, as he pulled her to her feet.

A dead silence came over the room, everyone stared in shock at them. Madeline looked down, guiltily. Alex had forgotten himself.

"What is it Sofia?" Alex asked, brushing off his behaviour. "I may be a king, but I'm still a gentleman to a lady in distress."

"Well, I suppose," she said, a doubtful look on her face.

"I'd do the same for any woman I had invited to dinner," he said smoothly. He sat back down, "Miss Black go and clean up. Once you're done, you and I will have to have a little chat about this."

Greg nudged him, "You need to be more careful mate," he muttered.

"You're giving me advice on how to act?" Alex replied. "You're poking a king."

"Right."

Madeline left, unsteady on her feet. She headed down to the servants' quarters and changed into another uniform. She wondered if she should head back, or find Sofia and tend to her. But then she remembered that Alex had commanded that she come back to see him for a talk. Heading back, her hands grew clammy, and her breathing shallow. She expected that he might have to reprimand her in front of everyone. Assisting her reflected poorly on him and reaming her out may be the only way to avoid suspicion. She held her breath as she opened the door, prepared to put on an act with Alex. But to her amazement, he was alone, sitting in his chair at the head of the table.

"Ah, Miss Black," he said, his devilish smirk on his face, swirling some brandy in a glass.

"Where is everyone?"

"I dismissed them. Explained that I needed to punish you without humiliating you publicly." He lifted his hand waving her to come towards him. "Come here," he said seductively.

501

She walked over with her hands behind her back. He grabbed her, his arms like trunks and settled her onto his lap. She giggled.

"You know I'm not angry with you?" he asked.

"I didn't think you were. To be honest, I thought you might yell at me in front of everyone. You know, to save face. I think you appalled Sofia."

He laughed, "Sofia's a very proper woman. There's not much that doesn't appal her."

"Isn't she the kind of woman you should be with?"

"Is Greg Umbridge the kind of fellow I should have around? I've never enjoyed the company of predictable people. They're boring."

She tittered, flirtatiously hitting his chest.

"I'm glad it happened. Now I can get some alone time with you," he said.

"What if I don't want any time alone with you?" she teased.

In an instant, he pulled up her up onto the table. "You destroyed dessert Miss Black," he began calmly. "You should be punished for such recklessness. Lift your skirts Miss Black, I want dessert." She squirmed playfully against him, but he pinned her down, kissing her hard. "Don't make me resort to giving you royal commands."

"Why don't you lift my skirts?"

Without much ado, Alex pulled up her skirts and sat in his chair.

Madeline parted her thighs and looked at her King, a come hither expression in her eyes, while he sat in his chair, feeling his sex grow rigid sexual desire.

"Spread those lips apart, for me," he said licking his chops.

Madeline arched her back slightly and reached down spreading her sex with her fingers. Alex stared at her awhile, a lewd expression on his face. He drew closer to her and breathed her in. "Mmm, I'm sure you already know I think you're alluring in every sense." He moved her fingers away and replaced them with his. Then he gave her a long lick up her cunt as if he were eating ice cream. Madeline moaned with each long lick, and soon he began switching between long licks and short ones, prodding inside her with his tongue, covering her sex with his entire mouth. It drove Madeline into a wave of small pleasurable orgasms. It was hot to watch her as she writhed on the table, but Alex desired more for her. Pulling back her lips with one hand, he began focusing on her small nub as he thrust his fingers inside of her.

Madeline reacted like a bolt of electricity had ran through her veins, arching her back, puffing and murmuring. Just then, she felt his fingers almost turning inside her, her body shuddered from the movement, she knew she was close. Her breath became shorter, then she felt his pinky playfully circle her asshole. She wailed, "Oh, God! Alex! No! You're going to make me cum all over the table!"

"Good," he mumbled between her pussy lips. He shoved the pinky inside her. The stimulation of having both holes filled and her clit tongued was too much. Bowing and squirming beneath him, she fell apart.

"AAAHHHHH!"

She came, covering his hand with her nectar. She could feel it trickle down to her bottom and onto the table. He gently tended to her as she collapsed on the table. He rose from his chair and picked her up and cradled her in his arms. He sat back down, resting her on his lap. She laid her head in the crook of his neck and kissed him, panting. He said nothing but took in the sound of her heartbeat racing against his chest. He placed his hand over it and smiled.

"Happy with dessert?" she asked coquettishly.

"I'm not done having dessert."

He put her back on the table and tore into the laces of her dress. She squealed his name, telling him to stop, all the while giggling. He threw the dress to the floor. She gazed at him as he began stripping his clothes off and casually kicking off his shoes.

"Close your eyes," he said giving her a warm kiss. He took the bowl of oil and slowly poured it over her breasts. She gasped, the hot bread that had been dipped into it earlier had made it warm and she could feel her nipples stiffen under the sensation.

"This will make things a little more interesting, hm?" he said as he continued pouring it across her stomach and onto her pussy, making her hotter and wetter than she was before.

"Mmmm," she crooned as it streamed between her lips and down the slit of her bottom.

He began kissing her stomach, his mouth moving towards her breasts. He began tenderly kneading them with his hands. He whirled his tongue around her nipples, gingerly biting them with his teeth. Her hips rose in response and she began grinding herself against the hard bumps of his abs.

"You're getting oil on my abs," he said pulling back from her chest.

"Oh," she said blushing.

"You can keep doing that, though."

They gazed at one another a moment before he went down kissing and sucking her breasts. As she slid her pussy down his abs again she could feel his cock bumping into her. He was hard. She reached her hand down, touching her oiled stomach as she did and grasped him.

"Hhhuuhhhh," he grunted feeling her warm oiled hand glide up and down him effortlessly. "Good God!" he muttered.

He stood upright and Madeline moved down the table, her hand still grasping him. She manoeuvred herself onto her stomach and propped herself up with her elbows.

He looked down at her knowing what she had in mind. "If you're thinking what I think you're thinking —"

Madeline didn't even let him finish his words, she languidly dragged her tongue up the underside of his cock.

"Madeline," his voice shuddered and his legs twitched. He weaved his fingers into her hair, gently brushing it. She wrapped her lips around the tip of him and looked up at him. His eyes melted into hers. Madeline smiled inwardly, she knew that look. He was her little puppet to do with whatever she wished. If she took her mouth off of him and denied him more, he'd probably lose his mind with desire ... then again so would she.

She tightened her lips and moved down him, motivated to make him do more than tremble and moan. She could feel him poke the back of her throat and she moved back and forth accommodating his length. When her nose reached his abdomen, she wriggled her head back and forth.

"Uhhh!" he moaned feeling his tip rubbing against the back of her throat. He could feel his balls begin to churn. She pulled back to his tip before she sucked in her cheeks and swiftly went back down, the oil taking her down there faster. She slowly pulled back again releasing her cheeks as she went. She continued this motion at a slow pace and Alex knew if she went any faster, he would erupt. She knew his body too well. Up and down his shaft she went sucking in her cheeks, releasing, breathing her hot breath on his oiled cock, driving him insane. Mad with lust, he pulled her off. "You're going to pay for that."

"I was hoping I would," she said rising and sitting down on the table in front of him. He grabbed her waist and guided his length to the entrance of her sex. He moved it about her slit teasing her.

She caressed his arm. "Alex," she begged.

He said nothing but smiled, his eyes smouldering.

"Now," she whined.

He grabbed the oil and poured it over both their sexes, massaging her as he did. Feeling the warm oil seep down between her cheeks she grew wetter with excitement. He grabbed her bottom and heaved it closer to the edge of the table. She lifted her legs onto his shoulders and clasped her hands around his neck. He forced himself into her, and she twisted her hips, in anticipation. The oil made both their bodies so slick; they both knew in moments he would be pounding and pistoning in and out of her relentlessly.

He began the onslaught, ploughing into her as he pulled her bottom to him. Their sexes crashing into one another, she could feel him in the deepest recesses of her cunt. Her arse sliding on the table, she crooned along with every grind. Soon she could feel her juices combine with the oil making their rhythm more fluid, and his strokes more powerful. Then, he hit her most sensitive spot.

"There Alex," she whimpered wanting the full assault. Alex charged into her harder than before, certain that if he went any harder, he'd split her in two. But she seemed to scream louder and louder with every hard plunge and became wetter. He could feel her juice coat his cock and his thighs.

"YES! THERE! THERE! AAAALLEEEEXXXXXX!" She held down on him like a vice, then pressed her lips hard against his. He groaned wanting his release, but still wanting to fuck her more. She parted from his lips and he looked down noticing a wet sheen on her breasts, he could have came from the sight of it. She was his. Every part of her being wanted to please him. But he wanted to please her more. He probed into her with long deep strokes making her reach her apex and cum several more times, before her arms finally released from his neck, her muscles too weak.

He quickly took her legs down from his shoulders and withdrew himself. She began to whimper, still in desperate need of him. He guided her onto her stomach. She felt her feet touch the floor again and she bent over the table excited for what was to come. But then to her surprise, she could feel him lift her arse into the air, holding her up by her hips. Propped up by just her elbows, she turned back, curiously and laughed. "Alex, you can't. You'll get tired holding me up."

"I know what I can handle, Miss Black. You'll tire before I do. I think you already have."

With that he slammed into her and she let out a yelp, her cunt still taut from her last orgasm. He grunted, bounding into her at a frantic pace. Soon he could feel her grip around his prick again. He grunted, lunging at a speed her moans couldn't keep up with, his heart hammering against his chest and his balls churning with the need to cum. But she shook and bucked screaming to climax before him. This drove him in to a carnal abyss, his body trembling along with hers.

"What are you doing to me?" he said shaking his head in disbelief. "I'm still hard."

It was then he looked down and noticed her glistening arse, ready for his cock. He grabbed the oil again and poured some onto himself stroking it up and down his shaft and tip. Watching her, he had the sudden urge to tongue her tight little hole. He leaned down kissing her cheeks, then began in circular motions around the soft opening. Madeline's eyes lit up. Her breath caught in her lungs as she enjoyed the sensation of Alex's tongue slithering about. He eventually moved on to probing her with his tongue, which had her moaning and scratching her fingernails into the table. He pulled back and poured some more of the warm oil down her bottom.

"Mmm," Madeline moaned as it streamed down to her cunt.

Moving toward her, Alex gently brushed her rosebud with his cock. Madeline relaxed her muscles and pulled back her cheeks again. Little by little, Alex pushed himself up inside the tight aperture, groaning as he did. She enjoyed as each inch went inside; the oil easing him in.

Pacing himself, Alex began to gyrate into her.

"Yes, yes," Madeline begged feeling the pounding of his prick. "More! Oooohhh yes, Alex! Harder!"

Alex obeyed and thrust himself hard into her again and again, but it wasn't enough.

"Alex! SIT!" Madeline commanded.

Stunned, Alex sat down onto his chair, bringing Madeline with him, sitting on his lap. She immediately took charge, grabbing the arms of the chair and rode his penis with her arse.

"HHuuHHhh OH MY GOD ... MADELINE ... FUCK!" he cried trying to keep himself from exploding inside her. Alex

508

pulled up her skirt and began massaging her sex, as she slid up and down.

"OOOhhhhh," Madeline murmured in pleasure, feeling his hand on her, "Oh, touch me Alex, touch MMMEEEEEE." She uttered a glass shattering scream, every muscle of her being contracting. She slapped the arm of the chair with her hand repeatedly as a force unlike anything she had ever felt ran through her body. She fell apart on top of him, cumming again and again. He came with her, shooting deep within her. She moaned and purred, revelling in his desire for her.

When her body finished spasming and her muscles eventually eased, he withdrew himself. They sat in silence for a few moments sharing soft kisses.

"I don't think you can use this chair anymore Alex."

He smiled, "I'll break it and throw it in the fireplace."

Once they had collected themselves, the two went about the room cleaning it. She grabbed a heap of napkins from the buffet table and began soaking up the oil from the table and herself.

"I can't believe we just did that," he said as he slammed his chair to the ground shattering it into splinters.

"What do you mean?" she replied, concern in her voice.

"We just don't think sometimes. I mean, I just," he trailed off. "Here, in the middle of the dining room. Someone could have come in. I don't want you to be imprisoned for –"

"You'd probably get it too, your Majesty," she interrupted as she nuzzled up to him.

"I'm not so worried about that," he said throwing the wood into the fireplace. "It would be a slap on the wrist for me. I worry about you."

"We're fine."

"I'm such a bugger. We were fine this time, but next time it may not be. Dolcezza —"

She interrupted again with a kiss.

He knew he wasn't going to win this discussion, so he surrendered gently nibbling on her bottom lip. "We need to get cleaned up. Towels aren't going to rid you of all the oil you got in your hair Miss Black."

When they finished hiding the evidence, he bade her good night then had a quiet bath. As he sat in the warm water, he wished that Madeline could be his wife. When the war was over and Sofia left, he could finally see her more frequently. Rumours would run rampant, but in time and with a little luck he could get Madeline into court; he could introduce her as a countess from another country. It would take time, probably years. She would need to be educated, taught proper etiquette and another language. He would also have to find a team of Lords willing to keep up the lie incase someone became suspicious of her being a fraud. He sighed. It was near impossible, but he needed to try.

Afterward, he decided to find Greg Umbridge for a night cap. Between Sofia, Madeline and being a king, it was difficult finding time for Greg. He missed their conversations and occasional brawls. He knew his friend's usual places; at this time of night, he would probably find him with a few friends in the Billiards Room. He went down to the ground floor and found him there, with Ben, Jack, and

Richard playing cards. Greg had a few drinks in him and was carrying on.

"Don't deny it Ben!" Greg said getting up from the card table, wagging his finger. "You've been tryin' to get with Mrs. Cotton. You like them older ones."

Jack howled in laughter nearly hitting the floor.

"Weren't you tryin' to mess with Miss Bram last time when we visited here in the summer?" asked Richard.

Ben chuckled, "I have no shame."

"From what'd I heard neither does Miss Bram!" exclaimed Greg, "so how does she ride?"

"Better than your clumsy, drunken arse would Greg," said Alex calmly.

The laughter stopped, they all turned and looked in Alex's direction, noting his presence. All of them broke down in laughter again, it was some time before it died down. "Gentlemen, I'll have to ask you all to leave," said Alex. "I need to speak with Greg about a few private matters."

The three valets rose from their seats and left the room. Alex sat down at the card table.

"So what brings you here?" asked Greg.

"I've missed you and your craziness," he said, giving him a light push at his shoulder.

"I've been wonderin'," Greg said swaying on his chair. "How do you plan to deal with Princess Sofia?"

"What do you mean?"

"Well, we jus' starting to invade France right," Greg said swinging his arms about. "We could win over that short little dictator bastard."

Alex laughed heartily, as Greg continued, "So, what will you do about your ladies? Both of them are going to expect somethin'."

"I know. My choice is Madeline."

"How do you think dat's going to happen?" He guffawed, pointing his finger at him. "If you send Sofia back to Spain then, what do you think the Lords are going to do?"

"I made a promise," Alex said simply. "I have to send Sofia back."

"Why?" he asked, sounding annoyed. "You can't marry Miss Black. If you didn't marry Sofia, the Lords would just send 'nother Princess your way."

It was true and Alex knew it. He was getting older. Twenty-four was fairly old to be a single king without an heir. He had been lucky that England had been at war with France for so many years. It had drawn the nobility to focus on political relationships between England and other countries in Europe. As soon as the war was over, he would be expected to find a suitable wife and produce an heir.

"What do you think I should do, Greg?" he asked, knowing his friend had already given this some thought.

"I dunno, but befor' ya send the Princess away, maybe you should 'ave a plan?"

Greg was right. The moment she left, Alex's schedule would be full of other princesses and highly regarded foreign nobles coming to visit. He cringed at the thought of having to entertain them, alongside the women at court who would also be clinging to him.

They stayed up chatting until the two in the morning. After, Alex went to his room, and after thoroughly checking his apartments with his guards, he climbed into bed. His thoughts raced; he could not be with Madeline if he sent Sofia away. He was going to have to make new arrangements. Complicated ones.

31

WAKE UP CALL

It was a House of Lords meeting like any other, but as Madeline walked along the aisle leading to the King, she noticed something odd. He seemed to be delighted about something. He was grinning from ear to ear. She grabbed his tray off her cart and climbed the steep steps of the pulpit. She began serving tea as he watched her out of the corner of his eye. She looked on the pulpit for a note, but there was nothing.

Then she heard some interesting words come from the Duke of Axford, "Now that he's been captured and taken to Elba, we really need to get down to business. You know, create a stable political climate."

She looked about curiously and began to open her ears to the conversation. In the past few weeks, the meetings had become more intense. Napoleon had lost his battle in Russia. Numbers of armies had been mounting against him. In the last meeting, it was announced that he lost a battle at Leipzig. It looked as though they had finally been able to capture Paris and Napoleon himself.

"The idea of sending him to Elba, to be an emperor of a small island – it's preposterous!" Lord Taylor shouted. "He'll escape and he'll wage another war. How can Europe be at peace? He is still a threat."

"I doubt that Lord Taylor," said the Duke. "How is a man to forge an army from an island with a few men? There is little Napoleon can do in exile."

Madeline's heart swelled with hope. The war was over. Napoleon was conquered. Princess Sofia could leave. She looked up at her King a wide smile on her face, but he was looking down at the Lords, deep in thought as they waited to hear his opinion.

"I agree with Lord Taylor," Alex said. "Napoleon may still be a threat to us. But I doubt he would use the men of Elba as his army. He is a resourceful man. He will find a way to escape, and when he does, he might try to reassemble his armies."

She went down the steps and began preparing the Duke's tray, giving fleeting looks at Alex, trying to catch his eye. She wanted to see his beautiful crystal gaze smile into hers. It wasn't just England's victory. It was theirs too. For weeks, their emotions had been hinging on the war and Sofia's stay at the castle. But something was off. He never looked in her direction. When she left, she knew he was intentionally ignoring her. She wondered if he did this because he did not want any of the Lords to suspect anything.

As the days passed, Madeline grew more frustrated. While she waited on Sofia and Alex was with them, he never made eye contact. It was as if she had become invisible. Though his ignoring her was upsetting, what scared her most was his sudden interest in Sofia. He was warmer toward her, being agreeable to the things she said. Even when she made absurd comments that Greg would snicker at, Alex defended and praised every word that came out of her mouth.

515

Madeline feared there was something between the two of them that she did not know about, and she could see she wasn't the only one that was cross about it. Greg was too. Every now and again she noticed Greg rolling his eyes or making faces behind Alex's back.

After several days, Madeline had enough. One day after having tea in the Crimson Drawing Room, Sofia decided to go for a nap. Finally, Madeline had an opportunity to have words with Alex. After settling Sofia in, she sped back down to the Crimson Drawing Room, storming through the doors. Alex stood by the window staring outside.

Madeline looked to Greg, who was sitting on a chesterfield, "Leave."

"What?" said Greg flabbergasted.

"You heard me."

"Let me tell you love, anything you've got to say to Alex, you can say in front of me. He –"

"GREG UMBRIDGE," Madeline yelled cutting him off, "do you ever know when you're crossing the line? Don't make things more uncomfortable. Leave!"

"Madeline," Alex began, "there's no reason to be rude. Greg, could you please leave?"

"Your Majesty," she said clenching her fists, "maybe you shouldn't be so rude. You've been snubbing me for days. Why?"

Greg looked between the two and realizing the seriousness of the situation. "I'll just be on my way then," he said and hastily made his way to the doors.

Alex turned away from the window to her, "I don't know what your problem is, but –"

"BUT WHAT? I don't know what you're playing at, Alex! Why are you acting as if I don't exist? I've also noticed you have been sweet on Princess Sofia lately."

"I've been doing a lot of thinking lately –"

"Good. If you've been doing some thinking, maybe you could tell me something." She put her hands on her hips. "If Napoleon is no longer a threat and Sofia and her family can go back, why haven't you sent them away?"

"I love you," he said his blue eyes sinking into hers. "If I weren't King, I'd marry you." He turned away from her, looking back out at the castle grounds. "I think we have to start looking at things differently. Someday I'll be expected to marry someone and produce an heir. If I can't have you, and I can't, then I might as well do what's best for my country and marry a princess."

Madeline smacked him hard across the face. She tried swinging her fists, but he held both her arms restraining her. He watched as she tried to compose herself, but tears poured down her cheeks. Kissing her cheeks softly, he held her close. He couldn't bear seeing the hurt in her emerald eyes, knowing what he had said tore her apart.

"In the carriage to Windsor Castle," she started in a choked voice, "you told me that you had no intention of marrying her, and now, you want to marry her?"

"I don't want to. I'm expected to."

"WHAT AM I EXPECTED TO DO?" she screeched, "WAIT ON HER HAND AND FOOT AND FUCK YOU TOO!"

She stormed towards the doors. He ran after her and caught her in his arms again. She tried to free herself, but his grip was strong.

"Dolcezza, I don't expect that from you!" he said in a desperate tone.

"THEN WHAT? WHAT THE HELL DO YOU WANT FROM ME?" she sobbed beating her fists to his chest.

"No. No," he said, guiding her head to his shoulder. "I was thinking that I could keep you at a private estate. You'll be the mother of my children and the woman I love."

She pulled back from him and looked upon his face with horror. His eyes were full of sincerity as he looked down at her he combed back some of her hair and kissed her softly. But she shoved him away. "I'm not going to spend the rest of my life being your dirty little secret."

She ran out the room, wiping her eyes. He fell back onto a chesterfield, crippled by her words. He knew that she would have a difficult time with his future plans for them, but he did not think she would consider herself his 'dirty little secret'.

Madeline paced about her dormitory. That he wanted to marry Sofia for his country and have her on the side, made her sick. She would rather he be a bachelor king with no heir, and Lady Susanna take the throne, than Sofia marry him and have his children.

She collapsed onto her bed. His marrying Sofia would only make them both miserable because he'd be living a lie. Life would become emotional and complicated. But the more she thought about it, the more she became aware that his life had always been this way. His mother had neglected him. His father had died mysteriously.

His uncle had been plotting to usurp the throne; there were assassination attempts. Maybe he was used to constant drama.

After their row, Madeline did her best to ignore Alex. That afternoon and evening she made sure she wasn't within his sight. She switched duties with Miss Van Gogh; preparing Sofia's evening wear, her make-up, drawing her bath and looking after her room. It was better than witnessing him doting on Sofia. After she finished dressing Sofia for bed, she went back to the dormitory.

As she lay under her simple bedsheets, she questioned whatever made her believe that Alex would stay true to his word. He was a king; his country would always come first.

32

THE RIGHT KIND OF WOMAN

Normally, Sofia didn't mind the company of her servants while a man courted her. But she questioned if Alex was comfortable with them being there. Recently, only Aletta had been around during their excursions and time together. But dismissing Aletta and not Madeline seemed unfair. So, after eating breakfast and getting dressed, she told them both that she would give them the day off. Alex had promised her to take her on a picnic. It was the perfect opportunity to see how he would behave without the presence of others. It was not proper for her to be without a chaperone, but she had heard he had often spent time with the ladies at court without chaperones. Sofia expected Alex would be more assertive if her maids weren't there. But there was still someone in the way – Greg Umbridge.

She knew Alex didn't mind Greg's company. But she hated it. It was weird to flirt with Alex while Greg was there. She did not know why, but sometimes she felt guilty for flirting with Alex when Greg was watching. She had wondered for some time how she would get rid of him. That morning, the answer came to her. She left her room on a mission to find where he slept. She sped down the halls where she found Mr. Tinney, who bowed as she passed, "Your Highness."

"Pardon me, Mr. Tinney?"

"Yes, your Highness?"

"Where would I find Sir Gregory at this time?"

Mr. Tinney made a kind of clicking sound while he thought. Often Sir Gregory Umbridge was recovering from the night before. He did not want the Princess to discover him hung over. But he could not lie to her either. "He's probably in his quarters. Most likely indisposed, though."

"Indisposed?"

"Yes, your Highness," he said breathing heavily through his nose. "He may have had a little too much to drink. You know Sir Gregory, loves a nightcap." He turned to walk away, and Sofia could hear him whisper under his breath, "Or twenty nightcaps."

Sofia shook her head and stormed down the hallway, determined that he would not join her and Alex on the picnic. When she reached his quarters, she barged through the tiny drawing room, that had only a card table, chair and a fireplace, then threw open the doors to his bedchamber. His room was nothing like she would have imagined it. It had large stained glass windows with beautiful scenes of the forest. Leaves were outlined in each tree, along with each blade of grass on the forest floor. Birds flew overhead, and deer peeked out from the brush in the scene. The brilliant colours shone through the glass and onto the hardwood floor. On the walls hung huge paintings of landscapes of the English countryside. However, not unsurprisingly among his armoires, planters and his bed, was a table with several whisky decanters on it, most of them empty. There were also several empty bottles on his fireplace mantle. She raised her brow realizing that the fireplace was double-sided with the one side in the drawing room and the other in the bedchamber. He was sprawled out on his bed, naked, an empty glass in his hand. Blankets strewn about the bed barely covered his bottom as he snored in a deep sleep. She looked away turning scarlet, but she had to speak to him. "Sir Gregory!" she shouted.

"Huh?" he said rousing as he turned to face her. A big grin grew on his face.

"Sofia," he mumbled, "you look lovely this morning."

"I wish I could say the same for you. Honestly Sir Gregory, do you have any class? You can't put on a bed shirt before you go to sleep?"

"What is the point of a bed shirt?"

She knew she was better off not answering his playful question, so she moved on to the reason for her visit. "The King and I plan to go on a picnic today."

"Yes, I know. I look forward to it," he jeered, lifting his empty rock glass into the air.

"Well, we have no need for your company."

"Really?" he said. He looked up at her, then sat up.

"What are you doing?" she asked as she noticed the blankets slowly unveiling him. He stood up, and the blankets fell from his body. She averted her eyes, her face feeling hot in humiliation.

"Just getting a pick-me-up," he said as he walked over to the whisky decanters and poured some more whisky into his glass.

"You have no decency."

"You're right, I don't. I really wish you'd just accept that. I've never been much of a gentleman, and I'm not going to become one 'cause you came to town, love."

"DON'T COME TO THE PICNIC!" she bellowed.

"Did Alex request this?" he asked.

"NO. I request this," she said hysterically, covering her eyes with her hand as he moved about the room in the buff. "That's a royal command. Don't come," she said wagging her finger, like a mother reprimanding a child.

He swirled his whisky in his glass, then replied, "You know your Highness, you could have politely requested that I don't come. I would have listened. No need to lose yourself and your class by bursting into my room uninvited and insulting me."

She shut her eyes tight and tried to make her way to the door. He laughed as she stumbled about. Knowing how ridiculous she must have looked, she finally begged, "Sir Gregory, if you'll be a gentleman, put on some clothes, or at least COVER UP."

"No need Princess, I'm not going anywhere or doing anything today."

"You are so annoying," she said as she moved about, her arms outstretched in front of her. He watched her for a while as she bumped into the plants and furniture in his room. "I suppose this is your way of serving me 'humble pie'?" she asked as she grabbed onto the leaves of a large plant.

"No. If I were serving you humble pie, your hands wouldn't be on a plant – they'd be elsewhere," he said in a tempting tone.

She turned up her nose, "Hmph!" she objected in a high-pitched whimper. It sounded so sweet, he took pity on her.

"Would you like me to lead you to the door?"

She said nothing but gave a long, deep murmur of defeat, brushing the toe of her shoe against the hardwood. He walked over and took her hand in his and led her to the door. He gave her hand a warm kiss.

"Always a pleasure to assist you, Princess," he said leaving her hand on the doorknob.

She opened her eyes seeing the large mahogany door before her as he stepped away. Quietly, she opened the door and shut it behind her, her palms sweaty and her knees trembling. She had never met anyone like Greg Umbridge. Perhaps that's why his devil-may-care attitude was refreshing and exciting.

After she had left, Greg assumed Madeline would have the day off, so he decided to see her. He felt somewhat guilty. He knew what he had said several nights ago had convinced Alex that Sofia needed to stay. Though what Greg said was true; the nobility would push another eligible 'candidate' for Alex to marry, persuading Alex to keep Sofia around was to fulfill Greg's own selfish needs.

Since their row in the Crimson Drawing Room, Alex had tried to arrange to meet Madeline in secret a few times. But, she never came. Though Alex never talked about it, Greg knew his friend was in pain. He was eating less and if Greg mentioned Madeline or Sofia, Alex would change the subject.

Greg went down to the servants' quarters to ask if anyone had seen Madeline and learned she had gone to visit the horses again.

He found her in the mews standing in front of one of its stalls petting the muzzle of a beautiful black horse. The horse's mane was almost a raven black and shiny as hers. It was a picturesque scene as she lightly touched her forehead to the animal. Watching her, he came to admire how naturally stunning she was. He could understand why Alex was so smitten. She had a grace about her like no one he'd ever met. Even a womanizer like Alex couldn't resist her alluring charm.

"Hello, Madeline."

"Hi Greg," she said shortly.

"What are you up to?"

"Just looking at the horses. It's my day off, and I don't want to run into his Majesty again if I can help it," she said. "I was about to take a walk about the grounds. Would you like to come for a walk with me?"

"Willingly," he said.

They left the mews silently walking about the grounds when he finally found the courage to start what he knew would be an awkward conversation. "You've been avoiding seeing Alex for some time now. He has sent for you a few times now, and you don't turn up."

"I'm not interested in seeing him at the moment."

"He misses you."

"Did he ask you to come and persuade me to go see him?" Madeline asked annoyed.

"No. But if this goes on much longer, he might. Please go to see him before he starts getting me to play messenger. I hate that."

She gave a look of understanding. It was not the first time things were awkward for him; it was the same the day he had to ask for volunteers to come to Windsor Castle. It was the same the day they rode in the carriage together though he did his best to make her feel comfortable. "Do you know what he expects of me?"

He shrugged.

"He expects me to hide away in some estate, so he can keep our relationship a secret. We'll have a few bastard children, but meanwhile, he'll marry Sofia and have children that will be the future royals of England."

He looked at her sympathetically, "I know that is difficult, but how else could you two be together? I mean unless he decided to give up the crown to be with you. You know it's not just a social acceptance thing. Hell, his father created laws specifying what kind of person his descendants could marry."

An abhorrent expression grew on her face, "That's disgusting. He never told me that."

"Because he did not want to. I don't think he can marry a commoner by law anyway. The only thing he can do is live out his life as a bachelor, and they'll keep tossing women at him, or marry Sofia."

She looked away embarrassed, "Is there any way he could he marry me?"

"He would have to abdicate the throne. But if he gives up the crown, the only other options are Lord Bathory or Susanna, and I don't think that would last too long. I could see them driving people to a rebellion."

"So you think I should go along with his stupid plan?" she asked incredulously.

"I hate saying this, but what more could simple commoners like you and I expect? I mean, I'm his best friend, but I'll never have more than being a knight. I would love to be a Lord and have an estate and leave titles to my family. But Alex and I both know it's too dangerous to reward me with a title. I'm sure if I were to have one, the House of Lords would argue against it until Alex had no choice but to strip me of it all. 'Sir' is the best I'll ever get."

She looked into the trees, reflecting on what he had said. "I understand what you are trying to tell me, but you know what? It's just not good enough for me. I don't think you understand how it feels. I mean, you don't have to keep your relationship with Alex a secret. I do."

"So you'd rather be a lowly maid than the love of his life?"

"The love of his life? I would be spending my days wondering if I really am the woman he loves while he lives a royal life with Sofia. Though Sofia isn't my favourite person, this isn't fair to her either."

He nodded his head, "'Bout time one of you said that. Truthfully, I think she's the biggest victim of all of this."

Madeline looked at him in disbelief. "Are you kidding me? She'll be happy as the Queen of England. She won't have to live a lie."

He grimaced. "That's just plain selfish. She'll be living a lie, and she'll find out eventually. She'll secretly live day to day with that humiliation, fearing that people will find out that her husband, the King, is in love with his maid. She'll be put in the middle of all this selfishness, with a man who doesn't love her. I know she isn't your favourite person, but you know what? She's quite a bit kinder than most princesses that I've had the displeasure of meeting."

She felt ashamed because it was true. "You're right," she sighed, "she doesn't deserve this."

"Damn right ... She is a little pompous though," he admitted.

"Yes, she doesn't seem to like you much," she chuckled.

"To be honest, I get a bit of a rise out of her. She is fun to tease."

Madeline shook her head, a smile tracing her lips.

"I think Alex is picking her because she is kinder than most of the upper-class women he has courted," Greg continued as they began walking down a path in the garden. "If another woman found out about you and Alex, there's a good chance she'd just have you killed. Sofia's soft hearted. I know Alex has told me he thinks she has a weak mind."

"Really? Why does he think that?"

"She tries too hard. He knows she'd do anything he asked ... Have you ever noticed that she flaunts her little breasts in low cut dresses all the while?"

"Are you blushing, Sir Gregory?" Madeline dared to ask.

"It's hard for any man not to notice that, love."

They were silent for some time as they walked toward the castle. He hoped what he had said would persuade her to go see Alex. Before they came to the castle gate, where two guards stood, he turned to her. "Will you see him then?"

"Doubtful."

"Come on," he whined, "you're being stubborn."

"No, I'm not. I've been thinking that perhaps I should leave the castle and go back to Buckingham Palace. I can't do what Alex is asking of me."

"Are you serious?" he asked shocked. "So, it's over then? Just like that?"

"I'll just continue to work at whichever residence he is not in."

"You'll only be kidding yourself, Madeline," he said shaking his head. "You're in love with him, and I doubt you could stay away from him for long."

"I love him, but if he expects me to live the rest of my life in this charade, then no, I can't do it."

"Do you think he's happy about this? Do you think he wants this?"

"He'll have two women, what man wouldn't want that?"

"Don't make it sound like this is something that he wants. He doesn't."

She said nothing. Greg grew more irritated with her, "I don't want to be the middleman. I'm not talking to Alex for you. If you don't want to be with him, you should tell him."

She was about to speak, but Greg had already marched off towards the small castle gate, asking the guards to let him in.

Madeline wandered off, towards a small forest of trees, her thoughts on Alex. She sat on a rock at the forest's edge and noticed her surroundings. The trees were tall and thin, and she could hear nothing but the wind rustling the leaves as they fell and tumbled across the forest floor. Hours went by, and some fog crept up around her.

Hours passed and dusk came. In the distance, she could see Alex galloping on Princess, slowing down when he had spotted her. He pulled Princess' reigns and stopped next to Madeline. "Greg tells me you don't want to be with me that you wish to go back to Buckingham Palace."

She said nothing, but looked away, giving him the cold shoulder. He dismounted from Princess, grabbed her by the arms and turned her so she was facing him.

"Why are you not talking to me now? I want to hear it from you. Are we over?" he asked.

"If you think marrying Sofia and sending me away to a private estate is a solution then yes, we are over."

"Dolcezza, it's the only solution!"

"No, it's not. Give up being king."

He looked down at his feet, "If I could, I would. But if I did, I'm quite sure this country would undergo some tough times."

"How so? We just won a war. I imagine the country should be doing well economically for some time."

He gazed at her, his eyes softening. "I don't mean to be a cad Madeline. I also don't mean to sound egotistical, but where would this country be if I weren't in power? Could you imagine Bathory or Susanna on the throne? How cruel they would be to common people like you?"

He was right. There would be a rebellion, just like there had been in France, and from what she heard, French commoners were enduring some hard times. She changed tact and continued to argue, "Why don't you just give me a title? Then you could marry me."

It was a good idea, but he knew that it was impossible. "This isn't like the olden days when a king could bestow titles and lands to whomever he wished whenever he wished. If I were to give you anything I would have to go through parliament, the House of Lords and anyone else that sees a problem with a woman having land. Unless inherited, it's against the law for a woman to own land. They won't allow it. Also, there will be suspicion to why I would give a common woman a title."

"Are you ashamed of me?" she asked.

"No!" he retorted defensively.

He went silent knowing that there was nothing he could say or do. She was angry with him and wanted to fight. He wondered if he should give her some time and space and maybe she would come to realize that his plan was the only way they could be together. He sighed slowly, "Do you really want to go back to Buckingham Palace?"

"Yes."

He looked away, trying to hide his emotion, "So, you and I … are we over then?"

"Yes." She did not want it to be over, she found it hard to fight back her emotion, but she could not live the way he was asking her to. If he cared about her, he would understand that and find another way. He gazed at her, trying his best to keep his composure. "I'll take you back to the castle then. Sir Ashton Giles will take you back to Buckingham Palace tonight. He has some business to attend to there."

He climbed onto Princess and extended his hand to her. She took it and they rode back to Windsor Castle, in an icy silence. She subtly wiped the tears from her face. His expressionless face confused her. She thought he would have reacted in fear of losing her for good. She thought he would promise he'd never marry Princess Sofia, but he didn't.

Overwhelmed with his own heartache, he continued to mask his hurt stoically; he could feel his eyes stinging with pain trying to hold back. He inhaled deeply, trying to sooth his tense body.

When they finally reached the castle mews, he dismounted and helped her off the horse. Then he took her into his arms, holding her tight. The dim light of the lanterns outside shone on his face and she could see the blood drained from it, pale and white even for his tan skin. He looked into her eyes, knowing she would do her best to avoid his gaze. After this, she would always work in a royal residence he was not visiting. He wasn't sure when he'd see her again. "If you ever change your mind, I'll take you back. If it's a hundred years from now, you'll always be the woman I love." His lips tenderly massaged hers.

"You can't do that," she whimpered, resisting him.

"Don't do this," he said, wiping the tears from her face. "You don't want to leave me, I know you don't."

She pulled away. "You're right. I don't. But I have to," she cried. "I can't do what you're asking of me. I'd hate myself if I became the kind of woman you want me to be."

She ran off, out of the mews and into the castle. He didn't follow. She had made her decision, and now he had to learn to deal with it. As she headed to the dormitories to pack her things and find Sir Ashton, Alex searched for Greg. It took Alex some time wandering through the galleries, the state rooms and recreational rooms.

Eventually, he found Mr. Tinney in the library, "Tinney, have you seen Sir Gregory?"

"Yes, your Majesty," he said bowing, "I believe he is in your apartments."

Alex left dumbfounded. It was an odd place for his friend to go this time of day, but Alex dismissed his curiosity and headed down to his apartments. He was so desperate to talk to Greg about the whole situation, he hardly cared that he was in his private quarters. He reached the large mahogany doors and stepped inside. To his chagrin, Princess Sofia was sitting across from Greg on the couch. Angry that she was there, Alex said nothing but stomped in and grabbed a decanter of whisky from one of the tables. He poured himself a glass and threw it back.

Sofia gasped as Greg watched in shock; he had never seen Alex be so ill-mannered. Worse, Alex began pouring himself another glass.

"Sofia, uh, it seems our King wants to play a drinking game," Greg laughed, trying to save Alex some embarrassment. "I know you're challenging me," he continued to joke as he jumped up and snatched the decanter out of Alex's hands. "I hope you're not challenging our sweet Sofia here," Greg said secretly giving Alex a forbidding look. Ignoring this, Alex tried to take the decanter back, but Greg held it out of his reach.

"I haven't had my drink yet," said Greg as he quickly grabbed a glass from the table, poured the whisky and tossed it back. Alex grabbed the decanter and poured himself another glass, drinking it in a single gulp.

"Two for one, let's see who's going to win," Alex challenged.

Greg furrowed his brow but poured two more glasses. He drank his, "Two for two."

"Three!" Alex said gulping another. He stumbled back into the table behind him. Sofia gave a gasp of alarm.

"Um, okay perhaps that's enough, Alex," said Greg.

"Oh no, ya don't! We aren't' finished yet," he continued stumbling about. "Whoever drops first."

"Please your Majesty," Greg said in all seriousness. "We both know it isn't going to be me."

"Your Majesty, perhaps you shouldn't play this game," Sofia warned standing up.

"No one asked you, Princess," Alex snapped.

She sat back down, silenced by her shock.

Greg grew angry. "Fine Alex," he said beneath his breath. "You will regret this." Greg poured more whisky into each glass and drank them both. He winced, "Doubles. Can you handle that your Majesty?"

"Certainly," Alex grabbed both glasses filling them and threw the first one back. He teetered and steadied himself on one of the wingback chairs, grasping both sides with his hands. Then, he crashed to the floor.

"Alex!" Sofia cried.

"I've got him," said Greg picking him up off the floor, "I think his Majesty needs to sleep this off."

Greg wrapped Alex's arm around his neck and held him at the waist, Alex leaned all his weight into him, and he buckled a little.

"Let's go," Greg said gruffly as he pulled Alex into his Bedchamber, leaving Sofia by herself. Greg dragged him to the bed and pushed him down. "You're a buggered arse," Greg scolded.

Alex looked aghast. Who was Greg to scold him for having a few drinks? It was ironic and funny. "Hhaaahaaahhhaaaaa!"

Greg was stunned. He had never seen Alex like this. "What the blazes are you doing?" The laughter died as Greg lectured him. "Tomorrow Bathory is going to be brought to trial. You don't think his conspirators are going to try to kill you tonight? And you're drinking?"

Alex observed the mix of concern and anger on Greg's face. Alex sat up unsteadily, stabilizing himself with his hands as the room spun around him, he tried his best to collect himself. "She's left me. She does-doesn't wan to be with me anymore. She went with Sir Ashton to Buckingham Palace."

"Sorry about that, mate. But what are you concerned about? She just wants to work at Buckingham Palace. That's not so bad."

"No. No. She ended it. It's over."

"That won't last long. I give it two days before you kiss and fuck again," said Greg.

"She meant it."

There was a long silence as Greg tried to find the right words to comfort him. "I don't get you. You're a king. It's easy. Just send to have her brought back here."

"She'll resent me if I do that. She wants me to come up with a solution ... so that we can be together. If I don't come up with that, there's no point in sending for her."

"You could always tie her to your bed. Don't think I don't know you probably tried that."

"Shut up," he said half laughing.

Greg snickered. There was another long silence and Alex frowned.

"Let her be for a while, and she will come to her senses," said Greg. "I mean, it's not your fault you have to marry a certain type of woman. She'll come to terms with that."

"I want to fix this for her. She's hurt. She thinks I'm trying to take advantage and have two women. Honestly, I wouldn't care if Sofia was seeing another man at court. Once she sees I'm not in love with her, hopefully, she will take a lover."

Greg said nothing, waiting for him to give his royal command. Greg was fairly sure what he was going to do.

"Send word to have Madeline brought back to Windsor Castle tomorrow," said Alex. "I can't stand feeling this way. I want this sorted out."

"You tried that earlier today. What are you planning to do now?"

"I'm not sure," he sighed. "But I don't want to start imagining life without her."

Greg found Mr. Tinney and instructed him to bring back Madeline from Buckingham Palace. But it was foggy and pouring rain. It would be too difficult to drive a carriage. It wasn't until the next morning that the weather was agreeable, and Mr. Tinney took one of the carriages. But when he arrived at Buckingham Palace, she was not there.

33

BOLD DECISION

After Madeline had left Alex in the mews, she went back to her dormitory and packed her things; the dresses Alex had given her, her mother's papers, her doll, and the cloak he had given her. She did not pack her uniform clothes. Where she planned to go, she would not need them. She did not like the idea of being his mistress, and she detested the thought of waiting upon him and the soon to be Queen Sofia for the rest of her life. Watching him living his life with another, or even hearing about it every day would be torture.

She caught up with Sir Ashton, who had been preparing a carriage with his luggage when she found him.

"Excuse me Sir Ashton," she said catching his eye.

"Oh Miss Black," he said startled. "What is it, my dear?"

"I've been given leave to go back to Buckingham Palace."

His thick grey brow furrowed. "But … are you not looking after Princess Sofia?"

"Change of plans, another servant will be taking my place. I've got some business to take care of."

He did not ask any questions but helped her with her luggage. Once they were on their way, he sat next to her with a book on his lap and stared out the window. The silence was becoming awkward for Madeline. "So, if you don't mind my asking Sir Ashton, why are you going to Buckingham Palace?"

He looked away from the window and considered her for a moment. "I'm going to speak with some of the witnesses for the trial. I just hope all this nasty business will end for his Majesty tomorrow. Lord Bathory has been a thorn in his side for some time."

"Yes, I had that impression."

"Some people theorise he might have killed King Charles."

"Really?" she said pretending to not know.

"Yes, you see the night he died, Lord Bathory's infantry had just met up with our battalion. He requested a meeting alone with the King that night. Later that night King Charles grew very sick and mysteriously died."

"But he was fairly old by that point, was he not?"

"Yes, but he was also a very healthy man. Strangely that same night, a rather large amount of belladonna was found at the camp."

"Lord Bathory poisoned the King?" she said. "If belladonna was found at the camp, why did you not charge him with treason?"

"There was belladonna at the camp, but that doesn't mean that he did it," said Sir Ashton. "There were thousands of other soldiers and Lords there. Also, his cause of death is still unknown."

"Does his Majesty know this?"

"Of course. Actually, he's the one that found the belladonna. More fanatical folk have theorised it was his Majesty."

She pursed her lips wondering why Alex had never told her. "What happened afterwards?"

"The next day his Majesty made history. I'm sure you've heard of his victory during the Irish uprisings?"

She nodded.

"Killed all those rebels by himself, brave lad."

She was nonplussed. Alex had told her that Sir Ashton had overheard a plot to kill Alex. Strangely, Sir Ashton did not mention this or the fact that Greg Umbridge had disguised himself as Alex that day on the battlefield. She realized that what happened that night and the next day was not common knowledge. It had been kept secret for some reason. Perhaps they planned to use it as evidence at the trial. "What was the King like as a boy?" she asked since they were on the subject. "Did it surprise you he had the courage to do what he did?"

"That's an interesting question Miss Black," said Sir Ashton. "Yes, and no. He was always a good soldier. I knew he was capable of doing it. But, he was quite young, still a boy. I've always been concerned how it would affect him emotionally. Killing a man is no easy thing, even when he is your enemy."

She nodded in agreement.

"He does take after his namesake in that respect though," he said tapping his book with his fingers.

"His namesake?" questioned Madeline. "Who was he named for?"

"Alexander the Great."

Not knowing whom Alexander the Great was, she looked down wondering if she should ask. She did not have an education. Was asking foolish? He noticed her bewildered expression. "Alexander the Great was a King of Macedonia and ruled an empire twice the size of what Napoleon's was," said Sir Ashton.

"Oh, gosh, that's quite something," said Madeline in amazement.

"Yes. His Majesty is a man of action too. Usually, it doesn't take him much time to decide what he's going to do."

Reflecting on his words, she wondered how long it would take Alex to take action on their situation. Would he come calling to Buckingham Palace later that night? Or would he let a few days go by, hoping that she would settle down? She looked down at her feet, a twinge of guilt came over her. She couldn't turn back on what she was planning, no matter how hard it was on him.

Sir Ashton continued the conversation, "What of you though Miss Black, I don't know very much about you. Where are you from?"

"There nothing to know, really," said Madeline shifting in her seat. "I mean, I grew up in London, started working for the Watsons when I was about fourteen, then came to work for his Majesty."

"What of your parents? Do you still see them?"

"No. Both are dead I think," she said, not entirely sure what had happened to her father.

He continued probing, "I'm so sorry to hear that Miss Black. Do you have any family?"

"No," she replied shortly, wishing he'd stop asking questions about her past.

He took the hint and began to look through some papers he had with him. She looked away thinking the conversation had finally ended. But then he started up again. "What did your mother and father —?"

"Enough about me Sir Ashton," she said quickly. "What about you? Where are you from?"

He didn't answer and went about reading the book sitting on his lap. For the rest of the carriage ride, there wasn't much conversation as she quietly reflected on what she was going to do when she got to Buckingham Palace.

When they arrived at Buckingham Palace, she went straight to her dormitory that she had shared with Marie. Marie was not there, and Madeline assumed she was still working. She sank onto her bed; she had missed her friend's company and had hoped she would be there when she arrived. She wanted to say goodbye.

She did not see Marie till dinner. She spotted her at one of the large tables eating across from Emma. She went over and sat down next to her, "Hello Marie, Emma," she said casually.

"Madeline!" exclaimed Marie in surprise. "What are you doing here?"

"They don't need too much help at Windsor Castle, so I requested to come back."

"It wasn't boring, was it?" asked Emma timidly.

"Oh no. It was fine, I just missed Buckingham Palace I guess," Madeline lied.

"Nothing interesting is going on here Mad," said Marie. "Windsor Castle is where all the action is. Is it true all the rumours of Princess Sofia?"

"What rumours?" asked Madeline.

"Oh, we constantly hear about how beautiful she is and how she's already smitten with the King."

"Oh yes, very much."

"Do you think he'll marry her?" asked Emma eagerly, a crestfallen expression darkening her face.

"Don't be silly Emma," said Marie. "The King is being a gentleman and a proper host. I'm sure he's just entertaining the Spanish royals until they can go back."

"Then why haven't they yet?" asked Emma, a quizzical look on her face.

"I'm not sure what his plans are concerning marriage," confessed Madeline.

"Well, he is probably seriously considering her," Emma said. "He's getting older. He should get married soon."

"Oh please, he's only twenty-four," said Marie.

"Doesn't matter, he's a king; he's expected to have more than just a couple of children to ensure the family name lasts," Madeline commented.

"King Charles didn't, he just had King Alex," laughed Marie.

"All the more pressure for King Alex to produce heirs," said Emma.

Madeline could feel a hole in her heart as the girls prattled on about whether Sofia could be the next Queen of England. Madeline and Marie finished their meal and headed back to their dormitory. Once in their room, Marie shut the door behind them. "All right, out with it Mad, what's the real reason why you came back here?"

"It's complicated," Madeline said simply, knowing she could never tell her, even though she and Alex were over.

"I'm going to be honest. I've heard things. And I sensed something before you left. You've been with his Majesty for some time now."

Unsure if Marie knew that she and Alex had a relationship, she tread carefully. "Yes. I've personally served the King a few times these last couple months."

"Hmph! If that's what you call it. Mad, I wasn't born yesterday you know. You and King Alexander have been seeing each other."

She looked in shock, "How did you know?"

"When your dormitory mate has a tendency to disappear at night, is sent to clean rooms which are already cleaned, and is chosen by the King's best friend to go to Windsor Castle, it's easy to put the pieces together."

"You're not angry at me for not telling you, are you?" she asked as she sank down to her bed.

"No," Marie said soothingly, "I don't blame you. If it had been me, I'd have the sense to keep my mouth shut too."

"Do you think anyone else knows?"

"I don't think Emma knows, but rumours have been flying around here," Marie admitted.

"Are you serious?" she said embarrassed, clasping her hands to her face. "Oh gosh, I hope no one at Windsor Castle knows ... Tilly."

"What? Tilly? Who are you talking about?" asked Marie curiously.

"Never mind," said Madeline, assuring herself that if Tilly knew, she would probably have tried to hurt her.

"People around here know that his Majesty has been spending time with a maid with black hair. Since you are new, not many people knew it was you."

She gave a horrified look, "Everyone knows? Does any of the nobility know? I mean —"

"Mad — stop, stop. Not every servant knows. You once told me that you used to hear rumours about the King in the marketplace when you worked for the Watson's. Do you remember any of those rumours coming directly from the Buckingham?"

She thought about it for a moment. It was true, for all the rumours she heard about Alex, they always came from other servants of the nobility.

"Being a servant for royalty carries a huge responsibility," Marie went on. "A kind of honour. We don't gossip to our friends or even our family about what happens behind these walls. This is the most respectable job any one of our class could have. Being disloyal to our King, takes away all honour and respect about this job."

She understood what it was Marie was trying to say. Gossiping about what happened behind castle walls did not only dishonour the King, it also dishonour the other servants who took pride in what they did.

"Besides you're one of us," Marie added as she sat next to Madeline on the bed. "I think it's kind of beautiful, you know, like a fairy tale."

"Well, the reality wasn't really a fairy tale. It was lots of sneaking around," she confessed. "Do you think everyone in Windsor Castle knows too?"

"Doubt it. Mr. Tinney is very strict from what I hear; he doesn't like the servants talking about the King, nobility or other servants. People have been fired for gossiping. If anyone knows, chances are they haven't shared that information with too many people."

It was a relief to Madeline, even though she and Alex were over, she did not want to be judged by the other servants. She was glad that Marie had figured it out, having someone she could trust to confide in was comforting. Though, she felt guilty for what she was going to say next.

"Marie," she began timidly.

"Yeah?"

"I have to tell you something."

"What?"

"I am going to run away from Buckingham Palace tonight."

"WHAT?" Marie yelped.

"Shhh!" Quiet, I don't want anyone to hear us!" said Madeline her eyes bulging.

"Mad, you can't do that," she whispered in a flustered tone.

"I have to. I can't live like this," she stammered as tears trickled from her eyes "I love Alex, but we can't be together. He can't marry a commoner or a bastard."

"You're a bastard?"

"Yes," Madeline admitted for the first time in years, not even Sissy knew this. "Please don't tell anyone, not even Alex knows."

"Your secret is safe with me," she reassured her.

"I can't sit around and watch him marry Princess Sofia to have an heir. I couldn't stand to clean these rooms day in day out. I wouldn't be able to stop thinking about it. Thinking about him. It would drive me insane."

Marie gave her a consoling look, "I suppose no woman could stand to watch the man she loved be with someone else."

"Would you come with me?" Madeline asked. "It'll be great, just the two of us."

Marie bit her lip, "Buckingham's been my life for some time Mad ... and now that I've met Harold, well I –"

"It's all right. I understand."

"I can see you off," she offered.

"That'd be nice. But could you help me with something?"

"What's that?"

"I need to borrow a horse."

"Are you crazy? You can't take a horse from the royal mews," Marie said rising from the bed.

546

"How else will I get a ride to downtown? I need to get to the bank. I can't live on the money I've made in these past weeks alone."

"You have a bank account?" Marie repeated in surprise.

"Yes. I've been saving money since I started working at the Watsons."

"Where will you go?" she asked.

"I'm not really sure yet," Madeline lied, knowing Marie would be questioned about her whereabouts.

"So how exactly do you want to do this?"

"I was thinking you could help me sneak into the mews and keep watch while I take one."

"That's daring. I can't do that. If we get caught, we'll both be punished." She tapped her finger to her cheek as she paced about between the beds. "You know what? I have a better idea; Harold has to go into London with another footman to pick up some food for the kitchen."

"That's perfect. What time will they leave?"

"Early in the morning, seven."

"Would Harold be willing to do this?"

"I promise you I won't tell him you're running away. I'll just tell him you're going to town on your day off. Once you get there, just tell him you are meeting someone, and they intend to give you a ride back."

Madeline thought for a moment, "You don't think he'd suspect anything?"

"Oh no, not if I ask him to do it as a small favour. I can go down to his dormitory to ask him now, I'm sure he will have no problems with it."

"That should be good then."

Marie left the room, closing the door behind her. Madeline stretched out on her bed and looked about the room, taking it all in. This would be her last night as a servant. The life she was about to lead was not as grandiose as Buckingham. But she knew she would rather lead a simple existence than be surrounded by lavish things and a gorgeous man, just dangling out of reach.

Madeline looked at the walls and all the beautiful drawings that Marie had done. Marie had talent. She captured so much beauty about Buckingham Palace; drawings of horses in the mews, servants working in the kitchens, and chatting in the parlour, carriages, statues and paintings. They were all beautiful, and if she took them all it would have made a beautiful memory book.

But then, the drawing of her mother caught her eye. She remembered how it felt to see her for the first time. Madeline realized how ironic it was that she used to think her mother was a fool for running away. Now, she was certain that Elizabeth had run off for a good reason. All her life, Madeline had felt that her mother was someone she could never understand, but at that very moment, she knew that there was no one she could relate to better. It sent chills down her spine. Looking at the drawing she could feel her mother's spirit with her, and she did not want to let it go. Then, Marie came back to the room and Madeline dropped her gaze.

"Marie?" Uh, this is a little strange, but I was wondering, could I have this drawing?" Madeline asked pointing at the drawing of her mother. "I don't know what it is. I just feel a kind of connection to it."

Marie paused. "All right," she said, not really wanting to give it away, but not wanting to disappoint her. "Harold said he'll take you. So, meet him at the servants' carriages at quarter to seven."

"I'll do that," she promised. "Thanks for the drawing Marie, it means a lot to me." She took it off the wall, folded it up and placed it in her bag.

Marie got a mischievous look on her face. "So it's your last night at Buckingham Palace. What do you want to do?"

She thought for a moment. There were all sorts of possibilities; taking off with a horse, trying on dresses in the Mistresses' Chambers. There was also the temptation of snooping about through the secret passageways and in the private rooms. But she just wanted a stiff drink. "To the Billiards Room!"

Marie laughed, "You can't be serious?"

"You bet I am. I could use a drink, and there's whisky just sitting there in decanters. Some of the world's best whisky. No one is going to come along in the middle of the night to check the room. Come on, haven't you ever wondered what it's like to indulge in what the rich can afford?"

"I don't know. Playing billiards and drinking is something men do."

"Want to try it?"

Marie thought about it for a split second. She knew because she was with Madeline there would be no consequences for this. If there were, it would be a slap on the wrist.

"Ah, why the bloody hell not?"

The two headed down to the Billiards Room and drank and played late into the night. Madeline shared how she and Alex got involved with each other. Marie was enthralled wanting to know more details as they grew drunker and louder. Eventually in the early morning hours, they went down to the Mistresses' Chambers and played dress up. Marie did hilarious impersonations of different ladies at court. Finally, around four in the morning, they headed back to the dormitory.

Madeline did not sleep well. She couldn't stop thinking about Alex and how difficult it would be to leave in a few short hours. She felt horrible for leaving him the day Lord Bathory would go to trial. She wanted to support Alex, but she reminded herself that Bathory had nothing to do with her decision to leave. Tomorrow was going to be a difficult day for Alex regardless of whether she left Buckingham Palace or not. But once Lord Bathory was sentenced, she was sure he would begin to feel better about everything.

34

LAST CHANCE

Greg stayed with Alex for the night, and slept in an armchair next to the fireplace. He had sent for four guards to go into the Bedchamber with him and watch Alex while he slept. With Lord Bathory's trial the next day, he wanted both Alex and Sofia to have as much security as possible. So, he also sent several guards into Sofia's room too.

At first, Sofia objected and tried to command them to leave, but Greg insisted, "Some people believe you may be the future Queen of England, you'd be a fool not to take the protection. What would I tell Alex if he woke up to find out that you were dead?"

"It's not proper for those men to be in my room while I sleep," she countered.

"It's for your protection. Besides, I just wouldn't send any guard to your room. Aletta can stay there as well."

Sofia left to go to her room as she walked through the galleries and halls she did not think about Alex and his unusual behaviour. Instead, she thought about the many sides of Greg Umbridge. Rude and ill-mannered one moment, responsible and taking charge the next. He was a complicated person to understand. Though she was thankful that Greg took care of Alex, she was upset that he sent her away.

She got to her room and with Aletta's assistance, got ready for sleep. She climbed into bed, with the guards standing at each post of her bed. Aletta sat in a large wingback armchair next to the large painting of English countryside on the wall. It was then Sofia realized something; she rose up on her elbow and looked over at Aletta. "Where's Miss Black?"

Aletta shrugged, "Mr. Tinney said she go to Buckingham Palace."

"That's not right," she huffed. "Someone should have told me. Who gave her permission to leave?"

Aletta shrugged again. Sofia crossed her arms and laid back into her mattress. Some people would have some explaining to do in the morning. It took some time, but she drifted off to sleep.

Madeline woke up around six and got changed into her periwinkle dress. She tried to sneak out her dormitory room without waking Marie. She turned the knob slowly when Marie whispered, "You're not really going to leave without saying 'goodbye'?"

She looked down guiltily, "I'm sorry Marie, I just didn't want to wake you."

"That's all right. You can wake me to say goodbye," she said propping herself up on her bed.

Madeline went over and hugged her.

"It's a shame you're going," said Marie. "I'm going to miss you. You're the first flatmate I had that I actually enjoyed spending time with. All my other flatmates were all stuffy, whiny old women close to retirement."

"I'll miss you too," she confessed. As Madeline said those words, she realized how true they were. Though she and Marie did not have much time together, Marie was her only friend besides Sissy. She hugged her tightly, "Keep an eye on his Majesty while I'm gone."

"You know if things don't work out for you, I'm sure there will always be a place for you here."

"I'm not too worried about that. I'll get by. I always do. Bye Marie," she said and headed out the door.

Madeline met Harold quarter to seven by the servants' carriages. He was there with another footman. The stranger gave her a grin, "You must be the beautiful lady Harold told me we'd have the pleasure of bringing to town. My name is Eric Alderton," he said tipping his hat, a salacious twinkle in his eye.

"Miss Black," she said shortly looking off to her side.

"If you need an escort about the city I'd be happy to accompany you," said Eric with a grin.

"Oh, um thank you for the offer. But I am going to be meeting someone in town," she said uncomfortably.

"Why are you bringing that large bag?" Harold questioned raising his brow.

"Oh, uh the person I'm seeing in London, I have to give them this," she lied.

"I'll put it on the back of the carriage," Eric said taking the bag and placing it amongst some trunks.

Harold climbed onto the driver's seat. She frowned realizing that she would have to share the coach with Eric. She could only imagine what kind of conversation would follow once they were alone.

Eric opened the door, and she climbed in and sat on one of the benches and began straightening the materials of her periwinkle dress. He sat next to her. "You don't mind me sitting next to you, Miss Black?"

"Well, to be honest, I'm not so comfortable with that."

He looked offended but moved to the other bench. "So I suppose getting to know each other is out of the question," he said testily.

"Yes."

"Well, that's quite snobbish."

"Sorry Eric, but I'm not here for you," she said. "I simply asked for a ride to town. Not a date."

He rolled his eyes, "Bitch," he whispered beneath his breath.

"What was that?"

"Nothing," he lied.

"Arse," she mumbled, glancing out the carriage window. He grew quiet as they rounded up the driveway and through the white marble arch. As they rode through it, she saw another coach riding near them. Both coaches stopped next to one another, and she could hear Harold speaking with the other driver. Her breath hitched as she recognized the face of a thin, gaunt man through the other carriage window glass. It was Mr. Tinney. She quickly ducked down. Her jaw dropped. Alex must have sent Mr. Tinney in the wee hours of the night to get her if he was arriving now. Eric had a baffled expression on his face. "Is there something interesting on the coach floor Miss Black?"

"I think I may have dropped something," she lied.

"What's that?"

"A small hairpin," she said pretending to search for it.

"I can assist you."

"That's quite all right. I'm sure I'll be able to find it myself."

She placed her hands across the floor, hoping that Harold would end his conversation with the driver of Mr. Tinney's coach. She grew nervous wondering what it was they were discussing. Were they talking about her? Was the driver explaining why Mr. Tinney was visiting? She was not sure, but she had spent some time searching the ground. Soon there was a silence, and she swallowed hard. Certain that they were on to her, she had reached over Eric for the door handle, but then the coach pulled forward, and she stopped herself.

"I thought you were looking for your hair pin Miss Black, surely it didn't just jump out the window."

"Yes, um, I just found it," she lied. "I was just wondering why we had stopped. I was about to ask Harold."

He looked at her suspiciously out of the corner of his eye. When they finally arrived in London, Madeline quickly said goodbye to them and explained that she was meeting her friend for tea, and would not need a ride back to the castle. Harold seemed to think nothing of it as he unpacked Madeline's bag and handed it to her, but Eric stopped him. "None of this makes any sense."

Harold chuckled, "What are you talking about Eric?"

"This servant girl comes from Windsor Castle and has a meeting with someone concerning the contents of this bag," said Eric suspicious. "Who would this girl know in London? What kind of business would she have with anyone? And tea at this time? It's too early for a spot of tea."

"You are quite nosy," Harold said quickly.

"Yes, it's rude to try to find out others' business," began Madeline. "But if you must know Eric, I'm meeting an old friend of mine that I used to serve with. We are having tea early because she does not have the whole day off."

"Oh," he said sheepishly.

"Anyway, I should be going," she said. "I know my friend is excited about seeing me again."

"Have a nice time," said Harold.

"See you," said Eric awkwardly.

"Thanks for the ride to town," she said and began down the foggy cobblestone street, her bag in hand, a free woman. As she walked, her heart sank. She wondered if a life without Alex, even a free one, was truly what she wanted. She reminded herself that it would be difficult at first, but as time went by, it would get easier. Eventually, she would forget about him and fall in love with another man, God willing.

35

MISERABLE MORNING

It did not take long for Mr. Tinney to find out that Madeline Black was not in Buckingham Palace. When he questioned her flatmate Marie Greenwood, she had said that she had not come to bed last night.

"And you told no one, Miss Greenwood? Your flatmate did not come to her bed last night, and you told no one?"

"It wasn't unusual behaviour for her. There were many nights she never came to bed, but she always turned up at breakfast in the morning."

Mr. Tinney thought this was strange, but regardless he had to give the news to the King. Lord Bathory's trial was to take place later that day at St. James Palace. He decided he would wait for the King to come and he could meet him there.

But there would be no trial. Around the time Mr. Tinney had learned of Madeline Black's disappearance, the guards of Curfew Tower found that someone else was missing. Lord Bathory.

In the early hours of the morning, when the guards went down to feed Lord Kinney and Lord Bathory breakfast, they found Lord Kinney dead and Lord Bathory gone. Not a sound had been heard through the night. Immediately after the discovery, the castle was put on high alert, and Alex and several Lords surveyed the dungeons.

But the scene was strange to Alex. It was dark and cold, each of the cavernous cells around the domed room was empty but one. He could make out a body lying across the cold stone floor in one of the dungeons. "Who is that man in the dungeon over there? Is that Lord Kinney?"

"Yes, your Majesty," answered one of the guards.

He walked over to the cell and looked through the iron bars. Lord Kinney's blue eyes were wide open, his cheek lying flat again the stone. His skin was ghostly pale and his mouth hung open. On his neck, there were purple bruises and red marks. He had died of strangulation, but his cell door was still locked. His body was right next to the bars. Obviously, Lord Bathory had killed him, but why he had was a mystery.

Other than Kinney's body and Bathory's disappearance, nothing else in the dungeons was amiss. All the cell doors were locked except two – the dungeon Lord Bathory had been in and the one across the room from it. None of the locks had been damaged; there were no holes in the walls or loose stones in the floor.

"What do you think?" Greg asked softly as he stumbled onto his knees, next to him.

"This had to have been an inside job," Alex replied in a hushed tone.

They stood aside at the wall, and the two began whispering and surmising what had happened as the rest of the guards and advisors investigated.

"You don't think anyone took Curfew passage to get here," Greg mumbled.

"It's possible. But they all have several locks, and only I have the keys."

"Who do you think did it?"

It was then Alex could smell the whisky on him. He frowned, disappointed that Greg would drink that early in the morning. "I'm not entirely sure," Alex said. "It would be wise to find out which horsemen or guards Susanna has been entertaining lately."

"Um, how should we go about getting that information?"

"Have Lord Taylor investigate."

"Right. Or I could," Greg said tipsily and turned to all the men in uniform in the tower. "Do any of you men know of a man in the guard or perhaps a horseman that has been buggering Miss Susanna lately?"

All the men stared at Greg, then to one another in shock.

Alex pulled him back, "Never mind. Can't you even try to be a gentleman sometimes?" he whispered beneath his breath. "Did you have a drink before coming here?"

"Your room was a scary place to be last night. I was expecting an assassin. I kept drinking after you passed out."

"I'm guessing you've been chewing on herbs again so I wouldn't smell it on your breath?"

"I don't want to hurt you Alex," he said laughing.

"Didn't work," he said, shaking his head.

A man short and stout pushed through the crowd of guards.

"Your Majesty," he said bowing to Alex and looking at Greg contemptuously.

Alex received him, "Yes, what is it?"

"I believe that I may know whom Miss Susanna has been seeing of late," said the man.

"Yes? Who do you think it might be?"

"Sir Stuart Cain. In the past several weeks, he and Lady Susanna have become quite close. He has been leaving the castle whenever possible to see her."

"Interesting," Alex said tapping his lip. "Sir Stuart Cain is quite a bit older than Susanna," he said shaking his head. The guards nodded their heads. "If this is true and he is the culprit that helped Bathory escape, then it's a shame. He fell for the oldest trick in the book."

"He was quite smitten, your Majesty," he continued. "He was saying some ridiculous things about running away to the countryside with her."

"Hmph. Susanna would never live in the countryside," said Alex. "Sorry, I didn't catch your name."

"Jacob Abbott."

"Yes. I think I remember. You're a family friend of Sir Ashton?"

"Yes, that's right your Majesty," he said beaming.

"Mr. Abbott, I would like you to tell Lord Cadogan all that you have just told me. If what you have said is true, and Sir Stuart Cain is behind all of this, you will be knighted."

"Thank you, your Majesty always a pleasure to serve."

A smug look grew on Greg's face. "Had I not said what I –"

"Don't start with me, Greg," said Alex in a warning tone.

"I'm just simply saying–"

"I get it, if you didn't ask, we would not have had that answer so quickly."

"Why am I not being knighted?" Greg joked.

"That's already happened. But maybe you were too drunk to remember that too."

"Aw shut up."

Alex chuckled, and the two left the men to their investigation. Though he was concerned about Lord Bathory, Alex was thinking about Madeline and was anxious for Mr. Tinney to come back to the castle with her. They began heading to the Octagon Dining Room to eat breakfast. It had been a busy morning, and they had not yet eaten. "I'll have Princess Sofia join us," said Greg as he marched on ahead.

"Wait," Alex called, "Why would you do that?"

"Well, she is still a guest here. It's rude to leave her and her family be. You're supposed to be their host."

"I realize that, but when Mr. Tinney comes with Madeline —"

"Then what?" Greg said annoyed. "Are you going to send the Spanish away?"

"No, I just —"

"Perhaps you should work out what you are going to do with your guests before you have her reenter your life. Besides, I don't think she will be too pleased to see that Sofia is still here."

"Never mind Greg, once I speak to her —"

"What else could you possibly have to say? Right now, you're a man of feelings and sweet nothings," Greg reminded him. "I'm sure you mean them, but what the hell are you going to do?"

He paused. He had no idea what he was going to do. He didn't know what excuse he could give Greg. Then a smile grew on his face. "I'm the King I don't have to explain myself to you." He walked ahead, leaving Greg standing in the hallway laughing.

"Oi I wish I had that excuse, then I could get drunk all the time!" Greg teased.

"Ha! If you were a king, you wouldn't just be drunk. You'd be walking about naked."

"You're a royal prick."

They continued to make their way to the Octagon Dining Room. Alex sent one of his servants to invite King Fernando and his family for breakfast.

"You need to have someone send word to St. James' Palace," said Greg. "They need to know that Lord Bathory has escaped, and Lord Kinney is dead."

"You're right. You wouldn't mind finding a messenger? I'll go to the dining room to receive the royal family."

He entered the Octagon Dining Room. To his surprise Sofia was already there, sitting on a red upholstered bench by the window. "Oh, hello your Majesty I've been waiting for you," she smiled. "Where have you been? I was starting to wonder if you weren't going to have breakfast with me."

"Lord Bathory has escaped from his dungeon cell," said Alex.

"Oh my! Have you caught him yet?"

"No. Lord Kinney was found dead though."

"What?" she said in disbelief. "Why would he be dead?"

"I'm guessing he didn't want to escape with Lord Bathory, so he was killed."

"How did he escape?"

"We surmise he got some help from the inside," Alex sighed.

"Really? Do you know who betrayed you?"

"We have a suspect. But don't worry yourself. It just means that I won't be going back to London for a trial. Everything is fine." He smiled, "Come to that, everything is fine in Europe as well. This Napoleon business is finally put to rest, hm?"

"Yes. It's good to hear that scoundrel has been sent to Elba," she said softly. She looked up at him and smiled sweetly, "But enough of politics, I wanted to talk to you about something."

"Yes, I had something I'd like to say as well."

"May I first?" she asked. "It's very important."

"Certainly. Ladies first."

"My father plans to take the family back to Spain, but I have enjoyed my time here so much, I was wondering if I could stay? I think we've become good friends."

His face froze, his mouth gaped. He wasn't expecting her to ask this. Ever. "Perhaps —"

Just then, King Fernando, Queen Isabelle entered the room followed by Greg. "I've rounded them up your Majesty," Greg said as they entered the room.

"Él dijo que sí papá!" Sofia squealed throwing her arms around her father.

Alex's eyes bulged.

"Excellent, you will let my Sofia stay," said King Fernando. "Should I expect a proposal soon, King Alexander?"

Greg stared at Alex and mouthed, "What?"

"Don't you worry, King Fernando, I'll return your daughter to you," Alex said hastily. She was just telling me she was enjoying her stay here and wishes to stay for a little longer. Don't worry you won't be losing a daughter."

King Fernando looked down, clenching his fists. Queen Isabelle put her hand on his shoulder and began speaking to him softly in Spanish, but the King's response was irritable, and he jerked away from her. He glared over at his daughter, who gazed at Alex, but he ignored her desperate stare. He no longer had any intention of being with her, and she needed to get used to the idea. Keeping her around for a while longer would be difficult, but he was beginning to fear that Fernando might punish his daughter behind closed doors.

Tension filled the room, but Alex ignored it as he sat down in his chair at the head of the table and everyone followed his lead. No one said anything. Then a servant came in the room with several fruit baskets and set them on the table.

"Ah fruit," said Greg awkwardly trying to start a conversation, but no one replied. The rest of the meal was eaten in silence.

Around lunch, Alex began wondering why Madeline had not returned yet. He sat with Greg, Sofia and Aletta, in the Music Room, listening to Sofia play the flute. "I thought she would be here by now, "he whispered to Greg. "What could the hold-up be?"

"I gather you want me to rudely walk out of Sofia's playing to find out."

"Rude is your thing," Alex smiled.

"Fine," Greg got up and began to exit the room. Sofia stopped and gave him a nasty look. "Nothing against your magnificent playing your Highness," said Greg. "I just have some business to attend to." He bowed and left as she continued to play.

Greg went to the servants' quarters to see if Mr. Tinney had returned. There was no one in the common areas that seemed to know anything. He went down to Madeline's dormitory room and checked the drawers and the armoires but found nothing.

"Bugger," he said to himself.

He left her room and went down to the service mews. There were several men there grooming the horses and doing maintenance on the carriages. Greg ran over to them. "Gentlemen has Mr. Tinney returned from Buckingham Palace?"

"No, Sir Gregory," said one of the men as he stopped brushing the mane of one of the horses.

"Oi," called another groom pointing in the distance, "isn't that Mr. Tinney coming up just now?"

They all looked. The head butler's carriage was coming towards them.

"I'm quite sure those are the horses Mr. Tinney prefers to use," said one of the horsemen to Greg. The carriage pulled up and came to a stop. Before the driver could come down to open the door, Greg pulled it open and looked inside.

"Sir Gregory?" Mr. Tinney said in surprise.

"Mr. Tinney, I take you heard of Lord Bathory's escape?" Greg said trying to act casual.

"Yes, yes, I decided to come the moment I was informed."

"Where is Miss Black?" Greg asked.

"Pardon? Miss Black?" Mr. Tinney said befuddled.

"Yes. Miss Black," said Greg impatiently, "where is she?"

"Right, right," Mr. Tinney said nodding. "Well, it seems that Miss Black has made an escape of her own."

Greg frowned. He withdrew himself from the threshold of the carriage and started making his way back to the Music Room. When he arrived at the doors, he could hear Sofia still playing. He rolled his eyes wondering if she would ever recognize Alex wasn't going to fall in love with her. He opened the doors and both Sofia

566

and Alex stopped and stared at him. "Tsk!" Sofia muttered beneath her breath and started playing again. He took a seat next to Alex.

"So?" Where is she?" Alex whispered.

Greg let out a deep sigh.

"Oh God. Greg, what? She won't come?"

"No. She's gone."

"What do you mean she's gone?" he said fearfully.

"She ran away. Mr. Tinney couldn't find her."

Slowly Alex's expression turned sombre. He got up, "Pardon me, Princess Sofia," he said and walked out of the Music Room.

Sofia stopped playing and stared at Greg accusingly, "What did you say to him?"

"Nothing, really," he said awkwardly. "Your playing was lovely," he said trying to change the subject.

"I swear, you are the most annoying creature on the face of this earth, Greg Umbridge."

He folded his arms, "That wasn't nice. Are you angry because his Majesty left?"

"I'm not taking it out on you," she said, feeling a twinge of guilt.

"Then why are you calling me annoying?"

"Because you are."

"Right, love."

She blushed, "Why else would I call you annoying?"

"I know why you call me annoying ... You like me. You like me a lot."

She gave an uneasy laugh. "Tsk. Like you? Why? You're rude."

"You're right," he said striding toward her. "I'm rude. I say what I think, and I don't care about the consequences. But being rude makes me honest, and you like that." He gently touched her cheek and leaned in toward her, but she pushed him away.

"You're living in a fantasy, Sir Gregory."

"And you're living in denial," he shot back.

She got up and headed for the door. "Put the flute away commoner," she called pretentiously as she sailed out.

She wandered anxiously through the hallways. She wasn't sure of where she was going, but she knew she had to get away from Greg. If she stayed any longer, she was sure he would try to kiss her again. Overwhelmed she plopped herself on a bench in the hallway. She sat tapping her foot in frustration. She kept thinking about Greg. She needed to stop. *I should be thinking of Alex,* she thought, *I should be angry with him. He's polite and sweet one moment, then rudely walking out on my flute playing the next.* She frowned. Alex always seemed as if he was somewhere else, living in his own world. Never with her. And Greg knew it too. He was there to witness Alex's indifference; it was humiliating. Even worse, Greg flirted with her; it was embarrassing to admit, but she enjoyed his attention. "Life would be easier if Greg Umbridge were king," she whispered to herself.

She sat stunned by her own words. If she wanted Greg Umbridge to be king, did that mean that she loved him? She laughed aloud to herself. She could never love someone as rude as he was.

568

"You only wish Greg Umbridge was the King of England because he would want to make you his Queen," she said trying to relieve her fears.

Greg left the Music Room to find Alex in the mews arranging a coach and a driver. "You're going to just up and leave?" Greg asked incredulously, "No announcement?"

"I saw Mr. Tinney on my way here," explained Alex, "I asked him about Madeline. He knew nothing, only that she was gone. So, I told him I had some affairs to take care of at Buckingham Palace and needed to leave immediately. Want to come with me?"

"Shouldn't we tell Sofia?" Greg suggested.

"No."

"That's wrong. You shouldn't leave without telling her you're going, mate," said Greg accusingly.

"Mr. Tinney will explain I had to leave and that it was urgent business."

"What will you tell her when you get back?"

"I'm not coming back without Madeline," Alex said. "If I do, I'll simply explain that it was something to do with Bathory."

The driver opened the door to the carriage. "Your Majesty," the driver said bowing as he opened it.

"Get in Greg," Alex ordered.

"I think I ought to stay here with Sofia. She'll need someone to comfort her."

"How will you comfort her?" asked Alex raising his brow.

A naughty smile grew on Greg's face.

"You want to take advantage of a woman's wounded heart, and possibly ruin her reputation? Not classy. Get in the carriage," Alex commanded.

Greg entered, hesitantly, still wishing he could say goodbye to Sofia. Once they were settled in their seats, the driver shut the door behind them.

Several hours later, they arrived at Buckingham Palace. It was dinnertime, but Alex wasn't interested in eating. He met with Sir Ashton Giles and demanded that anyone with any knowledge of Madeline Black's whereabouts be brought to him in the Throne Room.

Harold Vallant and Eric Alderton were interviewed first. Strangely, neither knew much of her disappearance, only that she wanted a ride to London to see a friend. This didn't surprise Alex; knowing how sly Madeline could be, she would know not to give them any information. Nonetheless, Mr. Eric Alderton acted as though her running away was foreseeable.

"She seemed like the conniving, lying type that would make a break for it," Eric said nodding his head. "Are you sure you want her back, your Majesty?"

After this comment, Alex dismissed them.

36

MADAM RAVINE

Late into the night, Lord and Lady Watson along with Sissy, Marie and Tilly entered the Throne Room. Sissy stared around the room in awe of its magnificence. Alex sat on his throne, unsure of how to present the ordeal as a casual one. A master concerned for his slave was unusual, so he would have to act as though he was infuriated with her running away. The group stood before him bowing and curtsying.

"You've all been called here today because you might have some information that may be useful to me," Alex said. "A slave of mine has run away, and we have no clues to where she has gone. Of course, any information you may have that leads to her location will be rewarded. The servant I speak of is Miss Madeline Black."

Despite knowing nothing, Lady Watson immediately spoke up, "Your Majesty, I had no idea. How awful for you! That wicked girl. If I were to guess that she went anywhere, I suppose she may have gone to look for her father."

"I doubt that." Marie piped up. "That man sold her to Madam Ravine. She hates her father."

"Where else could she go?" said Lord Watson.

"Wait. Stop," said Alex. He steepled his fingers, "Miss Black was sold to Madam Ravine?"

"Yes," said Greg slowly, "she told me that once."

Alex gave him a peeved look, "I wish someone had told me that," he said through his teeth. "Send a page to get Madam Ravine here now."

Greg left the Throne Room, and Alex turned back to the Watsons.

"Lord and Lady Watson," Alex continued, "do you know Madeline Black's father?"

"No," said Lady Watson aghast with the idea of being associated with a man like Madeline's father. "From what I was told by a merchant in London, her father was out on his luck. He didn't make much money as an actor, and needed to be rid of her to survive."

"That's not what happened. The merchant who bought her couldn't keep her," Lord Watson began.

"No merchant ever bought her," Lady Watson protested in her prettiest tone. "After I found out that she had been sold to Madam Ravine, I felt compelled to help her. It was an awful thing what her father did."

Lord Watson gave his wife a look of disgust, "When have you ever felt compelled to help anyone?"

"How dare you. You are unbel —"

"Stop quarrelling," interrupted Alex. He exhaled, "I would like to give each one of you an opportunity to speak. Tell me everything you know about Madeline Black – leave nothing out. Miss Greenwood, we will start with you."

Marie was surprised that she was chosen to speak first. "Well, I suppose um," she looked about nervously, worried what she might say would insult him. She had to be honest, but she was not sure how to do it without revealing their secret. "She did tell me she was going to run away," Marie began slowly. "She was upset you see, she was in love, but thought the man she loved didn't love her. It seemed he wanted someone else."

Alex sighed, feeling guilt-ridden. "Anything else, Miss Greenwood?"

"She didn't like speaking about the past," said Marie. "Especially about her family. But she did tell me before she left that she was a bastard."

"Really? What exactly did she say?"

"Um, she said the man she loved couldn't marry a servant, much less a bastard."

Just then, Tilly realized 'he' was not Sir Gregory Umbridge. She looked up at Alex, connecting the pieces. Fury seethed beneath her even expression as she imagined herself strangling Madeline Black.

Alex continued, "Thank you, Miss Greenwood." He turned to Sissy, "Miss?"

"Miss Sissy Hawkins, your Majesty." She curtsied.

"Miss Hawkins, how do you know Miss Black?" asked Alex.

"I came to Watson Manor after she did," said Sissy, rubbing her foot to the floor. "But when I first came, she kind of looked after me. Like a big sister."

"Did Miss Black ever tell you anything about her past?"

"Not much more than you've already heard."

He thought for a moment. He remembered that Madeline used to steal things from the Watsons and sell them in the marketplace in London. "Miss Black was a bit of a, um ... a seller," he began. "Do you know anything about that?"

Sissy quickly caught on and avoided looking at the Watsons, "Yes, I do. She used to um yes, be a seller and she would put her earnings in the bank. Under some other name."

"Do you know what name?" he asked intrigued.

"Don't know, sorry your Majesty," she said shrugging her shoulders. "There is one more thing though."

"What is it, Miss Hawkins?"

"I saw her. This morning. I had to go to town, and I ran into her."

"Really?" Alex said, his interest piqued. "What did you talk about?"

"She told me she was free," said Sissy abashed.

"Did she say where she was going?" he asked hopeful.

"To the bank to get money. She asked if I wanted to join her."

"But you didn't? Why?"

"Well, I don't like being a servant," admitted Sissy. "But I couldn't handle being out on my own. It's a scary thing for a woman to do that. I'm surprised Madeline did."

"Right." He turned his attention to the Watsons, "Do either of you have anything to add?"

Lord Watson thought on it for a moment, wondering if he should reveal that Madeline was the bastard child of Elizabeth Swan. It seemed Lady Watson did not know, or had conveniently forgotten. He questioned the King, "Sorry your Majesty, but will we be rewarded if the information leads to finding Miss Black?"

"Anything I find useful for her return, will be rewarded."

Since there was no reward and he had recently been put out of a job by the King, Lord Watson said nothing.

Greg re-entered the room, "It's taken care of; Madam Ravine should be here within the hour."

"Your Majesty?" Sissy piped up.

"Yes?"

"Sometimes Madeline used to talk about running away to the countryside."

He smiled, now he felt like he was getting somewhere.

"That makes sense," Tilly began, "I remember her once telling me she wouldn't mind joining a travelling act. You know, to see different parts of the country." An evil smirk grew on her face.

"I hope for your sake she hasn't done that mate," Greg said, pursing his lips.

"Well, it seems that there isn't much anyone can tell me to help me find her," he said disappointed. "I'd like to thank you all for the information you have shared."

The guests were escorted out of the Throne Room by several footmen.

"What do you think Greg?" Alex asked once they were alone.

"Should we put up missing posters?" Greg said trying to make him laugh, but he frowned.

"I've made some wretched mistakes. Please don't joke about this," said Alex.

"She can't go missing forever, mate."

"But what if she does? What if she goes to some other part of Europe? I never demanded the money back for that vase you know. She could buy a passage out of my life for good."

"Well, let's say she has Alex," he contemplated. "She would be a fool to do that. I mean how long do you think she could live off that money?"

"Huh. Around eight to ten years."

"What?" said Greg, realizing the magnitude of her disappearance. "You know though, other parts of Europe would still be a ridiculous choice for her," he said consolingly. "A woman travelling alone in war-torn countries? It would be stupid on her part if she did."

"I know," he rubbed his temples, "but she's more daring than most."

Greg nodded in agreement, "She's not irrational though. Who knows, she might have the sense to come back on her own."

"I doubt that."

"She is in love with you Alex, at least she seems to be. She was quite jealous of Sofia."

Alex buried his head in his hands, "I shouldn't have had her witness that. Taking Sofia on all sorts of excursions, dancing with her at balls, giving her everything I would offer a woman I would court."

"But —"

"No, Greg. It was daft. All of it. Everything I expected of her. Here, I was offering Sofia all of these things — but I offered Madeline nothing but to be my mistress," he said cringing. "She told me she couldn't live life being a dirty secret. It killed me when she said that. I took her for granted. I treated her like a common prostitute."

"If you weren't the King, you wouldn't have done any of that."

He shook his head, "If I truly love her, being a king wouldn't matter."

"Don't be too hard on yourself. You still have a country to rule."

"Great," he said sarcastically.

After a long silence, Madam Ravine entered the Throne Room. Her red hair colour was unlike any red they had seen in their life and her make-up was caked on. Alex could tell she was an older woman who once had had a beautiful face, and did her best to look youthful. She wore an emerald dress with matching emerald fur and elbow length gloves, and heavy, cheap jewellery. She wore a tight corset and gave Greg a little grin and a wink.

"It's always nice to get a sample before you buy," whispered Greg looking at her cleavage.

"You're ogling a fifty-year-old prostitute," Alex chuckled.

"Your Majesty," Madam Ravine said as she curtsied.

"Madam Ravine, thank you for coming on such short notice," said Alex. "Has anyone told you why I have summoned you?"

"No, but being in the business I'm in, I can imagine why. Are you looking for company? A special kind of lady?"

"No – I mean yes, I am looking for a woman –"

"Well, then tell me," she grinned. "What kind of woman are you looking for? What dirty –"

Greg began snickering.

"No, Madam Ravine, no," Alex interrupted. "I'm looking for Madeline Black. You owned her for a short time did you not? Her father sold her to you."

"Why yes, let me think. Yes, her father, was a big drinker."

"Who was he? What was his name?"

"Oh dear, let me think," she said touching her temple. "Isaac. Yes, Isaac Black."

"Where is he now?" he asked eagerly.

"Well, I'm not sure," she said looking away in thought. "From what I've heard, he'd drank himself to an early grave. But he was a drifter. So, I dunno if that's true."

"Oh."

"Did Isaac ever take a wife or a lady friend? Do you know the name of Miss Black's mother by any chance?"

"The 'whore' you mean?" asked Madam Ravine casually. "That's what Isaac always called her when I knew him. I have no idea what the woman's real name is. But when she left him, that broken heart of his never mended. None of my ladies could cheer him up."

"Do you know why she left him? Did she leave Madeline too?" Alex asked leaning forward in his throne.

"I wouldn't know anything about that. To be honest, I think that woman went out and ended up killing herself or some fool thing."

"Madeline Black was one of my servants Madam Ravine."

"Yes, I know, your Majesty. I tried to buy her the same day one of your men bought her," she said with a hint of annoyance.

"Madam Ravine, if Miss Black happens to come by to see you for any reason ..." he trailed off. "Bring her back here and I promise you, you'll be rewarded. It will be worth your while."

She laughed mirthlessly. "If she comes. I doubt that spitfire would come willingly."

Alex sat in silence watching the devious expression on Madam Ravine's face. His intuition told him that if she found Madeline, she wouldn't be bringing her back to him. "Thank you for coming here, and for helping us," he said dismissing her.

"Happy to be one of your subjects, your Majesty," Madam Ravine curtsied. She began making her way for the door when she stopped and turned. "Oh, and Sir Gregory, if you liked the sample, the guards can tell you where to find me."

"Much obliged," said Greg cheerfully.

"Usually that's what men say afterward," she giggled girlishly and exited the Throne Room.

"Oi," he said nudging Alex, "she's quite the business woman. Half her conversation was all about trying to get us into the brothel."

But Alex had a vacant expression, as if Greg said nothing at all. "Sorry Greg, nothing you could say right now could make me laugh. I know you're trying to help, but I'd rather be alone. Please leave me."

Greg looked at him concerned and hesitantly left the room, shutting the doors behind him.

By himself on his throne, Alex had never felt so empty and miserable. He wanted to cry, but refused to do it. He had not cried since the night his father died. He got up and paced about the room, hearing the echo of his feet on the floor trying to hold it back, but as he looked about the room, he was reminded of the first time he touched her, skin on skin, the warmth of her breath, the heat of her lips. Tears quickly fell from his cheek to the marble floor. He grabbed a decorative vase sitting on a table next to the wall, smashing it to the floor he cried, "MADELINE!"

The pieces smashed and scattered about. He looked about at them, wiping his cheek with his sleeve. As he looked up, he spotted his military tactics book sitting beneath his throne. He had forgotten he left it there months ago. He ran over to it and feverishly opened the book looking for her ownership pages. He turned the book upside down, and they floated to the floor. He picked them up and scanned through them:

Know all People by these presents, that I, Anna Ravine of the County of Surrey, England for and in the sum of sixty pounds to me in hand by Lord Watson, Baron the receipt where of I do acknowledge, have bargained for and delivered to Lord Watson, Baron

One female servant named Madeline Black.

To have and to hold the said girl Madeline to serve within his household and attend upon his needs. His Majesty, the King Rex, all executors, Parliament will hitherto recognised these papers of ownership. Signed on the fifteenth day of September in the year of our Lord One thousand eight hundred and one.

Signed,

Lord Watson, Baron September, 1803

The Lord Watson, Baron has sold

One female servant named Madeline Black

for and in the sum of two hundred pounds to his Majesty, King Alexander I signed in hand and sealed. On the Nineteenth day of August in the year of our Lord One thousand eight hundred and nine.

Signed,

Alexander Rex August 1809

The other attached papers were descriptions describing her age, weight, birth date and physical description. He groaned. He had hoped to see the name of her father or possibly her mother. Her past was shrouded in mystery. Why? He had the feeling that if he knew more about her past, he would find a clue to where she had gone.

But there was something else that confused him. How had a slave, managed to open a bank account? He looked back at the ownership papers and sat down again on the throne. He stared at them for minutes on end, waiting for the papers to reveal a secret he had not seen. But nothing came. Defeated, he folded the papers back up and put them into his book.

It was hopeless. He sulked for several hours, staring into nothing. Eventually, Greg re-entered the Throne Room, giving the shattered vase a curious look. "Alex, you've been here for hours," he said approaching him.

"I'm trying to think of a solution. But it's just not coming to me."

"Yes, but you need to eat something," Greg said patting him on the back.

Just then, Sir Ashton entered the room, "You've been here for quite some time your Majesty – musing, I suppose."

"Yes, Ashton," Alex said propping himself up in his throne.

Sir Ashton walked towards Greg and Alex, up to the throne. "I think it's time you leave the Throne Room, hm? Time to eat something. Maybe the answer will come to you when you're no longer thinking about it."

"If it were that easy," said Alex smiling faintly.

"Your Majesty, for as long as I've known you, you've never failed at anything. Everything you attempt, you succeed at. I'm sure it will be no different when getting Miss Black back."

Greg and Alex looked at one another, curiously as Sir Ashton turned to leave the Throne Room. Alex wondered how much Sir Ashton knew about his relationship with Madeline. "Sir Ashton," he began.

Sir Ashton turned back grinning, "My Lord, I've known you since you were a boy. How could I not know the kind of woman you'd fancy?"

Greg smiled shaking his head, whispering, "That man never misses a thing," as Sir Ashton left.

"Sir Ashton is right," Alex said confidently. "I'll get her back, and I'll make her my Queen."

"Right. Dinner then?" asked Greg.

"Yes, just keep me away from the drinks."

"No worries mate. I'll drink every bottle before you can get your hands on it."

"Don't get carried away," Alex said as he got up from his throne.

"When have I ever done that?" Greg replied with a grin.

37

BROKEN HEARTS

Sitting on her bed in her new home, Madeline began unpacking her things. The house had two rooms, one big and one small. The big room was a kitchen with a dilapidated table and mismatched chairs next to a fireplace. The small room was a bedroom with a single-sized bed and an armoire. The small room had a rather small door, and she had to duck each time she walked through it. It wasn't much. But it was hers, and she was free to do what she wanted whenever she wanted.

Opening her bag, Madeline began placing her possessions about her room. She did not own much. There were three dresses with matching pairs of shoes, a cloak, her bottles of rosewater, her mother's papers and a doll. It was all she had, and as she took each item out, she realized that all the things she had were given to her in one way or another by Alex, except for her mother's papers. She had stolen those.

It was twilight when she arrived, and there was no time to get firewood. She found a few matches and lit several candles about the house, looking for scraps of wood to burn, but found nothing. She was exhausted and frustrated. She had to get up early in the morning, and she had a cold sleep ahead of her.

She plopped herself on an old rocking chair by the fireplace kicking at the charred stones wishing she had something to throw in it. She looked at the run-down chair next to her. No one else would use it she reasoned with herself. She picked it up and threw it against the wall, and it broke to pieces. She built a fire with the rubbish, and began warming herself at the hearth. But the stone floor was cold. Her uniform she had worn leaving Buckingham Palace, couldn't keep her warm. She would need to buy some warmer clothes. In the meantime, she would use a blanket.

She went back to her room ducking to get through. She pulled a blanket off the bed. As she did so, the doll Alex had given her fell off the pillows. She considered it for a moment. It was a well-made doll. She brought it and the blanket back to the old rocking chair. She sat down and covered her legs. She began staring into the green eyes of the doll, with its black long braided hair and exquisite dress. She began to wonder if she really needed it. She and Alex were over. Why keep it? It would only be a painful reminder of the night he swept her off her feet and made love to her in the Mistresses' Chambers.

She softly brushed the doll's cheek with her finger. It was a beautifully crafted doll. It would be terrible to toss it out. She wondered if she should sell it. Overwrought with guilt, she immediately put the idea out of her mind. Selling a sentimental gift was in bad taste. Despite being angry with him, she could not disrespect him in that manner. She looked up from the doll to the fire, fiery red and orange a flame with heat, embers crackling. She looked down at her doll again. If she was going to let go of Alex, this was the best way to do it. Once she threw it in, she could never have it back.

She stood up and held it up above the fire, glancing at it one last time she slowly loosened her grip, then stopped and held on to it. The crystal blue dress the doll wore rode up slightly above the doll's petticoat, and there was something written in ink on the petticoat that she had never seen. She pulled back the skirt and read the handwritten inscription:

Every part of me tells me you were 'Made' for Majesty.

She slumped back onto the chair, staring at the words as they became blurry with her tears. She cried for some time before she drifted off to sleep...

Alex burst through the door. Startled, a pot she held in her clang to the floor. He ran over to her and took her in his arms.

"I can't survive without you, Madeline. Only you could be my Queen."

"So you won't marry Sofia?"

"I can't. I'm in love with you. Please, come back with me."

"It might take some convincing," she said looking up coyly into his eyes. He gave her a naughty smile and firmly kissed her lips. The two fell onto a large pelt of fur on the floor by the fire. He began undoing the laces to her dress, his lips moving about her neck and face ferociously. The desire in his eyes and his mouth made her feel as if nothing else existed in the universe. As he tore off her dress, she could feel him trace his fingertips across her scars, making them disappear.

"This is the last night you will ever wear simple clothes, Miss Black. The rest of your life will either be in the richest silks or naked."

She tittered and with his help, began tearing off his clothes. Soon, he was bare and standing in front of her. Her eyes absorbed his perfection as shadows and the dim light of the fire, glimmered on his tan skin.

His prick was hard, swollen and angry looking. She looked down in amazement. She hadn't even touched him. Seeing the predatory expression on his face, she smiled coquettishly. But before she could lay a hand on him, his lips were kneading hers, frenziedly suckling and exploring her mouth with his tongue and nibbling at her lips.

Soon he kissed her about her cheeks, ears, neck and shoulders. Moving his mouth to her to her breasts, he held each one in his hands and sucked at her at her flesh and buds. She crooned, the heat of ecstasy surged through her veins. She could feel her cunt swollen and moist with desire. She clenched his hair between his fingers, wanting to shove his head between her legs. But she couldn't. Pulling him off meant being deprived of a few moments of pleasure and she couldn't handle that.

Sensing her need, he slipped one of his hands down to her twat and began caressing it with his fingertips. She murmured, delighting in his every motion. He pushed a couple of his digits inside her teeming sex and plunged onwards and upwards. She immediately responded, all the muscles of her body tightening, "AHHHIIEEEE," she shrieked exploding onto him, her cum streaming down his hand. She gazed at him, light-headed, her vision of him was blurry. She ran her hand up and down his god-like perfection, fondling the ridges of his muscles as everything came into focus. She looked back down at his cock that was at attention, ready to please her.

"Mmmm," she whimpered as she reached out and grasped her hand around it. His body shivered at her touch, and he closed his eyes. She spread her lips about his hard pecks leaving a trail of kisses down his abs before she breathed her soft, warm breath on his sex. He combed his hand through her loose hair. Though she sometimes liked to taunt him, tonight she couldn't be bothered. She could already see pre-cum emerging from the slit in his head, and she wanted it. Gingerly licking it up, she raised her eyes up at him as his descended on hers.

He sighed and swallowed hard. To enjoy this for a while, he'd have to stay focused. But her ravenous eyes drove him wild, he always came faster if he looked into them. She loved cock; it was difficult to tear himself away from the excitement in her eyes.

She took his huge cock into her greedy hands and began sucking hungrily. She stroked him as she swirled her tongue about his head, a part of her wishing she could milk him like a barnyard animal. But if she did, she knew he couldn't enjoy it. As much as she loved his taste, she loved the expression of pleasure on his face and his moaning more.

Fortunately, it did not take long. Her sucking, petting and eyes quickly threw him out of orbit. He gasped, moaned and trembled, biting his lips. He wanted to hold out for longer to revel in all the pleasure she gave him, but it was impossible. In the past few months, she had become a maven to everything that thrilled him.

"UUHHHHHH!!" he groaned, surrendering to her, his twitching cock began to spurt his nectar. He moaned over and over as she eagerly swallowed shot after shot that filled her mouth. Cumming like he never had before, it was difficult for her to keep up. Some dribbled out onto her cheek, but she kept at him, wanting more. Induced by her thirst for him, he cupped her face releasing the final rush deep into her mouth, "Madeline," he whimpered.

She savoured the taste of him; she slowly licked it off her lips and scooped it off her cheek with her finger. As she brought her finger to her mouth, she saw more on his prick. She put it in her mouth and delicately brushed her tongue over him, cleaning the last bit off. He slumped to the ground. She caressed her hand along his abdomen. His eyes were sleepy, and she could feel his heart pumping through his stomach.

"You're going to get it now," he said his worn expression vanishing.

She giggled and tried to run off, but he quickly grabbed her waist, turned her and placed her on the floor in one effortless movement. "You're not getting away again, Miss Black."

He spread her knees apart and began leaving a trail of kisses up and down her thigh. She quivered beneath his warm breath as her pussy grew hotter and wetter. "Mmm," she sighed, "don't tease me, Alex. I don't like being teased."

He smiled, then opened his mouth sealing it around her he flicked his tongue across her clit, She wriggled her hips, across the fur beneath her. It tickled her arse, sending tingles up her back, making her tremble and buck. He grasped her hips, not wanting to part from her pussy.

That was the part that drove Madeline crazy about Alex; he was an expert the first time, every time. Whenever he ate her pussy, she couldn't help but to writhe and twist her hips at every stroke and fuck of his tongue. It was hard to lay still. If she didn't, he'd put her in her place until she came. As frustrating as it could be, he didn't mind; as long as he could hear her croon and have her sweet cunt juice.

Soon he began to fall into rhythmic motion, tonguing about her bud and labia. His untiring mouth gave her no rest. She murmured, her hands grasping at the fur pelt underneath her as she thrashed herself into his mouth. Her muscles tensed, climbing to the familiar sensation of orgasm, she cried out, pounding her fist against the floor, "ALEX! My ... GOOOODDD!!!"

He tasted her as she flowed into his mouth. He muttered, growing stiff again as he tasted her. She came again as she felt him moan on her. He lapped her up quickly as aftershocks crawled through her body. He began circling about her entrance and darted into her moving his tongue feverishly. Tremors spread through her, and she came again and again, an earth shattering scream escaping her. After some time of pants and wails, her mouth grew dry and her screams were soundless.

As she descended from her climax, the last throbs of pleasure coursing through her, he slowly thrust his tongue about her between soft murmurs. He could hear her heart drumming through her body, her breasts rising and falling as she heaved. When he could no longer taste her, he rose from her and lightly traced her belly with the tips of his fingers. "Are you all right?"

Drunk with sex, she could barely answer him, except give him a soft simper. He crawled next to her and cushioned her in his arms, pecking her forehead with his thick lips.

When she had finally caught her breath, she began to playfully stroke his cock, hinting that she was ready for him again. He quickly came to life, pinning her shoulders to the ground and positioning himself between her legs. "Thank God, it was driving me mental waiting for you."

She giggled. It was hard to believe that he'd ever get restless with his need for her. He always managed to keep such a calm appearance. On the other hand, he was always so excited and eager whenever he was given the opportunity. Holding her head in his hands, he rubbed his cock against her. Madeline grew anxious as he pushed about her hot sex, sending ripples of pleasure up and down her body. Their eyes met and he entered her, holding her gaze. "You know how I like it Alex," she whispered provocatively.

His lips met hers, sealing a promise to satisfy her. He began swivelling his hips about, warming her up for what was to come. She crooned, as he pushed into the sensitive velvet. Moving slowly at first, he soon began to pick up his pace. The louder she became the harder and faster he thrust into her. As she rounded her apex, she gripped onto him. Feeling her nails dig into his back he pounded into her harder and faster. They cummed together at once their pleasure interlaced, whirling them about like an unstoppable force of nature.

She fell back onto the soft fur, her chest heaving. His eyes lids heavy with the urge to sleep. Alex crept next to her and held her in the crook of his shoulder. "You all right, dolcezza?"

Madeline nodded, unable to speak because she was still taking long deep breaths. He slid his hand down to her sex, fingering her slowly. She sighed. She wanted to cum more. She stroked his cock, hoping it would spring to life and take her again. Though it did, he ignored it and continued kissing her as he fingered her. He slipped another finger in.

"Mmmm," she moaned kissing him, her sighs of pleasure on his lips.

"How many kisses will I need to satisfy my longing for you?" he asked as his lips intertwined with hers as they explored each other's mouths and lips. She could feel herself become wetter, moaning with hunger, and he slipped a finger into her arse, fulfilling her need. He rubbed circles into her button with his thumb, sending ribbons of ecstasy coursing through her.

She bucked a little, as he moved gently inside her. Madeline looked at him wide eyed. "More," she whimpered, "harder."

With a brazen glare, he began thrusting the three fingers and rubbing circles into her clit in a frenzy.

"Alexxx!" she cried. He looked up but only saw her eyes widen as she began to feel pleasure overtake her body. Inside of her, his fingers could feel her muscles clench.

"Oooohhh!" she murmured.

"Cum for me, dolcezza."

Her desire and love for him grew with his words, and she could feel a small rush of cum flow as she continued to breathe deep breaths.

"That's it," he said encouragingly.

He grinned as he slowly began twisting his wrist and his fingers delved her wet inferno more deeply. This was her undoing, "FUUUCCCKKKK! ALEX!" she screamed.

"WHOA! MADELINE!" he wailed as he felt her pussy and arse clench down on his fingers. She started writhing on the fur pelt, unable to control herself. He reached his other arm around her waist, pinning her down as a violent flood of sex juice released from her. It flowed onto the pelt, soaking it. Not able to contain himself at the sight of her cumming so much, Alex fell apart, "Ahhhh! FUCK! Madeline," he praised and came onto the floor.

He collapsed next to her, noticing that she had already passed out.

Hours later Madeline came to and looked around the room. There was no fur pelt on the floor. The fire had gone out. No Alex. Just a lonely girl, resting on a rocking chair by the fireplace. She cried out in agony and clutched the doll to her chest and breathed in the scented sandalwood feet. His smell. She inhaled again and again, tears flowing down her cheeks. She began to cry like she never had before. Her eyes became puffy and bloodshot, her chest heaving in pain as she tried to control her breath.

She had abandoned him, the only person that had ever loved and cared for her. "Alex," she cried as though he could hear her.

She picked up the blanket from the floor and fell back onto the rocking chair, rocking forward and back trying to soothe herself, smelling the doll. A part of her wanted to go back, but knew she could no longer do that. Going back meant tolerating the arrangement he proposed.

She knew in her heart that he was not trying to be a cad. But, as true as their love was, the arrangement of being his mistress wasn't right; the three of them would be miserable keeping up the charade. Until Alex realized that, she had to stay where she was. She hugged the doll more tightly and deeply inhaled his smell, her eyes closed a small smile slowly grew on her face. She knew her man. He wouldn't fail them.

OTHER BOOKS IN THE SERIES

Maid for Majesty Series

Forbidden Fruit (Book One)

Absence (Book Two)

Black Swan (Book Three)

Forbidden Fruit Erotica Version (Book One)

Absence Erotica Version (Book Two)

Black Swan Erotica Version (Book Three)

ABOUT THE AUTHOR

AJ Phoenix is the author of the #1 Best Selling Historical Erotica series *Maid for Majesty,* and lives on the shores of the Great Lakes in Canada. Her writing is not inspired by real life events. If such events did ever happen to her, her books would never have been written.

For more information about this author please visit:

www.maidformajesty.com

There's more to come in the series! Connect with A J through Facebook Twitter and Radish!

Made in the USA
San Bernardino, CA
02 July 2017